P9-DFU-552

Midnight Waltz

**Center Point
Large Print**

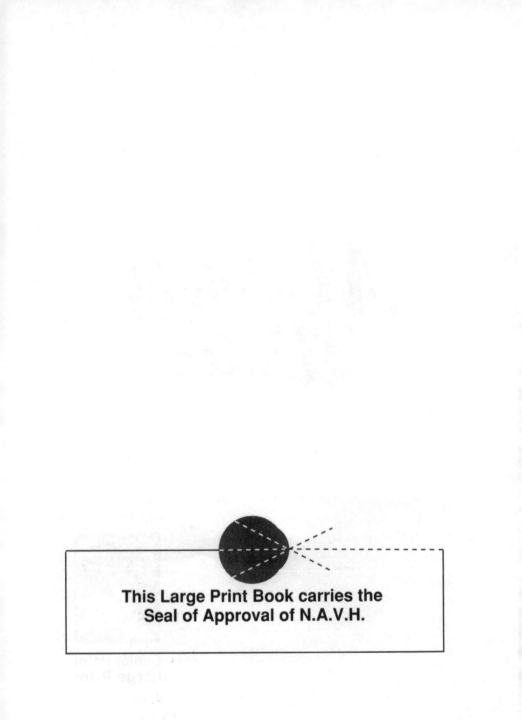

ॐ श्री गणेशाय नमः

JENNIFER BLAKE

Midnight Waltz

CENTER POINT PUBLISHING
THORNDIKE, MAINE

BOLINDA PUBLISHING
MELBOURNE, AUSTRALIA

This Center Point Large Print edition
is published in the year 2002 by arrangement with
Ballantine Books, a division of Random House, Inc.

This Bolinda Large Print edition
is published in the year 2002 by arrangement with
Random House, Inc.

The text of this Large Print edition is unabridged.
In other aspects, this book may vary from the original
edition. Printed in Thailand. Set in 16-point
Times New Roman type by Bill Coskrey.

US ISBN 1-58547-187-9
BC ISBN 1-74030-715-1

U.S. Cataloging-in-Publication Data is available from the Library of Congress.

Australian Cataloguing-in-Publication

Blake, Jennifer, 1942-
Midnight waltz / Jennifer Blake.
ISBN 1740307151
1. Large type books.
2. Romantic suspense novels.
I. Title.
813.54

British Cataloguing-in-Publication is available from the British Library.

Chapter 1

The force of the wind slammed the outside door behind Amalie Peschier Declouet, closing off the sound of the rain pelting on the floor of the loggia. She paused a moment on the braided rug to throw back the sodden hood of her cloak and to wipe the mud from her half boots. Raindrops gleamed on the soft brown curls of her hair, reflecting its odd, silver-blue highlights. The raindrops beaded on her dark brows and lashes and clung to the rose-petal skin of her heart-shaped face. In the salon where she stood, there was a massive mirror with a Chippendale frame hanging over a marble-topped table beside the rear entrance, but Amalie did not glance at it. Brushing distractedly at the droplets, she turned toward the door of M'mere's sitting room, which opened off the salon on the left, as the sound of voices came from that direction.

"I must refuse, of course, my dear Tante Sophia. That you would even think of such a thing is unbelievable, but that you would actually send for me and suggest it I find nothing short of amazing!"

"You are offended, *cher*, and it does you honor, but if you will only consider the matter without emotion, you must see that—"

Madame Sophia Declouet broke off in midsentence at Amalie's impetuous entry. Spots of hectic color appeared on the woman's high cheekbones with their stretched, crêpelike skin, and she flung a quick glance at the man who lounged in the chair facing her on the other side of the marble mantel. He came to his feet with controlled grace,

5

his dark blue eyes narrowing as he turned to face Amalie.

There was an atmosphere of strain in the wide room with its cream walls, elegant champagne-colored silk hangings, scrolled mirrors touched with gold leaf, and rosewood furnishings set around the edges of an Aubusson rug. The urgency of Amalie's message faded as she glanced from her mother-in-law to her guest, then back again. "Forgive me, M'mere," she said, her clear, low-pitched voice rather breathless. "I thought—that is, I expected only Julien."

"It is of no moment, *ma chère*." The older woman forced a smile as she recovered her composure. "Come, you remember Julien's cousin, Robert?"

"I believe we met at the wedding?" Amalie came forward to offer her hand.

"Naturally, you did," Madame Declouet said with a laugh that still had a strident sound. "It was Robert who stood up with Julien."

Amalie had a vague remembrance of the tall figure of a man at Julien's side on that day three months ago, but she had not been able to see clearly through her veil, and afterward there had been so many new faces. She had hardly known her groom then, much less his cousin, but she had heard much about Robert Farnum since. She said politely, "Yes, of course."

He took her hand, his strong, work-hardened fingers closing around it. As he bent his head in a perfunctory bow, the gray light from the windows caught in the waves of his dark hair. It also glinted for an instant in the dark blue depths of his eyes, revealing an expression of intent assessment.

Amalie met his gaze for a long moment. Her fingers tingled with warmth that pulsated up her arm to merge with the accelerating beat of her heart. She was suddenly aware of the masculine force of a man, of his will, purpose, and strength, in a way that she had never known with Julien, or even with Etienne, her first fiancé. She became still, unable to breathe, unable to look away, and quite unable to return his conventional greeting. For no discernible reason, she felt vulnerable, unprotected.

"Robert has been in the North on business, something about the machinery of his sugar mill, these past weeks," Madame Declouet prompted.

Amalie withdrew her hand with a small jerk, seizing, with gratitude, the topic offered. "Yes, so Julien told me. I trust your business was successfully completed, Mr. Farnum?"

He smiled, a movement of the lips that deepened the curved lines of past amusement about his mouth, but did not quite reach his eyes. "You must call me by my given name, if you please. And, yes, I was successful."

It was far too simply said to be a boast, but Amalie had the feeling that Robert Farnum did not often fail. She sent him a glance of frowning inquiry from under her lashes. His skin was dark, not with the olive freshness of the French Creole men of her acquaintance, but with the bronze color of one used to long hours in the semitropical sun of southern Louisiana. His brows were black and thick above deep-set eyes fringed with dark lashes; his nose was classically straight, and his lips were well defined, as if chiseled from granite, above the strong jut of his chin. His plain coat of dark blue broadcloth stretched over broad shoulders. Under it, his white linen shirt was open at the neck and tucked into the waistband of a pair of buckskin riding breeches. His cuffed boots were mud-splashed, but gleamed with the fastening chains of a pair of neat, smooth-roweled silver spurs. His kinship with her husband was obvious; they were much alike in coloring, height, and width of shoulder. It was in their manner that the difference between them lay.

"I am Amalie, then, Cousin Robert," she answered, willing her stiff lips into a smile and giving his name the French pronunciation that dropped the final consonant.

"Your cloak, *ma chère,*" Madame Declouet said, "it is dripping water onto the rug. Where have you been in this downpour?"

Amalie turned with relief. "Oh, M'mere," she said, giving her husband's mother the childish title that the older woman preferred, one coined by Julien when he was small, "that is what I wanted to tell you. I have come from the bayou. Sir Bent says that the water is rising, that it will be out of the banks before midafternoon and may well flood the lower rooms of the house unless a barrier of sandbags can be built. He has enlisted some of the other men from the quarters, but more must be ordered out, and M'sieu Dye is nowhere to be found."

M'mere frowned. "Ungrateful man, he is never close by when needed."

Patrick Dye was the overseer at Belle Grove Plantation, a swaggering Irishman with more sense of self-worth than responsibility. Try as she might, Amalie could not like him. Still, in this situation, he was the man they needed to organize the job and stay behind the field hands until it was done.

"Perhaps he went into town? If someone were sent after

him, he might return in time."

"And just as easily might not."

"What else can we do?"

That Amalie had come to the older woman, instead of to her husband, was not a matter for comment. Julien took no interest in the workings of the plantation and would be supremely indifferent to the prospect of mud in the house. The structure had, after all, been built on nine-foot-tall piers to form a raised basement with just that possibility in mind. The basement rooms were used primarily for storage and servants' quarters, though the dining room was also on that level. The main rooms occupied by the family members, however, were on the second floor. Any damage would therefore be slight. Julien would not take into consideration the appalling mess that must ensue or the effort it would take to clear it away.

As M'mere shook her head, Robert Farnum spoke. "You can leave it to me."

"You?" Amalie swung around to stare at him.

At the same time, M'mere said, "But what of your own place?"

Robert Farnum answered his aunt, ignoring Amalie's surprise. "The Willows sits on higher ground, if you will remember. I'll talk to Sir Bent, but I doubt the water will reach it. It never has before."

"We would be most grateful, then, if you are certain, *mon cher?*"

"I'm certain." Robert swung away from his aunt, moving toward the door.

"Wait," Amalie said, "I'll take you to Sir Bent."

He paused with his hand on the doorknob and the panel

of the door half open. "I can find my way."

"And you, my child, must go and take off your wet things," her mother-in-law said, an admonitory ring in her voice.

Amalie made a wry grimace, flinging back the edges of her cloak before glancing from M'mere to the man in the doorway. Robert Farnum's dark blue gaze was upon her, raking her from the crown of her head down the slender elegance of her body, more revealed than concealed by the damp garment she wore, to the toes of her half boots showing beneath the hem of her limp skirts. She did not think he had expected her to discover that swift and thorough appraisal, but that did not prevent the rush of hot color it brought to her hairline. Whatever it was she had been about to say was lost as a shiver caught at her, running along her nerves.

"Tante Sophia is right—at least in this," he said, his voice tight; then, flinging a hard stare at his aunt, he walked abruptly from the room with something akin to relief on his face.

In her bedchamber, Amalie gave her wet cloak to the upstairs maid who had come in answer to her ring. The girl exclaimed as she squeezed water from its hem into the slop jar then lowered her voice as Amalie nodded warningly toward the connecting doors that led into her husband's bedchamber. When opened, the wide, sliding panel doors could turn the two rooms into one, but they were closed now, as always. Julien never roused before eleven o'clock, sometimes not until noon.

The girl became solemn at once. The master of Belle Grove might turn a languid and indifferent eye upon the workings of the plantation, he might be petted and pampered by every person on the place from his mother down to old Sir Bent, but he was not a man to annoy with impunity.

In silence, Amalie permitted herself to be undressed and put into a wrapper of soft white flannel trimmed with ribbon and lace. When the girl would have released her hair from its pins to dry, she dismissed her with a smile, attending to the chore herself while her clothes were taken away to be laundered. With her hair streaming down her back and a tortoiseshell hairbrush in her hand, she wandered to the window. Rain still fell beyond the panes, just as quietly, as relentlessly, as it had fallen for the past weeks as winter turned into spring. It sometimes seemed to Amalie that it had been raining without ceasing since the day of her wedding.

Robert Farnum. No, she had no clear recollection of seeing him that day. Her attention had been concentrated on the man she was to marry. How excited she had been, how nervous. It had all happened so quickly. The letter from Madame Declouet to Aunt Ton-Ton proposing the match had been received in November, and by February of the following year, just before Mardi Gras, they were wed. The Lenten season had been the excuse; no one was married during such a bleak time. To have waited would have meant postponing the nuptials until after Easter, when everyone was ready to leave New Orleans for the country.

Amalie had been living with her great-aunt, Madame Antoinette Peschier, at her relative's home in the Felicianas. She had had no thought of marriage, and indeed, at the advanced age of twenty-four, had given herself up as a spinster.

She had been betrothed before, at seventeen, to Etienne Bawdier; a love match. Etienne had been the son of her father's dearest friend, a sweet young man: protective, gentle, cherishing. She had been radiant with happiness. Then had begun a chain of events, of deaths, that seemed to have no end. Her father had caught the gold fever sweeping the country and left for California. His letters had been fascinating reports until, abruptly, they stopped. A bundle of his belongings had been shipped home by a doctor with a scrawled note that shed little light on the manner of his death. For all that, it was no less final. The money he had taken with him to finance his explorations had been borrowed against their house and land, and it was not recovered. Amalie and her mother had gone into mourning and, when the mortgage fell due, moved in with Aunt Ton-Ton, there being no other close relatives.

Her mother had never quite recovered from the double loss of husband and home. She had grown quieter, more pale, by the month. Finally, just as the two years of official mourning—one in black and one in purple and gray—were coming to an end, she had succumbed to the wasting sickness. At least that was what the doctor in attendance had called it; Amalie had known otherwise.

With another year of black to be gotten through before the marriage between Etienne and herself could take place, his parents had sent him to Europe for a grand tour that had lasted not one year, but two. He had returned older, more mature, with a touch of cosmopolitan polish, but eager to make Amalie his bride at last. It had been early summer, but in the country that did not matter; the plans for the wedding had gone forward. He had ordered a special nuptial bracelet made to his own design in France and, two weeks before the wedding, had gone to New Orleans to take delivery of the valuable shipment. The month was June, the year 1853. Before that summer was over, yellow fever, the dread "bronze John," had killed ten thousand in the city. Etienne had been among them.

For two more years, Amalie had worn mourning, then the letter had come. Aunt Ton-Ton had known Madame Declouet, though that had not been her name then, since they had come to the Felicianas forty years ago as young married women, when the area was still a wilderness. The hardships and terrors they had shared had made them close. When Madame Declouet's husband had died, she had moved away, and later married again, but the two women had kept up a correspondence.

Arranged marriages among the Creole aristocracy, those of French and Spanish blood born in Louisiana, were not uncommon. The alliance of two families was a matter of grave importance, one not left to children. Even in courtship, there were matters that had to be weighed with care by the adults: the ability of the young man to provide for a wife, the size of the girl's dowry, the social standing of the families, the purity of the bloodlines—which must have no taint of *café au lait.* Often what seemed to be a love match was a case of careful maneuvering by the mothers of the couple. Then, even when all things were in order, the young man was never left alone with the girl, not even for the proposal, and was allowed a chaste kiss only after the betrothal was official. Such being the case, it had not seemed particularly strange that Madame Declouet should solicit the presence of her good friend Ton-Ton and her niece as her guests in New Orleans, with the object of approving the young woman as a bride for her son, Julien.

At first, Amalie had refused. She had been reasonably content as she was, living with her great-aunt, paying calls, entertaining visitors, and making herself useful about the house. She had known Etienne for so many years and had planned her life around him; since he was gone, she had wanted no other man.

Aunt Ton-Ton had been incensed. Amalie could not go on as she was, mourning the past, nor must she think that her poor old aunt needed her; hadn't she five children and fifteen grandchildren to see to her needs? Her niece would be a fool to let such an opportunity pass, for there might never be another, certainly not one with such advantages. As the wife of Julien Declouet, she would enjoy wealth and prestige. There would be jewels, gowns from Paris, the finest carriages, and journeys abroad, particularly to France where there were still family connections. She would reside in the Declouet townhouse in the garden district of New Orleans for the gala winter season, entertaining the famous and powerful, attending the opera, and appearing at the most exclusive functions. The spring and fall would be spent relaxing at Belle Grove on the Bayou Teche near St. Martinville, while the heat of summer would be tempered by the sea breezes at Île Dernière, the gulf spa of Last Island off the Louisiana coast where the Declouet family had owned a cottage for some years. And if such a prospect had no appeal, she must think of the companionship of a husband, of the love she would have for the children conceived in the union. What more could she want?

Respect, tenderness, caring? It had seemed that even these might be hers. Julien was a most attractive man, with great charm and address. She had thought when she first met him that he would be easy to love. Their courtship had consisted of two meetings, both closely chaperoned as was the custom. Even his proposal had been heard in the company of her aunt. On her acceptance, she had been awarded with a gentle kiss on her forehead. But there had been a promise in his dark eyes, and real liking. She had thought that, after all the dark years, everything was going to be all right.

The wedding, a large affair, had been a trial. She had been nervous of the five days of seclusion that tradition decreed must follow, but her fears were needless. Julien, with great understanding, had suggested that they use them to become better acquainted without the strain of intimacy. They had slept apart in the connecting bedchambers. Amalie had been so very grateful for the reprieve, for the sensitivity of her bridegroom's attitude. How high had been her hope for the success of the marriage!

Before they could settle down to life as a wedded couple, however, there were the bride's visits to be made, the round of calls upon relatives up and down the river and the bayous, allowing themselves to be entertained. Julien had insisted on buying a new wardrobe for Amalie first, cate-gorizing the gowns she had bought for her trousseau as dowdy, without flair. She had lived too long in mourning to know what was fashionable.

It could not be denied that he had excellent taste. He had made every visit to the dressmaker with her, helping to choose the fabrics that would best suit her coloring, poring with her over the copies of *La Mode Illustrée*, inspecting the fashion dolls that were just in from Paris. Even then, he had not been satisfied, but had swept her into the milliners for bonnets, hats, and veils to protect her from the sun; to the glovemakers for gloves of finest kid or silk; to the cobblers for slippers; and to the jewelers for pieces to add the finishing touches to her many ensembles. Never had she felt so petted, so cosseted and cared for, as if she were infinitely precious to him.

Then had come the night when she had awakened to find him beside her bed. She had felt the flutter of excitement as he lowered himself beside her. His kisses had been warm and sweet, his touch gentle, and she had been ready to be his wife, no longer afraid. He had held her, caressed her, removed her nightgown. Then nothing.

He had drawn away from her to lie staring into the darkness. She had not understood at first, had been afraid that in her inexperience she had done something wrong, something that had repelled him. She had reached out, trying ineptly to rekindle his desire, but he had caught her hands, holding her from him. In the end, he had cried, stifling the sound, choking on a grief she could not quite comprehend, though her own tears had wet her face. Twice more he had come to her: once aboard the steamboat as they had completed the required visits and once after they had arrived home to Belle Grove for the spring. It had been the same.

Amalie turned from the window, dragging the brush through the tangled dampness of her hair. The air in the room was cool and damp. A fire would feel good. She took a step toward the bellpull, then stopped. No, she could not stay in her room while the bayou rose to flood Belle Grove. She had to find something, anything, to do to help. She had discovered that keeping busy was an excellent antidote to thought and to repining. Not that she truly regretted her marriage. Julien was a good companion, when he chose to be, when he stayed at the plantation instead of seeking amusement in St. Martinville until the small hours of the morning.

There were those who would say that she was stupid to place such store on the physical union between a man and a woman, that she should be glad to be spared that burden. A number of times in the last years with Aunt Ton-Ton, the elderly women who came to call of an afternoon had forgotten Amalie's unmarried state and failed to lower their voices when they spoke of such things over the teacups. Amalie was not so sure. She was suffused at odd moments by an aching need to be held, to feel the strength of a man in opposition to her own.

She loved her husband, of course she did. At least, she sometimes felt a protective affection for him. He had many admirable qualities: consideration, generosity, the art of the well-turned compliment. He was a handsome man: dark, tall, with aristocratic bearing. And yet there were times when his grace, his effortless good manners, his smiling charm were an affront. There were times when she wanted to strike out at him, to do something wanton and wicked, anything to rouse him from his pose of studied indifference, to compel his attention and disperse the feeling of inadequacy as a woman that assailed her at weak moments.

And what did he feel for her? She could not be sure, but she greatly feared that his affection for her was tempered with rather too much concern for her comfort.

She went still. Could it be that the situation between

Julien and herself had been under discussion in M'mere's sitting room just now? That might account for M'mere's embarrassment and also the peculiar glances she had received from Robert Farnum. It was not every day that a man beheld a virgin wife. Certainly such a creature deserved a second look if only to see what it was that had prevented her husband from possessing her.

The slow heat of a flush rose to her cheekbones. No, it could not be. And yet M'mere was aware of the situation. The older woman had made the opportunity to ask delicately probing questions on at least a half-dozen occasions. The entire household could know, if it came to that. The maids who cleaned the rooms must be aware that she slept alone, that the sheets of her bed were undisturbed when she arose from them, and that the tin of purified, rose-scented goose fat left on the bedstand to ease her first tightness remained quite untouched. Or perhaps not. She sometimes rumpled the sheets and dented the other pillow as a matter of pride.

No. It was intolerable. She would not believe that her mother-in-law could have discussed such a thing with Julien's cousin; there could be no purpose to it. She was letting her imagination run away with her. Just because she was prey to misgivings about her unusual state did not mean that it was of overweening interest to anyone else. It was doubtless some boring business to do with the running of the plantation that had been the subject of debate between M'mere and her nephew. His interest in her had been merely curiosity to see how she was settling in at Belle Grove.

When Amalie emerged from her room a short time later,

she wore a crisp gown of rose poplin over only three petticoats and without a hoop to impede movement. With her
hair in a braided coronet on top of her head, she felt neat
and competent, ready to make herself useful. She moved
directly from her bedchamber into the salon, turning
toward the rear door that led out onto the loggia and also to
the outside staircase at the back of the house.

Belle Grove had been built during the early years of the
nineteenth century when every closet, chimney, and
enclosed staircase was taxed. As a result, the house had two
outside staircases, one in back and one in front, but none
inside; only two enclosed chimneys, but four fireplaces;
and armoires instead of closets.

The style of the house owed much to the influence of the
West Indies. The Declouet who had commissioned its
building had been a refugee from Santo Domingo after the
slave insurrection there. He had come to live near St. Martinville because he had illustrious, if distant, relatives there,
notably Alexander Declouet who had been commandant of
the Poste de Attakapas in the earliest years of the settle-
ment. Besides the raised basement, his house had a hipped
roof pierced by six dormers, three in front and three in the
rear. The overhanging roof line sheltered a pair of deep galleries across the front, supported by square brick columns
on the bottom and turned colonettes on the top, and with
upper and lower loggias on the back. French windows
topped by transoms opened out onto the upper gallery from
most of the front rooms, providing air and easy access to
what served as an outdoor living area. The lower gallery
was also much utilized.

Inside, there was no central hall. Each of the seven rooms

on the second, or main, floor opened into each other for cross ventilation. The salon cut through the center of the house with doors opening onto the gallery and the loggia. To the left of the salon was M'mere's bedchamber and sitting room and another chamber given over to Chloe, the older woman's godchild. On the right side of it were the bedchambers of Julien and Amalie; his at the back and hers in the middle, with another at the front known as the virgin's room. The last was furnished as an extra bedchamber but would, under normal circumstances, have been the sleeping place of any daughters born to Amalie and Julien as their family grew. The only entrance to it was through the room where Amalie slept, the lack of easy entrance and exit being to prevent dead-of-night clandestine visits to, or excursions by, those daughters as they reached marriageable age. Their sons would have been accommodated in the large, open dormer room under the eaves on the third floor until they reached the age when their boisterous conduct and profanity might become offensive to the ladies of the house. At that time, they would have removed to the *garçonnières,* those small, separate two-story buildings in the same West Indies style that flanked the house to the rear on either side, and were also used to accommodate unmarried male guests.

"Amalie! Wait one little moment, will you?"

Amalie, just starting down the steep stairs to one side of the loggia, turned at the call. A smile curved the generous lines of her mouth, lighting the somber brown of her eyes with the odd gray-blue rings around the irises. A rather plump girl of seventeen, her shiny, saucy black ringlets bouncing above her ears and a bell skirt of blue silk over an enormous hoop swinging around her, came sailing toward her from out of the salon. It was Chloe, and she caught Amalie's arm in a grasp that nearly overbalanced them both before Amalie snatched at the newel post.

"How clumsy of me. I'll break my neck one of these days, as Julien has told me a thousand times. Pray *le bon Dieu* that I don't break someone else's at the same time!"

"Yes, indeed," Amalie said promptly.

The girl laughed. "Yes, but is it not exciting? The flood, I mean, naturally. It has never happened before while I was here." Amalie glanced out over the railing of the loggia, beyond the *garçonnières* and outbuildings, to where the falling rain dimpled the silver channels of water that marked the rows of the waving blue-green cane spreading as far as the eye could see over the flatlands behind Belle Grove. Nothing could have been more peaceful. Her tone dry, she said, "Very."

Chloe stamped her foot in mock annoyance, her black eyes flashing and her mouth with its full lower lip set in a pout. "I think it is! And George is beside himself, but not, you understand, over the danger, at least not to anything human. It is his Eros that he worries about, the fool, and he goes now to see Robert, to beg sandbags to protect the ugly thing!"

"My dear Chloe how can you call it ugly?"

"With not the least little regret, I assure you. Anything that takes the attention of my lover from me is of an extreme ugliness in my eyes, an utter and complete hideousness!"

Chloe was not only Madame Declouet's goddaughter, but also a distant family connection. She had been taken in at the age of ten with the consent of her parents, who had been glad to be relieved of one of their brood of fifteen children. In the years that followed, she had been groomed with the prospect of becoming Julien's bride. It had been a mistake to rear the two together, however. They had grown to be like brother and sister, and siblings who did not get along at all well at that. Their disdain was fervent and mutual; Chloe had embraced Amalie on sight in her gratitude that it was she, and not herself, who was to wed Julien. And Julien lost no opportunity to point out Chloe's faults, from an overboisterous manner to a sagging hem. There was, however, a bond of affection between them, which may have been the reason for Julien's extreme caution about the girl's current *tendre* for George Parkman, the English landscape gardener hired to transform the grounds of Belle Grove into some semblance of a garden.

"I'm sure the Eros is a most valuable piece," Amalie said soothingly as she turned and began to descend the stairs.

"What matters that when George will risk his life for it while I am left unprotected?"

"I will grant you that it's hard to be deserted for a mere bronze statue, but we are in no danger."

Chloe sniffed as she trailed after Amalie. "He will catch his death of cold."

"The Eros?"

"George, of course! Though there is certainly no reason he should not, if he were alive, being quite—quite unclothed."

"George?" Amalie queried with as much innocence as she could muster.

"No, the Eros!" Chloe answered, turning fuchsia-red and

sending Amalie a dark look before she sighed. "George will have an inflammation of the lungs, I know it."

"But think how grateful he will be to have you nurse him."

Chloe's face brightened for an instant and a gleam came into her eyes, then she shook her head. "He is used to rain in England and finds our spring weather quite warm. I expect he will be totally unaffected."

"I only hope the men sandbagging may not all catch their deaths out in this rain; they must be wet through."

"The field hands are used to it, and Cousin Robert, too, for that matter, since he is forever riding over The Willows or hunting ducks and deer. The menservants from the house, however, may not be in such good case."

They had made their way from the foot of the stairs through the lower loggia into the dining room in the raised basement. Like the salon above, it bisected the house and was flanked on either side by storerooms, a butler's pantry where the food was brought before serving and the soiled dishes were stacked between courses, and a pair of bed-chambers used by the butler and the children's nurse, the last now empty. Skirting a vast mahogany sideboard with a bull's-eye mirror above it, they emerged on the lower front gallery.

The rain drilled down, spattering in on the brick floor. Through its silver shafts, they could see the dark figures of the men moving about beyond the drive that circled the house, a distance of some two hundred yards. There was purpose and will in their movements, much more so than earlier in the day. Along their line, a man rode back and forth on horseback, pointing, directing, shouting above the sullen roll of thunder. Nearer to the house, the great live oaks that dotted the lawn, giving the plantation its name, moved gently in the wind, their long gray beards of Spanish moss swaying. From the turretlike *pigeonniers* that flanked the gallery on either side, the pigeons, disturbed by the activity, took flight, becoming wheeling, soft gray shapes against the gray sky.

Because of its winding course, the bayou was named Teche from the Choctaw Indian word for snake. It was a fair-sized waterway, perhaps some two hundred feet across. In some ancient time it had been the channel of the Mississippi before the spreading stream known as the Atchafalaya had stolen the great river away, then lost it to its present wide course. Unlike the last two streams, there had never been earthworks along the slow-moving Teche. Since the level of the water had decreased so greatly over the hundreds of years and the channel was so deep, its own banks served to keep it in bounds except under the most severe conditions. This year, the spring thaw up north had been late and heavy, filling up the rivers and creeks, the bayous and swamps on its way south. The incessant rain of the past weeks on top of it was just too much.

The land between Belle Grove and the bayou was gently sloping, but the house and its outbuildings sat on a rise studded with moss-hung live oaks and magnolias, which stretched curving arms toward the water. It appeared that the dike of sandbags was intended to close the house in a semicircle with the ends merging with the rise, to prevent the overflowing water from reaching the house.

"Will they finish in time?" Amalie asked, almost to herself.

"If it can be done, Cousin Robert will do it." The answer came from Chloe with offhand confidence, the most impressive kind.

"He is rather a strange man," she ventured.

"What can you expect of one whose father was *un coquin Americain.*"

An American rascal. That was the name most commonly given to the riverboat men from Kentucky who in the early days had brought their produce down the river to New Orleans to sell. Their brash manners, their loud enjoyment of newfound riches, their propensity for rough-and-tumble fighting that destroyed property, had made them despicable to the longtime residents of the former French colony, and especially to the aristocrats among them.

"And yet, he is M'mere's nephew?"

The look Amalie turned on the other girl was mildly inquiring. It was enough. "Oh, it was one very great scandal, that, I tell you. Here was the beautiful belle Solange Declouet, toast of New Orleans and pride of her father's heart, and there was the crude giant from Kentucky in his rusty black suit, Jonathan Robert Farnum. The giant sees the dark beauty on her gallery and he stops, stunned into silence. He tries to enter but is not admitted; he shouts up to her, and she nearly swoons as she is carried inside by her mother and her maid. Then he is everywhere she goes. Her most acceptable suitor forces a challenge on the man and is bested, shot through the elbow. He bribes her maid to deliver a message. Solange meets him in the cathedral where she goes often to pray. He is enthralled. She is strangely drawn, but it cannot be. They meet again and are seen. A marriage is arranged in haste with the injured suitor. She swears she will not wed and prepares to go into the convent, to become a bride of Christ. The *Americain* hears, he abducts her, and they are wed by a priest at the far *Poste de Natchitoches*. Only after a son is born, does the couple become reconciled with her family."

"The son being Robert?"

"But of course."

"And the plantation, The Willows, was the dowry of Solange, since it is near the Declouet property?"

"Oh, no. The *Americain*, like his son, was a man of formidable success. He bought the land from others so that his Solange could be happy near her family."

"Then came M'mere, a young widow, to marry Solange's brother," Amalie mused.

"I think no, I think she was here already, married already. She was quite old when Julien was born, almost too old for children."

"I see. Robert seems to—to get on well with M'mere."

"That is not so strange. His mother died in childbirth when he was five or six years of age, and then not so long afterward his father and M'mere's husband were killed together in a boating accident while duck hunting. M'mere took the son of her husband's sister to her bosom to comfort him and so that he might be a playmate to Julien. Robert regards her as his second mother, with much affection, and perhaps, gratitude."

"Yes, of course. It's easy to see, then, why Julien and Robert are close, being so much of an age." Julien was twenty-nine, and Robert perhaps a year or two older.

Chloe nodded. "They are very great friends."

"So great that they were neither in a hurry to be married."

Amalie knew well enough, from what had been let drop in her presence about Robert Farnum, that he had no wife.

"Hah! Why should a man marry, tell me that? These males have their dancers, their opera singers, their quadroon *placées*. What is a wife, children, and domestic joy compared to such excitements? Some men even prefer to keep an assignation with a bronze statue!" Chloe smacked her hands together in anger, then, as she turned to look at Amalie, raised them swiftly to her mouth. "Ah, my stupid tongue! I was speaking in general, *ma chère*."

"I did not suppose that they—that either had been—celibate," she said with what she hoped was at least a degree of composure.

Chloe's face cleared. "You are not shocked, that is good. So many women pretend, which is a thing I detest. As for the other, I do not know, of course, but I have heard tales. Robert has never taken a *placée,* much preferring opera singers in the past, though there was a married woman a few years ago. They say she attempted to take her life by swallowing poison of the kind set out for rats when he grew bored with their assignations."

"To destroy another man's home is despicable," Amalie said.

"Yes. Julien has never done so, at all events. There was only his *placée,* a young girl arranged by M'mere since his father was not alive to see to it. But you may be easy. She was pensioned off before the wedding and he sees her no more."

"I see." She would not think of Julien with a quadroon mistress, a woman who had doubtless received his embraces, perhaps borne his children, something she might

27

never do.

"Would you rather I had not told you?" Chloe asked, her round face puckered with anxiety. "I apologize with all my soul, but my tongue runs away with me and I thought once you knew a part, it would be better if you knew the whole."

"But you should have no knowledge of such things your-self."

"Now that is stupid, exactly the kind of thing M'mere would say. How am I to know how to behave in the world if I am kept in ignorance of its ways?"

At that moment, Chloe's attention was caught by the shape of a man staggering through the rain around the end of the house. He was carrying a heavy bronze object inex-pertly wrapped in a gunnysack and was heading in the gen-eral direction of the *garçonnière*. She turned to call and wave, and George Parkman changed directions, stumbling toward the gallery.

Amalie lingered long enough to greet the Englishman and to help relieve him of his burden, then, as Chloe began to upbraid him, her gaze was drawn once more to where the men toiled in the rain. Her brown eyes followed the upright figure of the man on horseback, watching as he drew rein to lean with one hand resting on a hard thigh while he talked to a field hand. The back of his jacket glis-tened with moisture, molding itself to his broad shoulders and the muscled contours that narrowed to his waist. As he straightened, he swung around in the saddle, tipping his hat back with one hand as he stared at the house. Wrenching her gaze away, Amalie whirled and stepped back into the house.

Chapter 2

A malie went about her usual tasks in the house, checking up after the maids to see that the various bedchambers, with the exception of Julien's, had been tidied: the beds made, the slop jars and chamber pots emptied, and the carpets well swept. The butler's pantry was in need of cleaning, but it would have to wait. They were short of hands since the pair of men who normally did the heavy work in the house were down by the bayou; and Charles, the dignified Ashanti who served as butler, had his hands full keeping the maids from leaning over the gallery railing and waving their feather dusters in the direction of the work gang. She had parceled out the rations for the quarters and also those for the kitchen that day, using the keys to the various storerooms that hung from the silver filigree chatelaine at her waist. She had discussed the menu for the day's meals with the cook before going for her walk along the bayou. All that was left for the morning was a visit to the infirmary to treat the inevitable cuts, burns, aches, and fevers, using the much-worn copy of *Cunn's Domestic Medicine* that M'mere had bequeathed to her along with the chatelaine.

The amount of responsibility that her mother-in-law had placed in Amalie's hands in the past weeks was surprising, especially when M'mere's autocratic temperament was considered. She often wondered about the reason. Was it a form of testing, to see if she was capable of assuming the manifold burdens and responsibilities of looking after a large plantation? Or could it be that M'mere was not as well as she pretended? The older woman's carriage as she moved about the house was majestic, but also slow. Her manner at the table was superb, but she ate little of the many rich dishes that were set before her. She retired to her room each afternoon for what she called a period of repose, though from her appearance later it seemed she slept heavily but with little benefit. Her nights were disturbed, for Amalie, being a light sleeper, had awakened a number of times to hear her pacing back and forth in her chamber.

Stepping out onto the upper front gallery in search of a maid to polish away a set of greasy fingerprints she had found on a marble-topped table, Amalie paused to watch the men below. She shivered a little as a chill wind blew across the gallery, flinging rain in upon the cypress planks that formed the floor on this level and carrying damp mist to where she stood. The men looked so miserable as they slogged in the mud, shoveling the wet, black earth into gunnysacks and lifting them to their shoulders to carry them to the slow-rising dike. Such effort would call for strength and energy. They would need plenty of food and something hot to drink at noon, and it was doubtful that they could stop long enough to return to the cabins.

The visit to the infirmary and hospital building could wait, this one time. Amalie turned, making her way purposefully toward the back of the house and the outside stairs that led to the brick path in front of the *garçonnière* on the right and the kitchen located on its lower floor.

It was near midday when she made ready to leave the house once more with her cloak over her arm and an oiled umbrella in her hand. She paused in the middle of the salon, her attention caught by the snick of metal on metal, the scuffle of feet, and the flicker of movement on the front gallery. A tiny frown between her brows, she turned in that direction.

She halted in the doorway. The upper gallery had been commandeered for a fencing salon. Its two occupants were Julien, wearing only an open-necked shirt and slim trousers caught by straps under his bare feet, and his opponent and valet, Tige, the son of their butler, Charles, who was dressed much the same way. The épées they wielded were buttoned at the tips, but the two men had the protection of neither breast pads nor masks. The advantage in skill in the match was Julien's, but on his side Tige had caution, determination, and a superior reach. The bout was by no means uneven, for Tige had attended the *salle d'armes* of the great mulatto fencing master Bastile Croquere with Julien. Her husband had wanted a fencing partner always at hand and so had arranged that Tige be taught at the same time.

Julien flicked a glance in her direction. "Good morning, my love. How bright you look on this dull day."

"Thank you, Julien. You know of the rising water?"

"I know," he said, his reply a bit breathless as he recovered from the attack Tige had mounted at his first sign of inattention. "I suppose you think I should be out in the wet with Robert, saving us all?"

"It seems your cousin has the job well in hand."

"It appears so to me also," he said, flashing a grin as he parried a well-timed blow with ease, "but do you intend to join his crew in my place?"

"Hardly. If you refer to my umbrella, I mean to see that the men have something to eat and drink."

"A laudable mission. They will bless you, I'm sure, but

then you are already their *petite maîtresse.*"

"Yes. You have had breakfast?"

"Oh, yes. My wants are few and easily satisfied."

The double-edged words, the trace of irony, were not new. Amalie had learned to disregard them. They were, she thought, directed not at her, but at himself. Hard upon them, Julien advanced on his valet in a flurry of sharp-edged sword strokes, circling his opponent's blade, prising. Tige grunted, and his épée spun from his fingers while he stood shaking his numb hand.

"Again," Julien said, and, as Amalie turned away, the valet reached to retrieve his sword then bowed, sweeping it up in the fencer's salute in front of his brown, impassive features before taking his position once more.

The kitchen was kept separate from the main house primarily to avoid the heat of the constantly burning fire during the long summers, and to prevent the smoke and grease from staining the walls, to contain the cooking odors, and also to prevent the all-too-prevalent possibility of fire. Every time she was forced to visit it on a wet day like this one, however, Amalie doubted the wisdom of its placement.

Stepping inside the door, she shook out her umbrella and set it aside to drip before looking around her. A savory smell of apples and cinnamon, and also of stewing meat and onions filled the air. The cook, a massive, hard-fleshed woman with her head wrapped in a Madras kerchief and a spotless white apron over her blue dress, moved lightly between the fireplace and heavy worktable. Another woman stood with her hands in a tub of hot, soapy water on a bench near the door, while yet another was straining an iron pot of grease at one end of the worktable. At the other end stood a small Negro boy with a fried apple pie in one hand and a piece of charcoal from the fire in the other. He was drawing and under his small fist the shape of a woman's head with a kerchief tied about it, the ends sticking up like the ears of a cat, took shape. So exact a likeness of the dignified cook was captured in the simple lines that it was startling.

"Is everything ready, Marthe?" Amalie asked as the large woman turned to greet her.

"Indeed it is, Mam'zelle Amalie, and packed in the wagon, but who will take it, I don't know, me. M'sieu Dye just come and got that Zeke from the stables that harnessed the mule, took him down to the bayou just now. Charles is one fine man, a butler of the best, but it is not his place to leave the house, and besides, he has the great fear of beasts. All the others are with M'sieu Robert."

Amalie did not object to being addressed as mam'zelle. Only strange females with husbands in tow were given the title of madame. All women in a household, even to the crone with great-grandchildren at her knee, were called mam'zelle, just as she was also called the *petite maîtresse,* little mistress, while M'mere was the *grande maîtresse,* the big mistress.

"Perhaps the men could come as far as the kitchen, a few at the time?"

The cook shook her head. "M'sieu Robert will not allow it. No man may leave until the job is done. It is better so, for he has no time to chase those who do not come back, and even if he did, I think, me, that he would not like the job M'sieu Dye might have the others do while he was gone."

Dye, the overseer, had returned an hour or so ago. Amalie had seem him ride up, had seen, too, the confrontation between him and Robert Farnum. She had not been able to hear what was said, but she thought the overseer had not been pleased with his welcome.

"I will go."

The offer came from the boy at the table. He had thrown down his charcoal to stand watching them. Known as Isa, he had come to Belle Grove with his mother as a child. The mother had died in childbirth sometime later, and the orphaned boy had gone from one cabin to another in the quarters behind the house. A bright youngster of nine or ten, the straightness of his body was marred by a clubfoot. He could not keep up with the other quarters children, had difficulty in doing the small chores that fell to their lot, and so often took refuge in the kitchen were the cook tolerated him so long as he did not get in her way. Amalie had often seen him watching her when she came to the kitchen. Once or twice, he had even followed her back to the house. And on one occasion, the cook had shown her a charcoal drawing on the table surface of a portrait that was undoubtedly the *petite maîtresse.*

Amalie smiled at the boy, then gave a nod of decision. "Yes," she said, "and so will I."

It was such a short distance, when all was said and done, and the mule in the wagon shafts seemed docile enough, even rather bored, in spite of the rain that sleeked his brown sides. Amalie had driven out alone in her aunt's pony trap on many occasions once she was past her youth, tooling around the neighborhood on short errands not worth the effort of getting out the carriage. This should be no different.

Nor was it, the only problem being that she had to discard her umbrella to hold the reins. Tossing it aside, she pulled up the hood of her cloak, discovering that the rain had slackened to no more than a steady drizzle. With Isa in the back to watch the great granite-ware coffeepots, the kettles of soup, and the hampers of hoe cakes, bacon, ham rolls, and fried apple pies, she slapped the reins on the mule's back and turned the wagon toward the track that led around the back of the house, past the small summerhouse, and through the trees toward the bayou landing.

The men saw them coming, but did not lay down their shovels and sacks. Half their number at a time were released to go to the wagon, where they stood wolfing down the food, drinking the coffee and hot soup before it had time to cool. While the last group ate, Robert Farnum dismounted and walked along the curving line of sandbags, prodding them now and then with his foot. The bags were only three high along its length; not a great barrier, considering all their hard effort.

Amalie wrapped the reins around the brake handle and got down. Moving to the back of the wagon, she motioned to Isa to hand her a clean tin cup and a napkin. Wrapping a ham roll and a fried pie in the linen square, she filled the cup with hot coffee and turned to make her way toward her husband's cousin.

By the time she reached his side, the old, stoop-shouldered Negro who answered to the name of Sir Bent had joined him, talking in an earnest undertone. He pulled off his misshapen hat, ducking his white head toward Amalie in greeting as she neared them, but went on with what he had been saying.

"I don't like it, M'sieu Robert. Something, she be holding the water back. It should be three, four inch higher than she is, this I know. I think of the log jam up the bayou. What will happen if he is got bigger? What will happen if he has the water behind him and he lets go?"

Robert listened without interruption. The elderly man was known for his ability as a weather prophet. Whether it was age and experience that guided him or some sixth sense about wind and water, he commanded respect for his predictions, at least at Belle Grove.

"Moonshine," came a harsh voice from behind them. "The old fool is making excuses for being wrong, for causing all this extra work for nothing!"

"No, M'sieu Dye, I would not do that, me," Sir Bent protested. It was significant that, like most of the slaves on the place, he called the overseer by his last name. Their formality was an indication of mistrust rather than of respect.

The overseer was an Irishman with mahogany red hair, a jutting nose, and a short upper lip that gave the impression, intended or otherwise, of a sneer to his smile. He was only slightly shorter than Robert Farnum and of heftier build, especially in his barrel chest. Handsome in a florid way, he considered himself a ladies' man.

Robert sent the overseer a long look. "There may be something to the log-jam theory. There's been one building up for some time above us." The jams were caused by trees washed up from the soft, alluvial sandbanks of the bayou and its tributaries. As their roots were exposed by the water, they fell in and were carried along until they were stopped by a sandbar or a sharp curve. Every log that floated downstream from then on added to the natural dam.

Patrick Dye shrugged. "Believe it if you want, but you know they have to blast those things loose once they get matted up or else take a snag boat after them."

"Not always." Robert's voice was quiet, authoritative.

"Suit yourself. I still say all this is wasted labor." The overseer turned toward Amalie with a belated greeting, his hazel eyes moving over her, lingering on the soft curves of her breasts beneath the opening of her cloak before coming to rest on the food she stood holding. He touched the brim of his wide-crowned hat. "Ma'am. It was mighty good of you to bring something down here for us to eat. Is that for me?"

It was the first time she had seen the man without Julien being present. The look he had given her, added to the faint thread of insolence in his tone and his assumption that she would act as a servant to her husband's hired supervisor, brought a surge of anger.

"No," she said, her voice cold. "It is for Cousin Robert."

Robert swung toward her. "I'm sorry; I didn't notice." From the corner of her eye, Amalie saw the flush of chagrin that rode the overseer's face and the tightening of his mouth. The man deserved the snub, she thought, then forgot him as she gave the cup she held to Robert. She transferred it quickly, for she knew, as she freed her fingers of the handle, that the rim where he had taken it was hot. Even then, he stood holding it, his blue gaze meeting her deep brown eyes. "That is," he said, "I knew you were there, but not that you had brought this. Thank you."

Abruptly, the heat of the metal cup reached him, and with a soft oath he snatched at the handle with his free hand. One corner of Amalie's mouth twitched, but she schooled her features to remain calm. Proffering the napkin-wrapped food also, she said, "Not at all. It's the least I can do."

Leaving the three men, she returned to the wagon and began to repack the hampers, positioning the kettles and pots so that they would not turn over on the return trip. She looked around for Isa. He stood some distance away, near the edge of the bayou where cypresses and willows grew down to the water. His back was to her as he threw sticks broken from a rotted branch into the rushing current. She called to him, but he did not hear her over the sound of the water and the rain that had begun to pour down once more. She glanced at the mule hitched to the wagon. The animal seemed restive, shifting from one front hoof to the other, backing and filing, pricking his long ears and twitching water from them as he stared at the dark and muddy swirl of the bayou. The reins were secure, however, and she turned away, picking up her skirts as she started toward Isa.

Thunder rumbled, a low grumbling that went on and on, vibrating the ground. Amalie looked up, frowning. It was a moment before she realized that the sound was not coming from overhead, but from her right. Behind her, men began to throw down their picks and shovels. They turned to stare up the bayou and a yell rang out. Around the curve of the stream came a boiling yellow flood. In the seething, roiling water, twisting and turning like match sticks, were the dark, straight shapes of waterlogged tree trunks.

The men broke and ran. Amalie saw Isa stumble around, his mouth open in a cry as he hobbled toward her on his bad foot. The logs, borne on the raging wall of water, came on. They would crush anything caught in their path. The hood of her cloak flew back as she broke into a run. Her skirts flapped about her ankles, impeding her steps. Her footsteps splashed in the muddy water, and her breath was caught in her lungs. The edge of the bayou looked impossibly far away, as distant as the ends of the rows of cane that stretched away on its other side. She redoubled her efforts, snatching her skirts up to her knees. Then she had one arm about the boy, half carrying him as she swept him toward the wagon.

The rumble and roar of the water was in her ears. Above it, the shouts of the men as they scrambled toward the rise behind the house, the braying of the mule, and the thud as he kicked at the wagon had a thin, disembodied sound. Isa was gray and one of his hands was wrapped in the wool of her cloak. He was in pain from his twisted foot, she knew, but she could not help it. Her lungs were burning and there was a stitch in her side. Only a few more yards to go. The mule would be able to outrun the water, with luck. If not, there would be some protection in the wagon.

The reins had been loosened; she saw that as she hoisted Isa into the wagon seat. She grabbed for them with one hand while she clutched at the kick board with the other and set her foot on the hanging step. The mule reared, surging forward as his front hooves struck the ground. The reins flapped, jerking through her fingers. The wagon slewed to the side against the brake. Amalie's grasp slipped and then she was hurled backward. The ground came up to meet her with a force that took her breath away. The wagon loomed above her and she twisted frantically to the side as it was dragged, bucking and jibbing, away after the men. She saw Isa looking back, his mouth open in a scream, saw his black head disappear as he was flung to the floorboard.

She could hear nothing because of the thunder of the water. Jarred by the fall, she was disoriented, too, the shuddering of the ground under her. She pushed to her feet, swaying.

The pouring flood was coming nearer. Water was dashing out of the steep banks, foaming, washing around her ankles. She took a step toward the white bulk of the house, then the pounding was upon her. Water surged around her knees and she staggered. There was a blow at her back that seemed to whip around her, crushing her rib cage. Then she was lifted, turned. With a sobbing cry, she caught at the shoulders of the man who leaned from the saddle, holding her. At that instant, she saw the dark, water-soaked log as it was flung, spinning, above them. She was dragged against the horse as Robert Farnum lurched, expelling his breath in a short, soft curse that was edged with pain. He kicked his mount so that the horse surged forward, leaping away, then he straightened, drawing her up before him across his saddle bow to lie in his arms.

The water poured, sucking, around them, crashing into spray as the horse plunged up the slope, splattering them with bits of bark and leaf mold. Amalie, gasping at the sting of it in her face, was aware of the rigid grasp of the man who held her, of the board hardness of his chest and the bunched muscles of his thighs beneath her. Her breath rasped in her throat, and wildly she swung to look toward where the mule-drawn wagon was being dragged to a halt by the field hands at the top of the slope on the far side of the house. There were men in the branches of the live oaks, too, and scampering along the ridge toward the quarters.

Then they were out of the water. The sight of the others was cut off by the bulk of the house. The horse reached the top of the slope and stopped on the summit as Robert drew rein. They sat for long moments. It seemed to Amalie that her heart would burst in her chest, so hard was it throbbing, and she could feel the pound of Robert's heartbeat against her shoulder. She was trembling uncontrollably despite the hold that enveloped her. The rain drenching them was chill, streaming from her hair where her hood had been flung back, and yet between their bodies was a wet heat that grew, encompassing them.

Slowly Amalie looked up, meeting the dark blue gaze of Robert Farnum. It burned into hers, stark with an emotion she could not name, but which seemed akin to enraged pain. The rain made runnels down the bronze of his face, catching in the thick, wiry hairs of his brows, outlining his square jaw and the muscle that was taut in it, creeping into the open collar of his shirt and pooling in the hollow at the base of his throat. Between them lay a fierce tension, caused in no small part by the strain in the tendons and muscles of Robert's arms, as if he had been forced to embrace a hot stove.

A shudder ran over her. She forced herself to straighten, drawing away from him and lowering her lashes. Her voice was unsteady as she said, "I must thank you."

"Not at all."

The lack of interest in his tone was like a blow. Her eyes widened as she sent him a quick glance. His face was without expression, though he did not quite meet her gaze. "I insist. If you had not been there—"

"But I was, and I am grateful to have been of service. Shall we let it end there, Cousin Amalie."

The reminder of their relationship was, she thought,

deliberate. "As you wish, but I won't forget."

He inclined his dark head, then nodded toward the front of the house. "I think it is time I set you down."

For the first time, Amalie noticed that they had an audience. Julien and Tige, with a pair of the maids, stood at the end of the gallery. They were watching, apparently waiting to be noticed, for as she looked in that direction, Julien lifted his épée in salute. She raised her hand, forcing a smile as Robert walked his mount in that direction, rounding the end of the house and entering the water that flowed nearly a foot deep before the gallery. The water pressure behind the logjam had overflowed the sandbags. Now the bayou lapped around the columns of Belle Grove, flowing through the rooms of the raised basement. It was receding already, but, if Sir Bent was right, would rise again. The flood was upon them.

"A most gallant rescue," Julien called.

Did she imagine it or was there an edge to his tone? Amalie stared up at her husband as they drew nearer, stopping just beneath the gallery. Finally she answered, "Yes, was it not?"

"I saw what was happening, but was powerless to help. Never have I felt so useless in my life! I am in your debt, my cousin."

Robert moved his shoulders. "It was just luck that I was there."

"No." It was M'mere who made that quiet contradiction as she moved out onto the gallery to stand at the railing above them. Her voice flat, she went on, "It was meant. It is the will of *le bon Dieu*."

The man who held Amalie turned his head to stare at the

elderly woman with eyes narrowed to blue slits. "Blasphemy, Tante Sophia?"

"It is what I believe."

"That doesn't mean I can accept it."

"Can you not, when Julien is of the same mind?"

Robert swung, staring up at his cousin who stood straight and tall with his sword at his side. "Are you?"

A grim smile curved Julien's mouth. "I've found it is always best to agree with M'mere."

There was an undercurrent of meaning in their words that Amalie could not quite grasp, though she sensed its presence. She stirred, looking toward the stairs that rose to the left under the lower gallery as she grew stiff from the effort to hold herself away from Robert Farnum.

"Enough," M'mere said, sending a quelling frown from one man to the other. "Amalie is half-drowned, Robert, and so are you. I suggest you come inside."

"I will bring Julien's wife to the end of the stair, if he will come and get her."

"There's no need," Amalie said hastily. "I can walk."

"I insist."

Without giving her the time to argue, he walked his mount up onto the water-covered gallery and along it toward where the stairs ascended. At the foot he stopped and, as Amalie would have slid down to the steps, tightened his grip on her. Julien, having put aside his épée, moved with lithe grace down the stairs to the third step from the bottom. He gave his cousin a hard stare, then reached up to place his hands at Amalie's waist. As he swung her down, Robert leaned forward to steady her and she heard the hissing intake of his breath.

She turned on the stairs as Julien set her down, staring at Robert and remembering that looming, flood-swept log. "You're hurt."

"It's nothing, only a bruise."

At the head of the stairs, M'mere said, "Come up at once. It must be tended."

"Let me help you down," Julien said, reaching for the reins, offering his hand.

"I think it would be best if I went back to The Willows."

"Don't be a fool," Julien answered. "Am I going to have to drag you off that horse?"

"You could try."

Julien looked at the stiff way Robert was sitting in his saddle, the strained set of his shoulders. He let his hands fall to his sides. "In your condition, I don't doubt I could manage, but no one is going to force you to do anything. The choice is yours."

The two men stared at each other, blue gaze locked with brown. Amalie watched them with her brows drawn together over her nose as she tried to discover the point they were making beneath the surface of their words. She thought it concerned her, though how it could was more than she could see. Perhaps reaction to what had occurred such a short time before was making her fanciful. She was convinced that was the case when, after a moment, Robert gave a nod and, with Julien's arm bracing him, swung his leg over the pommel and slid from the saddle. Behind her, M'mere touched her arm. She turned, holding up her wet and sagging skirts, and straggled up the stairs with her mother-in-law's arm at her waist and Julien supporting Robert behind her.

Chapter 3

The rain stopped on the following morning, a blessed respite, though the sky remained overcast with only an occasional glimpse of the sun. The high water was with them for four days. For Amalie, it was a trying time. There were a hundred things that had to be done to make conditions livable for the human beings in her care and a thousand difficulties in getting any one of them completed. The dining table, chairs, sideboard, and butler's serving table had to be rescued from the lower floor, along with the china and crystal needed to set out a meal. Once brought upstairs, the wood pieces had to be carefully dried and polished to prevent water stains, then set up in a corner of the salon. Food, prepared earlier by a foresighted Marthe, had to be brought by pirogue from the kitchen and set out on makeshift benches on the loggia until dinnertime. Since the kitchen, being at ground level, was useless, a good assortment of utensils had to be taken up to a vacant room of the *garçonnière,* the fireplace of which must serve for cooking.

The upper floors of the *garçonnières* were dry enough, so George, along with his well-wrapped statue of Eros, was comfortable. Learning after a time from M'mere that Robert's injuries were a dislocated shoulder and massive bruising, neither calling for close nursing once the shoulder had been put back in place, Amalie had decided to give the Englishman company by issuing orders for a room to be prepared in the *garçonnière* for Julien's cousin instead of in the house.

The people in the quarters were safe enough since their

cabins were built on three-foot piers, but those who were in the infirmary had to be moved. A cabin was cleared for them and the changeover made without mishap.

The stables and cattle lots were another problem. The carriage and riding horses, and the plow mules, could not be left standing up to their knees in water, nor could the cattle kept for slaughter. The finer horses were sent with a pair of grooms to The Willows at Robert's insistence, while several other hands were detailed to drive the remaining animals to the back section of the two-thousand-acre plantation where higher land might be found.

The cisterns that provided the water for the house, and also those for the quarters, were underground, so there was the danger of contaminated water. It required constant vigilance to see that every drop used for drinking and preparing food was boiled. Even so, there was more than one case of bloody flux in the quarters. Amalie could only hope that no more contagious sickness developed.

The quarters children loved their watery playground and spent every waking moment splashing in the foot-deep water or in poling an ancient pirogue about the place. One morning, hearing the sound of hilarity coming from downstairs, Amalie found several of them floating up and down the dining room and paddling in and out the door of the flooded pantry. She felt something of a shrew for chasing them out, spoiling their fun, but consoled herself by the knowledge that it was for their own safety.

The danger was from water snakes. Washed from their hiding places along the banks of the bayou, they swam into the house, entering at the smallest crack or crevice, seeking dark corners for concealment. A pair of them were found entwined in the French crystal chandelier and the *chasse-mouches,* or punkah, that had hung over the dining table, and another was caught wrapped about the railing of the back stairs. Julien and Robert, and even George, had amused themselves after the first day by shooting the swimming snakes from the upper gallery with pistols, staging contests of skill and betting against each other. Despite the fact that Robert had his injured shoulder in a sling, the two cousins were evenly matched and the Englishman was not so far behind them.

Shooting was not their only amusement. They also seined for crayfish, contributing enough of those succulent creatures so that Marthe soon had a pot of gumbo simmering over the fire. They played billiards, wading around the table in a lower room of the *garçonnière* with their trousers rolled up to their knees, slipping in the mud that was slowly sifting out of the water. Card games held them for long hours, as did chess, checkers, and dominoes. After dinner, they sometimes cajoled Amalie into playing the Pleyel piano for them while they sang, or else snatched the embroidery from the hands of M'mere and Chloe, leading them out on the floor to dance. Often Julien arranged elaborate charades, sophisticated versions of favorite childhood games, or mounted amateur theatricals with the aid of the trunks of discarded clothing from the attic and Chloe's carefully hand-copied scripts. Chloe was particularly good at the last, having a decided flair for the melodramatic. She made a blood-curdling Lady Macbeth and was so passionate as Lady Sneerwell in *The School for Scandal* that George, watching her, tugged at his cravat as if it were strangling him.

Then there was Isa. He had wailed without ceasing until he was brought to Amalie after the flood broke, so great was his fear that she had been carried away. When they tried to remove him, he fought like a swamp cat, scratching and biting, kicking and butting with his head. Afraid he would be hurt, Amalie had signaled that he be allowed to stay with her. That first evening he had followed her everywhere, standing behind her chair at dinner, lying at her feet afterward in the salon. He had tried to enter her bedchamber, but denied that by Amalie herself with great firmness, had curled up outside her door where he slept through the night.

She had thought that his excessive devotion would wear itself out, but it did not. Isa was her shadow, at her elbow whenever she turned, beside her whenever she sat down. She finally took to sending him on errands as a means of parting him from her, but he always returned the instant his duty was discharged. Julien began to call him her page, only half in jest. By degrees she accepted him as such and came, in an amazingly short time, to depend on him.

Isa was with her when, as the water began to recede, Amalie gathered the two menservants and four maids and set them to shoveling and sweeping the mud from the lower rooms before it could dry. The accumulated silt was pushed out the door onto the front gallery, while buckets of water were poured over the floor and then swept out, taking the residue from the cracks in the cypress floors. So impervious was the wood that, other than being swollen, the floorboards had taken no injury. In the dining room, the plaster above the twelve-inch-tall baseboards was crumbling in a few places where the water had lapped up onto it, but it could be patched and whitewashed with little trouble. All in all, the damage was minor.

The mud on the front gallery was another problem. Being exposed to air, it had caked and hardened and thickened as the mud from inside was sluiced out on top of it, until it resembled nothing so much as a pigpen. Removing it became a job for the quarters children, though they did not know it was work. They were given scrapers, rags, buckets of water, and free rein to play in the mud all they liked. They squealed and skated, plastering each other from head to foot, but when Amalie returned a short time later, the job was well on the way to being finished.

"Isa," she said in voice loud enough to be heard over the racket, "run and tell Marthe to set out muffins and milk for my crew and also two for you for your hard work today."

Immediately the children crowded around her, reaching to tug at the enveloping apron she wore over her day gown of blue poplin and jumping up and down. "I'll go! Me! Me!" they shouted in excitement at the treat. Their hands left muddy smears on the pristine white apron, but she did not mind. Reaching out, she ruffled the tightly curled hair on one head, then another, laughing at their antics, infected by their joy in living.

Her tone light but final, she said, "Isa is my page and it's his place to go. But the sooner you finish up, the sooner you'll all get to the muffins."

Isa gave her a seraphic smile as, straightening his shoulders, he marched away toward the kitchen, his limp barely noticeable. The other children scattered, squabbling good-naturedly over scrapers and rags, sloshing water with abandon so that she had to step quickly out of the way. A little girl of perhaps four was not so quick. Her feet slipped out from under her and down she went, getting her home-spun dress wet and bumping her cheek. Amalie moved quickly as the child began to cry. She picked her up, setting her on her feet, and, kneeling, wiped her face and one of her small black pigtails with a corner of her apron. The little girl stopped crying. She put her finger in her mouth, then suddenly grinned. Amalie felt her own lips curve in an answering smile. On impulse, she reached out to give the child a small hug. For an instant, small brown arms were around her neck in a tight squeeze, then the little girl broke away, running and chanting in singsong, "Pretty lady, pretty lady."

For no good reason, Amalie felt the press of tears as she came to her feet. Half blinded, she did not see the man in the doorway until she was nearly upon him. Robert Farnum did not move aside to let her pass, but stood leaning with one hand braced on the frame and the other in his black silk sling. As he watched her, there was an arrested expression in his dark blue eyes.

It was not the first time in the last few days that she had turned to find herself the object of his regard. She could not accuse him of following her as Isa did, and yet he seemed to be everywhere she went. It was unnerving, that steady gaze. It made her conscious of her appearance in a way she had not been since she was fifteen, so that she fussed over dressing in the morning and made an effort to be graceful in her movements, even while despising herself for it. Now, scarlet rose in her cheeks and her heart throbbed in her throat with an odd apprehension, as if she had been caught out in some misdeed.

"You like children," he said abruptly.

"Why, yes, I . . . don't most women?" Her hands were clenched, she discovered, and she thrust them quickly into her apron pockets.

He reached out and, before she could draw back, touched the tip of his finger to the tear caught on the end of her thick lashes. His voice soft, he answered, "Some more than others."

She was assailed suddenly by the memory of being held close in this man's arms, of the hard planes of his chest against her back, of the ridges of his thighs under her, with the warm, wet heat burgeoning between them. There had been safety there, and something more that she did not quite understand or dare to examine.

"How is your shoulder?" she asked, glancing away from him toward where the children squealed and played.

"A bit stiff still, but well enough."

"I thought you were riding to The Willows today?" There had been some discussion of it at breakfast, with M'mere arguing against the exertion.

"I did go."

"Everything was in order, I hope?"

"Reasonably. There had been a small amount of seepage in some of the outbuildings, but no damage."

The sun emerged from the clouds just then, spreading its golden light over the slope before the house, bringing a welcome warmth. Abruptly Amalie could smell the delicious scents of the moss roses and sweet olive that grew along the side of the house and the sweet, fecund perfume of sun-kissed grass.

She swallowed. "It was kind of you to return. I'm sure

you have much in need of doing at your place."

"My overseer is a good man, trustworthy, with a sensible head on his shoulders, and Belle Grove is in worse shape as far as the fields go. Now that the water is going down, they need to be drained before more damage is done to the standing cane. The mill and its machinery needs attention, as do the barns and nearly every other building on the place. It will be a great deal of work over the next few days, even weeks."

The implication was plain. Robert did not trust Patrick Dye to do what was needed without supervision, nor did he think much of the chances of Julien giving it the proper direction. It could not be argued that her husband had little concern for the state of his holdings. His thoughts on arising late this morning had been for his barge, a pleasure boat he was fond of that had been torn from its moorings by the flood.

"Yes, I'm sure M'mere is grateful for your support just now. I . . . If you will excuse me, I, too, have much to do."

"I beg your pardon," he said, his features grave, "I didn't mean to keep you from your duties."

Was it irony that rang in his tones? She did not know, but neither did she stay to find out.

Whether it was the distinction bestowed upon him by Amalie's presence and his title as page, or his own growing confidence brought on by having a definite place at Belle Grove, in the days that followed, Isa seemed to grow in stature and to find a measure of acceptance among the swarm of quarters children. He still clung close to his *petite maîtresse,* faithfully executing the commission she gave him, but could sometimes be persuaded late of an evening to join in the games of the other children.

It was just before dark on such an evening that he came hobbling in haste up the stairs to where Amalie sat reading on the gallery in the last of the fading light. A steamer had stopped that afternoon on its way up to Breaux Bridge and put off two issues of the weekly *Le Courier De Teche*, along with sundry other items. She looked up from a letter to the editor deploring the brigandage, banditry, and murder rife in the parish as Isa came to a stumbling halt in front of her.

"Oh, mam'zelle! You must come, quick, quick! M'sieu Dye, he is hurting our Lally!"

"He is punishing her?" Lally was a quiet, attractive girl of the clear brown skin color known as bright. Nearing her sixteenth year, she worked in the quarters nursery while the women were in the field and had never given any trouble that Amalie knew.

"*Mais, non,* mam'zelle! He wishes her in his cabin and she does not want to go."

A grim light rose in Amalie's eyes as she put aside the paper and got to her feet. There was mute evidence among the younger quarters children of this propensity of the over-seer and the women themselves made no attempt to hide the fact. She had been taught to overlook the failing as being beneath her notice, but this was a different matter.

Still, she asked, "You are sure Lally was not willing?"

"She fights him and screams, but the others fear to help her. Come, mam'zelle. Please, you will come now!"

With Isa at her heels, she went down the stairs in a billow of skirts, rounded the house, and hurried along the path past the *garçonnières* and smokehouse, the stables and cooperage, to the quarters. She heard Lally's cries and pleadings before she reached the first of the cabins. A moment later, she caught sight of Patrick Dye on the muddy trail that led toward the overseer's house. He was striding along, hauling the girl after him by the arm. Lally's kerchief, which she wore while working, had fallen back so that her hair, finer and straighter than most, straggled around her face. Her mouth was swollen and there was a smear of blood where her lip had been split. She set her feet now, dragging the overseer to a halt and prising at his fingers on her arm. Patrick stopped, jerking around to cuff her cross the face.

"Release that girl this instant!"

Amalie, several yards away, had not meant to speak. The words seemed to spring to her lips of their own accord, filled with a cold and angry disgust. It was surprise, she thought, as much as anything else, that made the Irishman obey her.

Lally flung herself away, running to meet Amalie's steady advance, falling to her knees to clutch at the skirts of her mistress. "Help me," she sobbed, "I beg you in the name of the Virgin, help me."

The overseer started toward her with his hands clenched at his sides. Amalie lifted her chin, her brown eyes hard as she deliberately stepped in front of the girl. The man stopped.

"Now see here, ma'am, there's no need for you to concern yourself. This is a private matter between me and the wench."

"I disagree. I am told that you meant to force yourself on her."

54

Patrick Dye sent Isa, also half-hidden behind Amalie, a murderous look, "That's not the way of it at all. She was willing enough, but wanted promises first."

"No, no, I didn't," Lally cried, lifting her eyes, brimming with tears, toward Amalie's face.

"What kind of promises, M'sieu Dye?" Amalie demanded, her voice edged with contempt.

"Oh, she won't admit it now, but she expected to be my housekeeper, to be let off her other work so she could lay around the house doing nothing. It's what they all want."

"And is it what you always promise?"

"I don't promise 'em anything. It's an honor, it is, and they know it."

His conceit and his insolence in saying such a thing to her brought the rise of outrage. "Lally seems curiously ignorant of that fact. You will not touch her again."

He gave a snorting laugh. "I think this is a thing that should be settled between men. I'll speak to your husband. You had best leave us to handle it."

"I don't think you understood me—" Amalie began.

"And I don't think you understand about when a man wants a woman. After all, how could you?"

The breath left Amalie's lungs and she stared at the man with wide eyes, unable to believe he meant what she thought he did. He could not know of the situation between her husband and herself. It was not possible. And yet what else could he mean? Her hands were trembling with the chagrin and rage that gripped her, and she clasped them together until the knuckles gleamed white. For a fleeting instant, she wished that she was not too much of a lady to swear, then she opened her pale lips and spoke with icy politeness. "You are dismissed. You will pack your things and be gone from this plantation within twenty-four hours."

"Oh, no, lady, that I won't," the overseer said flatly.

Hard on the words came a deep and cutting masculine voice. "Would you care to repeat that, Dye?"

So intent were they on their quarrel that they had not seen the man walking his horse toward them. Isa had and was tugging at Amalie's sleeve to direct her attention that way, though she had paid no attention until that moment. As Robert spoke, she whipped her head around, her eyes black with temper. There was a spark of what might have been admiration behind his blue eyes as he caught and held her gaze. Then he turned back to the other man.

"Well?"

"What I meant to say was, well, only Declouet himself has the power to discharge me. My contract for the season has been renewed and it don't say anything about no woman—"

"That will do."

The overseer shut his mouth with a snap, squinting up at Robert. Though temper blazed in his eyes, it was plain that he had no wish to cross swords with Robert. The arrogance of the man had turned to bravado. Amalie saw it with a fierce gladness, though she did not allow it to show on her face.

Robert dismounted, drawing the reins over the head of his horse to form a lead that he transferred to his left hand. He favored that arm still, but had left off his sling two days ago and so was able to offer his right to Amalie as he said, "May I escort you to the house?"

"Certainly," she answered, the words clipped, "but this girl comes with me."

"Now there's no need for that," Patrick said, taking a step forward.

Amalie sent him a scathing glance. "There is every need. Lally, stand up."

The girl had stopped crying. She scrambled to her feet with a fearful look at the overseer, then moved with a crab-like scuttle to where Isa stood.

"It's a mistake to undermine my authority like this," the overseer insisted, his hot gaze moving over Lally's body in her shapeless cotton blouse and skirt.

"You did that yourself when you abused it," Amalie returned and swung to take Robert's arm.

Patrick Dye took a half step after them and Amalie expected him to try once more to stop them. That he did not, she credited to the hard stare Robert threw over his shoulder. In a procession, the two of them, followed by the horse and the two servants, drew away, leaving the overseer standing with his hands on his hips behind them. Remembering the last expression she had glimpsed in Patrick Dye's eyes, Amalie knew she had made an enemy.

"The insolence of that man defies belief," she said when they were well away. "I wonder that Julien continues to employ him."

"The hands produce under him and he has a good grasp of the cultivation of cane; to some that's all that is important."

"I can't abide him!" Robert's arm under her fingers was bare. He had removed his coat and rolled his sleeves to his elbows against the heat of the day, but would ordinarily have slipped back into the coat before entering the house since a gentleman never appeared without one. The touch of her fingers on his warm skin, with the play of muscle and sinew underneath, was peculiarly intimate, and it took an effort of will to keep them steady.

"It is true that only Julien can dismiss him. You intend to ask him to do it?" Robert sent her a long glance, a serious cast to his features. He glanced down at her hand on his arm, then looked away again.

"I do."

"Then I think I will have a few words to say on the man's conduct himself. Cane and the hands he may know, but he has no understanding of the land, no respect for its needs. And I wouldn't care to have a man on my property who would use the tone of voice to a lady that I heard just now."

Her emotions were in such turmoil, such a stew of anger and despair, of relief and stupid girlish consciousness of the man beside her, that she could think of nothing to say in answer except, "T-thank you."

It was perhaps an hour and a half later that Amalie stepped into the salon. She moved to the front doors that stood open to the night, leaning her head on the facing as she stared out over the bayou that was now back within its banks. The night was alive with the sound of peeper frogs, a constant chorus. The air was soft, scented with flowers. The darkness out on the gallery was inviting, or would have been, if there had been someone to share it.

She turned away, stepping to the piano. Seating herself on the stool and raising the lid, she let her fingers move over the keys. Of their own accord, they sought and found the notes of a fragment of Chopin. She needed something to soothe her, something to hold at bay the voices in her head that taunted her with the growing suspicion of the mistake she had made all those weeks ago. She let her mind roam, seeking something, anything, as a distraction.

This evening, she had taken Lally to her bedchamber where she had begun immediately to train the girl as her personal maid. M'mere had told her some time ago to choose one, but she had never found the opportunity. Lally was competent and intelligent, and her quiet manner suited Amalie perfectly. The girl would be safe enough sleeping in the old nurse's room downstairs for the night and after that there would not be a problem.

Her toilette had been rushed, from her bath in the hip tub to the donning of her gown of rose silk with its skirt of overlapping flounces. She had wanted to leave plenty of time to speak to Julien before dinner. Despite the lack of leisure, she had been pleased with the result achieved by Lally, especially with her hair. The girl had released the severity of her usual braided coronet, heating the curling tongs over the lamp to construct a cascade of curls down the back of her head. She thought Lally was not unhappy in her new position either.

It was seldom that Amalie ventured to knock on the connecting door between her room and Julien's, but after what had happened earlier she thought it warranted. Her husband had been surprised but welcoming. He had dismissed Tige. As he slipped on his shoes, made like all his footwear with a buckle trim on the side of his own design, featuring his initials cast in brass, he had heard her out in silence. He had asked a question or two when she had finished, but scarcely seemed to note her answers. Finally, he had shrugged and told her that Robert had already spoken to him about the affair. It was his opinion that they were both making a great to-do about nothing. She must keep the girl by all means, if she wished, but he did not care to be put to the trouble of finding a new overseer this late in the season.

She had been so certain that she could persuade him, that it would matter little to him whether the man stayed or went. He had refused to discuss it further, refused to credit how insolent the man had been. If she could have brought herself to tell him what Patrick had implied, that he knew they were not husband and wife in anything other than name, then he might have been swayed, but it had seemed impossible to put the matter into words. How did a wife tell her husband that another man had made a cruel joke of his lack of passion for her?

That was not the sole reason she had remained silent, however. She had not mentioned the scenes in her bedroom to a soul other than M'mere, and then only under close questioning. She could not imagine the older woman speaking of it to a man like Patrick Dye, not even if she had spoken of it to Robert. That left only Julien, and if her husband had mentioned her inability to attract him to the overseer, then she did not want to know it.

She looked up as she heard the sound of footsteps on the loggia stairs. Robert, moving with the lithe control of an outdoorsman, approached the open doorway and stepped inside. He was in formal attire of black broadcloth with a white silk cravat at the neck of his linen shirt. The stark contrast of colors gave his bronze skin a golden sheen. He was a distinguished-looking man, handsome in a rugged fashion if one cared for such things. Doubtlessly many women had in the past.

The room had grown darker. He crossed to the lamp that burned on the round mahogany table in its center and, picking it up, brought it to the piano where he set it down on the fringed shawl that was thrown over the top of the instrument. She smiled her gratitude for the extra light, and he moved away. She thought he stepped out onto the front gallery, and after a few moments, lost in the rippling notes of a sonata, then moving on to yet another piece, she ceased to think of him.

Music was an accomplishment required of her as a lady and she had no pretensions to being anything more than adequate at it. It had, however, been a solace to her in the years after the death of her mother and father and that of Etienne. Her great-aunt had not approved of displays of emotion, whether of grief or joy, anger or happiness. It was more acceptable for Amalie to allow her playing to express what she felt, more ladylike.

Ladylike. How she had despised that word as a young girl, how she had railed against all the stultifying conventions that hemmed her in, constricting her activities like so many layers of smothering petticoats. Now she was so used to them that she hardly noticed their weight, except to use them, at times, like a protective armor.

She thought of Julien and his bored refusal to dismiss Patrick Dye. For the first time since she was ten years old, she wished that she was a man, with a man's ability to impose his will. She might as well be a man, for all the good that being a woman looked likely to bring her in the long years that lay before her.

The last notes of Beethoven's Appassionata crashed around her, lingering in the air as she lifted her hands. Suddenly weary, she turned on the stool and raised her head. Somehow she was not surprised to see Robert on the other side of the room, lounging on a brocade settee with his legs stretched before him and his arms crossed on his chest. His gaze was upon her and in their dark blue depths was a remnant of that same intent appraisal she had discovered in them on that first morning in M'mere's sitting room. He lowered his lashes and his steady regard moved to the clustered curls of her hair with their shimmering blue highlights; drifted down the curve of her cheek to the smooth, white expanse of her shoulders and the delicate shadow that marked the division between the gentle globes of her breasts; then moved lower still to where the slender indentation of her waist merged with the fullness of her skirts. He was still, as only a man in absolute control of himself can be, then he looked up abruptly.

Amalie lowered her lashes, looking away, but not before she had seen it, not before she had recognized in the darkness of his eyes the cobalt blaze of desire. So intense was her concentration that she jumped, startled, as Julien appeared in the doorway.

"If the concert is over," her husband drawled, "could I interest anyone in a glass of sherry?"

Dinner was an endless meal. Julien had found his barge lodged against a tree downstream. It was three-quarters full of water from a stave in the hull, and he had taken four men from the work of plowing drainage ditches to raise it and tow it back to Belle Grove. The repairs to be made, the paint and gilding he would use to restore it, the material of cream-and-blue stripes he had in mind for sails and soft draperies to blow in the wind and to shelter the ladies from the sun made up his conversation. Chloe observed that boats made her bilious and he need not go to so much trouble on her account. Julien countered that, though it would be a severe strain, he felt that he might well be able to support a day without her company.

The quarrel that threatened was averted by George, who informed Chloe that she would, he was sure, enjoy sitting in the garden he had envisioned. The sandbag dike and the rich silt deposited on the front lawn by the flood had inspired him. He would have a reflecting pool formed in the depression where the soil for the sandbags had been dug in front of the house. There would be lilies and water plants around its verge. To make a fairy display in spring, he would plant soft-hued azaleas from China and drifts of spirea on the slopes that curved from the house around the pool. For the winter, he would have the dark greens of pines and magnolia leaves, and beneath them the shining foliage and tender blossoms of camellias. If Madame Declouet wished, there could be a formal French garden paved in brick, set around with hedge, and enlivened with statuary at the side of the house, but the more natural, English landscape would suit the bayou approach of Belle Grove.

Chloe agreed with him, exclaiming in a fashion highly pleasing to the Englishman, but was soon talking with just as much animation about the proposed visit of an opera troupe from New Orleans to St. Martinville, the notice of which she had seen in the *Courier.* Such engagements were not unusual; St. Martinville, for all its small size, was a mecca during the summer because of the planters who retired to their holdings that lined the Teche from Berwick Bay to Breaux Bridge, and of the healthful winds of that latitude, so different from the still, humid, pestilent heat of New Orleans. Julien entered enthusiastically in the discussion of the talents of the troupe, whom they had all seen in the city during the winter season, and before the meal was over they had planned an evening at the opera house.

They all rose from the dinner table which had been returned downstairs, and ascended to the salon together. In some of the American households along the bayou, it was said, the custom was for the men to stay behind after the last course had been taken away to drink brandy and port. No Frenchman, however, would find the attractions of the bottle superior to those of the ladies. The cynics claimed the momentary separation to be a mere convenience, one that allowed the different sexes to attend, without embarrassment, to those necessary functions brought on by long meals of many courses, each accompanied by wine. The Creoles, who saw no reason in these normal functions for discomposure, were amused. Everyone was human, were they not?

Amalie was persuaded to favor them at the piano. In an effort to lighten her mood, she ran through a medley of Stephen Foster favorites. Occupied with looking through the music for something else, she did not hear the beginning of the argument between Julien and Chloe. When she looked up, her husband was standing over the girl.

"Why should I listen to you?" he demanded. "Half of what you say is nothing more than pretense. What glorious self-indulgence, moaning over your fate while living in the lap of luxury, wanting for nothing. What could make your existence more exciting than to cast yourself in something approaching one of your leading library romances, to become the female half of a pair of star-crossed lovers!"

"Julien!" M'mere exclaimed in reproach.

"If we must talk of indulgence, what of you?" the girl returned with magnificent scorn. "You dabble in theatricals and play at art. Art, hah! You are no match even for poor Adrien Persac, who paints nothing but houses and cuts out his people from *Harper's* and *Godey's* to paste in front of them!"

"You being such a paragon of energy and creativity that you are able to cast aspersions? What of that last bit of Berlin work of yours, only half done and stuffed under the settee cushion for three months?"

"That will do!" Julien's mother cried, rising in agitation, then sinking back immediately with her eyes closed and her hand at her heart.

"M'mere!"

Julien was beside her in an instant, chafing her hands. Chloe caught up her fan that hung on her wrist and leaned over the older woman, plying it so vigorously that the lace on M'mere's cap fluttered about her pallid face. Robert moved to the liquor chest and splashed a little brandy into a glass. Returning with it to where the others clustered about his aunt, he put the glass to her lips, insisting that she drink. Amalie, who had risen to her feet, picked up the lamp on the piano and moved to put it down on a side table for more light. George, like a sensible man, stood back out of the way, though his color was high.

"Cut her laces," Julien said, his face creased with worry.

As Chloe made no move, Amalie stepped forward, but only to remove the brooch of intricately woven hair at her mother-in-law's throat and to loosen her collar.

The older woman sipped at the brandy, grimaced, and, as color came back into her cheeks, opened her eyes. "How silly of me. I must have stood up too fast."

Relief brought a smile to Julien's face. "Yes, I expect that was it."

"I will be fine now, you need not hover. If you would please me, my son, perhaps you would read something for us, as only you can. That man Longfellow's *Evangeline* would be pleasant."

"Of course, M'mere."

Julien found the small volume in the glass-fronted bookcase and turned to the beginning, taking a stance leaning against the piano. The others, in obedience to M'mere's will, found seats: Chloe beside the older woman on the settee, Robert in an armchair near the door, at the edge of the lamplight, and George beside him.

Amalie sank down onto a smaller chair beside the settee, turning it deliberately so that her face was in the shadow. Through the open door, the sound of the peeper frogs was loud in the quiet. A mosquito whined around her face and was gone. The night wind whispered softly in the live oaks outside, then died away.

Julien, his voice quiet, mellow, began: " 'This is the forest primeval—' "

Evangeline had been published some seven or eight years previously, but was still a favorite along the Teche. In eloquent style, it told the story of the expulsion of the French Acadians from Nova Scotia by the English in 1755.

Since many of those Acadians, seeking French-speaking compatriots and fresh lands to farm, had settled in Louisiana on the banks of the state's many bayous, including the Teche, the interest was natural. The long, lyric poem spoke also of Evangeline and Gabriel, young lovers on the verge of being wed, who had been torn apart and placed on separate ships, and of Evangeline's wanderings in search of her lost love only to find him, long years later, when she had become a nun and he lay dying.

It was said that the poem had come from a legend of the bayou country, one related by a young Louisianan named Edward Simon, while a student at Harvard College, to a writer named Nathaniel Hawthorne. Hawthorne had then told it to his friend, Henry Wadsworth Longfellow, who had used it as the basis for his work. The names of the real betrothed couple had been Emmeline Labiche and Louis Arceneaux. Three years passed before the couple was reunited at the *Poste des Attakapas*, which had been known for forty years now as St. Martinville. Emmeline had brought with her a wedding gown, carefully packed in her box, but on her arrival in Louisiana had discovered that Louis, who had given her up as lost, had married another. The girl, prostrated by shock, grief, and the rigors of the long journey from Nova Scotia, died, and was buried in the Catholic cemetery behind the church of St. Martin de Tours.

Julien did have a sense of the dramatic. His voice rose and fell, playing on the emotions and bringing an immediate sense of reality to the poignant story. When his last syllable died away, Chloe sniffed, wiping at her eyes with the edge of her hand. M'mere gave a long sigh. Shortly afterward, they all began to drift toward their bedrooms.

Amalie, putting away the music at the piano, was one of the last to go. Julien glanced at her once or twice as he replaced the book he had used in the bookcase. They were alone as she started toward the door to her room.

"Amalie?"

Her brown eyes were dark with surprise as she turned. "Yes?"

"I'm sorry that I had to be so disobliging about Patrick," he said as he moved to stand before her. "He could be replaced, but the trouble is there's no guarantee the next man would be any better, and he might well be worse."

"I suppose."

"I realize you don't like him, but there is no need for you to associate with the man after all."

"Am I to ignore him when I see him in the quarters?"

"If you like. So long as you tolerate him, there is no need to be polite."

"He seems to operate under the same rules."

"Meaning?" her husband queried, frowning.

"That Patrick Dye's behavior this afternoon was most discourteous."

"His manners may seem coarse to you, but you can hardly expect otherwise. He's an overseer, not a gentleman."

She gave a stiff nod. "If you are satisfied, then I must be also."

"Ah, Amalie," he said, catching her arms and sliding his strong swordsman's hands along them to cup her elbows, "I knew you would see reason. It's a small matter, in all truth, not worth quarreling over."

There was a hint of pleading in his voice and in his smile. He was exerting his considerable charm to bring her to share his opinion. As much as she might disagree, she was gratified that he would make the effort. She shook her head. "It's your responsibility after all."

"So it is. Good night, *ma chère.*" He leaned to press his firm lips to her forehead before releasing her.

There was a tiny frown between Amalie's brows as she watched him walk out onto the loggia where the main entrance to his bedchamber was located. How odd of him. He seldom kissed her except to salute her hand with playful gallantry. She could count on the fingers of one hand the number of times she had felt the press of his mouth upon hers, and then it had been the most fleeting of pressures. And yet this kiss had held the warmth of affection, the feel of benediction, and, yes, a trace of possessiveness.

Chapter 4

Lally was waiting for Amalie in her bedchamber. As the girl unbuttoned her gown and took it off over her head, untied the tapes of her cage-hoop skirt and petticoats, and unhooked her corset, Amalie allowed her thoughts to return to Julien.

If theirs had been a normal relationship, she would have thought her husband was showing signs of jealousy. He had been disturbed the day of the flood when he had seen her in the arms of his cousin. Robert's continued presence seemed to make him edgy, though she had it from M'mere that there was nothing unusual about her nephew taking his meals with them or making use of the *garçonnière.*

Throughout their boyhood, it had always been taken for granted that Julien and Robert would eat where they found themselves at mealtimes and sleep where they were when darkness fell. So often did they borrow each other's clothing that it was difficult to tell at any one time what item belonged to whom. Even now, the two men got along well for long periods while they laughed over drinks, telling tales of their many hunting and fishing expeditions together and boyhood outings and pranks. And yet their conversations were often halted by uncomfortable silences as they stared into their glasses, and Julien's black eyes sometimes rested on his cousin with a brooding look in their depths. Was Julien's resentment simply because of the way Robert had taken charge at Belle Grove since his return, despite his own reluctance to do so himself? Or was it because of his cousin's interest, no matter how guarded, in his wife?

She did not think she was flattering herself. Something about her had caught Robert's attention. She was not overly concerned, however. Her husband's cousin was a man of honor. If she were any judge of character, there was not the least need to fear that he would step beyond the line of acceptable behavior. Doubtless it was a momentary thing, one that would fade without encouragement. And there would not, of course, be any encouragement from her.

Amalie suppressed a grim sigh as she lifted her arms so that Lally could slip her nightgown of white batiste over her head. The material was soft and filmy. The fullness of the skirt, with its deep hem embroidered white on white by the Ursuline nuns, fell from a high, scooped-neck bodice that was also embroidered. It was one of an even dozen, all similar in style, provided by M'mere as a part of her trousseau.

Lally took down her hair and brushed it until it hung in a light brown curtain touched with shimmers of blue down her back, reaching well past her waist. The maid then turned down the bed and, when Amalie was in it, let down the mosquito baire, lowered the lamp, and went out, closing the door behind her. Her footsteps died away in the quiet house.

Left in semidarkness, Amalie became aware of the crack of light under the sliding doors that led into Julien's bed-chamber. She thought of her husband, preparing for bed with the aid of Tige, but though she listened, she could hear no sound from the next room. She turned her head toward the gleam of moonlight shining in through the windows with their hangings of rose silk.

The same silk hung from the tester of the bed on which she lay, drawn back on either side at the head, while the silk that was gathered in a starburst arrangement on the under-side of the great wooden frame overhead was of palest blue, the traditional color of the bridal *ciel de lit,* or bed ceiling. The room loomed large around her, decorated with an enor-mous French armoire of rosewood; a dressing table skirted in gold brocade to match; a washstand with china pieces on its marble top that were painted with roses and twining vines; a set of steps beside the bed that contained a hidden well for her slippers; and a pair of bedstands on either side of the bed. There was also a Louis XVI velvet-covered arm-chair beside the open window. Oppressed suddenly by the lack of air beneath the mosquito baire, Amalie swung it aside, slid from the high bed, and moved to the chair.

She sat down, tucking her feet under her, and covering them with the long length of her nightgown. She breathed deeply of the fresh night air, scented with roses and honeysuckle, as she leaned her head against the velvet back. Beyond the window, the moonlight silvered the leaves on the live oaks and dusted the hanging rags of Spanish moss with powdered diamonds. Through the tree branches, she could catch a glimpse of the mirrored surface of the bayou as it wound around past the side of the house.

Her gaze narrowed as she caught a flicker of movement. A man was standing under the trees; his face and hands were a pale blur, though his clothing blended into the darkness. He moved, wandering toward the water, stepping into a shaft of moonlight, moving out of it again.

Was it Julien or Robert? She could not tell. From his size and carriage, it might have been either. Still, it was Robert who made a habit of being up and about early and Julien who kept the late hours and late risings.

If it was her husband, what was he doing out there? A dark garden was not his usual haunt. Was he disturbed by the softness of the night, the fecundity of the season? If so, she could understand it. She could indeed.

Thrusting herself up from the chair, she swung away from the window and climbed back into her bed. She spread her hair over the pillow to keep it from under her, then closed her eyes with determination. After a time, the stiffness left her body and she slept.

It was a touch that woke her. Warm and exquisitely gentle upon her breast, it sent a shiver of desire along her senses to rout her dreams and leave her flushed and conscious. She opened her eyes. The moon had set and the room was dark.

A shadow loomed beside her on the high mattress, a presence as much felt as seen. A man's hand was on her breast, cupping the tender globe with care and caressing the nipple through the thin material of her nightgown.

She started, her hand coming up to catch his arm as she whispered, "Julien?"

The word was smothered as he leaned over to find her mouth with his. Firm and smooth, his lips brushed the sensitive surfaces of her own with the touch of fire. She felt the heated flick of his tongue as he tasted the sweet and vulnerable corners, testing the moist line where they came together for resistance. There was little. Amalie, seduced by a new sureness in her husband's touch and the insidious creep of languor along her veins, hesitated only a moment before she allowed her lips to part.

With a low sound in his throat, he took instant advantage of that soft, tentative surrender. He probed the moist and tender recesses of her mouth, teasing, exploring, increasing the burning demand until hesitantly, driven by a deep need, she touched her tongue to his. The bed ropes and the mattress creaked as he joined her on the bed. He caught her close to him and she could feel the hammering of his heart in his chest. She reached out to smooth her fingers along his forearm, closing her hand slowly upon the ridged muscles.

On a ragged breath, he lifted his head. His warm mouth trailed a fiery path of kisses along her jawline and up the slim curve of her cheek to her temple. He brushed his lips over her closed eyes, feathering the salt-flavored lashes with his tongue, and spanned the space between her brows with a gentle kiss. He inhaled the clean fragrance of her hair mixed with the scent of vetiver from the pillowcase on which she lay, then, with the urgency of a thirsty man seeking water, sought her mouth once more.

This was new, his passionate pleasure in the feel and taste of her. Recognizing it brought the release of some closely held fear deep inside Amalie. She clung to him, sliding her fingers to his shoulder and along it to the column of his neck. With her breath fluttering in her chest, she twined her fingers in the crisp hair that grew low there, pressing herself against his long length. The firmness of her breasts thrust against him, her lower body came up against the incredible hardness, heat, and rigidity of his masculine form. Through her batiste gown, she felt his nakedness, his need of her. Her heart swelled, throbbing against her ribs as she realized that this time there would be no disappointment, no tears.

"Amalie—"

The husky syllables had the sound of a plea and a prayer. His fingers, warm and slightly rough, once more found the swell of her breast and its soft covering. They followed the low neckline of her nightgown, searching for and finding the tiny pearl buttons that held it closed. The fastening yielded to his sure movements. Slowly, carefully, he drew aside the fragile cloth. She felt the cool night air upon her skin, the warm touch of his breath, then his mouth was upon the arch of her throat. A tremor ran over her as she felt the flick of his tongue at the hollow at its base. It increased as he sought lower for the firm mound of her breast that trembled with the thudding of her heart.

She made a soft sound, almost a protest, as he drew back, but he only shifted higher, tugging the nightgown down her shoulders and freeing her arms as he pushed it lower about her waist. He bent to bury his face in the valley between her breasts, breathing in her sweetness, then his mouth slowly began to ascend one peak, circling it with meticulous care as he tried its texture and resilience. Amalie held her breath, her senses expanding. Her skin seemed to glow with warmth. Then, as she felt the heat of his mouth close upon her nipple, she arched toward him.

She had not known it could be like this, like a fire in the blood, had never guessed how wanton her nature was. This was a woman's duty, or so she had been taught; how was she to know it could also be a woman's pleasure? The women in the quarters had always averred so, but ladies were different. Or were they?

She raised her trembling fingers to touch his face, smoothing its planes and angles, putting a tentative fingertip to his mouth, which held her nipple as his tongue caressed it. Delight burgeoned inside her, spreading, bringing a fullness to her loins.

Leaving one nipple taut and wet, he sought the other with no less patience. So enthralled was Amalie with the sensations he brought forth that she scarcely noticed his hand at her waist sliding the nightgown lower, brushing the folds from her abdomen as he pushed the sheet aside and drawing the soft cotton material from beneath her. It was only as he swept the last covering from her, dropping her nightgown over the side of the bed, that she felt her nakedness. She shivered, not with cold, but with reaction, yet before she could move, he had captured her mouth with his firm lips, and his hands, gently marauding, were upon her once more.

He spread his hard fingers over her breast, flicking the

nipple with his thumb before smoothing his palm downward over her ribs to the slender indentation of her waist. He flexed his fingers to span half its narrow width easily, then pressed downward to clasp the tender curve of her hip. She drew her breath in at that intimate touch. It remained trapped in her lungs as he turned his hand, brushing the backs of his fingers across her abdomen to the small and silken triangular pelt at the apex of her legs and slipping them between her thighs.

His touch, insidious and constant, brought the molten surge of desire. The prickle of gooseflesh moved across her skin, and she moved closer, drowning in the need to be a part of him, to make him a part of her. The taste of his mouth was sweet, and the assurance of his touch upon her was like a balm. The muscular hardness of his frame was the perfect complement to her softness, its hollows and angles fitting with precision to her curves. His heart vibrated against her, and in the tension of his hold she could sense his rigid control. In an ecstasy of giving, she eased her thighs open, allowing access to her moist flesh. As he took it, she gasped at the stinging pain.

He had found her unbreached maidenhead. He went still, making a sound in his throat that might have been a stifled exclamation. He withdrew his hand and his kiss became gentler, as if in apology.

Amalie turned her head, her voice a thread of sound whispering against his cheek as she said. "The goose fat on the bedstand."

"No need," came his soft answer. Before she could protest, he had raised himself above her and leaned down to place the warm wetness of his mouth where he had touched.

The natural moisture, her own and his, was enough. When he drew her to him moments later, his entry was easy, with no more than an instant of pain that was soon banished by the soothing rhythm of his movements. In passionate gratitude, Amalie clung to him; then as her pleasure grew, she moved against him, wanting—needing—to have him deep inside her, and deeper still. The blood raced in her veins; her skin was dewed with perspiration. The shocks of his thrusts shivered through her. She welcomed them, rising to meet their endless power, their effortless strength. Her breasts and her mouth were swollen. Tears rose unbidden to her eyes, tears of ecstasy and relief from her fear that she might be forever denied this joy. They were also tears of completion, tears of love. She moved her head from side to side, pressing her palms to the hard muscles of his shoulders as he kept his weight off her.

It crept in upon her, the ancient magic—vivid, devouring, an explosion of wonder. It held her transfigured, this balm to the rite of womanhood. There was nothing but the man and the moment, and herself encompassing both in an exultation so intense that it had an undertone of pain. She cried out as she felt the rush of release and was caught close in a painful hold as the man above her plunged deep, then was still.

The tears would not stop. They overflowed her eyes and tracked down her temples into her hair. She made no sound, trying to control her ragged breathing, trying not to give herself away. She swallowed hard, but still they came.

He eased from her, rolling to his side and drawing her against him. She was lying on her hair and he pulled it from under her, smoothing the silken strands over her shoulder and brushing them from her face. He cupped her cheek in his hand and pressed his mouth to her forehead, then brushed her eyelids. At the wetness of her lashes, he drew back.

"What is it, *chérie?*" came his whisper.

She shook her head. "N-nothing."

"Did I hurt you?" The words were soft, with a hint of pleading.

"No," she said vehemently. "I . . . It's just that you—that we—always before—"

He touched his finger to her lips. "Shh, I think I understand."

It might have been that, or it might have been his arms around her and his hand stroking her hair, but finally the ache in her throat eased and the tears ceased. She relaxed against him with her head pillowed on his arm and her legs entwined with his. She spread her hand over his chest with its light furring of hair, feeling the steady beat of his heart beneath her palm. The warm male smell of him filled her nostrils and his strength supported her. She took a deep breath and let it out slowly.

"It was difficult, the waiting?" he asked, his voice a thread of sound. His hand strayed down her back to where her hips were pressed against him.

She managed a small nod.

"The next time, then, should not be so long in coming."

It was a moment before she took his meaning and even then she was not certain. She tilted her head back, staring at his dark shape there in the darkness, caught by the thread of amusement in his tone that had sounded odd for Julien. Then her doubts were routed as his mouth closed over hers, and his grasp on the curves of her hips brought her against the lower part of his body that was heated and hard once more.

Some time later, in the early hours of the morning, he left her, sliding from the bed and stooping to pick up his clothing, or perhaps his dressing gown from the floor. She protested sleepily and was rewarded by a swift, hard kiss. Still, his footsteps retreated and she heard the scrape of the sliding doors that led into his room as they opened, then closed once more.

"Mam'zelle looks well this morning."

Amalie, sitting at her dressing table, glanced at the maid who was putting up her hair. There was a knowing light in the girl's eyes which was overlaid by shy affection. It was the bed, with its all too obvious stains on the sheets, that caused it. Silently castigating herself for being too drowsily content to rise early and remove the telltale signs, Amalie did what she could to remedy matters.

"Thank you, Lally. I think you know why."

"Mam'zelle?" The maid was the picture of innocence.

"I don't mind that you know of my private affairs since you are so close to me, but I would be most unhappy to learn that they were being gossiped about in the quarters."

"Ah, no, mam'zelle, this I would never do. So much I owe you for saving me! How could I repay you by telling such things behind your back?"

"I was sure I could count on your loyalty."

"But, yes, mam'zelle," the girl said fervently as she paused in braiding the glistening strands of hair she held, "always."

When the maid had departed, carrying the sheets to be

laundered, Amalie took a last look at herself in the cheval mirror that stood in a corner. She did look well. There was soft color on her cheekbones and radiance in her eyes; her skin, above the modest neckline of her gown of lavender cord muslin trimmed with slate ribbon, had the sheen of a pearl. She felt as vibrant as she looked, for the days that stretched before her now seemed filled with promise when they had been empty before.

Swinging away and moving toward the door, she was aware of the glide of her thighs together, even clothed as they were in pantaloons, in a way she had never noticed before. The swing of her hips, the seductive swish of her skirts, made her feel more womanly than at any time in her life. It was peculiar but true, and the knowledge brought a smile of wry amusement to her lips.

As she pulled the door open, Isa nearly fell into the room. He had been sitting with his back against the door, patiently waiting. Now he scrambled to his feet, picked up the thick pallet on which he had slept, and straightened its meticulous folds before tucking it under his arm. At a sign from her, he scampered ahead to open the door out onto the loggia, then stepped back while she passed through the opening. He paused to put his pallet away in the wooden box that held a clutter of odds and ends—riding hats and crops, umbrellas and oilskin capes—then came thudding down the stairs after her in time to dodge around and open the door to the dining room.

There was a scraping of chairs at her entrance as Julien and Robert came to their feet. Amalie paused in surprise. She had expected to find only M'mere at the table since they usually breakfasted together. Robert was in the habit of eating much earlier, often waiting at the kitchen door for a biscuit and ham to eat with his morning coffee, downing it while standing up, before swinging into the saddle and riding out over the plantation. He might, indeed he often did, eat a second breakfast on a much grander scale with Julien, when her husband could bring himself to face food before noon, but was seldom present when she had her own.

"Good morning," she said, sending a smiling glance from under her lashes toward Julien standing at the head of the table. Isa had pulled out her chair at the foot and she slid into it while the men resumed their seats.

Julien returned her greeting shortly, his dark brown eyes not quite meeting hers. Robert's answer was civil but brief, and there was a grim set to his mouth as he flicked a look from his cousin to her. Amalie's face lost some of its animation. It was M'mere who filled the breach, asking her how she had slept and making some comment about the early warmth of the day.

Isa donned his serving vest of white homespun, which was laid ready on a chair beside the door. It was just like those worn by the menservants who could be heard talking in low voices in the pantry. He filled a coffee cup from the service set out on the sideboard and brought it to her carefully. She helped him place it properly, then he took her plate and, raising the domed silver covers of the chafing dishes, chose for her two buttered muffins, a slice of ham, and a peeled and sectioned orange. She thanked him with a fleeting smile as he set the food before her. Taking up her cup with stiff movements, she took a sip of the hot, aromatic coffee.

Julien's lack of response, his failure to show any sign of

his own pleasure at what had passed between them, was dismaying. And yet what had she expected? A passionate embrace? The ardent look of a lover? No, nothing quite so dramatic, but surely there should have been some indication of their changed relationship.

Then again, Julien's reserve might simply mean that he did not care for public displays of affection. It was borne upon her just how little she knew of the man she had married, how little she had learned in the months they had been wed. He was a private man, and had, since their return to Belle Grove, been living his life very nearly separate from her. Surely that would change now?

Summoning composure, she raised her voice enough to be heard at the end of the long table. "You are up early, Julien."

"I didn't sleep well." The words were deliberate, almost surly.

"Didn't you? It might be easier for you to sleep at night if you got out of the house more during the day—went riding perhaps."

"In your company?"

Her gratification that he had taken her meaning banished the shadows from her brown eyes. "Yes, if you like."

"Today?"

"I'm sure I could make the time."

"I regret to disappoint you, but I am seeing to the refurbishing of the *Zephyr* this morning."

The *Zephyr* was the name of his sailing barge. She lowered her gaze to her plate, toying with a piece of muffin. "I see."

"Robert, now, slept so well that he was late rising and has

not yet made his inspection tour. I'm sure he would be pleased to have your companionship."

"I would be delighted," Robert said without hesitation.

She slanted a quick look at her husband's cousin, at the same time aware of M'mere's anxious gaze upon her son. Her voice subdued, she answered, "Another time, perhaps. I—I've just remembered that I must set the women to cutting out shirts. Several of the hands are looking quite ragged."

"Your devotion to duty is overwhelming," Julien commented, leaning back in his chair and pushing his plate with its untouched food away. "How lucky I am to have so diligent a wife."

"Indeed, and so understanding," M'mere said, her tone sharp.

Her son paid no attention. The irony in his eyes as they met Amalie's direct gaze was disturbing.

"I do the best I can," she said.

"So accommodating," Julien murmured.

There was a loud scraping sound as Robert pushed his chair back. He threw down his napkin and left the table, flinging himself from the room. M'mere jumped up with a soft, disjointed excuse and hurried after him. Julien frowned as the door closed behind them, then sighed, pushing his hand through his hair.

"I must beg you to forgive my ill-humor, *ma chère*," he said. "You were not the cause, and it was wrong of me to turn it in your direction."

It was a moment before she could answer. "It doesn't matter."

"But it does. I would not have you hate me."

"I could not do that," she said and was aware the moment the words were spoken of their truth.

"It might be better if you did." He got to his feet abruptly and moved from the room.

"Julien?" she called after him, but he did not stop.

How long she sat holding her coffee cup in the air, she did not know. It was Isa who disturbed her absorption. Stepping to her side, he bowed, then took the cup from her grasp and carried it to the sideboard where he emptied it and refilled it with fresh, hot coffee. Then he brought it back to her and she drank it gratefully. Leaving the cold muffins and ham on her plate, she got to her feet and moved from the dining room out to the back, in the direction of the quarters.

It was a long day, and a strained one. Amalie kept busy, trying not to think of the night that had past or of those that were to come. She set the women to work cutting and sewing summer clothes for the men, one of the two sets of clothing made by the plantation women each year. Since there were seventy-five hands on the place, it was a large job. When it was well under way, she visited the infirmary, then returned to the house and set the spring cleaning in motion.

Though it was not yet officially summer, the sun in this southern latitude was growing hotter. It was doubtful that they would need a fire again until fall, so the fireplaces could be emptied of ashes and cleaned. The carpets needed to be taken out and beaten before being sprinkled with tobacco against moths and stored in the attic. The walls and ceilings had to be brushed down, the woodwork washed with whiting, and the picture frames and gilding dusted.

The windows and mirrors needed washing and polishing, the furniture rubbed with oil, the marble surfaces cleaned with silver soap, and the brass finishes made bright with vinegar and soda. It was perfectly natural, of course, that in the midst of this upheaval there should be afternoon callers.

It was a trio of ladies who rode up to the door in their carriage. The Mesdames Lulu and Marie Oudry were widowed ladies, elderly friends of M'mere, and accompanying them was the granddaughter of the eldest, Mademoiselle Louise Callot, a giggling girl a bit younger than Chloe. The two older women wore stiff and rustling black, which made the skin of their faces look incredibly pale and their eyes like small bits of obsidian. Louise, in virginal white, was slyly demure. Once seated in the salon, the elder of the pair declared that they had brought dear Louise to enjoy younger company than they could provide. Her father and mother were presently traveling in Alabama, but would soon return to collect their daughter; at the same time they would call upon dear Sophia and Julien, combining the most gratifying pleasure with commerce, as it were.

The last reference was to the fact that Monsieur Callot was a cane and cotton factor. His firm had handled the selling of the sugar produced by the plantation for some years, and due to some distant connection, the families were quite friendly, visiting often during the winter season in New Orleans.

The main burden of conversation during this visit fell on Julien's mother and Chloe, since they were nearest in ages to the visitors. As the favorite topic of the two older guests was which of their mutual acquaintances was ill to the point of being at death's door and who had passed through that dreaded portal, and Louise's main interest was herself and her most recent conquests on the battlefield of the ballroom floor, Amalie could not feel too badly about being left out. Still, she was put to the trouble of ordering cakes and the *eau de sucre* suitable to the occasion and was forced by convention to lend her presence. She spent the time plying her needle on a damask tablecloth in need of mending until the visitors had left.

She discovered a short time later that Robert had deserted them. He had returned to The Willows, sending his valet to remove his possessions that had gradually accumulated in the Belle Grove *garçonnière*. He would still keep an eye on the place, of course, and would often be in and out, but he had thought it best to leave. M'mere affected to have no idea of what had caused his sudden decision. Amalie thought she knew. As difficult as it was to believe, she thought the reason was Julien's possessiveness of her.

Amalie had never considered herself of more than average attraction. Her great-aunt had always emphasized the passing nature of physical beauty and the importance of internal grace. Vanity had not been encouraged. Amalie knew her coloring was a bit unusual, but she was also aware that it lacked the dramatic effect of blond or auburn prettiness. She had no reason now to think that her husband's manner was due to a desperate passion for her. His jealousy, if such it was, could only be accounted for by comparing him to a dog with a bone. She had become precious in his sight of a sudden because she had caught another man's eye.

It was not an assessment to Julien's credit, any more than it was to her own. She did not like the conclusion she had come to, but could see no way, given the circumstances, that it could be avoided.

At dusk, she stood leaning against a colonette on the upper gallery watching the pink and lavender afterglow of the sunset reflected on the bayou and the wheeling of the pigeons as they made ready to roost for the night. In front of her was the fresh-turned earth where George Parkman had begun his reflecting pool. She could see, off to one side, the Englishman and Chloe strolling about under the trees while he waved his arms explaining his vision of floral loveliness once more. Behind her, she could hear the scratch of a coal on the gallery floorboards where Isa was drawing. She should tell him to stop, make him clean the charcoal away, but she did not have the energy or the heart. He became so absorbed in his pastime and was so innocently pleased with the results.

A pigeon swooped low and fluttered to perch on the railing just down from where she stood, then began to sidle nearer. He was gray with white-tipped wing feathers, a blue, green, and purple iridescent sheen to the ruff at his neck, and red legs and feet. Chloe sometimes fed them breadcrumbs and toast crusts here in the morning, and that was doubtless what this bird expected from her. The pigeon cocked his head, making his cooing, warbling sound, his manner as ingratiating as he could manage it. Amalie laughed, a soft sound.

Isa looked up, then his charcoal moved in quick strokes. A moment later, the image of the pigeon was there on the floor. She glanced at it, then moved to stand beside him as he squatted over his drawing.

"What a marvel you are, Isa," she said, "I wonder what

you could do if you had more to work—but of course!" As he looked up at her with patient inquiry in his dark, liquid eyes, she went on, "You must go at once to Lally. Tell her I require my box of paints from the top shelf of the armoire. Then find Charles and say that I desire a length of wrapping paper."

He wrinkled his brow. "You are going to paint, mam'zelle?"

"Don't you think I could?" she teased him.

"Mam'zelle can do anything."

Touched by his faith, she suppressed a smile. "I had lessons some years ago, but, no, I am not going to paint. You are."

His eyes widened. "Me, mam'zelle?"

"If you will cease standing and asking questions, and go get the things I have requested."

Never had she seen him move so quickly. She was afraid, in truth, that in his eagerness he might stumble and fall down the stairs. His lameness troubled her more than it did him, she sometimes thought. There was nothing that could be done about it, however.

The light was going and Amalie lit a lamp in the salon, spreading the paints and paper in its glow while Isa ran for a glass of water to use to spread the watercolors. She showed him how to pick up the watercolor with his brush, to make a wash for the sky, and a few other pointers that she remembered, then stood back and watched him. His touch was quick and unerring; the expression on his face was one of rapture. So intent were they that they swung around, startled, as a voice came behind them.

"An apt pupil, but are you sure this is wise?"

"Cousin Robert," she exclaimed, "I thought you had gone back to The Willows."

His smile was rueful. "I had, but M'mere sent an urgent summons on a matter of business and here I am for dinner again."

"Dinner? Is it so late?"

"I'm afraid so."

"And I haven't changed. You must excuse me." She turned to Isa, directing him to put the materials away and run to the kitchen for his meal. She permitted him to serve her since it was what he wanted to do, but she could not be comfortable thinking that he was hungry while doing it and so insisted that he always eat first.

The boy closed the box of paints and put them under his arm, then went away bearing the waterglass in one hand and carrying his still-damp drawing between his forefinger and thumb of the other. Amalie nodded to Robert and moved toward her room.

"Wait, please."

She turned, a smile curving her mouth though there was a questioning tilt to her head.

"It's none of my affair, but do you think it right to treat that child the way you are doing?"

Her smile faded. "What way is that?"

"Making him into a pet, pampering him, keeping him near you in the house."

"Do you think he should be sent out with the others, made to labor in the fields, to do a hard day's work?" Her brown eyes had grown hard, a glint of steel in them, and there was a sting in her words.

"No," he answered, his own voice stern, "but what will

become of him when you grow tired of the game? Or, later, how will he feel when he is no longer a child, no longer permitted to follow you about like a puppy?"

"If you are suggesting that I will put him out—"

"I've seen it happen before."

"You've never seen me do such a thing!"

"Possibly not, but what you are doing may well be worse. He is bright and talented, but it is forbidden to teach him. You may not be able to prevent yourself, and then what? There will be no outlet for his knowledge and little for the art he may produce. He will know only frustration and discontent. What payment is that for his trust or his love?"

She turned from him in a whirl of skirts, but did not move away. Over her shoulder, she said, "I—you may be right. But am I to ignore him, to let him go back to being taunted and laughed at by the other children? That would be equally cruel and such a waste!"

"It isn't easy to know what to do for the best."

"He might not remain a slave since he has little value as a workman. There are thousands of free Negroes in Louisiana."

"Most of them were freed years ago before the process became so entangled in legalities."

It was one of the great ironies of recent years that the very actions of the abolitionists—encouraging the slaves to seek illegal freedom—had brought about laws that made it much more difficult for an owner to free one at will. There had been a time when it was not uncommon for manumission to be bought by the slave himself, or by his relatives, or else be awarded for valor or special service. Now the most certain way was for freedom to be stipulated in the master's will.

Finally she said, "I can only do what I think best."

"Yes. I did not mean to insult you."

"I'm sure you didn't." She turned her head to give him a level look, then left him.

It was later, much later, after dinner was over and the house was still, when the door between her bedchamber and her husband's eased open. Julien came toward her, his movements quiet. He drew back the mosquito netting. She felt the give of the mattress under his weight, then his arms were around her, gathering her against him.

"Forgive me," he whispered against her throat before his warm lips captured hers. "Forgive me."

She pressed against him with an inarticulate murmur, her arm going around him to clasp his shoulders. Her blood raced in her veins and deep inside she felt the quickening of anticipation. But for some unknown reason, perhaps because she had spoken so frankly to him that evening, the face that she saw in her mind, before she forced it from her, was not that of her husband. It was the face of his cousin, Robert Farnum.

Chapter 5

The planned visit to the opera gradually evolved into an all-day excursion. First there would be Sunday morning mass at the church of St. Martin de Tours, followed by breakfast with friends at the Hotel Broussard near the landing. Then in the afternoon, as was the custom in New Orleans itself, would come the opera, Meyerbeer's romantic spectacular *Les Huguenots*. At the end of the entertainment would be a dance sponsored by a number of the patrons, of whom Julien was one, and held in the grand hall of the hotel.

Due to the length of time they would spend in town, it was thought best to put up at the hotel in order to have a convenient place for the party to rest and change clothing. Moreover, if they were to be at the church before the bells ceased to ring, they must be close at hand. It was decided, then, that they would drive into St. Martinville on Saturday evening.

The ladies would naturally require their maids and the gentlemen their valets. The Hotel Broussard was well enough as such hostelries went, but M'mere preferred to take her own sheets of heavy monogrammed linen, pillows, a rug or two, and a few trinkets—a lamp and a picture or two—to make her feel at home. The hotel's chef was adequate, but did not have their own Marthe's light hand with pastry, so a supply of croissants, biscuits, and muffins must also be taken, as well as some of Belle Grove's superior hams, sausages, preserves, and jellies. Charles must come to announce callers and of course Isa would be indispensable to Amalie; would there not be messages of all descriptions to be carried?

It was a cavalcade that stood ready before the house, then, on Saturday afternoon. The wagon, with the supplies already loaded and the servants seated in it, was first on the drive, ready to leave in order to reach town far enough in advance to have everything ready for their arrival. Julien's elegant new Studebaker buggy, with the glaze finish on its dark green paint and gilded scrollwork, was next. Behind it was the victoria, somber and elegant, with the top laid back, while to one side was Robert's saddle horse calmly cropping grass.

Amalie watched from the gallery as Robert waved to the driver of the wagon, giving them the order to start. The sun glinted on his dark hair as he turned toward his horse, untying the reins from the hitching post. He put his foot into the stirrup, and the muscles in his thighs and lean hips flexed under his doeskin riding breeches as he mounted. The big bay horse sidestepped, throwing up his head in high spirits, but Robert controlled him with firm hands, his seat in the saddle easy, excellent.

"Mam'zelle?"

Amalie turned to see M'mere's maid, Pauline, in the doorway that led from the older woman's bedchamber out onto the gallery. "Yes?"

"Your pardon, but the *grande maîtresse* would speak with you."

They were on the point of departure; M'mere should be ready to go down. "Is anything the matter?"

The woman, an elder sister to the cook, Marthe, and not much younger than M'mere herself, only shook her head. As Amalie moved toward her, she stood aside so that Amalie, in hoop skirts, could enter through the French window without crushing the material of her gown.

M'mere was dressed in gray silk with a black silk mantle thrown around her shoulders and a black bonnet, with the hanging curtain of lace at the back of the neck called a *bavolet*, upon her head. She was kneeling at her prie-dieu, a small padded bench with hand support that sat beside her bed. Her lips moved in silent prayer for a few moments more, then, crossing herself, she sighed and pulled herself to her feet.

"I did not mean to keep you waiting, *ma chère*," she said, the soft crêpe of her skin creasing as she smiled. "Journeys always require the intervention of *le bon Dieu* for safety, do they not?"

"Yes, M'mere," Amalie answered, sensing that some reply was expected of her.

"Before we go, however, I have a small gift for you."

"No, really, you have given me so much—"

"It is but a token of my love and gratitude for the happiness you have brought my son." There was a dressing case sitting on the high tester bed and beside it a small jewel casket. The older woman moved toward the last and, taking it in her hand, lifted the lid.

"I am his wife; it is my duty—"

M'mere ignored the protest. She removed a tray, then lifted out a box covered in blue velvet. She took Amalie's hand and placed the box in it. "You have shown understanding beyond most and I honor you for it. Please do not disappoint me by refusing."

Amalie lowered her lashes to the box she held. She was by no means certain that her understanding was as great as M'mere thought. In the past weeks, Julien had come to her perhaps a half-dozen times. Each occasion had been a union of supreme physical pleasure, an emotional upheaval so intense she could hardly bear it, and yet when they met again the next morning, it was if it had never happened. He was surly and impatient much of the time, though now and then he would smile upon her with his old, wry affection. So lacking in ardor was his manner during the light of day that she had come to feel he was merely using her, that she was a handy receptacle for his seed; that his visits were a mere duty. For the sake of her own pride, she had tried to remain unresponsive under him, to resist the passion he aroused in her. She could not. Always when he left her there in the dark, departing as if to sleep with her until dawn was a task he could not undertake, she was bereft.

"Open it, *ma chère!*"

Obediently Amalie raised the lid. Inside on a bed of white satin lay a necklace of sapphires and diamonds set about with seed pearls and with eardrops to match. It was jewelry for a young woman, a new bride, combining the seed pearls of youth with the more sparkling stones of sophistication.

Amalie looked up, her eyes brimming with tears. "Oh, M'mere."

"*Tiens!* Do not make so much of so small a thing. You are to wear it for the opera and the dancing afterward, naturally. T'will be most becoming, I do declare."

The older woman was pleased by her reaction, that much was evident from the shining warmth in her faded brown eyes. Amalie forced her lips to curve into a smile, saying simply, "Thank you, M'mere."

"You are entirely welcome, and now we must go before Julien and Robert storm the stairs to fetch us."

Julien would have preferred to travel on his barge. It lay at the rebuilt landing before the house, its white paint bright, its cream-and-blue-striped sails wrapped about the mast, and its draperies and awnings rolled tightly so that they would not be faded by the growing strength of the sun. There wasn't room for them all on its cushioned deck, however, and the windings of the bayou would have added miles to the distance they had to cover. Moreover, Chloe had refused most absolutely to be a party to any such idea. She was quite unwell on the water and did not intend to arrive at the hotel the color of asparagus to please Julien's whim.

There was one advantage the barge had over the victoria; it did not kick up dust. There was a great deal of traffic on the road and a brown cloud of dust hung in the air, coating the cane that grew up to the grass-lined verges and turning the live oaks about the houses they passed brownish gray with its powder. So thick did it become at times that they had to cover their mouths with handkerchiefs. Chloe complained that it was Julien's fault since he had bowled away ahead of the heavier carriage with George up beside him, leaving them to eat the cloud of fine dirt he had stirred up. She was only partly right. They were not alone on the road.

Near St. Martinville, they came upon a house with buggies and flatbed wagons drawn up around it so thickly that people could barely walk between them and wheeled traffic had to thread its way around them where they lined the road. Children, wild with excitement, chased each other in circles, men stood in groups laughing and drinking from the jugs that were making the rounds, while on the front porch of the house sat the elderly women, rocking and holding the babies. Under one tree was a trio of black iron pots nestled in coals with younger women with aprons about their waists standing over them, stirring. Beneath the spreading branches of another tree a trio of fiddlers were tuning up. The sound of laughter and the smell of cooking seafood drifted on the air.

"What is it? What's happening?" Amalie asked.

"It's a *fais do-do,* a party in the Acadian style," M'mere answered, inclining her head in stately fashion to the elderly women on the porch, who nodded back just as gravely.

"Everyone comes," Chloe added. "They eat and talk and listen to music, and then when the children are asleep, the courting couples and grown-ups dance the rest of the night away. They will all go to mass in the morning, then they will go home."

There were not as many Acadians, or Cajuns as they were called by the Americans, in the Felicianas as there were along the bayous such as Lafourche and Teche. Amalie had heard of the *fais do-do,* of course, but this was the first one she had come across. "They look as if they are going to have fun."

"Oh, yes, much fun," Chloe agreed. "But so are we!"

In spite of the young girl's prediction, Saturday night was spent quietly. They had settled into their suite, a series of bedchambers opening onto a small salon, and Amalie was relieved to find that she had a room to herself. After an early dinner, they moved out onto the upper gallery of the square-built, red brick hotel, where they enjoyed the view of the Teche that flowed on their right. They were regaled by the conversation of a number of their neighbors, among them the elderly Oudry ladies and Mademoiselle Callot, who had elected to follow the same plan for the morrow. They were also honored with the exalted company of several members of the opera troupe who were staying at the hotel.

After a time, George, tired of watching Chloe hanging onto the words of the rather portly tenor, took her off for a stroll to see the grave of Emmeline Labiche, said to be Longfellow's Evangeline. Julien drifted away to see what other amusements the town had to offer. M'mere settled in for a long discussion with the Mesdames Oudry over the pattern for a new altar cloth planned for the church. Robert fell into conversation with a fellow planter about the cane crop and the new machinery he had bought in Philadelphia for his mill. A few minutes later, however, the planter's manservant stepped out onto the gallery with a message from Madame his wife about some difficulty with getting one of the children to sleep in a strange room, and Robert was alone.

Amalie watched as Julien's cousin got up out of his chair and went to the balustrade, leaning with one shoulder against a column as he stared out over the bayou. She allowed a little time to pass, then got to her feet and moved to join him. There was a dark green vine running along the railing. The railing was covered with the small white stars of jasmine, and its fragrance engulfed her as her skirts brushed against it when she stopped at his side. He turned his head to give her a small smile, then looked back at the water.

The Bayou Teche ran, slow moving, yellow-brown, and tranquil, no great distance away. It was difficult to think of it being out of its banks and running through the streets of the town not so long ago, so very peaceful did it appear now. Houses lined the verge, set back behind screens of bamboo cane and the drooping limbs of moss-hung live oaks. Directly before the hotel was the ancient tree known as the Evangeline's Oak, said to mark the spot where the boat carrying Emmeline Labiche had landed at the end of her long and perilous journey from Nova Scotia, where she had met her Louis and been told of his faithlessness. A small breeze whispered through its branches, stirring the ferns that grew on its lower limbs and gently swaying the gray streamers of moss.

Amalie moistened her lips. Without looking at Robert, she said, "Did you know that the Spanish moss is a sign of Indian bereavement?"

"Is it?"

"It's said that once a princess and a brave lived on the banks of the Teche. They were much in love and were to be wed. Then the princess became ill. On her death, she was buried at the foot of an oak. In his grief the brave had asked for her long black braids and he placed them on a limb above her grave. In time, they turned gray with age and the wind blew the strands from tree to tree. Finally, all the trees were hung with mourning in the land of bayous, from the headwaters to the gulf."

"A charming legend." His tone was warm, with a note of indulgence.

"Sir Bent told it to me."

He nodded toward the oak before the hotel. "Do you know what the Acadians say of Emmeline and Louis and their oak?"

"About their meeting beneath it?" She plucked a leaf of the jasmine vine and began carefully to curl it in her fingers.

He shook his head, sending her a smiling glance. "No, about the end of the story. They are a happy race and prefer a happy ending. The laws of the church say that marriage is a sacrament broken only by death, so they can't have the pair together in life, but they say that their shades meet beneath the oak. They claim that if you listen carefully when the wind blows, you can hear them laughing—and making love."

There was something in his voice as he drew out the last words that gave her an odd feeling around her heart. Trying for a light response, she said, "I think I like that ending better myself, though I'm not certain that you didn't make it up. It was kind of you, but then that is one of your virtues."

"My virtues?" He turned to face her, a brow lifted in a look of puzzlement tinged with scorn.

"You don't like the term? I was only trying to find a way to say that it was kind of you to act as escort for M'mere on this outing. I'm sure it isn't what you would prefer."

"You are mistaken. There can be no question of kindness where it concerns Tante Sophia. I have received so much from her over the years that I can't begin to repay her and am therefore always at her service when she has need of me. But, in this case, I suit myself also. I am certainly enjoying this outing."

His words confirmed what Chloe had told Amalie about him, explaining his devotion to the fortunes of Belle Grove. She did not comment, however, saying instead, "Are you? I was certain you would not like to leave The Willows."

He swung around so that his back was to the column, giving her his full attention. "Why do you say that?"

"You have been near the house so little lately that I was afraid you had found much that needed your supervision, many things neglected while you were with us during the flood."

"This is a busy time of the year," he answered, his shrug only emphasizing the evasive reply.

"Still, you don't deny that you have been avoiding us?" She tilted her head, slanting a quick glance over his bronze features. She saw the frown that came and went between his brows. "That's too strong a word, surely?"

"Is it?"

"I ride over the fields at Belle Grove often."

She nodded. "I've seen you from the loggia, early of a morning, but you don't come into the house."

A smile cut into the planes of his face. "I thought I might have worn out my welcome."

"You know better than that," she countered with a shake of her head. "Are you sure that you—that Julien hasn't a quarrel of some kind with you?"

"None that I can think of."

His answer was even, immediate, and yet his eyes had narrowed so that the thickness of his lashes shielded their expression. She swallowed. "I have this feeling that that isn't quite the truth. Perhaps it's I who has offended you."

"That could never be," he said quietly.

The timbre of his voice sent a tremor along her nerves. She summoned a smile. "Then I hope—"

"Permit me," he said abruptly and reached out to touch the gentle swell of her breasts just above the neckline of her gown.

The shock of pleasure took her breath. She stepped back in haste, feeling the imprint of his fingertips as if it were a brand. Her eyes widened as she stared at him, the blue-gray shadows intensifying in their brown depths. She thought she saw a flush darken his skin, though it was impossible to be certain in the failing light. He made an abrupt movement with his hand and her gaze dropped to his fingers that he held out to her.

"Oh, a spider," she said, hearing the faintness of her tone, which she was unable to prevent. Was it relief or regret that gripped her? She could not tell. She did recognize the sudden wave of desire that had swept over her at his nearness.

She was not only a wanton in bed, then, but while fully dressed, in company, and with a man not her husband. How could it be? She had taken her wedding vows with devout belief and intent. She had never considered herself in the least promiscuous, or particularly susceptible to the needs of the flesh. And yet she had responded to Julien as she had not dreamed it was possible to do, and now she had felt the same heated need with this man. Could it be that her character was so depraved that, having been aroused to passion after so many barren years, she could feel it for any man?

"It was on the vine, I expect." He tossed the small, brown insect over the railing. "You were saying?"

It was a moment before she answered. "Nothing. Just that—that hope you will come to see us more often. It would please M'mere."

"And you?" he asked, cocking his head to one side.

"And me, too, of course," she answered and, smiling firmly, moved away. As she reached her chair beside her mother-in-law once more, she looked back. Robert was watching her. His face was without expression, but the hand that had touched her was clenched into a fist at his side.

High mass on the following morning was a most solemn and moving occasion. The church of St. Martin de Tours was fairly new, having been built over twenty years before, though there had been a rustic chapel of the same name on the site since 1765. A trim building of plaster over bricks with massive doors and windows set in Roman arches, it had a steeple of perfect proportions that was matched by a cupola of white wood at the rear and decoration beneath the entablature of stylized crosses. Inside the stations of the cross were beautifully detailed statues. The roof was supported by fourteen large Doric columns that soared above the box pews, while above the altar was an enormous painting by Jean François Mouchet of St. Martin. The magnificent old marble baptismal font had been a gift to the parish from King Louis XVI.

The priest, Père Jan, was everything an ecclesiastic should be: benevolent, caring, concerned with community matters, yet, in speaking of matters of sin, stern.

Amalie, in company with the other ladies, emerged soothed, in mind and body, and ravenous. An enormous breakfast greeted their arrival back at the hotel: fried ham, bacon, hot cakes, waffles imprinted with a pineapple design and drowning in fresh sweet butter and cane syrup, biscuits, snow white hominy grits made yellow with yet more butter, hot coffee rich with cream, hot chocolate and milk. It was recommended that they rest in their rooms before the rigors of the afternoon and night, but Chloe had other plans.

Neither Robert, Julien, nor George had attended mass. The Englishman and Robert were on hand to eat breakfast with the ladies on their return, but then the latter vanished into the gentleman's parlor with a second cup of coffee and a newssheet. Julien had gone out earlier and Tige could not say where, though when pressed he admitted that something had been mentioned about a cockfight. He was able to assure them, however, that M'sieu Julien had not gone far since he had not ordered his buggy. Chloe, much delighted at the last bit of news, sent at once to have the vehicle hitched up and brought to the front of the hotel.

It was George who came near to canceling her arrangements. Informed that he was to have the honor of tooling Chloe, with Amalie as a chaperone, around the streets of the town, he had categorically refused. It just wasn't done for a gentleman to take another's conveyance and horses out without his permission, particularly when the gentleman in question was hardly more than a hired workman. All Chloe's protests, temper, and tears would not move him, nor would he agree that his position, as she claimed, was that of an artist. He was living on the generosity of the master of Belle Grove and could not, would not, impose upon him.

It was left to M'mere to save the outing, which she did by not only promising to explain the matter to Julien on his return but by virtually ordering George to remove her goddaughter so that she herself could rest.

Chloe, once she had her way, could not have been a more amiable companion. She pointed out the houses of the well-to-do, giving an amusing, if somewhat malicious, account of their ancestry and habits. She took them up and down the well-laid-out streets, past the opera house that had been in operation for over sixty years, the two banks, the courthouse, the male and female seminaries. They circled around past the hotel once more, then, a few blocks later, turned to cross the draw bridge that spanned the Teche, built to allow steamboats to ascend the river in high water to Breaux Bridge. In this area, Chloe promised, were yet more opulent dwellings to be viewed.

George was not happy with his part in the outing, no matter how many times Chloe tried to tell him that Julien would not care a picayune's worth for his scruples. Yet the press of his inamorata against him, as the three of them were seated abreast on the narrow seat, her sunny chatter and faint perfume, seemed to resign him to whatever Julien might say on his return. Chloe incurred his disapproval once again, however, as they took a winding road that led away from the bayou.

With her shining black curls bouncing about her ears and her black eyes bright, she looked around. "How very unusual. I don't think I've been down this— Oh!"

"What is it?" Amalie asked, leaning to see the girl's face beneath the brim of her straw bonnet lined with pink silk.

"I *have* been this way before."

"Yes?"

"I came with M'mere, last fall, though the way was dark so that it looked different. We were driven in the carriage, but it was her maid Pauline who was our guide."

It sounded so unlikely that Amalie frowned, saying, "I don't understand."

"Nor I," George added.

"We came along this road and stopped at a house with crêpe on the door. I stayed in the carriage while M'mere went inside. I don't think she expected me to understand where we were, and I might not have except for an exchange between Pauline and the driver. Actually, M'mere was paying a condolence call at that house just there. It is the house of Julien's *placée*. The girl's young brother had died, a suicide."

Amalie turned her head swiftly to look at the house they were passing. It was small, built of whitewashed cypress with a wide front porch and a high-pitched roof that held a sleeping loft. The entrance to the loft was gained by a steep outside stairway leading to a trapdoor in the porch ceiling. It was shingled in cypress shakes and had a chimney of glazed mud and deer hair over a framework of cypress laths. Set back from the road and with a live oak on one side and the green umbrella of a chinaberry tree on the other, it was neat, clean, and totally nondescript, giving nothing away.

"I think this is far enough on this road," George said, a flush beneath his thin skin.

At the next opportunity, he turned the buggy, then, as they headed back toward town, began with great determination and detail to tell them of a sea captain he had met that morning on the gallery. It seemed that the man was just back from China. While there he had met another captain who had been stowing vast numbers of shrubs and plants scavenged from the countryside on his decks. Carefully settled in pots with arrangements to keep them watered during the long sea voyage, they were to supply the market that had developed in the southern United States for such exotic plant specimens. George had spoken to the elder Madame Declouet and she had graciously agreed to allow him to travel to New Orleans as her agent when the ship came in, with the authority to purchase as much of the cargo as he thought might be suitable for Belle Grove.

Amalie paid little attention as she thought of the woman who had been her husband's mistress. Chloe was also pensive. Receiving little help with the conversation, George went on to speculate on the camellias and azaleas and other plants that might be included in the shipment. Chloe bore with him for some minutes, then turned on him.

"You have no trouble asking M'mere about your precious plants; why can't you ask Julien again to allow us to be betrothed, even if we are not yet to marry?"

George sent an unhappy glance at Amalie, who did her best to appear deaf. "He said he would consider the matter again if you were still of the same mind after a year. What use is it to press him?"

"That was only an excuse because he thought I didn't know my own mind. But I do; you know I do. You could at least try to explain."

"It's an awkward thing, as I've tried to tell you. I'm a younger son; my prospects are not the best. It would be extremely presumptuous of me to try to persuade your guardian to overlook these things. I'm only surprised he hasn't shown me to the door already for my pretensions."

"How can you speak of pretensions, you, the son of an earl? And I refuse to believe you are so poor. You traveled from England and across America, had just come from the wilds of some place called Wisconsin when you reached us!"

"It was a legacy," he said patiently, in the tone one uses for an old story. "I thought to use it to see your country and compile a book on its flora that would make my reputation as a botanist and give me an entrée with the kind of people in England who can afford to hire a landscape architect. But the money is nearly gone and there's little to show for it."

"You think too much of money," Chloe complained. "With us, family is much more important and yours is above reproach. I will have a generous dowry and there is plenty of room at Belle Grove."

"You expect me to live on your relatives?"

"What is so wrong with that? It's often done; they will not mind."

"I'll mind," George said forthrightly.

"But you could work on the gardens, if you felt the need to be useful, and perhaps write your book. I could help you find specimens and copy out your pages. It would be no different from now, really, except that I would be your wife."

For an answer, he merely shook his head.

Chloe, angry in her disappointment, flounced back against the seat, making it jounce on its springs. "You are afraid of Julien. You think if you push him too far he might send you away before your precious garden is done. That's all you think about, dirt and flowers, flowers and dirt!"

"Be reasonable—"

"How can I be reasonable when you won't make the least effort to gain our happiness? I don't want to be an old maid left to make tapestry. I want to be your wife!"

"I should never have spoken to you before I had the permission of your relatives. If you did not know of my feelings, you would not be so unhappy."

"Unhappy? I am miserable! But the fault is not yours, it's Julien's for making us wait. Promise me you will speak to him. Promise me!"

"Please, Chloe, my love. You are making Amalie uncomfortable, besides drawing the kind of attention I'm sure you would not want."

"All right!" she cried, sitting up straight. "If you won't speak to him, I will!"

He sent her a hard look. "As you please, but you will not say that you are my emissary, for Julien gave me his word two months ago that he would consider my proposal again next winter and I am confident he will stand by it."

Chloe did not speak again, but neither Amalie nor George made the mistake of thinking that she was any less determined. She sat staring straight ahead until they had reached the Hotel Broussard once more, then got down without a word and mounted the steps. Amalie followed her, leaving George sitting and staring at a spot between the horse's ears until, rousing himself with a shake, he sent the buggy rolling back toward the stables.

An appreciation for opera and the theater had been brought to Louisiana by the earliest French colonists. Not burdened by the puritanical distrust of such worldly pleasures, they had continued to enjoy the samples that came their way by means of traveling troupes. It was in New Orleans that the first resident opera company was established on American soil, long before the cities on the Eastern seaboard considered themselves able to support such a thing.

The music was all-important. Snatches of favorite arias could be heard on the street, coming from a French Quarter courtyard, sung by a laundress swaying down the street with her basket of linens on her head, or hummed by a small boy selling fish in the French market. There were heated arguments over the relative merits of different singers that often led to duels. The divas and tenors of the hour were showered with floral tributes on the stage, fêted in the best homes, applauded spontaneously in the restaurants, and showered with gifts. When a performance reached its climax of passion, power, and musical beauty, it was not unusual for young ladies to swoon or for hardened rakes to brush away traces of tears. And nowhere in the world were the cries of bravo and encore more fervent or longer lasting.

The opera was also a social occasion, however. It was a time for women to dress in their finest, for men to bring out their most gallant manners, and for young belles to do their utmost to attract every man of their acquaintance to their sides in the family boxes during the intervals. These intermissions were also the time to greet friends and exchange gossip, to scrutinize the toilettes of everyone present, and to stroll and drink punch, though everyone was always in their places when the curtain rose again. The gala operas of the summer in St. Martinville were no different.

Dressing for the opera, then, was a most important occupation. It required the most elaborate arrangement of the hair that one could conceive or that one's maid, or the hairdresser called in for the occasion, could manage. The gown was correspondingly ornate, especially since nearly every woman in the crowded opera house would be wearing the same color. A visitor to New Orleans had once exclaimed that the ladies in their boxes at the French opera were like an enormous bouquet of white roses, and it was a rare woman indeed who cared to depart from such a pretty conceit.

Amalie's gown was of shimmering white tarlatan with a

wide lower skirt composed of six layers of narrow flounces edged by a ruche of lace, an upper skirt that was drawn up in poufs and secured with streamers of slate-blue ribbon, and a heart-shaped bodice with ribbon-trimmed pouf sleeves that draped over her arms. Her hair was drawn up in a cascade of curls with ribbons twisted among them, while around her throat and at her ears were the sapphires M'mere had given her. Because of the sleeves and the warmth of the evening, she did not feel the need of a wrap. Taking up her fan and a handkerchief, she stepped from her chamber into the sitting room of the suite.

As if on signal, M'mere and Chloe emerged from the room they shared. Chloe, her face and shoulders fashionably pale from the application of white pearl powder, wore white satin with an overskirt of lace caught at the knee, the waist, and the bodice with nosegays of her favorite blush-pink roses. M'mere was in palest pearl gray, as became her age and widowed status, but wore a shawl of white silk heavy with silk sewing fringe over it.

"Very pretty," the elderly woman said to Amalie, satisfaction in her fine old eyes as she noted the necklace she wore. Accepting the compliment on her own appearance, she swept Amalie and Chloe before her from the room and down to where the three gentlemen were waiting on the front gallery.

Robert turned as they emerged, and in his eyes as they rested on Amalie sprang the warmth of admiration. He started forward, then, as Julien swung about and advanced upon her, stopped abruptly.

"*Ravissante*," her husband said, taking her hand and raising it to his lips. There was pride in his face as he surveyed her and his hold on her fingers tightened a fraction before he turned to his cousin. "Do you not agree, Robert?"

"How could I fail to do so?" came the ready answer, and Robert inclined his head in a gesture of homage, his smile expressing nothing more than polite agreement. But as he glanced toward Julien, Amalie thought she caught the flick of hard challenge between the two cousins.

They were amazingly alike in their black broadcloth and white linen that was almost an evening uniform for men, and were easily the two most handsome men on the gallery. And yet in the limpid light of the waning afternoon, they were also unlike. Julien was the more elegantly attractive of the two with satin lapels on his coat and a more intricately tied cravat. His dark eyes glinted with some private amusement and his mouth was mobile, pursed now as he glanced from Robert to his wife. There were lines and shadows of dissipation about his face, the paleness of which was nearly a match for that of Chloe. Robert's face was bronze and stern, giving nothing away, though the curve of his bottom lip was sensual in its strength.

George, ignoring the byplay, went straight to Chloe and offered her his arm. M'mere stepped forward to slip her hand through the crook of Robert's elbow, giving him a small tap on the wrist with her fan for his neglect. He turned with an apology and a ready compliment for the older woman, his grin for her playful rebuke devastating in its naturalness. Julien placed Amalie's hand on his arm, and they all left the hotel, setting out to walk the short distance to the opera house, from which direction could be heard the tuning up of the orchestra on the still, languid air.

Meyerbeer's *Les Huguenots*, the offering for the afternoon, had been applauded by the opera lovers of southern Louisiana for seventeen years, since it was first presented in New Orleans in April of 1839. Despite the fact that the audience was always overwhelmingly Catholic while the story was a tragedy concerning the persecution of Protestants in seventeenth-century France, its reception was not thought odd. The appeal of the piece was in its setting, its grandeur, its dramatic spectacle, and its romantic score. The hush as the curtain went up, the sighs, the groans as the story progressed, the applause and shouts of bravo after the arias were ample testimony to the seriousness with which those present regarded the entertainment.

The first interval came quickly. Now was the time to see and be seen, and in the case of unmarried girls like Chloe, to attract eligible males to their boxes. The number of young men who put in an appearance would be carefully noted by everyone present and a young woman's popularity judged accordingly. It was a surprise, then, when Chloe got to her feet as the curtains were closed and the lamps in the box turned up.

"Where are you going?" M'mere asked, her voice sharp. "I thought I would walk with Amalie and Julien, if they don't mind."

M'mere glanced to where Amalie and Julien stood at the door leading from the box, then back to her goddaughter. "But what will people say if you aren't here?"

Chloe lifted a round white shoulder. "I care not at all."

"If you wish for some punch, perhaps M'sieu Parkman would—"

"He can stay to keep you company since I'm sure Robert has calls to make."

Robert, leaning with his shoulders braced against the back of the box, sent a long, level glance at George, who looked away, then to the girl. "Don't, please, my dear Chloe, arrange my time for me. I'm content where I am."

Chloe stamped her foot. "I only want to speak to Julien!"

"Lower your voice," M'mere hissed, "and try for a little conduct. Everyone is staring."

Julien made a sudden, impatient gesture. "If you must come, then come, but I warn you I am in no mood for one of your scenes."

The plump, black-haired girl accepted the ungracious invitation with alacrity. As they reached the corridor, she twined her arm into his on the opposite side from Amalie, smiling up at him and chattering about the play and the people who nodded to them as they strolled up and down. Julien's resigned expression took on a sardonic tinge, especially as she drew them toward a secluded corner near the entrance.

Finally Julien said, "All right, Chloe, you may consider me sufficiently softened to hear you. What is it that you wanted to say to me that is so important?"

"If you are going to take that attitude, I might as well not speak!" Chloe's expression was indignant as she turned on him.

"Very true. Shall we go back?"

"No! No, I—I thought since you are so happy in your marriage to Amalie that you might feel differently about my desire to wed George. We are so much in love, and there is no reason why we should be kept apart."

"Aside from the fact that he has little means to keep a wife."

"You know that is merely an excuse. We could live quite comfortably at Belle Grove."

"And would you continue to respect a man willing to agree to such an arrangement, one who would cast both himself and his wife on the charity of her relatives?"

"You make it sound so degrading and it need not be at all! Anyway, George isn't willing. He is fully aware of his obligations, but what are we to do? I don't want to wait until he makes his mark as a landscape designer."

"Yes, very likely you would be an old maid by then."

"What a hateful thing to say! Just because he is not a planter or a lawyer or something equally boring and respectable!"

"He is, that I can see, nothing at all."

"You will regret those words one day when he is famous for designing great public parks and pleasure gardens!"

"No doubt I shall, if I live to see it," Julien said, still polite in the face of Chloe's growing wrath.

"Go ahead and sneer! George is an artist, which is more than may be said for you! What claim do you have to usefulness with your drinking and fencing and airs of a gentleman while Robert runs Belle Grove?"

"That will do." Julien's voice was hard.

"You think you are artistic, with your elocution and grand arranging of plays and games and your floating about on your barge contemplating the clouds. You don't work at anything. You have no plan, no goal, and yet you dare to cast aspersions on George!"

"I dare more than that," he answered, a flush on his face and his mouth tight. "I dare to say that you won't marry your English popinjay. I won't give my consent, not even if George screws up the courage to ask me again himself, though I would certainly respect him more for it."

"It isn't George, not really. It's just that you think everybody at Belle Grove belongs to you, that we should all bow to your every whim without daring to have a thought of our own, and certainly without daring to feel what you think we should not. Well, I don't belong to you; I never have and I never will. I'm going to marry George, and if you try to stop me, you'll be sorry."

There was a small silence as Chloe stared at Julien with her bosom heaving and tears of rage in her dark eyes. It was broken as Robert cleared his throat behind them.

"I don't like to intrude on such a fine exhibition of temper, but your voices are penetrating to the box and M'mere is upset. She begs that you will resume your seats. I suggest that you obey, unless you would, both of you, prefer to return to Belle Grove on the instant with Tante Sophia in a swoon on the seat?"

To emphasize his words there came the bell chime for the second act curtain.

Chapter 6

They did not leave the opera house; that would have been to attract attention indeed, but neither did they linger in St. Martinville when the evening's entertainment was done.

The ball had been pleasant. A string quartet had provided the music. The early supper, spread on sideboards in the dining hall, had been good though nothing extraordinary. Chloe, her expression defiant, had given George three dances, then whirled over the floor with a succession of young men with earnest faces that were flushed from the champagne they had drunk. Julien had stood up with Amalie twice, guiding her around the room with verve and reckless gaiety. He had then solicited the hand of his mother and had been rebuked, with a smile, for his impudence. The next time Amalie looked around, he was gone.

Robert had not come near her. He had fallen prey to one of the hostesses for the occasion, who had taken him off to dance with her daughter, a shy blond girl who kept her eyes on his cravat. After that, he had retreated to the gentlemen's parlor where a serious game of poker was in progress. It had been Monsieur Broussard, the owner of the hotel himself, who had volunteered to extract him when M'mere declared herself fatigued and anxious to rest in her own bed. Amalie, prohibited as a young matron from dancing with any other than her husband or male relatives, had been more than ready to leave her place beside the older woman and return to Belle Grove.

Their bill had been settled earlier, their trunks had been packed by the servants who had loaded them and themselves on the wagon that had then set out while the opera was in progress. All that was left was to order the carriage and depart. Julien could not be found, so George was forced to mount into the carriage with the ladies. He found it no hardship, however, for the long ride in the darkness was an excellent opportunity to press close to Chloe on the seat and to hold her hand under the fullness of her skirts. He had also the felicity of having the young girl place her head on his shoulder for the last part of the journey. Worn out with excitement, Chloe alternately talked to the Englishman in a drowsy voice or dozed.

M'mere was preoccupied, staring out into the moonlit darkness with her head resting on the padded gray velvet upholstery. The look on her face was worn and faintly apprehensive. Amalie sat trying not to listen to Chloe and George or to the steady hoofbeats of Robert's horse as he rode alongside. She studied her hands clasped together in her lap and wondered what had become of Julien. There had been some mention of yet another cockfight, but there were a number of taverns and gambling houses along the road leading south to New Iberia. She thought of the house of his quadroon mistress, also conveniently close, then dismissed it. Hadn't Chloe said that the woman had been paid off at the time of his marriage? There was no reason for him to call on her, especially considering his nighttime visits to her own bedchamber. He would be along after a while when he discovered their absence from the festivities.

At Belle Grove, Chloe was shaken awake. M'mere was helped down with care by Robert, who gave her his arm up the stairs, while George assisted Chloe's stumbling steps and Amalie trailed behind. In the sitting room, good nights were said and Amalie turned toward her bedchamber.

Lally was waiting for her. She helped her mistress from her clothes and put her into her nightgown with a dressing gown of lace-edged batiste over it. She took down her hair and brushed it into a shining cascade, then offered to bring a glass of warm milk from the kitchen. Amalie shook her head with a smile and sent the girl away. As the maid reached the door, however, she called her back.

"I saw no sign of Isa just now. He did return with you all right?"

"Oh, yes, mam'zelle. But that Isa, he was so worn out from all the sights and from fretting that he could not go with you to the opera, that he went sound asleep on the way home. Charles put him down in the kitchen on a pallet."

"I see. Thank you."

The maid bobbed a curtsy and went out, closing the door softly behind her. Amalie stared at the panel for a long moment, then moved to blow out the lamp. She glanced at her high bed with its steps and filmy draping of mosquito baire, then skirted it, moving toward the window. She pushed it wide, flinging back the jalousies.

The night air was soft and warm, heavy with the scents of roses and honeysuckle and the sharper lemon-tang of magnolias. The moon was waxing full, but the hour was growing late, and it hovered ready to set, shedding only a dim light. Nothing moved. The trees were still, their branches and leaves faintly silvered. The summerhouse in their deeper shadow was a pale shape, without definition.

Amalie breathed deep, leaning her head against the window facing. She was a bit weary, but not sleepy. She felt on edge, her muscles tense. She was not certain what caused it; it seemed to come more from the atmosphere around her than from any particular reason. There had been the quarrel, of course, and before that the odd exchange between Julien and Robert. There was Julien's desertion, too. Still, she did not think she had been affected to any great degree by those things. Nor, she told herself fiercely, had she been disturbed by the scene with Robert the evening before.

No. It was just the natural result of an overstimulating occasion. She closed her eyes, hearing again the music of the opera, the passion and the pathos, the soaring voices that touched the heart with their beauty and inflamed with their ardent outpourings of desire and love, hate and fear.

Was that it? Had she been so affected by the music that she now longed for her lover? Was she so thoroughly enamored of her husband, so awakened by him that she felt the need of his caresses? It was a novel thought and yet she did not shrink from it. She did enjoy his touch, the sensations that he aroused in her. She was exhilarated by the strength and hardness of his body against her own. It gave her pleasure to press herself to him, to feel the play of his muscles under the skin, to seek the devouring warmth of his mouth.

She swung away from the window, moving to the center of the room. She stared for long moments at the pair of dark rectangles that were the doors leading to Julien's bed-chamber. After a moment, she sighed, letting her shoulders droop. It was an immodest woman who sought out her husband, surely? And in any case, he had not returned.

She turned her gaze instead to the door into the salon. Moving toward it, she drew it open and stepped out into the darkened room. There was a crack of light under the door of M'mere's sitting room. As she listened, she thought she could hear the sound of footsteps, moving up and down, back and forth. Then the elderly woman could not rest either. Was it Julien's absence that troubled her or was it Chloe's entanglement with the Englishman? M'mere was the kind of woman who worried about those close to her. It was an endearing trait, but not a restful one.

The outside door from the salon to the front gallery was locked. Retracing her footsteps, Amalie tried the one that led onto the loggia on the opposite side. It, too, was firmly secured. She stood still for a moment, then turned back into her own bedchamber, padded across to the connecting doors, and grasped the knob, sliding one panel open. She half expected to see Tige as she stepped into the room, but her husband's bedchamber stood dark and empty. The outside door that opened from it directly onto the rear loggia had been left unlocked, awaiting Julien's return. Amalie wondered if Charles was still on duty, but, no, she thought she remembered M'mere dismissing him. Julien had his key, of course, and could be depended on to drop the heavy bolt into place after him. She slipped outside, closing the door behind her.

Her bare feet made no sound on the cypress treads of the stairs. Without slippers or wide skirts and the heavy fullness of petticoats, she felt amazingly unencumbered, as light and free as the night air that wafted under her nightgown. The brick floor of the lower loggia was cool, faintly gritty. The grass of the backyard, between the two wings of the *garçonnières*, was wet with dew and she held the hems of dressing gown and nightgown above it. Skirting the brick-topped cistern on the left, she moved between the big house and one *garçonnière,* out into the side yard.

A call, distant and haunting, sounded. She stopped, listening, feeling the rise of gooseflesh on her arms. After a moment, it came again and she let out her breath on a soft laugh. It was an owl quartering the fields for mice and giving his hunting cry. Or had it been a plea for a mate? She did not know; still, it was a comforting feeling to know that she was not the only creature awake in the night. She glanced toward the quarters beyond the outbuildings, toward where the rows of cabins with their cypress porches and brick chimneys sat still and dark. Sometimes the men roamed at night, going as far as the next plantation where they often had women, and she supposed that the quarters at Belle Grove were visited in their turn. She had little fear of molestation herself, however. Any who discovered her presence would take care that she did not see them. The penalty for doing otherwise was too dire to risk.

The last gleam of moonlight disappeared below the horizon. The night closed in. Protected by its soothing denseness, Amalie moved on. She lifted her face to the damp, dew-laden air, breathing in the scents that were carried on it. The increasing smell of roses and honeysuckle was like a drug to her senses, expanded them. There were beauty and freedom in the night and she reveled in them, shaking back her hair so that it rippled down her back, dropping her skirts and letting them flow around her, heedless of the damp.

The summerhouse off to the right was a ghostly blur under the trees, a pale beacon. She turned toward it with sure footsteps, moving beneath the trees, touching a low-hanging limb, running her fingers over the curve of the trunk of an old live oak, her progress unhurried but steady.

The small, rectangular building was built of whitewashed lattice work on a framework of cypress supports topped by a roof of cypress shakes. It had two door openings, a brick floor, and a bench for sitting that ran around the walls. Designed as a sheltered vantage point from which to view the bayou that ran before it, it was also a shady retreat in summer and the destination of walks in winter. A blush-pink running rose grew up one side of the convenient lattice trellis, while Hall's honeysuckle had invaded the same end, twining and twisting upward until it lay in a drift over the roof. Their combined mass created a dark and perfumed bower.

Amalie stepped inside the back entrance and strolled across to the front. She could hear the soft gurgle of the bayou as it eased past, but could catch only a faint sheen now and then of the water. She crossed her arms over her chest and leaned to rest one shoulder against the door facing, staring out into the night with unfocused eyes. Her thoughts were aimless, unconnected, and she had neither the wish nor the will to control them.

There came a soft grating sound behind her. She turned her head, but it did not come again. The shift of the rose canes and honeysuckle vines, she thought, they were often used by nesting birds. Or maybe a frog or lizard taking sanctuary. After a moment, she relaxed, returning her gaze to where the bayou glided in the night.

"Don't be alarmed," came the rustling whisper of a deep voice at her ear as strong arms closed around her. "It's only me."

She stiffened, coming erect, but the grasp in which she was held did not loosen. One firm hand held her elbow while the other closed gently over the swell of her breast. "Julien! I—I thought you were still in town."

"I've just returned."

"So I see," she snapped, stung by the trace of mockery in his tone, though an instant later she was not certain that it had not been directed at himself.

"I rushed to your side the instant I discovered you were bound for home. Doesn't that deserve some reward?"

The soft words were spoken at her ear. His warm lips brushed her cheek, trailing toward her mouth. She turned her head away. "I might, if you had not left me stranded at the dance while you pursued your own interests."

"You would prefer that I moon about you like a callow, lovesick youth? It isn't the fashion, *mon coeur,* for a man to be too obviously smitten by . . . his own wife."

Surprise parted her lips as she swung back to him. He took immediate advantage of that unguarded moment, setting his warm mouth to hers, turning her to him, and enclosing her within the iron bands of his arms. What was the point in fighting him? He was there and so was she. Amalie, caught in the surge of desire, swayed against him.

The buttons of his waistcoat and the studs of his shirt pressed into her. His warmth enveloped her with the smell of starched linen, the faint spice of bay rum, and his own maleness. The tang of brandy was on his tongue, a heady taste as it mingled with his sweetness. She pushed her hands upward to clasp them behind his neck, drawing him closer as she moved her burning lips on his. He smoothed his hand over the silken curtain of her hair, closing his fingers upon it, then opening them wide again to spread them over her back and pressing lower to draw her against his male hardness.

She wanted him. She wanted to feel her bare skin against his, to take him within her in wild abandon. The force of her need was shocking and she tore her mouth from his, hiding her face in the curve of his throat. He held her, his lips brushing her hair, his arms tightening until she could scarcely breathe. She could feel the thudding of his heart and the tension in his body as he fought for mastery of his need of her. Then his chest rose in deep breath. He let it out slowly, his hold loosening.

His withdrawal was a tangible thing, hardly won. She could feel it and a soft protest rose in her throat. She clung to him, sliding her fingers into the crisp waves of his hair. With eyes closed and lashes trembling on her cheeks, she lifted her mouth for his kiss.

He spoke her name on a quiet sigh, the single word an entreaty, an apology. An instant later, she felt the searing hunger of his mouth on hers. It was a reckless possession, one that would not be denied. The pressure, the burning invasion sent excitement swirling through her. The strength of his grasp brought her to her toes. She strained against him, the rasp of the material of his waistcoat upon the peaks of her breasts making her shiver as they tightened into points. His hand settled on the curve of her hip, his fingers biting deep.

The world shifted dizzily and it was a moment before she realized that he had slowly revolved as he held her, turning from the open doorway to the center of the summerhouse. In that deeper darkness, he went to one knee, drawing her down with him. Then he released her, shrugging quickly out of his coat to spread it over the floor and slipping her dressing gown from her shoulders to add to the makeshift pallet.

She needed no urging but sank down upon it with him. He lay on his side above her, brushing his lips over her brow, tracing the curves of one small ear with his tongue, barely closing his teeth upon the lobe. He paused for the space of a heartbeat, as she reached out slender fingers to unbutton his waistcoat, to slip the studs of his shirt free, then he continued his explorations.

The shape of her form beneath the gauzy batiste of her nightgown snared his attention. He molded the angle of her collarbone with his fingers, caressing the hollow beneath it, letting his hand climb the gentle, cloth-covered mound that rose below. He sought the hollow between it and its mate and swooped downward, skimming the lift of her ribs and finding the small sink of her navel. The resilient flatness of her abdomen drew his touch and, after it, the firm structure of her leg. He continued downward to increase his grip, drawing up her knee, then, without pausing, swept back down upon the sensitive softness and heat, the intricate folds of tender flesh at the juncture of her thighs.

Her breathing quickened. She was alive in every pore. In the center of her being there flared a vivid and joyous sensuality and she welcomed its racing in her veins. She slipped her hand inside his shirt, threading her fingertips through the fine curls that grew there, delighting in their vitality. She touched a pap and felt it contract, then spread her hand over the layer of muscle that covered his ribs and hardened his waist; with the backs of her knuckles against his abdomen, she slipped her fingers into the waistband of his trousers.

He drew back, shrugging from his waistcoat and shirt, unfastening his trousers and removing them as he kicked off his low dancing shoes. Then he reached to strip her nightgown upward. She pushed herself in to a sitting position as he drew it off over her head. The night air touched her skin and she shivered, then his arms were around her once more, pulling her against him, molding the slender curves and hollows of her form to the force and strength of his own. His hold tightened. It was as if he would imprint the feel of her upon his hard body against the chance that he might never touch her again. She clung to him, snared in his fierce embrace, yielding to the growing abandon inside her that was fueled by the leashed violence she sensed in the man who held her.

She did not care that this coupling in the open would be scorned as depravity by any who heard of it. She did not care if they were seen. Nor would it be cause for concern if the Teche should rise to engulf them or the sick old world go spinning to its end. Nothing mattered except this wild rapture, this furious glory.

With a hoarse sound deep in his throat, he lowered his arm, lifting her knee and drawing it across his lean flank. She felt an aching vulnerability, then he was inside her, filling her, pressing deep and deeper still. The sense of completion was so intense, the assuagement so gratifying that she was lightheaded, almost as if intoxicated. Then she eased down upon him, moving in the surge of newfound strength, wanting, needing his answering force.

It came, a powerful gathering of muscles. He carried her with him up and over onto her back, rising above her. She encompassed him, accepting the shocks of his thrusts. They vibrated through her taut muscles, an endless excitation that gathered, blooming and exploding in soundless wonder inside her.

She was a part of him and he of her: inseparable, fused, two pieces of a whole. There was nothing, no reality, no dreams, that did not include this miraculous joining. What purpose had the night but this? What use the perfume of flowers except to incite its magic? Hidden by the darkness, drowning in the scent of roses and honeysuckle, they strove together with limbs entwined and fervent breaths mingling. Seeking surcease, they found exultation; reaching for pleasure, they touched splendor and felt it settle around them.

The owl hooted, a mournful noise not far away. A breeze sifted through the lattice, whispering across their damp flesh. The petals of an overblown rose growing through its crisscross trellis shattered, falling softly to the brick floor. They did not stir. Amalie's head was pillowed on his arm, his face was buried in the tangled swath of her hair. Their bodies were melded together at the hip, enmeshed.

"*Je t'aime*," he whispered in quiet reverence. "I love you."

She opened her eyes. "Oh, Julien—"

For the fraction of a second he was utterly still, then he moved to place a finger on her lips. When she was obediently silent, he lifted his head and pressed a brief kiss where his finger had been. He eased his arm free and rolled from her. As she levered herself up, she could hear him in the dark, finding his trousers and shoes and getting into them.

"What is it?" she asked.

He did not answer, but reached to help her to her feet. He bent to pick up their clothing, then handed them to her. When she had clutched them to her breasts, he leaned to place one arm under her knees and the other behind her back, lifting her high against his chest.

"What are you doing?" There was a quiver of a laugh, or perhaps something else, in her voice.

He brushed her forehead with his lips, his answer a low

sound at her ear. "Putting you back where you belong."

"You mean—Oh, put me down."

For an answer, he stepped from the summerhouse and, ignoring her low-voiced protests, strode over the dew-wet grass, treading his way through the trees. He skirted the corner of the big house past the *garçonnière* and moved to the loggia. Without pausing, he climbed the steps to the upper floor and approached the only door left unlocked. He stopped before it. Resigned, Amalie reached down to turn the knob and push it open.

He hesitated a moment in his own bedchamber and Amalie thought he meant to put her in his bed, but then he moved on toward the sliding door that led into her room. So well balanced was it that it opened to the thrust of his shoulder and he stepped inside. Surefooted even in the dark, his strides took him straight to the high bed. He placed her on it, then took the clothes she still held.

She reached out before he could move away, touching his wrist and curling her fingers around it. Her voice low, she said, "Don't go."

Did she imagine the tension that corded the tendons of his arm? It was gone in an instant as he answered with the softness of a sigh, "How can I?"

She slid across the bed to make room for him. He let fall their clothes and paused long enough to strip off trousers and shoes. The bed ropes creaked as he put his knee on the mattress, then he lowered himself beside her. His arms encircled her and he settled her head upon his shoulder, then allowed his hand to rest on her hip while his mouth brushed the fragrant silkiness of the hair at her temple.

Her arm curved behind his back, holding him to her. Her

breasts were flattened against the iron wall of his chest and her thigh was between his. Their bodies fit together with perfect naturalness, as if they were made for each other. Smiling in the dark at the thought, she inched closer still, pressing her lips to the pulse that throbbed at the base of his throat, touching it with her tongue to taste the salt of his skin. Her smile widened as she felt the stir of his reaction at her groin.

"Go to sleep, *chérie*," he whispered.

"I'm not really sleepy."

His hand moved upward, skimming her waist and coming to rest on the curve of her breast. His thumb brushed the soft peak to stiffness. "Nor am I."

Sated, near exhaustion, she slept some time later with the feel of his hands upon her hair, stroking the tangled satin skein of its length from her face. She did not know when he left her.

The sun was shining brightly when Amalie left the house trailed by Isa and dressed in a riding habit of blue pelisse cloth with *mousquetaire* cuffs trimmed with braid and braided frog closures on the jacket. She had been up long enough to have dispensed the food from storerooms and smokehouse, eaten breakfast, approved the menus for the day, and checked on the summer clothing being made. Now she meant to visit the dairy, located at some small distance from the house, and to oversee the weeding in the vegetable garden that supplied the kitchen. But before she did, she meant to enjoy a brisk ride.

Her mount, a chestnut gelding, was waiting near the front door. She nodded with a word of thanks to the groom who held him and also a pony for Isa. The man was disappointed that he would not be riding with her, she thought, but she would not be going far and there was Isa to send for help if the need arose. She stepped to the mounting block and sprang to the sidesaddle, hooking her knee over the horn and adjusting the long fall of her skirt to cover her boot in the stirrup. She gathered up the reins, adjusted her flat crowned hat with its jaunty plume, and turned to watch as Isa was helped onto his pony.

She was tired, with sore muscles that had never given problems before. It was not surprising, she considered with the glimmer of a smile as she recalled her strenuous night. Regardless, her odd malaise was not physical. She had been disappointed to find Julien gone that morning when she awoke. It was almost a betrayal, that creeping away from her, after what had passed between them in the night.

She had come close to barging into his room, waking him up to demand why he had left her. It had been a peculiar shyness that had prevented her. Julien in the daytime was so different, so much more formal, than he was at night. His words of love had seemed sincere, so infinitely right those few short hours ago, but in the light of day they rang oddly. If he had looked at her with nothing more than his usual mocking affection, she could not have borne it.

She took the wagon road that led past the clothes-drying yard, smokehouse, cooperage, and plantation chapel toward the fields. The last building, small and boasting a miniature steeple though the bell hung on a post outside the door, had been installed by M'mere. The elderly woman came to pray there at times, though it was used mainly by the slaves. The diocese sent out a priest at irregular intervals to hear confession and to hold mass. Amalie saw at a glance that whitewash was needed on the exterior after the rains and made a mental note to order the painting done.

It was pleasant riding through the fields, listening to the rustling of the cane. The light morning wind swept over the endless stretches, tossing and bending it like waves in a green sea. The sun shimmered on the blades, as if sparkling over water. It was not yet hot, though it would be later in the day. The summer was deepening fast. In a few weeks, the fever season would be upon them, and it would be time to think of removing to Île Dernière. She was looking forward to that. She had never seen the gulf or the ocean. The Felicianas, being somewhat higher in elevation than New Orleans and away from the swamplands, had been considered a healthful country. The main reason, however, was that she and her great-aunt had not been able to afford an annual trip to the seaside or some watering place such as Saratoga, White Sulphur Springs, or Salt Springs. Sea bathing was said to be quite beneficial and also enjoyable. One had to be properly dressed, of course. She must remember to mention to M'mere the possibility of having a costume made.

The crop had been little damaged by the flood. If anything, it had benefited from the rich silt deposited about the roots as the water receded; it appeared rich and green and unusually tall for the time of year. Barring high winds later in the season, disease, or an early frost, they should make a good profit come cutting time.

Far over the fields, she caught sight of a work party. At the same time, she heard the braying of a mule and now and then a call. The cornfields, where the grain was grown to feed the livestock as well as providing food for the humans, started just there. The hands were plowing, cultivating the middles between the rows of young corn, and hoeing out the grass. A man on horseback sat in the road watching. For a moment, she thought it was Patrick for she had recognized his loud voice, then she knew the seat was too good, the shoulders too straight. A moment later, she caught sight of the overseer standing under a tree.

The rider was Robert. He turned his head as the sound of the horses reached him and lifted a hand in greeting. Amalie waved her riding crop, but did not go nearer, turning instead down a track that would take her back to the house by way of the dairy and the kitchen garden.

"M'sieu Robert, he's a good man," Isa said from behind her. She had almost forgotten the boy was there. She turned to give him a smile. "Yes, he is."

"Not like M'sieu Dye."

"No," she agreed, her tone clipped.

"Why did we not stop to talk to him then?"

He was frowning against the sun, but there was only curiosity in his voice. "He was busy and I didn't want to get in his way; besides, I have things to do."

"He comes to the big house sometimes, not always. If he comes today, I will show him my picture of the turtles who swim in the pool of M'sieu George."

The boy's smile was mischievous. Amalie knew she should not encourage him, but could not prevent the grin that tilted the corner of her mouth. The Englishman had been considerably upset that morning to find not only a trio of turtles sunning themselves on a piece of driftwood in the center of his pool, but a small water moccasin undulating across it and breaking up the still, reflecting surface. Cousin Robert, she was sure, would appreciate the drollery.

No matter how it might have looked, she was not avoiding the man. Of course she wasn't. What reason had she to do such a thing, after all? He had touched her and she had felt some small physical reaction. It had meant nothing except that she was a normal woman with normal responses. She wasn't going to make it into something mysterious and fraught with emotion. There was no point. None at all. He had seen nothing out of the way about it, she was sure. She would forget it, put it out of her mind. It would be as if it had never occurred. She had forgotten it until now. Julien had helped to banish the memory.

It was churning day in the dairy. Amalie directed the women as they scalded churns, lids, and dashers, then drew up the milk from the dairy cistern where it had been hung to cool in crocks set in buckets. She did not leave until they had skimmed off the cream to go into the churns and begun the long process of agitating the milk that would bring the butterfat to the top.

In the garden, she surveyed the neat rows of vegetables bordered by strawberries and sprawling plots of herbs, with tangles of raspberries growing on the enclosing fence. The English peas and cabbages were almost gone, the spinach and the lettuce trying to go to seed. The shallots were good for the summer; the mustard and radishes would last a while longer, as would the Irish potatoes, though the last were getting too large for boiling and would have to be dug before long. The string beans and the squash were coming on, however. They would be ready to eat in a few days, and following them would come the butter beans and okra. She set the old man who tended the plot to weeding and gave orders for greens, onions, and potatoes to be brought to the kitchen in time for the noon meal, then turned back toward the house.

Since she was returning the back way, Amalie left her horse at the stable and walked toward the house with Isa skipping awkwardly at her side. She slowed her steps to accommodate his slower pace, then, as they neared the kitchen, sent him to get a glass of water for himself and to order water and coffee to be brought to her wherever M'mere might be. The older woman did not get out much, but enjoyed hearing the report of what was happening about the place.

On the loggia, she started toward the backstairs, but glanced through the open dining room toward the front gallery as she passed the door. The front door, like the back, stood open to the soft air. A shadow lay on the gallery floor, cast by the warm, slanting sunlight, and she caught the faint murmur of a voice. Swinging her long skirts from under her feet by the loop over her wrist, she started in that direction.

It was dark in the dining room compared to the outside. She paused for a moment to allow her eyes to adjust to the gloom. The table had been set for luncheon; there was a fly buzzing in the frosted glass flycatcher in the center of the table, an angry sound in the quiet. The plates had been turned upside down to prevent more flies from crawling into them, as had the water-glasses, except for one. Amalie reached to turn it down, then skirted the table, moving toward the door.

"But I tell you I don't want to wait!"

"Not so loud, my dear Chloe, you'll wake her. My advice is to cultivate patience. That's the surest way to get what you want."

The first speaker was without doubt Chloe. The second voice, firm, yet so quiet it was barely above a whisper, was one with which Amalie had become most intimately familiar in the past weeks. She stepped out onto the front gallery with a smile rising in her eyes and her lips open to speak.

She stopped abruptly. Chloe sat in a rocking chair, her arms folded across her chest and a pout on her face. M'mere lay with her head resting on the back of an arm-chair and a shawl over her lap, her eyes closed in sleep. A man, tall and dark, stood leaning with his back to the railing and the sun, his face in shadow. It was not Julien, however, but Robert.

A suspicion struck her, one so terrible in its implications that for a moment she could not see, could not hear. It was beautifully logical, perfect in its application to the circumstances, and yet required such concerted deception, such disregard for her welfare, her sensibilities, that it was inconceivable.

And yet she would have sworn that the quiet masculine voice she had just heard was that of the man who had said he loved her, the man who had made love to her in turbulent bliss in the summerhouse the night before, the same one who had come to her all the nights before.

Chapter 7

obert came erect, his dark blue gaze fixed on Amalie's pale face. Chloe sat up, facing her. "My goodness," the girl said, "you look as if someone had hit you."

With an enormous effort, Amalie collected herself. She managed a shaky laugh. "A touch of the sun, I expect."

"What—what?" It was M'mere, rousing, blinking. She turned her faded gaze, catching sight of Amalie. "Is that you, *chère?* Do come and tell me what you have been doing."

She had to have a moment alone. Grasping at an excuse, she said, "Yes, in one instant. I must run up and wash my hands. I—I've ordered coffee. I hope you will stay, C-cousin Robert."

She included M'mere and Chloe in a vague smile, but though she glanced in the direction of the man who stood there, she could not bring herself to meet his gaze. Whisking around, she crossed quickly to the other end of the gallery and mounted the stairs.

On the upper gallery, she entered the salon, threading through its furnishings to get to her own door. She swung into her bedchamber, closing the door behind her before she came to an abrupt halt. She took a calming breath, letting it out slowly. After a moment, she forced herself to move to the washstand. Her hands trembled as she poured water before bending to splash her face. Taking up a linen towel edged with tatted lace, she blotted the droplets, staring at herself with wide, stricken eyes in the mirror.

No. It could not be. It was impossible, unthinkable. She

had made the same foolish mistake before, hadn't she? That first day she had met Robert, when she had come upon him talking with M'mere in the sitting room, she had thought it was Julien she heard. She was upsetting herself for nothing, simply because the timbre of their voices was similar.

Or was she?

She flung down the towel and swept around, staring at the doors that led into her husband's bedchamber. She took a step toward them and then another. Swiftly, before she could change her mind, she moved to thrust the doors open and step into the other room.

Heavy draperies at the French windows kept out the morning light, and also the air, so that the room was close and steeped in gloom. Julien lay sprawled across the bed on his stomach with the sheet bunched about his waist. He wore no nightshirt, for he was naked above the waist, but she thought she could see the line of the waist of his under-drawers just above the sheet. The sound of the sliding doors opening had roused him, for as she approached the bed he opened one eye. Seeing her, he quickly shut it again.

She reached out to put her hand on his shoulder, giving him a slight shake before quickly drawing back. "Julien?"

He raised his eyelid again. He sighed. "Yes, *chère?*"

Moistening her lips, she asked, "What time did you get home last night?"

He considered the question, then gave a low groan, stretching and turning to prop his elbow on the pillow and rest his head on his hand. Finally he said, "I'm not sure I remember. Anyway, it is indecent to fling such questions at a man at this time of the morning and expect him to answer without so much as a sip of *café au lait* for his nerves."

"Coffee you shall have if you tell me how long you remained in town behind us, and what you did when you returned."

"Is this a test, my sweet?" he asked, studying her white features and her hands, which were clasped in front of her. "Did I do something stupid last night?"

She lowered her lashes to stare down at her hands as she gave a quick shake of her head.

He raised up, pushing himself higher in the bed. His voice sharpened. "Did I hurt you then?"

"No, no," she said hastily.

"Then perhaps I said something I should not have? If so, you must hold me excused. I'm afraid I may have had a little too much to drink."

She looked up to find him watching her, his dark eyes intent. "You didn't seem at all intoxicated."

"You flatter me, *chère,* I fear. I'm a clumsy oaf at times. If I displeased you in any way, I beg you will forgive it, for I swear it was not intentional."

His voice was low, the timbre rough with sincerity. Was it the same? She did not know. It could be. She took a deep breath. "Do you remember anything of what happened last night?"

"A little," he said and, holding her shadowed brown gaze, let his finely molded mouth curve into a smile.

It had been him; what else could he mean? Her answering smile was tremulous. She asked in a rush before she could change her mind, "Then why did you leave me?"

He frowned and it seemed there was swift and cogent thought in his narrowed eyes. "You mean, after . . ."

"Yes. After."

He made a deprecating gesture, then rubbed a hand over the dark bristles that shadowed his face. "I thought to spare you this sight in the light of the morning. Besides, the truth is, I've slept alone for too long."

The last comment had a flippant ring. If he had been drunk the night before, she thought, then she might well prefer him that way. Pushing the idea from her, she said, "I'm sorry I woke you. If you would like to come down, Robert is here. We are just going to have coffee."

"I think," he said slowly, "that I can do without seeing my dear cousin today. I'll take mine up here."

"As you like," she said and turned away toward the door.

"Amalie?"

She swung back. "Yes?"

"Nothing," he said and flung himself back on the pillows, closing his eyes.

Amalie, after ringing the bell for Tige, changed quickly from her habit into her hoop skirt and a gown of pale gold poplin, then returned to the lower gallery. She had collected herself and her manner was spritely, even rather gay. Isa had arrived behind the coffee, bearing his drawing of turtles. She drew him forward, encouraging him to show it not only to Robert, but to the others. He was shy, primarily because George had joined them over the coffee tray, but the boy relaxed as the Englishman laughed, enjoying the joke at his expense.

Several times Amalie found her gaze straying to Robert. He paid little attention to her, however, as he rallied George on his turtle pond or teased his aunt about her napping, pretending that it was her late nights of dissipation that was the problem. Amalie was amazed at herself that she could have thought this virile, self-contained man would stoop to pretending to be Julien merely to take advantage of his cousin's wife. He could have his choice of beautiful women, or so Chloe had said, something Amalie saw no reason to doubt. She should also have remembered that, other than the night before, Julien had always come from his own bedchamber into her room. For Robert to have taken his place would mean that Julien had to be a party to any deception, and her husband was far too proud and possessive to consent to such a thing. Nor was there any possibility that it had been only on one occasion, the night before, that she had been betrayed. The man who had made love to her then, and the one who had taken her virginity with such tenderness, were without doubt one and the same. His touch and his kisses had been identical. Of that much she was certain.

The thought of her disturbance over the brush of Robert's fingers two evenings ago intruded, but she dismissed it. That had been a mere affliction of the nerves. To consider otherwise was too degrading, and yes, confusing.

Still, When Robert rose to take his leave at last, she stood watching as he kissed M'mere on the cheek and gave Chloe a quick hug, but when he inclined his head to her in farewell, she did not give him her hand.

If she had wanted to brood over her foolish suspicions, there would have been no time. That afternoon a carriage pulled up on the drive. A man, portly and hearty, with hair of the color known as pepper and salt, got down, then handed out four ladies. It was M'mere's friends, the Mesdames Oudry, with Mademoiselle Louise, and the girl's mother and father, Monsieur and Madame Callot, who had come to collect her after her visit. They would be staying a few days, perhaps a week or two, before returning to the city.

Julien was on hand to greet them and to help entertain the gentleman. Since Monsieur Callot was the factor who handled most of the plantation supplies as well as the selling of the sugar crop, the two had much to discuss. Julien might take no interest in the growing of the cane, but the profit from it was important to him. Juleps were ordered on the lower gallery and the women, to escape the talk of business, retreated to the upper gallery with tall glasses of *eau de sucre* and orange flower water.

The time generally allotted for a visit came and went. The elderly ladies talked on, unnoticing. Chloe and Louise giggled together at the far end of the gallery, from whence came such enlightening scraps of conversation as "He has a most noble brow," "La, his air, quite dashing," and ". . . so dangerous he makes one quake; he has met his man on the field of honor no less than fourteen times and has always drawn first blood!" Amalie tried to enter into conversation with Madame Callot, but the woman wanted only an audience. Overweight in the manner that causes a pouter-pigeon bosom, she was also overbearing. Before two hours had passed, she had indicated that she considered St. Martinville a provincial backwater; that she thought Julien sadly indolent, but not to the point where a wife of sufficient energy could not redeem him; and that country slaves were far inferior to those reared and trained in the city. She had favored Amalie with her own recipe for

orange flower water that included just a bit more laudanum, fretted about the absence of candied violets, her
favorite afternoon delicacy, on the refreshment tray, and
said forthrightly that Isa, who spent the time seated at
Amalie's feet, would be better employed in some more
useful occupation such as shooing the chickens that wandered into the front yard back to the rear areas where they
belonged.

The scrape of the men's footsteps on the stairs had the
sound of deliverance to Amalie's ears. She was far too opti-
mistic. Julien, discovering that he and his man of business
had much more to thrash out between them, had not only
invited the entire party to dinner, but had sent a wagon for
their baggage and personal servants so that they might
spend the night.

Regardless, dinner was not so difficult since it was
enlivened with a discussion of Île Dernière: the riding and
picnicking, the walks along the beach where one searched
for shells, and the music and dancing available at the hotel.
Madame Callot did not approve of sea bathing for ladies,
no matter how healthful it was considered, and was quite
frightened of the wind storms that sometimes came off the
water. But she was unable to dampen her daughter's enthusiasm. Monsieur Callot ate heartily, and with gusto, of
turtle soup, ham, turkey with oyster sauce, fresh greens
chopped with boiled eggs and covered with bacon drip-
pings, parsley potatoes, hominy, and a variety of custards.
All of the dishes were served with a choice of red or white
wine, and after these had been removed, dried figs, raisins,
and almonds were offered with madeira. During the meal,
however, Monsieur Callot talked of little except the

Lucullan feasts that the simple meal Amalie had provided brought to mind. He did, however, praise Julien's cellar and permitted himself to be persuaded to take a taste of brandy after the meal, a mere pint or so.

Where their guests were to sleep had presented a problem. All the rooms on the second floor were in use except for the virgin's room. Amalie intended to remove herself to the smaller room, giving her own chamber to Monsieur and Madame Callot, but the factor, with a wink at Julien, refused to disturb the arrangements of a couple so newly married. He and his wife would take the smaller room and be glad of it. He was so adamant that Amalie could only agree, though it meant that the couple would be forced to parade through her room every time they entered and left their own.

The disposition of the elderly ladies was easier. They would take Chloe's room, next to M'mere's sitting room, and Chloe and Louise, being younger and more agile, could sleep in the third-floor loft. With a resigned shrug, Amalie had given the orders to have the rooms made up. After all, it would only be for one night.

But the visit stretched to a second day and then to a third. A week went by. At first, Julien arose early to entertain his guests, taking Monsieur Callot out in his buggy to view the fields and to inspect the sugar mill and arranging floating excursions on his barge. Toward the end of the week, however, discovering that the other man was happy sitting on the gallery with a mint julep at his elbow, he resumed his old habits. Madame Callot had more forcefulness, however. She followed Amalie on her rounds, talking every minute in voluble fashion and pointing out her own way, necessarily superior, of doing things—from the making of jelly to the disciplining of unruly slaves. Chloe and Louise were forever whispering in corners to the disgust of George, who made great progress with the preparation of the beds for the shrubs he expected to put in them. The two girls disturbed M'mere, however, who retreated more and more often to her room to rest.

In order to gain a little breathing space, Amalie decided, quite ruthlessly, to throw Robert to the wolves by suggesting that the two girls ride over, with a groom in attendance, to visit him. The scheme gained several hours of quiet, but was not without repercussions. The two girls not only brought Robert back with them to dinner but had hit upon the idea of a soirée, which they saw no reason why Amalie should not arrange for their enjoyment.

The long glance Robert gave her, the momentary pause before he took her hand and bowed over it in greeting, brought the memory of her folly back to her. She had flushed, not the least because she was suddenly aware that he was more observant than she had supposed. She was convinced that he had noticed her withdrawal at their last meeting. He could not guess the reason for it, of course; still, her guilt for her ridiculous suspicions made the smile she gave him a little warmer than usual.

They stood on the lower gallery. The girls had gone on upstairs, despite the early hour, to begin dressing for dinner. Except for Isa, her constant shadow, they were alone for the moment.

There was a slight frown between his dark blue eyes as he stood staring down at her, retaining her fingers in his firm grasp. "You are sure you don't mind setting another place? If I will make too many, just say the word, and I'll go away."

"No please. You know you are always welcome." She summoned another smile. "Besides, it seems I have exhausted everything that can possibly be said to our guests and I look to you to help keep the conversation going."

"Fresh blood?"

"Something like that," she agreed wryly.

"I had heard of your guests through the plantation grapevine, then Chloe had a great deal to say today about this past week. She happened to mention, too, that it was you who suggested she bring Mam'zelle Louise to see me."

He missed little, it seemed. "I am sorry if it was an inconvenience."

"It wasn't exactly convenient. Mine is a bachelor household, you know, with very little to offer ladies in the way of refreshment and no one trained to attend to it in any case. But never mind. If it helped you, I'm glad to have been of service."

His usefulness did not stop there. He dominated the remaining afternoon and evening, paying gallant compliments to the older women, meeting Monsieur Callot on his own ground in a discussion of business affairs, and stunning Louise into near silence with a glance or two from beneath narrowed lids that carried more animal sensuality than she was used to arousing in the opposite sex. He became Amalie's shield against Madame Callot, questioning the woman's every statement and discovering in a spuriously judicial fashion the advantages of his hostess's way of arranging matters. He was powerless to prevent the development of the plans for the soirée, but did manage most adroitly to turn it into a farewell party for the Callots and Oudrys.

And yet his presence was a reminder that Julien had not come to her at night since their guests had descended upon them. Amalie tried to tell herself that it was because of the Callots sleeping so close by, likely to barge through her chamber at any time. Still, she could not help but fear that she had spoiled the tender relationship growing between them by her questions and demands.

Amalie was sorry to see Robert leave that night, so grateful was she for his support and so comforting had it been. Still, she had his word that he would not fail to come to the soirée in two days' time. She went to bed with her brain teeming with the many things that would have to be done: the invitations to be written out and sent around by a groom; the food and drink to be served; the music; the house cleaning and decorating; her own toilette. This would be her first large-scale entertainment and she would like for it to be a success. With Robert to distract her guests and Julien to help enliven the evening, she began to think she might come through it with some small credit. Thinking of the epicurean feast she would serve, some-thing guaranteed to astonish Monsieur Callot, she finally slept.

It was early, well before sunup, the next morning when she visited the smokehouse and storerooms to pass out pro-visions. In the cool dimness of the raised basement area under the house, she checked the long rows of nine-pound loaves of sugar, the barrels of flour, the cases of olive oil, and the casks of brandy and whiskey. Moving candles boxed up by the gross and homemade soap in stacks already cut into bars, she checked over the racks of bottled wine and the shelves holding dried fruit, preserves, and pickles. She gave a satisfied nod as she stepped out into the dining room, waited for Isa to follow, then locked the store-room door behind her. Pulling a piece of writing paper from under her arm, she began to make notes as she walked toward the loggia.

Outside, she looked up to see Tige moving toward the stairs carrying a brass can of shaving water from the kitchen. That meant that Julien was up then. Nodding to the valet, she finished her notations, put the paper into the pocket of the apron she wore over her morning gown, and started up the stairs after him.

As she reached the upper loggia, she saw Patrick Dye standing outside the door of Julien's room as if he had just come from inside. His head was bent, and catching the solid clink of gold, she saw that he was counting the coins in the sizable roll that he held in one hand.

"Is there something I can do for you, M'sieu Dye?" she inquired, her voice cool.

So intent was he on what he was doing that he had not heard her approach. His head snapped up and his hand closed over the gold. With a quick gesture, he pushed the handful of coins into the leather purse he held. He stored the purse in his pocket and took out a pocketknife. He flicked it open and began to use the long blade to clean the dirt from under his yellow fingernails. He smiled at her then, though there was a wary look in his eyes. "No, my dear Madame Declouet, there's not a thing you can do for me, at least, nothing you would."

She stiffened at his suggestive words, lifting a brow. "Did you wish to see my husband?"

The slight stress she had put on the last word had no effect. Giving a slow shake of his head as he put his knife away, the overseer said, "I've just spoken to him."

"Then you must not let me keep you from your duties."

"Well, now," he drawled, putting his hands on his hips as he surveyed her slowly from head to toe, letting his gaze finally rest on her breasts that rose and fell with her growing anger, "you're certainly the kind of woman who could."

"I find your manner offensive, M'sieu Dye. I suggest you leave!"

"Oh, quite the lady of the manor, aren't you? What are you going to do if I don't? Tell your husband? That didn't get you far before, now did it?"

She clenched her hands into fists in her apron pockets. Behind her, she was aware of Isa edging backward toward the wooden storage chest and glancing at the stairs as if watching for help or preparing to run. "If you think Julien will overlook insults to his wife, then you are much mistaken."

"Are you sure now? Are you sure Julien Declouet cares a damn what happens to his virgin bride?"

Shock that the man would dare say such a thing to her ran along her veins, then was crowded out by sheer rage. She wanted to strike his crudely handsome face, but chose words as weapons instead. "I am his wife, indeed, M'sieu Dye, no virgin bride, and if you think that means nothing to a man like Julien, you have much to learn!"

His face went blank with surprise, then he gave a sneering laugh. "So he finally got the job done, huh? Too bad. I thought I might console you one of these days. But it's not too late to give you an idea of what you're missing."

He reached for her arms, dragging her against him. His hot, wet lips grazed the corner of her mouth, and she cried out in raging disgust as she jerked her head to one side, trying to pull free. She twisted and turned, but his fingers bit into her arms, holding her against him. She kicked out, but hampered by her skirts, could make little contact.

She heard the crash of a lid closing, the thud of running footsteps, then came the slashing of blows, rising and falling, striking the overseer on the sides and back.

"Let go!" Isa shouted as he belabored the man who was twice as tall as he was with the riding crop he had taken from the storage chest. "Let go of the *petite maîtresse!*"

Patrick pushed Amalie from him so that she stumbled against the railing. With a growl in his throat, he turned on the boy, snatching at the crop and wrenching it from his hand. He swung a fist, catching Isa on the side of the head. The blow sent the boy spinning backward to smash into the wall.

"I'll teach you to hit a white man, you little black bastard," the overseer growled, clenching his fist on the crop as he started toward Isa.

Amalie hurled herself at the man, reaching for his uplifted arm and clutching at him so that her fingernails sank through the cloth of his shirt into the soft skin on his belly and she was half riding on his back. He wrenched around toward her, then froze as the door to Julien's bed-chamber was snatched open.

"What in God's name is going on out here?"

Julien paused in the doorway, tying the belt of his dressing gown. There was a wet towel around his neck that Tige had been using to soften his beard. His hair was tousled and his face flushed from the heat of his shaving water.

Amalie released Patrick and stepped back. She lifted one shaking hand to push at the tendrils of her hair that had come free of her braided crown. "This man insulted me, put his hands on me, and struck Isa."

"He what?" Julien demanded, his dark eyes blazing as he turned to the overseer.

Patrick laughed, rubbing at his scratched belly with one hand. "I only wanted to teach her a thing—"

Julien moved so fast that the crack of the backhanded slap rang out before the overseer knew what had happened. Dye's head snapped back with the force of the blow. He brought his hand up, and dabbed at the blood that appeared at the corner of his mouth, his brows drawing together in fury and disbelief.

"My wife," Julien said softly, "needs no instruction from you or any man. Touch her again and I will kill you."

"Aren't you forgetting a thing or two here?" Patrick blustered with a sidelong look at Amalie.

"Would you care to remind me on the dueling field?"

At the silken sound in the voice of the master of Belle Grove, the other man's eyes widened. "Here now, there's no call for that."

"It might well suit my purpose to force a meeting, though it would pain me to accord the honor to one so obviously not a gentleman."

The overseer licked his lips. "I don't hold with dueling.

It's against the law."

Julien smiled. "The law is blind to the practice in this state, *mon ami,* or at least so slow in tending to its duties that the sheriff seldom reaches the field of honor until all parties have fled."

"There're a few things I could say—"

"But you won't, will you, on the off chance that it isn't necessary? That being the case, you will apologize now to Madame, my wife, and also to her small protector."

"The devil I will!"

"Or else."

Amalie, hardly listening to the exchange, had turned away to kneel in a billow of skirts beside Isa. There was a bruise on his cheek and a lump on the back of his head, but his eyes were unclouded and his handclasp firm as she helped him to his feet. Still, the deadly quality of her husband's last words reached her so that she looked up.

The two men were watching each other, their features tense, as if searching for signs of weakness. Abruptly, Patrick Dye looked away. He jerked around toward Amalie, ducking his head. "I forgot myself, Madame Declouet. I hope you—and the boy—will overlook it."

He did not wait for a reply, but blundered past her with his face set and fiery red. He clattered down the stairs, then they saw him striding away toward the quarters with his head down and his hands knotted into fists.

"Are you all right, *ma chère?*"

There was concern in Julien's dark eyes as they moved over her. Amalie wanted to fling herself into his arms, to be held safe. Instead, she nodded.

"If that man ever so much as looks at you with disrespect

again, I want to know it."

"Yes, of course."

"I . . . Perhaps it would be a good idea if you were to lie down for a few minutes, have a glass of wine."

"It isn't necessary." It might be just as well that he had not allowed her to give in to the moment of weakness, of longing to be near him. She felt much stronger now, well able to control any tremors of disturbed nerves.

"As you wish," he said. "If you will excuse me, I'll get dressed."

"Yes. I . . . Julien?"

"*Chérie?*" he said, turning back.

"I wanted to talk to you about entertainment for tomorrow evening."

He smiled, a slow curving of the mouth that lit his face. "Leave it to me."

So happy was she to be able to do so that the answering smile that rose to her brown eyes was light. She did not move until the door had closed upon him, then she herded Isa into the salon. There she moved to the liquor chest and poured a small amount of wine for him as well as herself after all. It was not until she had taken her glass out onto the front gallery, not until she stood tasting the semisweet, stimulating liquid reserved for ladies, that it came to her. The position of the overseer at Belle Grove was oddly privileged. Not only had he been privy, in a way she found inexplicable, to knowledge of her private affairs, but the fact was that in spite of what Patrick had done, regardless of the violence of Julien's reaction to it, there had been not the least suggestion of discharging the man.

There was no opportunity to question Julien concerning

Patrick Dye. His time was taken up by his duties as host in the next thirty-six hours, and, in addition, he seemed more remote since the contretemps, though in truth he had become more and more so from the time he had stopped visiting her bed. She had thought there might be a few minutes during the afternoon before the party to speak to him, but Madame Callot had gone into a fury of packing, calling for tissue paper and the loan of extra boxes, causing much extra laundering and ironing as she made ready to leave early the next morning. The hurrying of the maids and valets here and there as they tried to make their various mistresses and masters ready for the party, each demanding to use the washtub and drying lines, the flat and crimping irons that Madame Callot's people were monopolizing, brought inevitable squabbles that had to be smoothed over. Then there were the last-minute crises with food, wine, and table arrangements. In the end, it was time to dress before it was all done. Amalie was so happy to see the signs of the imminent removal of their guests, however, that she resented none of the calls upon her.

Lally approached her new duties with great seriousness. Amalie had fully intended to wear the first thing that came to hand in the armoire, but the maid had laid out one of the gowns Julien had chosen for her in New Orleans: a lavender-blue silk with a waist that narrowed to a point in front, a skirt of draped fullness finished with a deep flounce, and a bertha of ecru lace shot with lavender ribbon. Lally fastened a small cluster of mauve moss roses where the bertha met between Amalie's breasts and tucked another low at the back of her head to nestle against the soft figure-eight into which she had twisted her hair. She stepped back with such an air of triumph that Amalie, recognizing the girl's pride in her accomplishment, especially against the competition of the Callots' worldly-wise servants from New Orleans, was warm in her praise.

She also had reason to congratulate Marthe and the kitchen staff. The dinner, set before twelve couples from neighboring plantations and St. Martinville in addition to Robert and those already in residence at Belle Grove, was a triumph. The bounty seemed to have no limits and included two kinds of soup, two kinds of seafood, three roast meats, various vegetable dishes, salads, breads, pickles, and preserves. One dish, a masterly concoction of roasted fowl reminiscent of Roman times, consisted of a dove stuffed into a quail, the quail into a guinea hen, the hen into a duck, the duck into a capon, the capon into a goose, and the goose into a turkey, each bird boned and the whole served in thin transverse slices.

The sideboard was loaded with pies, cakes, puddings, and fresh blackberries dusted with sugar and covered with thick cream. It was voted, however, to wait upon dessert until later in the evening since all were too full to do justice to the array.

Music for dancing was provided by two fiddles and a banjo from the quarters, with Amalie at the piano for certain pieces. The furniture in the salon had been pushed back against the walls, the rug taken up and the floor polished, and the double front and back doors, plus the French windows, thrown open to the night. They began with a reel and swung without pausing through a schottische, a polka, and a waltz. The young couples, friends of Chloe's and of Julien's, seen often at various balls and picnics and other outings in the past years, laughed and called gay comments as they swept past each other. Dancing, perhaps because of the opportunity it gave for touching in a manner forbidden in any other situation, or because it was an outlet for their unused energy, was their passion and greatest joy. They seemed tireless as they whirled around the floor with the gowns of the young women fluttering and billowing and getting under the feet of the men. Watching them as her fingers rippled over the keys of the piano, Amalie felt matronly for the first time. She had never been as light-hearted as they were, or so it seemed, due to the years of mourning and her extended betrothal. Compared to the youthful exuberance of those on the floor, she felt tired and worn.

"Madame, will you honor me?"

It was Julien, bowing before her, taking her hand, and drawing her from behind the instrument without waiting for an answer. He whirled her out onto the floor to the strains of a waltz. His movements had the liquid grace of excellent muscle control; his guiding touch at her waist was light but firm. He shortened the length of his steps to hers, his timing perfect, so that she seemed to float effortlessly, swept by the lilting rhythm carried on the music. She smiled up at him, her spirit light, her tiredness vanishing. He watched her face, his own features relaxed, though in the depths of his dark eyes there was a tinge of what might have been pain.

They danced again and yet again. Twirling in her husband's arms, Amalie noticed Robert dancing with Louise for the third time. There was a possessive grip to the girl's fingers as they clasped his and animation on her face. Her giggles trilled across the floor, and so abandoned were her movements that her hoop dipped and swayed, showing her ankles above her silk dancing slippers with their small curved heels. Amalie sent Robert a laughing glance and he gave a wry shrug. It appeared that the effect of his smouldering glances had quite worn away and the result was his partner had developed a most obvious *tendre* for him. Madame Callot, instead of interfering, looked on with a complacent smile on her large, white face.

It was when the music swung to an end that Robert returned Louise to a seat beside her parents and turned away. He moved quickly toward where Amalie stood fanning herself beside Julien near the French windows. He inclined his head, a grin cutting grooves into the planes of his face.

"Your pardon, cousin," he said to Julien, "but may I borrow your wife?"

Amalie felt Julien stiffen. She slanted him a brief look before glancing at Robert. His expression had turned abruptly wary. To break the odd tension, she adopted a teasing tone, saying to her husband's cousin, "Are you in need of protection then?"

"More in the nature of someone to throw the hound off the scent. I swear I feel like a buck that's been flushed out of the swamp."

"The hounds," Julien said, his manner relaxing, "being, er, female?"

"Exactly."

Amalie tilted her head. "You could turn and embrace your pursuer."

"I thank you, no. There would be one giggle too many

157

and I would be forced to strangle the—"

"Bitch?" Julien supplied, his tone bland.

"I didn't say that," Robert protested and, without waiting for permission, offered Amalie his arm, leading her out onto the floor.

She was breathless from dancing; that was the cause of the rapid beat of her pulse, the constriction in her chest, the glow of color across her cheekbones. It was the unaccustomed exercise, too, that left her weak and a little giddy as she was held close in his arms and whirled across the floor. She looked up at him and found him watching her face, his own features taut, closed in. A tremor ran over her and she looked away at once.

"I owe you an apology," he said.

"Oh?"

"I failed to ask if you cared to dance with me. If you would rather not, you have only to say so and I'll take you back to Julien."

She summoned a light tone. "Don't be ridiculous. Why should I object?"

"I'm not sure. Perhaps it is my turn to ask if I have offended you." His voice was deep, not at all light.

"If you continue in this vein you may well do just that. You are one of the family and I am fully aware of all you do for us here at Belle Grove. I hope we need not stand on such ceremony as to worry about petty misunderstandings."

"Not on my account, certainly, but you have become so much a part of the plantation I sometimes forget that you are newly come among us and may not understand our ways."

"Good. That is just the way I want it."

Her voice was firm, her smile did not falter; he seemed to accept her open air. Still, it was not so much later that she wished she had not dismissed the subject so quickly.

It was during a break in the dancing while the musicians, Sir Bent on the lead fiddle, paused to rest and take something to drink. Some of the older people trailed down to the dining room in search of their delayed dessert while the younger ones settled for punch and a stroll in the night coolness on the long upper gallery. Amalie had spread her skirts, taking a seat on the storage chest on the back loggia. For the moment, she was alone. She was assailed by a spasm of guilt. As hostess she should be seeing that her guests were being taken care of, particularly those below in the dining room. It was true, however, that M'mere was downstairs and Julien in the salon. Perhaps that would be sufficient.

The last was confirmed as she heard her husband's voice raised in an announcement. Getting to her feet, she moved to the door of the salon, listening. It was a game, an embellished version of blindman's buff. Someone would be "it," in this instance Julien himself. He would be blindfolded and turned around several times for the sake of confusion. But then, instead of staggering here and there in pursuit of those without the control to be silent, he would order the lights lowered. Those to be captured would be at just as much of a disadvantage as the pursuer. In addition, anyone caught would have to pay a forfeit as well as having to do the catching the next time.

There were shouts of approbation from the men and cries of scandalized glee from the young ladies as the obvious extra benefits of the game became evident. Two or three of the older ladies left as chaperones looked at each other with raised eyebrows, but none spoke to forbid it. In less than a moment, a blindfold had been produced and applied, and the candles in the chandelier overhead and several candelabra had been snuffed.

Louise's giggles could be plainly followed as she darted here and there. There were startled gasps and a muttered oath or two as some collided with the furniture or each other. Most tried to move away quietly as Julien blundered near, but the scuffle of boots and slippers on the bare floor, the brush of trouser legs, and the rustle of petticoats was loud in the shifting darkness.

Amalie turned away, moving back outside toward the far corner of the loggia where the railing met the wall. She wasn't in the mood for games. She doubted the wisdom of this one, but it was probably harmless enough and would doubtless end as soon as the adults below discovered that the lights were out. In the meantime, she was too weary to mind. She would be happy when the evening was over and she could seek her bed.

It was not a sound that alerted her, but a presence. She turned her head to see the broad-shouldered shape of a man, seen faintly in the glow spilling from the dining room out into the yard below, coming toward her. Julien had noted her out here then, she thought, smiling a little. Gathering her skirts around her, she backed carefully away toward the corner. He swerved, coming nearer, bearing down upon her in that deeper darkness.

Then he was upon her, reaching out to draw her against him, his hands, gentle and familiar, moving over her, spanning her waist, cupping her breasts. His voice was a husk of sound as he said, "Amalie, *chérie,* I claim this as forfeit."

His mouth descended upon hers with honeyed sweetness, molding her lips with the warmth of his desire. His arms tightened as he probed deeper, exploring, reveling in her willing response. The need of him rose in her and she strained against him, feeling the dig of his waistcoat buttons. So intense was her hunger that she swayed off balance, supported only by the strength of his hold.

Then came the scratch of a match beside them. Its small yellow fire blossomed bright and hurtful to the eyes. Startled, Amalie drew back. She turned, half-blinded, aware of the stillness of the man at her side, the protective circle of his arms. Her gaze moved beyond the trembling flame, up the arm of the man who had set it alight, seeking his face.

Julien.

His blindfold was in his hand.

And the man who held her was Robert.

Chapter 8

A malie lay in her bed with her hair spread in silken splendor over the pillow and her eyes wide as she stared up into the canopy of mosquito netting above her. This time she could not deny it. There could be no mistake. The man who had taken her in her marriage bed was Robert. The man who had made love to her in the summerhouse was Robert. The man who had intimate knowledge of her body, who had possessed it inch by careful inch, who had melted her very bones with desire and given her the most sublime joy was Robert.

She felt defiled.

By what right had he so deceived her? How was it managed? Why?

How had she come to allow him into her bed? He and Julien were very similar, but also very different. She could remember a brief moment that first night when she had thought her husband more assured, even, yes, changed. But how could she have dreamed of such a substitution? It was inconceivable that Robert would dare to use her in such a way, that he would chance recognition and flaunt the strict conventions that bound them. So improbable was such behavior that it was beyond thought. Perhaps therein lay the secret of her gullibility.

He had said he loved her and that was the greatest deception of all. There had been no need, surely, to carry the ruse so far?

She was an adulteress. Though innocent of blame, she had sinned.

No, no, no. It could not be. She would not believe it; she did not want to believe it. Normal, ordinary people did not do such things. She was deceiving herself, confused by her own so recently awakened passion. It was only a coincidence that her husband's kisses and his cousin's were the same. Doubtless most such caresses were similar. She had little experience of such things, but how much difference could there be in the physical act of touching the lips together?

Robert was attracted to her just as she was to him. He had meant to steal a kiss, nothing more. Or perhaps it had been a game, one of Julien's devising, that had made Robert pursue her at the soirée. He had implied as much, hadn't he, when he had seen her shocked face? What had he said? *"It was a stupid wager and a cruel one. I beg your pardon most abjectly."*

But then he had been forced to say something, hadn't he? The circumstances had required some effort to propitiate her, no matter what.

The doubts that clamored in her mind had been tormenting her for a full five days. She had slept little that first night after the soirée and not much more since. She had seen her guests off and hardly noticed regaining the peace and privacy that she had so desired. She wanted answers, but was so appalled at what they might reveal that she had kept a fairy lamp burning beside her bed every night. She had been determined to see the face of the man who came to her now that her room was her own once more.

No one had come.

She was not certain what it meant. If Julien had been disgusted by her behavior or embarrassed by his own, he might be avoiding her. She had it from Lally that he had gone into St. Martinville on most nights since the party, returning in the early hours of the morning. His afternoons were spent fencing, practicing at target shooting, painting as he drifted on his barge—anything conveniently away from the house.

Then again, if her lover was indeed Robert he would not care to continue his seduction in the lamp's glow. She did not think there was anything else to keep him away unless it was his conscience. He could not know how strongly she suspected him unless the presence of the lighted lamp itself made it obvious.

The fairy lamp that sat on the bedstand beside her sputtered, its light wavering. Amalie turned her head to look at the small lamp of deep rose glass with its base and chimney of the same color. The soft pink light it gave, diffused by the gauze of the mosquito baire around her, gleamed across her cheekbones and highlighted the curves of her breasts above the rounded neckline of her nightgown, giving the tones of her skin a soft, delicate shading of color. Again the flame danced on the wick with a fluttering sound.

It could not be low in oil; Lally had filled it only that morning. Amalie lay watching it for some time, but the sound did not come again. At last she turned away, closing her eyes, lifting her arm to cover them against the light. She was used to sleeping in the dark and could not become accustomed to the brightness of the room. She was strongly tempted to plunge the room into darkness. If no one had come in five days, they might not be coming at all.

That was not a pleasant thought, regardless of her suspicions. Was she never to know the embrace of a lover again, never to feel his caresses and the mounting excitement they brought? Was she condemning herself to that sterile existence by her own actions? It did not bear thinking of, and yet what else could she do?

She could accept what came. If she had been committing adultery, it was not by her own choice, but at the instigation of others. Given the circumstances as she understood them, she could guess at the reasons. Who was she to say they were not valid? How could she deny the undertaking? It was not as if there was any personal gratification in it. Was there?

When she finally slept her dreams were disturbing, filled with murky images and unappeased desire. She tossed on her pillow until her hair twisted around her like confining bonds and her nightgown rode up about her waist. She feared the darkness, but was pursued by a glowing spot of light that grew brighter, threatening the world with fire before fading without reason. Relief crept in upon her. She settled on her side, clasping her pillow in the darkness that swayed and whispered around her.

The first touch was light, the merest brush, but the sensation it brought was like a gentle flame. It came again, more firmly. Sweet arousal flowed in her veins, rising with incredible swiftness to the heat of a fever. She stirred and felt the warmth of a body against her, the weight of a hand upon her breast. Her limbs felt weighted, her mind dark yet pulsing with the need that rippled through her. With a soft sound in her throat, she turned and her mouth was taken in the heat of a kiss that commanded, implored. Strong arms tightened around her; she was drawn against the hard body of a man. He held her close, then heaved himself above her. Her nightgown was pushed higher, then his knee eased between her thighs. He pressed into her, gathering her close as he laid his face against the smooth curve of her neck.

She came awake to the liquid surge of desire. Mindless in its grasp, she reached out for the man above her, spreading her hands to run her palms along his sides and around to the ridged muscles of his back. He was still.

It was not what she wanted. She moved against him, turning her head to brush the faint roughness of his face with her lips.

He let out his pent-up breath with a rush, rising above her and setting a rhythm that in its exultant strength catapulted them into the fury of uncontained ardor. It engulfed them, a buffeting storm of passion with an edge of violence and an undertone of remorse. It carried them in its vortex, lifting them higher and higher. As one, they soared, transfigured, beyond mortal cares. They were ageless and nameless, without past or future, without earthly ties. They belonged to the night and to each other and were bound only by the joining, the white-hot ascent of pleasure that burst around them in a moment of brilliant beauty, then left them drifting, spent.

Sometime later, he withdrew from her, easing to lie beside her. Amalie shifted and stretched cramped muscles. She lay for a moment, breathing quietly and evenly as she stared into the darkness. Then she rolled to her side, reaching out and sweeping aside the mosquito baire to touch the bedstand, feeling across it to the fairy lamp. The rose glass was still warm, the key that raised and lowered the wick turned all the way down as if it had been turned out.

In the drawer of the stand was a tin box of matches. She extended her reach, finding the teardrop pull of the small drawer. It rattled as she caught it in her hand.

"Don't," came a rough whisper behind her, commanding for all its urgency. "Please don't."

She lay for a long moment, listening to the thudding of her heartbeat before she answered. "I must. Don't you see that?"

The only answer was the shift of the bed behind her and the wafting of the mosquito baire as it was thrust aside. Then came the rustle of clothing.

He was leaving. She wrenched herself higher in the bed, snatching open the drawer, fumbling for the match box and sliding it open. The first match she took out broke as she scraped it along the box top. The second spit, then flared up. She swung with it in her hand, but all she saw through the film of the mosquito netting was the dark opening where the sliding door into Julien's room stood open. Then she heard plainly the sound of the knob on the outside door turning.

She shook out the match without bothering with the lamp. Thrusting her nightgown down, she swung her legs over the side of the high bed and slid down. She ran to the open door, slipping through and moving quickly toward the outside entrance.

She stopped abruptly. She stood with her hair swirling slowly around her, her eyes fixed as she stared into the blackness of her husband's room. She had her answer. It could not have been plainer. Julien would not have run, would not have scooped up his clothes and flung himself like a criminal into the night. What need had he for flight, after all? He had a legal right to be in her bed. He was her husband. And the truth could no longer be denied. The man who had just left her, in spite of everything, regardless of the unlikelihood of it, was and always had been Robert.

It was unendurable. She must talk to Julien.

That resolve made in the night was not so easily kept when daylight came. She had tried it once before and what had come of it? Evasion, a sense that she was being disloyal even to consider that such a low subterfuge might have been used against her.

How could she ask her husband flat out if he had allowed another man access to her bed? Could she expect an honest answer when Julien's pride as a man and the tenuous harmony of their marriage might hang on keeping the truth from her? Did she, in fact, really want confirmation?

If she put a stop to the clandestine visits, it might be as well to pretend that they had never happened. That was the wisest course. The results would be the same as if she had never discovered the truth. There would be a surface politeness that would allow her to continue as Julien's wife.

The alternative was not as pleasant. Annulment of the marriage on grounds of nonconsummation was clearly impossible now, and divorce, even if it would be sanctioned by the church, was a difficult proceeding involving the state legislature. The reasons for dissolving the marriage would have to come out and the scandal that must erupt would be a terrible ordeal to face. Even then there was no guarantee that a divorce would be granted, especially if Julien, with his wealth and influence, opposed it. And what of afterward? What kind of life could she have as a woman legally free but spiritually bound and haunted by the past?

She could return to her aunt, of course. Aunt Ton-Ton would allow it without question and would become her champion once she knew the truth. But she was not sure that she could return to being a mere niece after having been the mistress of her own establishment. She was fond of Julien and found him to be charming company when he chose to exert himself. There was little chance that he would force his attentions upon her, it seemed. Why, then, could she not live in peace as his wife so long as she could prevent Robert's clandestine visits? But could she prevent them without enlisting Julien's cooperation, without talking to him?

Her thoughts went around in circles through the morning and afternoon of the next day, still without coming to any real conclusion. A part of the time she thought that she was being practical in her decision to hold to her marriage; for the rest, she castigated herself as a coward for not denouncing Robert while she had the opportunity, for not tearing herself from his arms and striking out at him. She had been taken by surprise, had been uncertain of his identity, she tried to tell herself, but she knew well that the reason was her own weakness. It was her desire for him that had prevented her, the entrancement of his touch, the sweet drug of his kisses—those things and nothing more.

So confused were her feelings and ideas that when she walked out into the yard in front of the house in the soft twilight of late afternoon and saw Julien's barge drifting in toward the landing, she hesitated between running and staying. He was lying back among the pillows, staring up at the cream-and-blue-striped sail that was lavender in the fading light, as Tige brought the small vessel in. He sat up as he saw her and lifted a hand in a casual greeting. As the barge bumped the landing, he swung to the gunwale and sprang out on the wooden dock, catching a line and securing it before turning toward her.

"Is anything wrong?" he called.

"No, no," she said as she realized he thought she had come on purpose to meet him. "I was just walking."

"I'm glad that you have the time, you are always so busy." He came up beside her and she turned with him to walk back toward the house.

She sent him a surprised glance, for she had not thought he noticed what she did. "I've done little else except receive callers today."

"I take leave to doubt that," he said dryly. "But never mind. Is everything going smoothly? No more problems with Dye?"

"Everything has been fine." She had scarcely thought of Patrick Dye since the incident on the loggia. That was one thing about the situation in which she found herself; it left little room for other worries.

"That's good."

They walked on a few steps. "Julien?"

His smile was easy as he turned his head, his expression expectant but relaxed. The words she wanted to say were a jumble in her mind and in her fear of hurting him, she could not bring them into order. Snatching at the first safe topic that came to the surface of her thoughts, she said, "The Morneys' groom came a little while ago. We are invited to a cotillion ball they are giving in two weeks' time."

"That should be pleasant."

His glance was quizzical, as if he suspected something else was on her mind. She hastened to reassure him. "From the number of invitations in the groom's basket, everyone in the country is to come. Are you sure you want to go?"

"I don't see why not. They came to our soirée, and it would be rude not to allow them to entertain us in return. Besides, we have to have some amusement to make the days bearable."

"If you are sure, I'll write an acceptance." After a second, she went on, "There are a few cases of fever in the quarters. I've begun treating them with quinine bark."

He sent her a sharp look. "You must be careful. It would

not do for you to become ill now that—"

He stopped as if holding back what he had intended to say. She turned her head to stare at him. "Now that what?"

"You must be aware that the state of your health is important to me."

"Yes, but why now?"

He smiled, his dark eyes steady on her face. "The usual reason for brides of a few months, *chérie.*"

"Oh," she said as comprehension came, "I see." His concern was that she not endanger her health at a time when she might be expecting a child.

"You have been looking particularly well of late, even radiant. I don't suppose you have anything you might like to tell me in that regard?"

It was a question that she had considered. More than enough time had passed; still, she could not be sure. Her courses had not appeared, it was true, but she had not kept close account of them. There had, until the last few weeks, been no need. It was a possibility the implications of which she did not care to face. After a moment, she said, "I don't think so."

"Too bad."

In his smooth voice there was the sound of genuine regret. Why it should matter to him, she could not imagine, unless he was tired of giving up his room for Robert's entry, tired of being the cuckold. There was no time to ask, however, for they were at the door of the house. Inclining his head with his usual charming deference, he took his leave in order to bathe and change before dinner.

It was a quiet meal and soon over. Julien excused himself, saying he had an engagement in town. Amalie took a book to bed and lay reading until she was certain he had gone, then got up and took a length of ribbon, wrapping it around the knobs of the sliding doors so that the panels could not be pushed open. She had thought she would not sleep for listening to see if the doors were tested, but she did. When she awoke again, the sun was shining.

She walked into the dining room and came to an abrupt halt. Robert was at the table. He lounged back in his chair with a booted foot thrust in front of him and a cup of coffee in his hand. He came to his feet as he saw her in the doorway and moved to draw out a chair, holding it for her.

There was an awkward pause. Amalie's customary self-possession had deserted her and she could not bring herself to smile or to move forward. She stood staring at Robert with the color draining from her face. M'mere turned from the letter she was reading to look at her, one gray brow lifted in inquiry. Chloe, who had been talking in an undertone to George, glanced up, frowning. George swallowed hugely, a wary look coming into his pale blue eyes.

"Good morning, *ma chère,*" her mother-in-law said, her voice soothing. "The most marvelous thing. The plants from China have arrived in New Orleans and I am to have first choice of them." She waved her letter. "I have this from the ship's agent, brought out by special messenger this morning. George is to set out at once to see to it."

"How nice," Amalie replied. Her tone was breathless, but at least she was able to speak, able also to move forward with some semblance of normality, despite the tremors that ran through her. She did not look at Robert as she seated herself in the chair that he held, though she could feel his gaze upon her averted face as if it were a brand. When Isa,

172

trailing behind her as was his habit, filled her coffee cup and brought it to her, she was happy to have the chance to turn from her husband's cousin.

M'mere went on in a light tone, describing the route George would follow: he would take the steamboat at St. Martinville to descend the Teche to Bayou Boeuf, where he would transfer to the New Orleans, Opelousas, and Great Western Railroad just opened through to the Boeuf in February of that year. The railroad, traveling over the so-called trembling prairies and through the remote "Devil's Swamp" at the fantastic rate of thirty miles per hour, would see him in the city in half the time it would take to travel the tortuous river route from the Teche through the back bayous and rivers to the Mississippi, then downriver to New Orleans.

Chloe was reluctant to have him go. It seemed she feared the possible attractions of the city belles and her George's susceptibility to their charms. He tried in vain to tell her that he was interested only in the plants and in seeing them safely back to Belle Grove. She would not be consoled and begged him to speak to Julien before he left, as if she thought some permanent commitment between them would curb his inclination to wander.

As George looked more and more harassed, Robert, who had returned to his place, intervened, asking if the year was not too far gone for the planting of shrubbery that must go through the heat of a Louisiana summer. Brightening, the Englishman treated him to a long lecture on the chances of shrubbery shipped in soil-filled pots and barrels, such as these would be, withstanding both the long voyage from China and the transplanting, including the various methods of shading and watering that might be used to cause them to disregard their change of nationality.

Amalie let their conversation wash around her without attempting to join in it. She crumbled the roll and ate the blackberries and cream that Isa brought while searching her mind for some excuse to escape as soon as there was a lull.

Robert saved her the trouble. Before she was aware of what he intended, he had excused himself, drained his cup, picked up his hat that lay on the table, and was striding toward the door. She watched him go, an expression on her face that was half relief, half unacknowledged grief. At the door, he swung back, his hard gaze seeking and holding hers. She could not look away in time, but was forced to hold that intent regard. A muscle stood out in the hard plane of his cheek and the line of his mouth was grim. And in his dark blue eyes was the reflection of her own desolation.

How was she to go through the rest of her life meeting Robert everywhere she turned? There could be no escape from it, for he was in and out of Belle Grove as much as in his own place. To see him, to know what had happened between them, and yet never to speak of it, never, ever to acknowledge it, would require more strength of will than she possessed; she was sure of it.

So disturbed was she by the meeting that she hardly noticed when George took his leave to supervise his packing or when Chloe trailed away with a handkerchief pressed to the corner of one eye. Her attention was caught only when M'mere turned to her and reached to place her cool fingers on Amalie's wrist.

"Now, *ma chère,* tell me what it is that ails you. Are you

sickening for something?"

"Not at all," Amalie said hastily, afraid that M'mere might hint at the same thing Julien had the evening before if given the least pretext.

"You cannot pretend that you are entirely yourself."

"I appreciate your concern, but it's just—just a bout of stupid melancholy," she said, making a valiant effort to smile.

"Has Julien upset you?" M'mere asked, her eyes narrowing.

"No, nothing like that."

"Then—" The older woman hesitated, then went on. "Then have you quarreled with Robert perhaps?"

Amalie's head came up. "Why do you ask?"

"I am a foolish old woman, I expect, but I thought you quite liked Julien's cousin. It seemed just now, however, that your feelings might have undergone a change. If you find you cannot abide him after all, I might speak to him, ask him not to come to us so often."

Was there a reason for M'mere's words? Did she suspect what had taken place and think to discover a reason to keep Robert from Belle Grove? It would be an underhanded trick to restrict him to his bachelor household now after years of welcome.

"When he is one of the family?" she inquired, making her voice light with great effort. "That would be a great cruelty in me, would it not? And there is not the least need of it, I assure you. Robert and I are friends and cousins by marriage, and—and get along together very well. I am only a little out of sorts this morning, that's all."

M'mere was not entirely satisfied with her answer; still,

she probed no further. After a time, Amalie left her to go about her duties.

The day passed swiftly, not the least reason being because Amalie filled it with every task she could discover. Another was because she dreaded the night and what it might bring.

She dressed for bed in nightgown and wrapper and allowed Lally to brush out her hair. The maid and Tige had become rather friendly of late and it was easy to discover that Julien was once again absent on his own concerns. The knowledge did nothing to calm her. When Lally had gone she paced the floor with her layers of soft batiste swirling about her ankles, up and down, pausing now and then to listen as the house grew quiet and the hour late.

More than once she glanced at the doors to Julien's room with their ribbon lock still in place. A strong man could force it or a resourceful one insert a knife through the slit between the doors and cut the ribbon. It was more of a sign than a protection, a signal of her reluctance to participate any longer in this farce.

If Robert had any sensitivity, he would recognize and honor it.

She whirled away, moving beside the foot of the four-poster bed, curving her fingers around one carved post and letting them slide down it to the counterpane, running them over it to the other post. She gripped that post of polished wood until the carving bit into her palm.

Abruptly she released her hold and stood still. Why was she so agitated? Was it fear that Robert would come or distress that he might not?

She flung back the rippling curtain of her hair. She was

being foolish. This situation was not of her choosing; her permission had been neither asked nor given. If pain was to come from the exposure and cancellation of the arrangement, it was through no fault of hers. If she had found joy in it, it was innocently indulged.

What cause had she to hide away and wear a trench into the carpet while beating her breast? She did not bear the guilt here. She had been duped, maneuvered with no more compunction than might have attended an attempt to breed a promising mare. Why then should she hide herself away or protect others by her silence?

Cold anger brought the blue shadows in her brown eyes into prominence as she swung around, moving toward the secured door. Her movements were deliberate as she released the ribbon tie and opened the sliding doors. That done, she turned back to cross to the bedstand where she took out the tin box of matches, then leaned to blow out the lamp that burned beside the bed. Sweeping around again, she moved past the foot of the four-poster and stepped through the door opening.

The room was empty. Tige never waited up for Julien's return anymore. The reason for that was obvious now, though when she had first learned of it, it had seemed like consideration in her husband to allow his valet to sleep. Closing the doors behind her, she shut herself into her husband's darkened bedchamber.

She was familiar with the room not only from the few times she had looked in on Julien, but also from frequent inspections to see if it was being kept in order by the maids. Now she moved with care to the washstand on one wall where a large lamp with a fat round outer globe of painted china, as well as an inner chimney, sat. She put down the box of matches. With careful hands, she removed the globe and chimney and set them to one side, then turned the key to raise the oil-soaked wick. She located the slipper chair that sat to one side and drew it close to the washstand. Taking up her box of matches once more, she sat down in the slipper chair and prepared to wait.

Chapter 9

An hour passed, and a half hour more. Doubts of the wisdom of what she was doing crowded in upon Amalie, but she dismissed them. She refused to think, concentrating instead on every sound in the old house and outside of it. There was no wind tonight, only the soft, fecund stillness of summer with its bell-like trilling of peeper frogs and the shrill rasp of crickets.

So attuned was she to the noises of the night that she heard the first quiet scrape of a footstep on the backstairs. Amalie came to her feet and, in the same motion, took a match from her box and held it poised to strike. As she stood waiting, her senses leaped to an almost painful alertness. Still, there was not another sound until the knob of the door that led onto the loggia began to turn.

It swung open on silent hinges, revealing a dim gray rectangle that was crossed momentarily by the tall shadow of a man, before it closed once more. He moved from it with the soundless grace of a swamp panther, only the slow brush of his trouser legs marking his progress across the room. He must have lifted the weight of one of the sliding doors, for it opened on its brass track with scarcely a whisper. He stepped through the narrow opening.

It was enough.

Amalie struck the match and, with a hand that trembled uncontrollably, touched its sulphur yellow flame to the wick of the lamp. She whipped around then, half afraid the man would bolt, would try to leave by way of her door into the salon, perhaps stumbling over Isa sleeping outside. It did not happen.

Robert stood braced in the opening, one strong hand on the sliding panel door. He faced her squarely, his bearing erect and the look in his dark blue eyes bleak.

She had not really believed it. In spite of all the arguments she had used to convince herself it was so, she realized at that moment that she had not thought it possible, had not wanted to think so. Sickness moved over her. She stared at him with her brown eyes wide and accusing until, abruptly, the heat of the burning match she still held reached her fingers and she shook it out with a quick, final gesture.

In a voice so hollow it was unrecognizable as her own, she asked, "Would you like to explain what you are doing here?"

"I think you know." His voice was steady, but the grip of his hard brown hand on the door was so tight that the ends of his fingers were white.

"You meant to take Julien's rightful place, of course, I understand that, but it doesn't tell my why."

"It was not by my own choice—"

"Oh, I give you credit for that much!" Her tone hardened as her anger revived.

"Not," he added deliberately, with the reflected flicker of

the lamp flame in the depths of his eyes, "that it hasn't been my very great pleasure."

"It was a despicable act."

It was a moment before he answered, then there was a ragged edge to the words. "Would you have preferred to remain a chaste and untouched bride?"

"That has nothing to do with it!" she cried, swinging away from him. "What I want to know is what set the masquerade in motion, what made you begin?"

"Can't you guess?"

She lifted her chin. "I suspect it was for the sake of an heir for Belle Grove."

"Exactly."

"And you lent yourself to such a subterfuge? I thought you a man of honor!" She turned back to him, her brown eyes blazing with contempt.

The color drained from under the bronze of his skin. "I thought so once myself; now I'm not so sure. But in this, I have come to see, I am as much a pawn as you."

"You could have refused! No such choice was given me!"

"I did refuse, at first."

The tight sound of his voice, his words, triggered a memory. It had been in the sitting room, that first day that he had returned to the plantation, the day of the flood. His rejection of some request, quickly dropped when she had entered, the strain she had felt then and the niggling suspicion that she had been the subject under discussion came back now with a rush.

"M'mere," she said, almost to herself.

"M'mere," he agreed.

"How could she?" Amalie's voice had dropped to a low note.

"She and my uncle worked all their lives for this place, building something of permanence for Julien, a heritage for their descendants; a piece, if you will, of immortality. Like the great estates of France and England, it was to be handed down through the generations—except that it appeared there would be no more."

"But any child that you and—that is, any child I might bear would not be of her blood."

"But it would be of her husband's, through his sister's child, myself."

"Then why not just give Belle Grove to your children?" she demanded, her self-possession fraying.

"And allow it to be swallowed up with my own holdings? Besides, since I am unmarried, there was no guarantee that there would be children, not in time, and not that M'mere could take as her own to mold and nurture."

"In time?"

"You must have noticed that she isn't well. She doesn't discuss it, but she visited several doctors in New Orleans last fall. That is why—"

"That is why she hurried to arrange Julien's marriage to me," she finished as she stopped.

"Does it matter?"

"No. No, what matters is this intolerable situation. It must stop, it must, do you hear me?"

"I do, and so will the rest of the house if you—"

"I don't care! Don't you realize? I am an adulteress! That may mean nothing to you, with your married mistresses, but it does to me!"

"My what?" His brows closed together in a frown.

She ignored his angry question as the words held back for so long came tumbling from her lips. "You may say what you please, but no one forced you to—to come to my bed. You came of your own will, without a thought of how I would feel. You came to satisfy your own lust, to foist off your bastard on Julien by base trickery."

"That isn't so!"

"How can you deny it?"

"Julien knew," he said, his voice hard.

She had known he must, but it was another thing she had not wanted to accept. "So you had my husband's permission. But what of mine? What of mine?"

He stared at her for long moments, then took a deep breath and let it out slowly. He released the door, moving toward her. "You are upset and who can blame you? It will be better if we talk about it later, when you are calmer."

She stepped backward away from him and was glad when he came to an abrupt halt. "There—there isn't anything to talk about. I want your word that you will not come again. That is all that I require from you."

"Amalie, be reasonable." He moved another step forward.

"I want it now," she cried, recoiling.

The lamplight carved his face into a bronze mask of planes and hollows and wavered in the blue darkness of his eyes. She was aware, even in her furious determination, of the magnetism he held for her. It was not fear of him that caused her retreat, but fear of herself, fear that she would weaken, fear that if he asked her to let him stay, she would not be able to deny him.

"Amalie?" His quiet tone made a soft entreaty of her name.

"Get out! Get out!"

His head came up and his eyes narrowed. "I'll go because I would as soon not have an audience for what is between us. But we will talk, Amalie. That much I will promise you and nothing else, nothing else at all."

He swung from her, striding to the outside door. It closed quietly behind him.

Amalie was glad that she had put a stop to those clandestine visits. They had been demeaning, an animalistic groping in the dark without loving affection or the grace conferred by the spiritual tie of marriage. She could not have borne to continue them. It was unfair, then, that her bodily responses that had been brought so gently and thoroughly to life should torment her so that she was unable to enjoy the triumph.

In the daylight hours, she was strong, she could despise Robert Farnum with a free heart. It was in the moonlit stretches of the night that she tossed without rest, hugging her pillow, a prey to needs she had not dreamed of before he had come to her. It was at night that she wanted him, that she remembered only the excitement of his touch, his tender strength, and most of all, the desolation in his eyes when she had sent him away.

A week passed, and the best portion of another one, and still they had not talked. It was not for lack of effort on his part. He was often at Belle Grove, but since George's departure Chloe had kept close to Amalie, and her unabashed curiosity and tripping tongue made it necessary for him to be discreet in her presence. If Chloe failed, there was always M'mere.

Amalie would not have thought that Robert would have been put off by the older woman, but so it proved. While his aunt was in the room, he never by word or deed indicated that their relationship was anything other than that of cousins by marriage. It seemed that his purpose was to protect M'mere. It was a motive that Amalie could well understand. There was something fragile about Julien's mother these days. Her face was often creased with lines of anxiety, and there was a look of pain on her features as her gaze rested upon her son. She spent many hours at her priedieu, and when she was not occupied in that manner, often sat staring into space.

Even knowing what the elderly woman had done, Amalie could not bring herself to accuse her or even to discuss it with her. A part of the reason was convention; one did not speak of such things. A part of it was the difficulty of finding the proper words. But there was also the fact that it was possible that M'mere's burden of guilt for it was heavy enough. And then there was a final thing. For all that it had been M'mere's suggestion, it had been Robert alone who had acted upon it.

On one occasion, Robert persuaded Lally to deliver a note to Amalie. She had returned it unread, of course. The most disturbing thing about the incident was the veiled glance the maid had given her. It had forced Amalie to face a few unpleasant facts. Lally, in her friendship with Tige, was in a position to know that, due to his nocturnal habits, it was unlikely that Julien had been sharing her bed. At the same time, Lally was well aware that someone had, from the state of the sheets the following mornings if nothing else. The presence of Robert, his attention to her movements, made it easy to guess that he was the man. How long could it be before everyone on the plantation knew? How long before it became common gossip at every breakfast table along the Teche?

Robert came upon her early one day in the middle of the second week while she was in the dairy. She emerged rolling her sleeves with their lace edges down after showing a new girl how to squeeze the whey from churned butter to make it more compact. The sun was in her eyes and she did not see him waiting there, holding the reins of his horse. It was only as she looked around for Isa and saw him standing with his hands in the waist of his breeches, staring up at Robert as they talked, that she became aware of him.

"Good morning," her husband's cousin said.

The low timbre of his voice sent a tremor along Amalie's nerves, but she disregarded it. She returned his greeting in colorless tones, turning to the boy. "Come, Isa, time for your drawing lesson."

"First, Isa, would you lead my horse around to the front hitching post while I talk to your mistress." Robert extended the reins, the request quiet, yet authoritative.

Isa looked from one to the other, a frown between his eyes. He knew well that the *petite maîtresse* had no desire to be alone with M'sieu Robert, but the habit of obedience was hard to break.

She gave him a reluctant nod, disinclined to involve so innocent a pawn in their quarrel. She stood watching as Isa moved away slowly, leading the big bay stallion.

"I want you to come riding with me, Amalie," Robert said without preamble. "We could go to The Willows. You've never seen it and it would not seem strange for us to stop there for a few moments for something to drink after our ride."

She swung to stare at him. "You must be mad!"

"That may well be. You are driving me insane with your damned elusiveness. Why won't you speak to me? What are you afraid of?"

She ignored the last. Her face set, she began to move toward the big house. "We have nothing to talk about, nothing at all."

"You know that isn't so." He shortened his stride to suit hers as he fell into step beside her.

"What can there be?" she cried, an edge of distress in her voice. "It has ended. It's over."

"I won't accept that," he answered, the words tight with control.

"What else can you do? Your attentions are already too noticeable. I don't know what they may be saying in the quarters."

"What?"

She told him briefly of Lally's friendship with Tige, of the girl's change of attitude.

"M'mere would not be pleased if talk starts," he commented, his tone pensive, though his thick brows were drawn together over the bridge of his nose.

"Can't you see, then, that you must leave me alone?"

"I'm not M'mere."

"Meaning you don't care what's said of you? How very nice it must be to be a bachelor, free to flout the rules of

God and men!"

"Don't press me, *chérie*," he said softly.

"It seems to me that the shoe is on the other foot," she said. They were nearing the house. The laundress hanging lengths of toweling on the line looked up to watch them as they skirted the drying yard. Another, stirring clothes boiling in a black pot over a wood fire, tried to shoo away the group of boys, none older than ten, who were playing with homemade wooden wagons in the beaten earth of the path where Amalie and Robert were walking. As they started to scramble to their feet, Amalie waved them back down and moved around them.

"What about that ride?" he asked, the question abrupt.

It was only a few more steps to the back loggia. Amalie thought she could hear Chloe's voice coming from the dining room where the girl was discussing what she would have for breakfast with Charles. She made no reply.

He reached out, snagging her wrist in a hard grip and spinning her around so that her skirts belled out over her hoop, piling against his boots. "I asked you a question."

"It doesn't deserve an answer," she snapped.

"I will have one, anyway, here and now. Or would you prefer that I come for it tonight?"

"You will find my door locked."

"That won't stop me."

Was this the man who had held her with such gentleness? It seemed impossible. "Julien has been at home of an evening more often lately. I don't imagine he will permit you to molest his wife in any way you please."

His grip tightened. "I will have an answer, no matter what it takes."

The thought of the two men, close since boyhood, brawling over her in the middle of the night was not a pleasant one. Nor was the idea of having it all brought out into the open between the three of them. Amalie glanced around from under her lashes. If she did not make up her mind soon, she could spare herself the worry of what Julien might say, for everyone on the place would be a witness to their involvement. The laundresses and the boys with their wagons were watching with undisguised interest.

"Very well," she said with a slight catch in her voice. "I'll ride with you."

He gave a short nod, though there was no relenting in his features. "I will be here, early."

He was as good as his word. When she walked out onto the lower gallery the next morning with her crop in her hand and the extra fullness of her habit skirt thrown over one arm, she found him waiting for her. The sun was not yet up, but he was not alone. He was talking to George, while one of the Belle Grove grooms walked his stallion and Amalie's mare, which she had ordered brought around.

The Englishman had returned late the previous afternoon. He had ridden out from St. Martinville. The shrubs were being towed on barges up the bayou in the care of a couple of men from the seagoing vessel assigned to see that they came to no harm. They would arrive by noon at the latest. George had come on ahead to make certain that everything was ready for them. Already there were men with shovels busy on the rises that curved toward the bayou, digging planting holes according to a carefully set pattern of stakes.

The evening before George had been voluble on the

rarity and beauty of the specimens he had found awaiting him in New Orleans. He talked so much about them, bemoaning the few that had not survived the voyage, and exulting over the different varieties and how they might best show to advantage, that Chloe, feeling herself ignored, had become pouting and sulky.

Julien had been present, as had become his custom in the last week. His cutting comments had not helped matters, however. Having reduced Chloe from sulkiness to sullenness, and then to tears, he had taken himself off to read in his bedchamber.

M'mere, after saying everything suitable concerning the way George had carried out his commission and expressing her keen anticipation to view the finished garden, had gone away to her bed. Amalie had been forced to sit as chaperone while George coaxed Chloe into good humor once more, though she had thought he looked less than his genial self when it was done.

The Englishman seemed none the worse this morning, however. He wore his oldest clothes and, as he talked, stood where he could see downriver in the direction the steamboat and barges would come. If he found anything in the least odd in the early ride Robert and Amalie planned, he was much too good-mannered, or good-natured, to show it. He gave them a cheery wave as they set off down the drive, then turned at once to direct the organization of a bucket brigade formed to bring water from the bayou to store in a large tank, water that would go around the plants as they were put into the ground.

As she returned George's wave, Amalie saw Julien. He stood on the upper gallery with an épée in his hand. It was impossible to see his face from that distance, but he held the slender sword as if it were a dagger, with the point stabbing into the gallery railing, and his other hand was clenched into a fist, resting on his hip.

Amalie faced forward again without calling Robert's attention to his cousin. A moment later, they were out of sight, hidden by the low-growing branches of the live oaks. Still, she could not forget that last sight of Julien there on the gallery, could not prevent herself from wondering what had been in her husband's mind as he watched her ride away with the man who had betrayed him with his wife.

Isa was not with her. He would have been, but in the dining room while she sipped a quick cup of coffee, he had shown her a drawing that he had just begun of Belle Grove and the hands at work on the new garden. It was good, amazingly good. Beyond the aesthetic value, it was a record of what the house looked like at the present time, something M'mere might enjoy having. Since it had seemed more important to let him get on with it than to have his company, she had allowed him to stay behind. He had spoken wistfully of what a good view he might have of the house, if he could only cross over to the opposite side of the bayou, and the last thing she had done before stepping out of the house had been to leave orders that Isa was to be rowed across as soon as the sun was up.

The morning was pleasant, the air fresh and sweet and exhilarating despite the warmth that hinted at greater heat later in the day. It was good to be out, to feel the movement of her mount beneath her. It was almost possible to forget why she was here, though it was not as easy to forget the man who rode beside her.

It seemed strange not to have Isa riding along on his pony at her heels. She was becoming attached to the boy, perhaps too attached, but he was so willing to please, so grateful for any attention she spared him. She wondered if Robert was right, if she was treating him like a pet and raising expectations that could not be filled, all for the sake of the boost to her ego of having him at her beck and call. She did not think so, but it was difficult to be sure. She truly wanted to help Isa, but it was possible that she was only hindering him. She wanted to give him pride and confidence in himself, though it might be that these were things that would not serve him at all. Pushing such thoughts from her, she drew her composure around her and began to talk in the light, inconsequential vein that would, she hoped, ward off intimacy.

The Willows was a two-story mansion of soft rose-red brick with green shutters and a slate roof. It was built in the Georgian style with neoclassical adaptations that included a gabled portico on the front with white columns that soared from the ground to the architrave to shelter upper and lower galleries, the top one being railed with wrought iron in a design that was airy and simple. A second portico jutted out on the right, a carriageway for protection from the elements for arriving and departing guests. In the rear overlooking the bayou was yet another portico to match the one that faced the road, making it impossible to say with any certainty which of the two main porticoes was on the front and which on the back. Massive oaks hung with moss surrounded the house, giving it an air of coolness and seclusion.

They dismounted at the side entrance, entering a hallway

that met the main hall at right angles. Robert showed her around the salon, the library, and the ladies' sitting room; those few rooms that might be considered safe for a female to visit in the company of a man. Every surface gleamed with polish and there was a hint of beeswax and warm oil hanging in the air, as if it had not been long since the last thorough cleaning. His behavior was impeccable, that of a polite host, but in the sitting room as she looked around at the rose hangings and white-and-gold paper, she caught him watching her in the mirror that hung at a canted angle above the fireplace. The look in his eyes made the heat of a flush rise to her face before she turned sharply away.

Coffee, lemonade, and cakes were served to them on the lower gallery that looked out on the bayou. They talked of Robert's parents, of the building of the house when they were newly married and the difficulties, then, of bringing materials and furnishings to this isolated area. Such was the constraint that lay between them, however, that Amalie almost wished he would abandon his role of a gentleman, that he would have done with politeness so that they both might say what had to be said and she could go home again.

The coffee was finished. He rose to help her from her chair and to lead her back out to their mounts, and still he had not spoken. As they rode away, Amalie sent him a puzzled look from under her lashes. Why had he insisted she come here if he had meant to entertain her exactly as he would M'mere? It was obvious that he had urged his staff of servants to great efforts to have everything ready for her, nor would it have surprised her to learn that he had left orders for them to keep their distance once the refreshments were laid out. And yet he had been a model of propriety.

Was that it? Had he decided that it was not proper to set out to seduce her in his own home, among his people who had close ties to the quarters at Belle Grove? If so, she should be grateful for his forbearance. Instead, she felt singularly frustrated. This meeting had loomed in her mind as an ordeal to be endured. She had expected to pit her wits and knowledge of what was right against his most practiced flatteries and fervent appeals. She had thought that he might even stoop to physical coercion, when all else failed. To find herself returning to Belle Grove with her weapons still untested was deflating enough to make her wonder if she had misjudged, or, at the very least, misunderstood him.

It was strangely gratifying, then, to have him suddenly reach out and take her bridle, swinging her mount's head around toward a faint trail that led from the road down toward the bayou's edge. She protested and her hand tightened on the crop as if she would strike out at him, but it was more a resistance in form than in fact. She realized in amazement that she was not at all averse to having it out with him beyond the reach of prying eyes and listening ears. It would be a welcome luxury.

They drew up in a small clearing at the water's edge that was overhung with oaks and carpeted with clover. The dew still sparkled here on the lobed leaves in the rays of the sun; it splashed as warm as bathwater against Amalie's boots as Robert helped her down. She moved to stand under the biggest oak, leaning against it to stare out at the water. He led their mounts a short distance away, tying the reins to a low-hanging limb with enough slack so that they could crop the thick, lush grass at the edge of the clearing.

"I'm glad you came to The Willows."

The words were quietly spoken as he came toward her, yet they carried a hint of tension.

"It's a lovely place," she said conventionally, then added, "I can see why you are proud of it."

He dismissed her comment with a quick movement of one hand. "I have often pictured you there, in those rooms. I've wanted to be alone with you there, in the light of day."

"Please," she said, an odd constriction in her throat. "It would be better if you didn't say things like that."

"Would it? I'm not so sure. There is much I have wanted to say to you, so very much." He paused, but when she made no answer, went on. "I couldn't bring myself to do it back there. I could say the reason was because I didn't want to spoil your memory of your first visit to my home, but the truth is I didn't want to risk spoiling my own."

She searched her mind for all the reasoned and harsh words she had meant to use against him. They were gone. She moistened her lips, beginning unsteadily, "I am a married woman—"

"I know that!" he lashed out. "That, of all things, I know too well. It doesn't keep me from wanting to see you in my house, to watch you undress and see you lying naked in the lamplight on my bed, to look into your eyes as I make love to you."

There was a hush in the clearing as the rawness of the words and the pain that etched them lingered on the air.

"You—you can't."

"So I've told myself, times without number. That doesn't

make it any easier to accept. I am haunted by the thought of you, don't you see? Dear God, if I had known it would come to this, I would have run from you as a man fleeing damnation. Never, never would I have so much as touched your hand."

"Why did you?"

He sent her a quick glance, as if startled by the question. "I thought you had it figured out. Lust was the reason, wasn't it? Jealous, unbridled, conniving lust."

"I never said that," she protested, stung by the bitterness in his tone.

"It was what you meant."

"What else was I to think?" Her hands were clenched at her sides and she brought them up to press against her abdomen.

He stared at her for a long moment, then gave a slow nod. His voice flat, he said, "I came to you that first time because—oh, because it was M'mere's request, the only thing she had ever asked of me in return for the care, the acceptance, the love she had given without stint since my own mother died. Because I saw how beautiful you are and how wasted on Julien. Because of the feel of you in my arms the day of the flood. Because of the special warmth of your smile when you played with the children in the mud after the water went down. Because I am a man, and the thought of so lovely and untouched a woman so near, mine for the taking, a gift, was more than I could bear. Because—oh, because I looked at you that first day in M'mere's sitting room, with your hair hanging in wet wisps about your face, with raindrops like tears on your cheeks and such concern in your eyes, and I knew you were mine. You were mine, and though it was too late to make you my wife, I could still have you, for I had just been told exactly that."

Her heartbeat pounded in her ears. Her skin felt as if it were on fire from the frankness of his words and some more basic response to them. Slowly, in an effort of control, she unclenched her fists and clasped her hands together. The words she forced past her throat were no more than a whisper. "It was wrong."

"Yes. It was meant to be only an interlude, a few brief nights of love before you could discover the substitution. It wasn't enough."

"So you came again and again."

"I couldn't stay away. Tante Sophia saw it at once; she tried to warn me, but already it was too late. She and Julien had given a traitor the key to the treasure room and there was nothing they could do to keep me out."

"A traitor?" she asked, sending him a quick look.

"I was supposed to be acting in their interest and I deserted it for my own."

A wry smile twisted her mouth. "They didn't really try to stop you, not even after the soirée. Julien could have, easily enough. All he had to do was lock his door."

"That would not have been honorable, by his code, since it was for his sake that I was recruited. Though lately I've seen signs that he was growing restive. His incapability as a man is of the mind, not the body. My greatest fear was that in seeing how desirable you were to me, he might find in himself the ability to assert his rights as a husband."

"Out of jealousy?" she asked, doubt threading her tone.

"In part, but also because he finds you attractive. If he did not, he would not have agreed to the marriage, no matter how persuasive Tante Sophia was. I think, in fact, that he cares for you as much as it is in him to care for any woman."

There was an odd expression on his face as he finished speaking, as if he wished he could take back the words. She gave a slow shake of her head. "That may be, I don't know. I feel sometimes as if I hardly know Julien at all."

"Few do."

"And yet you are one of the few."

"Yes," he agreed and looked away out over the bayou. "I know him well enough to know that this marriage of yours was a mistake. I know that you will never be happy in it."

She would not agree with him, for that would be disloyal. She tried a small shrug instead. "I must be; it's too late for anything else."

"No, it isn't."

"What do you mean?"

He moved nearer, taking her hand, though he kept his gaze upon her gloved fingers. "You could come away with me."

She jerked her hand away. There was contempt in her tone as she said, "Just like that? You are suggesting that I give up everything and move in with you—as what, your mistress? And all for the sake of a few clandestine visits in the night."

"We could go to Paris. The social climate there is very accepting of such liaisons as ours must be."

"Some parts of it, you mean! Not everyone accepts the demimonde into their homes."

"There would be enough that we need not feel like outcasts. I am not a poor man; you need not think we would starve in some garret. At least we would be together."

If he had spoken of love instead of his haunted need of her, she might have listened. But that he could think she would turn back on respectability, security, family, and friends to live with him in sin merely to escape an unsatisfactory marriage was enraging. That he could consider that the fact that he had money would make a difference only added to her wrath.

"Please say no more," she said in heated tones as she swung away from him. "I have been insulted quite enough."

He shot out his hand to catch her arm. "I meant no insult."

"Did you not?" she cried, her brown eyes glittering with anger. "Let me inform you that I am not a—a demi-mondaine put here for your enjoyment! I have had enough of being used when and how you wish. Why should I run away with you for more of the same? I told you once: All I want from you is to be left alone!"

"You don't mean it." The words had a grating sound.

"I was never more sincere in my life!"

She wrenched her arm from his grasp, moving across the clearing toward her mare. He caught her in a single, lone stride. His hard fingers bit into her forearm as he hauled her around. As she tipped back her head to look at him, her hat with its veiling fell from her hair and she dropped her skirt so that it trailed in the dew-wet grass.

"That isn't all you wanted not so long ago," he said, his eyes dark blue as his gaze raked over her face.

"No!" she gasped as his meaning reached her. She

pushed at him, twisting in her arms, but his hold was like steel.

"You turned to me on the night after the soirée with all the fire and sweet passion that any man could ever dream of finding in a woman."

"I—I thought you were Julien."

He gave a short laugh. "Oh, no. Before that night, maybe, though I think you had begun to guess. But from the moment I kissed you, like the fool that I was there in the midst of your guests, you knew."

"I couldn't know, not for certain," she said with an edge of panic in her voice. "Then when you came I was asleep, dreaming—"

"Dare I hope of me? No matter. You gave yourself to me knowing full well who I was, accepting that knowledge for the sake of the desire of the moment, and without a thought for Julien. That is something you had better remember, *chère* Amalie, before you become too involved in condemning me!"

She tried to pull away from him again, avoiding his hard gaze. "Let me go!"

"Not until you admit it." He pulled her toward him so that she fell against his chest. Only the single thickness of the material of her riding habit, plus one petticoat, lay between them as her thighs pressed against the ridged muscles of his legs.

"That isn't the way it was!"

"Then why did you try to light the lamp?"

She flashed him a look of acute dislike. "If you were so certain I knew, why didn't you let me?"

"Because," he answered, his voice grim, "the pretense

199

would have been at an end. You would have been forced to denounce me, to adopt this pose of outrage, and I couldn't bear that, not then, not after we had been so close."

She went still. Her breasts rose and fell with her breathing. She could feel the jarring of her heart against her ribs. He was so close now, so very close. The sun slanted with a blue gleam across the waves of his hair and etched his bronze features in bold relief. She could see herself reflected in the twin mirrors of his eyes, while at the same time they were as bottomless and soothingly blue as the sea's depths.

"It isn't a pose," she said, though the words had a shaky, uncertain sound.

"Isn't it?" he queried softly, his attention upon the tender curves of her parted lips as he lowered his head to touch them with his own. Against their smooth, moist surface he said again, "Isn't it?"

Chapter 10

I t was a challenge, one made not only to the mind and spirit, but to the senses. His mouth was warm, tasting faintly of coffee, as he molded its firm contours to her own. Her lips burned under the pressure, leaping with exquisite fire as his tongue probed their sensitive inner lining, then pressed deeper, enticing her response.

She wanted to withhold it, to remain aloof, to retain a degree of anger and a little dignity. Her body, recognizing the touch it had come to crave, betrayed her. She swayed closer. The sun was dazzling behind her closed eyelids, its touch on her skin like a caress. Her sense of right and wrong receded, replaced by a heated longing that took no notice of such questions. Her hands, which were pressed against his chest, slowly closed on the lapels of his coat, holding him to her. With a small sound deep in her throat, she touched her tongue to his, drew back, then slowly allowed it to entwine with his.

Around them rose the sweet scent of trampled clover, blending with the smell of starched linen, the faint spice of bay rum, and the lingering perfume of the vetiver always used in her armoire that wafted from the folds of her habit. The last increased as he released her arms, smoothing his hands over her shoulders and down her back to the slim curves of her hips. He held her to him and she could sense the strength of his heated desire for her. Deep inside her a taut fullness burgeoned. Her clothes were suddenly too tight, too heavy. She longed to feel the sun and the warm air upon her bare skin.

His lips moved to the corner of her mouth, tasting the delicate fold, probing it. They traveled, warm and smooth, over the skin of her cheek, the curve of her jaw, the tender turn of her neck, as if savoring the resilient softness. He inhaled deeply, filling his lungs with the delicate natural fragrance of her body, the sweet essence of her. He caressed the back of her neck, settling upon the thick knot of hair at her nape. The pins made a soft clatter as they were released one by one into the clover.

The satin tresses loosened, sliding, cascading down her back. He sank his fingers into the soft warmth of them as he nuzzled the vulnerable arch of her throat. He trailed lower, toward the pulse that throbbed at the fragile hollow, but it was protected by the lace frill of her blouse and the small amethyst brooch that nestled there.

"Amalie," he whispered, the syllables a paean of longing.

She wanted him. She had been taught all her life that the desire to act was the same as the deed, so in this case she stood condemned already. Moreover, it was not a new sin, but one repeated over and over, both knowingly and unknowingly. And yet could this sweet singing in the blood be wrong? It did not profane, but rather was true and natural, and therefore sacred. She had been wed to Julien, but it was Robert who had consummated the marriage. In an odd way, it was as if she had married both men: one in spirit, the other in the flesh. The terrible thing was, she realized in a moment of startling clarity, that if Julien should ever seek to exert his physical claim as her husband, that joining would seem the adultery.

She drew back slightly in the circle of Robert's arms, removing her gloves and lifting her hands to the brooch at her neck. So unsteady were her fingers that it was a moment before she could release the catch, then it was free, the amethyst winking lavender-blue fire as it lay in her hand.

He stared down at it, a suspended look on his face, then with grave care he took the gloves and small piece of jewelry from her, slipping them into his pocket. His fingers went to the tiny, mother-of-pearl buttons that held her blouse closed, and eased them from their holes. Then his hand dropped lower to release the steel hooks that held the braided frogs of her coat. A few more buttons and the front of her blouse lay open. Carefully he drew the edges aside, revealing the blue-veined creaminess of the swells of her breasts above the low, ribbon-shot eyelet neckline of her camisole and the lift of their shape outlined under the fine lawn, the nipples contracted with desire.

He spread his fingers upon her rib cage, sliding them upward to cup and hold the gentle globes. "I knew you would be beautiful in the light," he murmured, "but not so beyond compare."

His hands were warm, beguiling upon her. It needed a supreme effort of will to lift her own and catch his wrists, stopping his movements. Her voice husky, she said, "Someone will see, here. Could we—that is, perhaps we could go back to The Willows?"

"There are watching eyes there, too. This is as safe as anywhere for us." The strong bones of one wrist moved under her grasp as he brushed his thumb over the peak of her breast.

He was right. Surrounded as they were by family and servants, there was no real privacy, no place they could be certain they would not be discovered. "This must be the end of it, here, today. There is no other way."

He did not answer and the thick screen of his lashes shielded his expression as he watched the firm curves he held in his hands tremble with the pound of her heart.

"You do understand, don't you? I—I am flattered that you would give up everything you have here to take me away, but it wouldn't work. After a while, you would grow bored—"

"Never."

"You would," she insisted. "And I would be guilty and miserable. We would grow to hate each other."

"If I told you that I love you—"

"Don't! There's no need, not now. Besides, it makes no

difference, don't you see?" She swallowed hard against the tears that rose in her throat. "Oh, Robert, please kiss me now and let it be for the last time."

He took her lips with a hard hunger that seemed to have an undercurrent of fury, too. It was because she had resisted him, she thought, as she released his wrists, lifting her arms to clasp them around his neck. His hands slid down to her uncorseted waist, his fingers nearly meeting, closing upon it as if he would break her in half. Her breasts were flattened against his chest, the buttons of his waistcoat and the studs of his shirt gouging into her. She gasped.

Abruptly his hold loosened, his lips, his tongue caressed her mouth in wordless apology. He raised his hand to her shoulder, brushing the sleeves of her basque jacket down her arms, freeing her from it and tossing the garment aside. In the same way, he removed her blouse. Slowly, tentatively, Amalie served him the same way sliding his coat from him, working with one hand at his cravat. It required more dexterity and greater concentration. She trailed her lips to the corner of his mouth, testing the firm, tucked corner with its faint roughness of close-shaved stubble, tasting the spice of bay rum on his chin before she rested her forehead against it.

She let the ends of his cravat hang loose while she pushed the gold studs from the holes of his shirt, leaving them hanging in one side. She unbuttoned the waistcoat, then inserted her fingertips in the line of his open shirt, brushing them through the hair on his chest before pushing the edges wide.

She heard his sharp exhalation before he began to shrug out of his coat. He stepped back and stripped it off, spreading it on the ground. Taking her hand, he knelt, drawing her down with him.

Slowly, then with growing haste, they finished undressing each other. The sun poured down upon them, gilding their skin and touching it with shadings of apricot and peach, with bronze and copper, shimmering in their hair with blue fire. It was embracing in its warmth, blinding in its brightness, a pagan sun, benign and enduring. It shimmered along their arms and shoulders as they pressed close and glimmered with a pearl sheen along Amalie's limbs as Robert sank down, drawing her to lie on top of him.

She braced herself on her hands that grasped his shoulders. The peach-colored peaks of her breasts grazed his chest. Her hair fell forward, spilling around them in a shining, protective curtain. He caught her hips, kneading them, holding her to him, and his eyes were sea dark and secretive with desire. Her breathing quickened as she felt the hardness of his manhood between her thighs, its gentle probing. There was a stillness, a waiting, moist and hollow, inside her. She eased backward, holding his gaze, the movement slow and undulating. By infinite and heated degrees she encompassed him, taking him inside her. At the utmost limit of fullness, she stopped.

He smiled, an easy curving of his mouth that denoted uncomplicated joy. Satisfaction rose into his eyes and something more that made her catch her breath as if in pain. The tears that shimmered in her brown eyes overflowed, clinging to her lashes. A tremor ran along her arms and turned to trembling.

With a wordless exclamation, he caught her to him, levering himself over, taking her to her back to relieve the strain on her arms. He twisted, lowering his mouth to take her breast, lapping at the nipple with the rough velvet of his tongue. She touched the crisp waves of his hair, closing her eyes, hardly aware of the wet track of tears into her hair. Without her volition, or so it seemed, her hands caressed the column of his neck, smoothing the muscles that were knotted across his shoulders. She spread her palms over the sun-warmed skin, aware of his tensile strength, vitality, and powerful control in every nerve in her body. She felt a wanton need to abandon herself to him, holding nothing back, while at the same time there was a thread of grief in the far reaches of her mind that already mourned the fact that this binding of her body to his would never come again.

He had not agreed.

The knowledge flitted across her mind as she felt the touch of his fingers, insistent and arousing, at the most sensitive and protected portion of her body. She made a soft sound deep in her throat, closing her eyes more tightly. Reality and questions of right or wrong faded. Nothing mattered but this perilous rapture. It was hers. Nothing could take this from her. Nothing ever would.

He captured her mouth with his and sank deep into her, then locked the muscled strength of his legs around her, rolling with her into the fragrant, dew-laden clover. It was warm and wet and sweet around them. Pagans both, primitive and beatified, they bathed in the sweet and soft liquid of dawn, thrusting against each other, straining together.

Never in her life had she felt so voluptuous, so free. Her damp skin glowed with the hot flush of passion. Her blood leaped in her veins, racing, surging, suffusing the lower part of her body as she rode him now with frenzied effort, then turned with him once more to lie beneath him. Her muscles were taut, the tendons tightly strung. Her hands clung, taking him deep, urging him deeper with every plunge. She wanted their bodies to blend beyond parting, to forge a memory that would link her to him for all time.

Her senses stretched, soaring, hovering. The darkness behind her eyes became blacker. Her breath caught in her throat. Her hands closed convulsively upon his arms. There was a giving feeling inside her.

It burst upon her in blood-red wonder, a glorious magic, ageless, without limit. It was a silent storm, an internal violence. At its peak, he plunged into her one final, shuddering time, holding that ultimate penetration. She gave a low cry, arching against him, then they were still.

It might have been only a moment, or ten minutes later, that he gathered her to him, turning on his back in the clover and pulling her to rest on his chest. Their breathing eased. The combination of dew and perspiration that glistened on their bodies turned cool, drying away. A mocking bird called nearby. A grasshopper landed beside them with a small, clicking sound. The waters of the bayou made a quiet, gurgling noise.

"I hope," Robert said, his tone threaded with easy, satisfied amusement, "that there is no poison ivy in this particular spot."

Amalie smiled without opening her eyes. "Or redbugs."

"Damn," Robert said, stiffening.

Redbugs were tiny, blood-sucking insects of the tick family known elsewhere as chiggers. Their bite was far from dangerous, but could itch with unbelievable persistence. That he would swear at the thought was not surprising. Amalie felt a chuckle rising inside her, but before she could make a sound, she was rolled from him to the grass. He heaved himself up to a crouch, turning his broad back to the bayou and screening her from view while he reached for the skirt of her habit. She tried to sit up, but he prevented her with a hand on her shoulder as he flicked a glance around behind him.

She saw it then, the shape of a triangular, striped sail in cream and blue. There was only one vessel on the bayou that sported such distinctive canvas and that was Julien's barge. It was drifting past along the bayou, brilliant in the sun with the water sparkling and chuckling around it, an object as vivid and useless as a butterfly. Tige, at the tiller, was hidden by the puffed sail, but his master among his cushions was not. Her husband was sitting up, pushing a straw hat to the back of his head as he came to his feet. On his face was a look of startled rage and he was staring straight at them.

The barge was rocking at the landing with its sail furled when they finally reached Belle Grove. They had been in no hurry to return. It had taken some time to find Amalie's pins and to repair the ravages to her appearance, then they had ridden slowly, allowing the hot sun to dry their damp clothing. Amalie was not certain she was grateful for the respite, however. It might have been better if Julien had pulled into shore and vented his anger upon them then and there. That he hadn't was most likely due to the presence of his valet. Whether Tige had seen them or not, he had given every indication of overlooking them. It would not have done to force their indiscretion upon his notice. Still, the thought of the confrontation that must come filled Amalie with dread and ineffectual anger.

They had spoken little, she and Robert, each preoccupied with their own thoughts. She wondered what he was thinking as they rode along, but the impassive planes of his face gave nothing away. Did he regret what had happened? She did not think so. Did she? She was not sure. She should, of course.

George's shrubbery from China had been delivered. Pots and barrels by the hundreds, big and small, covered the slopes before the house and sat around the edges of the pool. The steamboat that had pulled the flat barges carrying them had gone again, back down to St. Martinville. M'mere, with a sunshade over her shoulder, was strolling among the plants while George, at her side, pointed out the finest specimens. Of Chloe there was no sign, nor was there of Julien.

Robert and Amalie dismounted before the house. M'mere lifted a hand to wave. George shouted to them, telling them to come and see his beauties. Amalie, knowing her appearance could not stand close scrutiny, shook her head, calling that she must change first. Their friendly greetings were a relief, however. It did not appear that Julien had spoken of what he had seen.

Amalie draped her riding skirt over her arm and moved toward the house. As Robert fell into step beside her, she glanced at his set face. She waited until the groom, who had come to take their horses, was out of hearing before she spoke in low tones. "You don't have to come in with me. It might even be best if you did not."

He sent her a steady blue glance. "I can't let you face him alone."

"You could, but you won't."

"As you say."

The implacable sound of his voice was an indication of how unlikely it was that she could persuade him. In truth, she did not want to try. Inclining her head, she moved before him to the gallery and across it at an angle to the outside stairs. She reached up to take off her hat as she climbed toward the upper gallery.

"Don't stop there," Julien said from the landing above her, the words weighted with sarcasm, "you may as well take off the rest in public, too. As a matter of fact, I don't know why you bothered to put your clothes back on."

"Julien, that will do." Robert, his tone hard, spoke from behind her.

"Will it indeed? And am I to turn a blind eye to the two of you disporting yourselves as naked as Adam and Eve where any passerby might see you?"

"It was merest chance that you saw us."

"Mischance, you mean! I would not have dreamed you would be so lost to the behavior due your good name—or my wife's—my dear cousin. I thought better of you."

"Please, Julien," Amalie said, stung by the scorn in his voice, "it wasn't like that."

"No? Am I to believe it was a moment of uncontrollable passion that made you so careless? How very touching. But I have no intention of standing by while the two of you brand me the betrayed husband for all the world to see simply because you cannot exercise a little self-discipline."

Robert moved up to take Amalie's arm, climbing with

her to the upper gallery so that Julien had to step back out of their way. His voice grim and a little weary, he said, "It won't happen again."

"I should think not! It's time this masquerade ended. The purpose is almost surely accomplished, or so says Tige, who had it from my wife's maid. If Amalie is with child, then there is no point in continuing."

Amalie was aware of the sharp glance Robert flung in her direction, though she could not bring herself to meet his eyes. She was aware, too, of the approach of M'mere just below them, hurrying to reach the lower gallery.

"I agree," Robert said.

It was Amalie's turn to look swiftly at him then, her own brown gaze shadowed. His hard features gave nothing away. She looked to her husband and saw a smile of satisfaction slowly widening on Julien's sensitive mouth.

"I confess that after this morning I had not looked to find you so reasonable," he said to Robert.

"You had better hear me out."

"Oh?" Julien's tone was suddenly wary.

"I agree that it's time this thing was ended. It should never have begun, but that scarcely matters now. I wanted to take Amalie away before I knew about the child, but there is nothing that can stop me from doing it now."

"No! No, no, no," M'mere cried in agitation as she stumbled up the stairs. "You don't know what you are saying. Only think of the scandal! It cannot be, it must not be!"

Robert's voice was quieter, but no less determined, as he faced his aunt. "I'm sorry, but to leave it as it is would be insupportable."

"You agreed. You promised. Only think what you are

saying, *mon cher*; we would never be able to hold up our heads again." The older woman's hands were trembling as she held them out to him and her face was pale with a line of perspiration across her upper lip.

"I never knew it would be like this. It was wrong of you to ask it of me and foolish of me to think I could do it."

Julien took a stride toward Amalie, catching her arm, dragging her against him. There was in his face a peculiar expression, almost like terror. "I won't let you take her, do you hear? She's my wife and she will stay with me where she belongs."

M'mere moaned, clasping her hand over her heart. Robert reached to take Amalie's other elbow, as much to steady her as anything else as Julien jerked her away.

Inside Amalie a fearful anger grew. That they could quarrel over her as if she had no will of her own and plan her life without consulting her was added to the distress she still felt for the way that she had been used by them all, duped into providing an heir for Belle Grove. Julien's fingers were digging into her arm and she wrenched it from his grasp, at the same time coming up against Robert. He released her elbow, catching her in the circle of his arm.

Julien snatched her wrist, twisting it as he yanked her away from his cousin. "So you choose him do you? You found out who had been sneaking into your bed and decided you liked being his whore? I should be glad I found out what a bitch I married, a fornicating adulteress who cares nothing for her marriage vows, one who will run after anything in trousers that will give her what she wants!"

There was a red haze of pain behind Amalie's eyes, running from her twisted wrist. The virulent words washed over her, their overlay of truth making them sink like burning shafts into her mind. Then there came the rush of a hard blow, a grunt, and Julien went stumbling backward to crash into the gallery railing.

Robert, his hands still balled into fists, stood over him. Julien, sprawled on the floor with one shoulder braced on the balusters, stared up at his cousin. He reached up to touch his cheek where a livid bruise was already forming. A cold look came into his dark eyes. His voice soft, he said, "You will meet me for this."

"Julien!" M'mere cried in stricken tones.

"Don't be a fool," Robert said tightly, his gaze never leaving his cousin's face.

"Why not, if you are determined to expose me as one, if not worse."

Robert straightened. "That was never my intention."

"What will it take to make you fight me? Shall I make it a question of—of my wife's honor, or lack of it?"

"Julien, my son," M'mere moaned, her agony in the sound.

There was a taut silence. Finally Robert spoke, his voice quiet, without expression. "The choice of weapons is mine, I believe."

A fierce joy sprang into Julien's face. "Do I dare hope you will choose swords?"

"No," M'mere whispered. Amalie, her eyes wide in horror, made not a sound.

"There is no reason why I should be a fool just because you are so inclined," Robert said tightly. "Pistols, at twenty paces."

Julien smiled, satisfaction shining in his dark eyes. "Tomorrow at dawn. The usual ground."

M'mere crumpled to the floor and lay unmoving.

By the time Robert had lifted his aunt and taken her into the salon, Amalie had loosened her collar and her stays, and her elderly maid had brought her vinaigrette and waved it under her nose, M'mere had regained consciousness. She would do nothing except cry and moan of *la scandale,* however, waving away the glass of wine brought to her as well as the orange flower water.

Robert took his leave when he saw that she was all right, it being awkward under the circumstances for him to remain. It was certain he also had a number of arrangements to make for the meeting: the finding of seconds and a physician willing to be present, the making of his will. Amalie tried not to dwell upon such things.

She stayed with M'mere for some time, helping her to her bedchamber where the older woman stretched out upon the narrow accouchement bed that sat at the foot of her large four-poster. They talked, M'mere rambling on about the night that Julien had been born on that very bed on which she lay, of how terrible the birth had been but how glorious the outcome. She spoke of what a beautiful child he had been, how naughty, how spoiled, how beloved, and of the days when he and Robert had been inseparable. She did not speak of her fears, but they were there, hovering at the back of her every word, patent in the quiver in her voice, the restlessness of her gaze that turned often to her prie-dieu.

At last Amalie made her escape. In her bedchamber, she

rang for a bath, then took off her habit and folded it away on the topmost shelf of the armoire. There were grass stains on it and traces of dirt that should be cleaned at once if it was to be wearable. She didn't care. If she never wore it again, never saw it, she would be just as happy.

Perched on the seat of the hat tub, so called because it looked much like a man's hat with the crown filled with water and the wide brim angling out to catch the splashes, she turned a small cake of rose-scented soap in her hands. In her mind the events of the morning had an unreal feeling. She could not make herself understand that she had allowed herself to be seduced into making love in the broadest daylight beside the bayou, that she had been seen by Julien, and that her husband and her lover were now to fight a duel over her. Such things did not happen to well-brought-up young ladies. How had it come about that they had happened to her?

She tried to think of what she could have done to prevent it. There seemed little. They had all been in league against her from the beginning: M'mere, Julien, and Robert. When she had first begun to suspect that she was being duped, she had tried to speak to Julien. If he had called a halt then, it might not have come to this. If he had stayed at home more, instead of leaving her to Robert, if he had realized himself how deep his resentment ran, it might have been avoided.

The names he had called her had been hurtful. She had not deserved them, at least, not until today. She had been innocent until this morning, but for what had taken place between her and Robert there beside the Teche, she had no excuse. It made no difference that it would never have taken place without the trickery that had gone before. She had accepted it, even invited it, of her own will; she could not delude herself into thinking otherwise. Still, the coarse and degrading things Julien had said had nothing to do with her or with what she had shared with Robert.

It was strange. She blamed Robert for what he had done, and yet she could not despise him for it. Was it because of the way he had come to her, with tenderness, with infinite care for her pleasure, or was it only because she knew now how very much she would have missed if he had been more the gentleman?

She had questioned his honor that night when she had trapped him in Julien's room. It was a blow he had felt, she knew. And yet he had tried to protect her at every turn. Even this meeting between him and Julien—

No. She would not think of that. She would think of what she was going to do to get through the rest of this day and the night that must pass before she would know the outcome of the duel. She closed her eyes, thinking with feverish intensity of the tasks that needed doing. The copper in the kitchen needed polishing against verdigris poisoning. The supply of tallow dips for the quarters was running low and there was a large stock of grease and ashes that should be used for the candles. There might be callers in the afternoon—but no, everyone would be too busy making ready for the ball—

The Morneys' ball. It was this evening. They must send their regrets at once. They could not put in an appearance, not now. To laugh and eat and dance knowing all the while that the two men who were her partners would try to kill each other at dawn the next morning would be too much.

She could not do it. Nor, she thought, was M'mere capable of the effort.

She was wrong. When she had hurried through her bath and dressed in a fresh gown of cool batiste, she went at once to the older woman's room. She found her sitting up, watching as her maid brought out one ball gown after the other. She looked up, summoning a smile as Amalie entered. The marks of distress were still on her lined features, but they were overlaid by a precarious calm.

"Have you decided, *chère,*" the older woman greeted her, "what you will wear to the ball?"

For an instant, hearing her even tones, Amalie was forced to wonder if her mother-in-law was quite well. "I only just this moment remembered it. You don't mean to go?"

"We cannot do otherwise."

"But surely we can hold ourselves excused?"

"And have everyone say we were too ashamed to show our faces? I think not."

Amalie moved to sit beside the older woman. "No one will know why we have chosen not to appear."

"How little you know a small community such as this if you think so. Julien must have seconds to attend him and Robert the same, plus the physician. Five men. It will be amazing if one of them does not whisper the news to his valet, his wife, or to someone else. Depend upon it; there will be rumors flying on this evening."

"Oh, M'mere, on top of all the rest?"

She was required to explain. When she had finished, M'mere's face was stern. "There is no loyalty anymore. Everyone prattles and snickers behind their hands. It cannot be helped. If we fail this evening, everyone will know that the worst they may hear is true. If we go and smile as usual, there will be at least some small doubt."

"But is it worth it?" Amalie pleaded. "You have not been well lately."

"It was the worry over my stupid interference. I should not have done it; I know that now. I can only say I thought it for the best."

"Perhaps it was."

M'mere reached out to touch her hand. "You only say that to make me feel less at fault, but I know better. The blame is mine and had been from the beginning. I have done you a great disservice, my child. I will try to make amends, I promise you. I only pray you will find it in your heart someday to forgive me."

"Please, you must not talk this way," Amalie began, but M'mere waved away the protest and, perhaps because she knew it was false, Amalie did not pursue it. She got to her feet.

"If I am to go this evening, I had better make preparations."

"Yes. If you are going to the kitchen, will you tell Marthe, if you please, that I will have a light luncheon in my sitting room?"

She agreed and was turning toward the door when a knock fell on that panel. She moved to open it, then stood staring in surprise as she saw Patrick Dye standing there.

He was leaning on the frame, his mouth pursed in a silent whistle. He gave her an impudent glance that lingered on the rounded softness of her bosom, before nodding and looking past her. He straightened without haste and took a step into the room. "You sent for me, Madame Declouet?"

"Yes, m'sieu," M'mere agreed, but said no more until Amalie had left the room, closing the door behind her.

The material of Amalie's gown was an iridescent silk of the color known as *l'heure bleu,* a soft gray-blue that shaded to lavender in the folds. So as not to distract from the uniqueness of the fabric, the style was plain, with a perfectly smooth bell of a skirt, a pointed basque at the natural waistline, and a bertha of blond at the rounded neckline. Its simplicity and rather somber color suited her mood.

It lay on the bed while Amalie, wearing nothing more than her wrapper, sat before the dressing table as Lally put up her hair. She had requested a simple style in keeping with the gown, not the least reason being that she had a headache beginning just behind her eyes and did not think she could bear anything more elaborate.

The maid drew the long, silken strands back from a center parting, easing them into deep waves at either temple, then made a thick knot at the nape of her neck. She brought out a headdress in the shape of a pair of fern fronds made of lavender velvet that she fastened at the back of Amalie's head. Finished, she handed her mistress a hand-mirror.

Amalie turned on her chair so that she could see the sides and back of her head. She smiled at Lally in the mirror. "Very nice, as always."

"I try to please." The girl, a little flushed at the compliment, turned away to pick up the silk stockings that would go on next.

At that moment, the sliding doors opened. Julien, in a long dressing gown of claret velvet with black cord edging, stepped through. He lifted a brow, a sardonic smile curving his mouth as he saw the surprise on the faces of both Amalie and her maid; then, with a nod toward the other door, he said to Lally, "Leave us."

Amalie got slowly to her feet, her hand going to her throat to clutch the edges of her wrapper together. The thought uppermost in her mind was Robert's fear that Julien might decide he was able, after all, to enforce his connubial rights. Had the prospect of losing her given him that resolution? There was about his mouth a firmness that hinted as much.

When the door had closed behind the maid, he turned to her. His voice rough, he said, "Don't look at me like that. I didn't mean to hurt you this morning."

"It was nothing." She searched her mind for something to say to distract him. "I'm sure it was an unpleasant moment, seeing the two of us as you did."

"That is no excuse for the way I acted toward you. I am bitterly sorry for what I said and did. To turn on you, after what was done to you, and with my full knowledge, was unforgivable. I can't explain what came over me; I'm not sure I understand it myself. I can only hope that you will not condemn me too harshly."

He was staring at the pattern of the rug at her feet as he spoke. That made it easier. Her voice stifled, she said, "If it seemed that I had no regard for your name that I bear, or for your standing in the community, you must know that it isn't so. I will not willingly do anything again to jeopardize it."

"I can ask no more."

A silence fell. He frowned at the rug and shoved his hands into the pockets of his dressing gown. She swallowed. The ormolu clock on the mantel chimed softly. They glanced at it. He cleared his throat.

"It must seem strange to you that a husband would allow another man access to his wife."

"I—yes, it did, but Robert explained."

"Did he? I would like to have heard that. Did he tell you why?"

"In part."

He looked up at her, his eyes narrowed as he met her steady gaze. After a moment, he drew a deep breath and let it out slowly. "I must be grateful to him then."

She took a step toward him, reaching out, though not quite touching him. "If that's so, then couldn't this sense-less duel be stopped? You were the injured party, couldn't you—"

"No. I can condone what you did, but not his part in it. Robert betrayed a trust. He did it in full recognition of what it would mean, and if left alone, will continue on the same course. I cannot allow that."

"Please. Please don't go on with it. I—I will do anything you ask."

A twisted smile tugged the corner of his mouth. "Out of fear for his safety or mine? Or need I ask?"

"For both. Because whatever happens will be on my conscience." It was the truth, she found, as the words left her lips. She touched his arm then, her brown eyes dark with appeal.

He lifted his hand to her cheek, his face softening as he brushed its smoothness with one knuckle. "How very beautiful you are; the ideal of most men: charming, industrious, passionate, incredibly sweet. Almost, I could be tempted."

She waited, her breathing suspended. How she would do what she had promised, how she would live with herself after, she did not know; still she did not shrink from him.

He let his hand fall. "But to have you as my wife, adorning my home, gracing my table, if not my bed, is all I can ask of you, all I will ever ask."

Chapter 11

The Morney house was in the classical style: a Greek temple built in a square with columns on four sides supporting the roof that protected a lower gallery, though there was none at the second-floor level. Less than two years old, it was, by the standards of St. Martinville, a trifle pretentious, a bit nouveau riche. No one allowed such a judgment to stand in the way of accepting the hospitality of the Monsieur Morney, however. Their host was an excellent man, with good taste in wine and the discrimination to prefer living in town and seeing after his holdings along the Teche to keeping greater state on lands he owned on the Mississippi River. He had a plump, laughing wife who set a sumptuous table and who had presented him with a living proof of her affection every other year of the twenty-four they had been married. As a result, the couple had two sons and three daughters of marriageable age, and were unstinting in their arrangement of entertainment for them and their friends.

The house was three stories in height, the third floor being an open room with a polished floor, wainscoted walls hung with mirrors, and arched windows that could be opened wide for air. This enormous room was officially designated as the ballroom. For all its elegance, however, its location was not the best. At this time of year, the heat rose from the lower floors, lingering after the sun had gone down. On this evening, the resulting warmth, combined with that of nearly two hundred active guests, was such that every lady not taking part in the dancing was vigorously plying her fan, and the gentlemen, encased in close-fitting coats, were seen surreptitiously wiping their faces with their handkerchiefs.

The crowd thronging the room included not only young people, but every age group—from the recently married to grandparents. A cardroom had been set up in what was normally a back sitting room downstairs, and a number of gentlemen and older ladies had gravitated toward it. There was a constant coming and going up and down the great curving staircase that was a feature of the main hall, mainly to the pair of guest bedchambers with attached sitting rooms, which had been designated as retiring rooms, one for the ladies and one for the gentlemen.

The musicians in a corner, hidden by ferns on stands, played with a will. The punch, cooled by tinkling chunks of ice brought in at no small expense by steamboat, was popular. The candles in the chandeliers with their tinkling lusters and ropes of crystal beads added to the heat, wavering in the vagrant draft from the windows and the air stirred by the exertions of the dancers. The bouquets of roses and cape jasmine wafted fragrance in the warmth, competing with the perfumes of the ladies. Silken gowns of soft pastel tones gleamed in gentle contrast to the unrelieved black of the evening attire of the men. In one corner stood their host with Père Jan and one of the itinerant priests who made calls about the parish. The murmur of voices and the ripples of laughter vied with the strains of a waltz. Despite the closeness of the night, everything was colorful and bright, and everyone seemed in high spirits and determined to have a good time.

Amalie, sitting to one side, alone for the moment, wondered if all was as it seemed, or if those who swung with such carefree abandon about the floor were just better than she at hiding their misery. Did they each hold their secrets and fears, and smile in spite of them?

Were there fornicators and adulterers among the crowd? It was indeed likely, though few would be women like herself. Females were so hemmed around with servants, with the conventions that said they must never be alone with a man not a close relative, never venture out of their homes without the protection of a male, that few opportunities presented themselves. It was easier for a man. Illicit love was, to an extent, even encouraged in unmarried males so as to preserve the ladies from their ungoverned desires. Afterward, there were opportunities in plenty for them and many wives who preferred that they look elsewhere in order to prevent in some measure the constant round of pregnancy.

And yet, women had desires, too, Amalie had discovered. Perhaps it was wise to hedge them around with restraints, as long as such a premium was put on their chastity. The purpose, of course, was to protect the sanctity of the male bloodline, to insure that a man did not give his name to a child not his own. How much easier, and more reasonable, it would be to trace the descent through the female line. It would make no difference, then, whose child a woman carried.

She came to her feet as if propelled then, glancing around self-consciously, strolled around the edge of the dance floor. She had danced a polka and a waltz with Julien earlier. He had brought her punch and left her with M'mere. A short time later, the elderly Oudry sisters had sought out her mother-in-law, taking her off with them to the cardroom. George had come by in search of Chloe and, seeing her on the floor in the arms of a dashing, mustachioed Creole youth, had begged Amalie to honor him. He had steered her carefully through a gavotte before hurrying off to overtake Chloe as she left the floor.

They seemed to have made up their differences, for they were now going down the room in a reel. Chloe was laughing as she clung to George, nearly oversetting him with her exuberance. The Englishman, suffering more than the others since he was not used to the climate, was perspiring so heavily that he held his handkerchief in the hand that was at Chloe's waist to keep from staining the silk of her gown.

The music ground to a halt. Chloe spread her fan to wave it before her partner's face as they moved toward the punch bowl. Watching them, Amalie smiled a little. It was a shame that Julien could not see how well matched they were as a couple. "May I have this dance?"

She swung to find Robert at her elbow. She summoned common sense, trying to ignore the accelerated beat of her heart. "I'm not sure it would be wise."

"Nothing between us has been wise. Why begin to count the cost now?"

"Because we are not the only ones who will pay."

"Very true," he said, a wry smile rising to his eyes. "Shall I stand here and talk to you or take myself away?"

Amalie had seen already a number of oblique glances cast in their direction. There could be little doubt that it would be best if he moved on, perhaps to ask some unattached female to take the floor with him. She could not, somehow, bring herself to suggest it. "As you prefer."

"I prefer to dance with you. It's such a perfect excuse for holding you in my arms." Before she could protest, he had encircled her waist with his arm and whirled her out onto the floor to the opening strains of a waltz.

They moved together in perfect naturalness, two halves of a whole; dipping and gliding, he guiding, she responding. It was as if their bodies kept time to a different rhythm, one more elemental. His eyes were cobalt as he caught her brown gaze, holding it as they circled the floor. Her skirts swirled around them, brushing his trousers, wrapping around his legs in silken intimacy. The correct distance separated them; her fingers lay lightly in his, held at the proper angle, and his hand barely touched the corseted turn of her waist, yet it was as if their bodies were entwined, merged. Other couples pressed around them, the skirts of the women softly clashing in the turns, but they might have been alone.

There was a curious ecstasy in this public portrayal of a private ritual. It affected Amalie with languor, with a need to press closer that was so intense that the effort to refrain left her giddy and disoriented. His nearness, his touch, were reminders of other places, other times. The expression in his eyes was seductive in its assurance and lack of reserve. She swayed toward him, the shadows banished from her eyes, her lips moist and parted.

Still, there was a part of her mind that found his disregard of the consequences of what they were doing, of what would take place on the morrow, disturbing. She could not prevent herself from wondering if he wanted everyone to know of their affair, if such it could be called. She had to ask herself if perhaps he had wanted them to be seen that day beside the bayou. Could he face his dawn appointment with such composure because he had no fear or because he was certain of the outcome?

She did not like the tenor of her thoughts. Their cause was not hard to find, however. By the manner of his approach to her bed, he had made it difficult for her to put her trust in him. He seemed capable of anything in her mind and therefore was suspect. It was unfortunate, but it was something she could not help.

The music seemed to go on forever. Amalie, torn by the conflicting emotions, felt the beginning of a headache behind her eyes. It had been threatening all afternoon, but now it began to make itself felt. She frowned a little.

"Is something wrong?" Robert asked, his tone laced with concern.

"I wish I could go home now."

"So do I wish it, with me," came his swift answer.

"I'm serious."

"You think I'm not?"

"I'm never quite certain, with you," she said, searching his face.

An arrested look came over his features, but before he could speak, the music swung to an end. They were joined at once by Chloe, who came barreling down upon Amalie, taking her arm.

"I must talk to you a moment," the girl said, her gaze troubled. "Come with me to the retiring room, if you will."

Amalie allowed herself to be borne away with only a quick backward glance for Robert. He was staring after her, she saw, before she turned to prevent Chloe from dragging her into the path of a servant collecting punch glasses. She slanted a quick glance or two at the girl as they descended the stairs, but could tell little from her tight-lipped expression. She could guess what had upset her; doubtless it was some news of the duel. What she could not know was how much Chloe had been told.

There was a pair of matronly women in the sitting room when they entered. They made no haste to depart, but leaned by turns over the mirror that hung above a marble-topped empire table, talking of ways to prevent their husbands from snoring and the trials of the change of life. When they had finally trailed away, fanning themselves and pressing handkerchiefs to their upper lips, Chloe checked to be certain that no one was in the connecting bedchamber, then came back to face Amalie.

"I was never so near swooning in my life, a real swoon, as when I heard just now of this duel between Julien and Robert. It is a great lie, I know. It must be. Tell me that is what it is."

Amalie glanced at the girl's agitated face, then looked away past her shoulder. "M'mere did not tell you of it?"

Chloe turned away, sinking into the nearest chair. "You—you mean it's true?"

"I'm afraid so."

"Why was I not told? Why am I treated like an ignorant child who is never consulted?"

"I can't say. Perhaps M'mere did not want to upset you."

"Upset me! What if one of them is killed? I would have had no warning, no hint of such a thing."

"Please, don't."

"Don't. It can happen if they meet! But they must not. They must be stopped."

"Has there ever been a way to stop two men bent on a duel?" Amalie's tone was shaded with bitterness. She moved away to where a window stood open to the night. From above could be heard the music of the ball and the faint shuffle of the footsteps of the dancers.

"Ah, Amalie, you don't understand. They are like brothers."

"Those who have been close know best how to hurt each other and so find forgiveness harder."

"What do I care if they forgive, so long as they aren't killed! It is M'mere I am thinking of. If either is harmed, she may never recover from the blow."

Amalie reached up to rub at the pain between her eyes with the tips of her fingers. "You may be right."

"If the cause was known, it might be possible to do something." There was a tentative sound in Chloe's voice and, as Amalie turned to look at her, her black gaze was intent.

"Did your informant not venture a guess?"

"I was not informed; I only overheard someone talking and the moment they saw me, they changed the subject. Though from the way they sounded, I doubt they knew."

"Then you will have to ask M'mere."

The girl's eyes narrowed. "I have this feeling, Amalie,

that you could tell me, if you would."

"Why should you think so?"

"I'm not sure," Chloe answered slowly, "It's just a feeling."

There was no time for more as a laughing group of girls swept in, chattering and exclaiming, filling the room with their wide skirts. To Amalie's relief, they hailed Chloe and swept her away into the bedchamber with them. Taking advantage of the opportunity, she made her escape.

All the chairs near the windows in the ballroom were taken. The only ones that were left were those in the corners where the air scarcely moved. George, catching sight of Amalie as she took a seat, came to stand talking to her for a time, offering to bring her a glass of punch. The beverage was wet and cool, but much too sweet. It did nothing for her headache and made her feel a little ill after a few moments. When George deserted her as Chloe reappeared, Amalie sat holding the cup in her hand for a time, then gave it to the small maid who came around with a silver tray.

A pair of young married women came to sit near her. Their voices were carrying over the music as they talked of recipes, the sicknesses of children, and the ills of being *enceinte* during the summer months. They spoke of the advisability of traveling while in that interesting condition, weighing the benefits of being at a watering place during the fever season against the possibility of causing a miscarriage.

Amalie, with a particular interest in the subject of their conversation, listened without appearing to, languidly plying her fan. The two women, with relatives in New

Iberia, just down the bayou, soon turned to rather desultory gossip, however. They were considering going to Île Dernière for the summer, primarily because it was rumored that one of the better-known young women of their acquaintance was going. She was Frances Prewett, the daughter of Mrs. Moore who owned several thousand acres in the vicinity and who had originally been married to a Weeks, though was now widowed for the second time. Only a year older than Amalie, Frances had also been married and widowed twice. She was apparently living at the family home, the Shadows, with her two children, a boy and a girl, from her first marriage to a Mr. Magill. Though still clinging to her black clothing, she was beginning to take an interest in getting out again. An extremely attractive young woman with excellent prospects, it was likely, or so thought her friends, that she would marry again, if only to give her two youngsters a father.

Widows. The subject was a reminder of how constant death was in this part of the country, of how easily it could come to snatch away loved ones. It was not something Amalie wanted to dwell upon, not now, with Julien and Robert pledged to meet in the morning. She got to her feet, moving aimlessly, the ache in her head so intense that her vision was not too clear. When Robert came toward her, she halted, putting out her hand to him in distress.

"What is it?" he asked, his voice low as he caught her hand, searching her face.

"Could you take me home? My head is pounding and I haven't seen Julien in ages."

"Nor have I seen him. I will take you, of course. Let me find M'mere."

He was back in a moment. His aunt did not think Amalie should go, but if it was truly necessary, then she herself and Chloe as well, would stay for the sake of appearances. It must not be said that they were all routed.

M'mere did not mean to be unkind, Amalie told herself as she lay back against the carriage seat. The evening had been a strain for her also, perhaps more so since Julien was her only child. Still, Amalie felt like a coward, even knowing that matters would not have been helped if she had stayed to be exceedingly ill.

The night air was blessedly fresh and cool. Robert's presence beside her in the dimly lighted carriage was comforting, though he did not try to talk. She was glad that he did not press himself upon her. Such conduct was inappropriate, somehow, even if she had been able to respond. She slanted him a quick glance as the carriage rumbled along. He seemed rather remote, as if his thoughts were elsewhere. It came to her that this was the way they might have ridden together if there had been nothing between them, if he had been no more than the cousin of her husband.

How much better it would have been if it was so. Or would it? She did not know. Her head was pounding too violently for her to decide.

At Belle Grove, Robert got out and helped her down. Charles, who had been waiting up for them, opened the downstairs front door as they approached the house. Robert bade him send Lally to Amalie, then kept his hand under her elbow as she climbed the stairs.

At the top, he paused. "I won't come in with you since I have to take the carriage back for M'mere and Chloe."

"Yes, it was kind of you to see me this far."

"Kind?" His tone was amused. "I was grateful for the opportunity. I only wish you had not had to be ill to give it to me."

He had taken her hand, holding it in his hard fingers. Behind them, a lamp burned in the salon. It threw its yellow shafts of light out onto the gallery floor. The glow was reflected in Robert's eyes, giving them an odd sheen. Amalie did not pretend to misunderstand them. "Is there no way this duel can be stopped?"

"Not if Julien doesn't wish it."

"It's so stupid," she said fiercely.

"I agree, but, as you know, the choice was not mine."

"You could have ignored his insults."

"True, but then there is the fact that I do owe him some reparation."

"That's stupid!"

He gave a low laugh. "I suppose it is, and also a bit unusual. I was to seduce his wife; that much was agreed upon. If it had stopped there, it would have been all right. What he objects to is the tampering with your affections."

"I rather thought it was the public display."

"That, too, but the main thing was that I failed to allow you to go on thinking that he was your lover as well as your husband. For all his resentment of the subterfuge, it was important to him to have you think just that."

"He is so proud," she said, her voice quiet.

When he did not answer, she looked up at him, realizing that the same words applied to Robert Farnum as well. He was watching her, his blue eyes black in the uncertain light.

"If I don't come back," he began.

"Please! Don't say a thing like that."

"I only wanted to tell you that, regardless of how I should feel, I regret nothing."

"Oh, Robert."

"I don't expect you to say the same, but I will take a kiss with me to remember."

He caught her to him, his eyes searching hers before he lowered his mouth to take her lips. She yielded, moving against him, savoring the hard, sweet pressure as if she would never know it again, needing its sting as an antidote against the pain that was suddenly like an open wound inside of her. Her breasts ached as they were flattened against the hardness of his chest. In her throat was the salty taste of tears. Her hands clenched on the collar of his coat.

He stepped back, his breathing hard. He inclined his head, turned, then went quickly down the stairs. Behind Amalie, Lally came to the door of the sitting room, pushing it open.

"Is everything all right, Mam'zelle Amalie?" she asked, her tone soft.

"No," she answered. "It hasn't been in some time, and never will be again."

If Amalie had not known there on the gallery that she was in love with Robert, then she would have known it by the dawn of the next day. She slept little, going over and over the things that had happened since she had come to Belle Grove, gathering together bits and pieces—things she had seen, a glance, a smile, a word, fragments of things she had heard. There was so much, and yet so little, that had concerned Robert, so very little.

How had it come about that she had drawn so close to

this man of American blood? The act of merging their two bodies in the dark was not enough to make it so. She admired his concern for M'mere, his constant attention to the needs of the plantation, his attitude toward those who worked under him. He had saved her from injury, taken her part against Patrick Dye, and even, at times, against Julien. But it was more than that. It was something in the man himself, an integrity, a sense of excitement, of strength; but it was also an elemental attraction that had no cause.

She should think of him with scorn, but she could not. His face filled her thoughts, and it seemed impossible that she could ever have thought the man who had made love to her was any other. The thought that he would never do so again, no matter what the outcome of this duel, was a bitterness inside her. If there was a minor shedding of blood, some small injury to satisfy honor, then Julien would see to it that Robert never came near her again. If Robert killed Julien, then he might well be in trouble with the law, but more important, she did not think she could bring herself to ever wed him, even if he should ask it. Of the other possibility, that Julien would kill Robert, she tried not to think.

She heard M'mere and Chloe when they returned, but there had not been a sound from Julien's bedchamber. Her headache receded somewhat, but did not go away. Finally, sometime in the small hours of the morning, she took a few more drops of the laudanum she had had earlier and slept at last.

She came awake with a start. Her heart was beating fast and she felt a fearful certainty that she had missed some important appointment. Beyond the rose draperies at the windows, the day was dawning, golden-edged, as the sun began to rise. The duel. It must be over.

She swung from the bed without ringing for Lally. The maid must have been listening for some sound from her, however, for she appeared as Amalie was getting into her petticoats.

Amalie looked up at her. "Is there any word?"

"No, mam'zelle. What shall you wear? The muslin with the dots or the striped pink?"

"Anything, it doesn't matter," Amalie said impatiently as she stepped into her slippers.

Dressed finally in the dotted muslin, she swept from her room into the salon in a swirl of skirts. She spared a quick smile for Isa who crouched beside her door with a pad of paper and a pencil on his knee, then moved toward the settee where Chloe sat huddled in a corner in her dressing gown. M'mere was standing at the open front door, staring out over the bayou, while from the back loggia Charles appeared with a coffee tray.

Amalie looked at Chloe, who shook her head. The girl's eyes were red-rimmed from sleeplessness and her hair straggled down her back. As she made no move toward the tray the butler had placed on a side table, Amalie stepped to it and poured, handing her a steaming cup. She glanced at M'mere, then poured out another cup and, with it in her hand, moved to stand beside the older woman.

Her mother-in-law was telling her rosary of jet beads and silver. She stood for a long moment, her lips moving, then sighed, crossed herself, and put the rosary away in the pocket of her voluminous skirt. She accepted the coffee Amalie offered with a wan smile.

Amalie longed to be able to comfort her, but what was there to say? She could think of nothing that was not trite and most likely untrue. She knew that for her own desolation there were no words that would help, and so she said nothing, only standing quietly beside the other woman, staring out at the oaks and the new shrubbery, at the silently moving waters of the bayou.

There was a movement beside her and she looked down to see Isa carefully holding out her own coffee. She thanked him with a smile and a touch on his shoulder, and he went back to sit against the wall. For long moments there was no sound except the clink of china cups on saucers, the soft scratch of a drawing pencil, and the calls of the birds in the trees beyond the gallery.

The grating of footsteps on the lower gallery came to them. The sound echoed on the treads of the stairs. It was possible that the victor in the contest had cut across the fields from the main road instead of coming along the drive on his way from the meeting place in a field of oaks nearer to town. Amalie put down her cup and moved forward in time to see the top of a man's head appear as he mounted to the second floor.

"George," she said, the word a near gasp. Behind her, Chloe gave a quick exclamation, setting her cup down with a crash as her other hand went to her disordered hair. Jumping to her feet and drawing her wrapper around her, she whisked herself from the room as the Englishman stepped over the threshold.

He looked around as if expecting to find at least one of the duelists there. When he did not, he lowered his voice to the timbre reserved for funerals and asked, "Any news?"

Amalie shook her head in the same way that Chloe had done earlier. For something to do, as much as because hospitality demanded it, she sat down and poured out coffee for George, handing it to him. He stood with it balanced uncomfortably in his hand until M'mere, seeing his dilemma, moved to seat herself so that he could do the same.

They talked in stilted phrases. Chloe returned, having made herself presentable. Charles brought more coffee and a platter of buttered brioches. They all took one of the latter and sat fingering it on their plates, with the exception of George, who ate two and reached for another before he noticed the look of reproach that Chloe cast in his direction.

At the sound of hooves on the drive, they went still. The horse was moving quickly. They heard the jingle of the bridle as it was pulled to a halt. Amalie looked at M'mere, but she was staring straight ahead, her face whiter than the lace of the cap tied under her chin. Chloe reached for George's hand. Amalie clasped her own in her lap, turning her gaze to the opening door.

The footsteps on the stairs were firm and quick; the tread across the gallery floor the same. The figure of a man filled the doorway. He carried his hat and his crop in his hand and there was a frown on his face.

Chloe gave a stifled cry. M'mere closed her eyes. Amalie came slowly to her feet.

Robert stepped into the room. His voice grim, he asked, "Where is Julien?"

Chapter 12

It was Amalie who broke the silence. "What do you mean?"

"I mean," Robert said, his features stern, "that Julien did not appear on the dueling field."

M'mere sat with her hands clasped on the arms of her chair. Chloe jumped up as she exclaimed, "Impossible!"

"It's perfectly true." Robert's answer was as hard as it was short.

"What can it mean?"

George had risen as the ladies had. Frowning, he said in his ponderous way, "It's as plain as can be. He has forfeited, admitted that he was at fault."

Chloe turned on him. "There are other ways he could have done the same thing without branding himself a coward! He could have spoken to Robert or fired into the air."

"Couldn't have spoken this morning," George answered, pursing his lips. "An apology on the field just isn't done. He could have deloped, fired skyward, of course, as you say, if he had wanted to give his man a chance to put a hole through him."

"And that is just what he would have done! I do not always agree with Julien, but I know well enough that he would never run away."

Ignoring their exchange, Amalie said, "We all took it for granted that he had gone to meet you. Since he did not, it may be that he overslept, that he is still in his room. Perhaps he is even ill?"

"My own conclusion," Robert agreed and swung to stride across the room, pushing into Amalie's bedchamber. He crossed it without a glance and thrust open the sliding doors that led into Julien's room.

It was dim and quiet, with draperies still drawn. The four-poster stood with a smooth counterpane and the bolster in place beneath the pillows in their embroidered shams. It was too early for the maids to have straightened the room. The bed had not been slept in.

They had all trailed along behind Robert. They stood staring about the room, except for M'mere, who moved to the head of the bed where she put out her hand, smoothing one of the pillows. Chloe, looking around in bewilderment, said, "Where can he be?"

"An excellent question." Robert swung toward Amalie. "Where is Tige? He may have some idea."

They rang for the valet and he came hurrying to the house from the kitchen. He turned gray under the brown of his skin at the sight of M'sieu Robert awaiting him in the salon, but stood waiting to learn why he had been summoned. At the question of the whereabouts of his master, he looked blank.

"I don't know, m'sieu. You did not—that is to say, he is not injured?"

"Not by my hand," came Robert's grim answer. "He said nothing about not returning last night?"

"No, m'sieu. He said to me that I am not to wait up for him, but that is all. He often tells me this."

"Does he often not come home at all?"

"Sometimes, m'sieu."

"Did you have any idea that he might not put in an

appearance on the dueling field this morning?"

"Not appear? But, no, m'sieu!" the valet said, his eyes mirroring his shocked amazement. "He would not have done such a thing."

"My thought exactly," Chloe declared.

"On the occasions when he stayed late in town," Robert said, "do you have any idea where he might have passed the time?"

Tige glanced at Amalie. "Not since his marriage, m'sieu."

Amalie had allowed Robert to conduct the interrogation, as they all had, but now she stepped forward. "Am I to understand that Julien did not return with the rest of you last night?"

"He did not," Robert said.

"I heard nothing to indicate that he came in later, but if he did, if he got back too late to rest before riding out again at dawn, then his dueling pistols should be gone." She turned to the valet. "Tige, are they in his room?"

It took a moment to check. When the valet returned, he inclined his head. "Yes, mam'zelle."

Julien had left the house the night before for the ball. He had disappeared from the festivities early and had not been seen since. His bed had not been slept in, no clothing was missing from his armoire other than the evening wear he had worn, and his dueling pistols were in their mahogany case in the cabinet where they were always kept. He had failed to keep an appointment on the field of honor, failed to send word either to his opponent or to his family. There could be only one explanation; he had been prevented in some way. Nothing else, given Julien's nature, made sense.

Tige was dismissed. Those left in the salon looked at each other. M'mere spoke, a slight quaver in her voice. "An accident, perhaps?"

"Yes," Chloe cried, "that must be it."

Robert shook his head, frowning. "Julien is well known. There could be no question of who he was, in that case, even if he could not tell them. A message would have been sent here."

"Unless," Amalie said, "The accident has not yet been discovered. He was riding last evening, as you were. He might have been thrown and is lying somewhere."

"There have been a number of robberies lately of travelers and men who venture into the wrong kind of taverns and inns," Chloe added.

"Yes." Robert's tone was repressive as his glance touched M'mere, who sat so pale and still in her chair. He looked then to Amalie, and in the blue depths of his eyes there was a bleak, haunted expression before he shielded it with his lashes. "The first step will be to retrace our route into town, then make inquiries there. I'll do that at once."

"If you don't mind the company," George spoke up, "I would like to come with you."

"Two of us might cover more territory," Robert agreed.

They left within the hour. Watching them ride away, Amalie thought that times like these were when it was hardest to be a woman. How she longed to be doing something—asking questions of people, scouring the countryside—anything except sitting in one place and waiting for someone to find out for her the thing she most wanted to know. It would have been thought shameless for her to have ridden with Robert and George. Though they had not said so, she knew they would scour every low tavern and gambling den in the area; for her to have gone into such places would have been a shocking thing, proof that she was without the tender sensibilities expected in a lady.

In truth, she was not sure she had such sensibilities. She should have been prostrate with the blow of discovering that her husband was missing. Instead, she was restless, consumed by the need to go and look for him. It was fear that drove her, fear for the safety of a man for whom she had come to feel a fondness, but, more than that, it was guilt. She could not help wondering how much her affair with Robert had to do with her husband's disappearance. She thought, from the look she had seen in Robert's eyes, that he felt the same.

It was almost eleven in the evening when the two men returned. No one had gone to bed, though Chloe and Amalie had tried to persuade M'mere that it would be best for her to retire. The older woman had sat up, telling her beads and saying little. She seemed to have shrunk, her eyes sinking back into her head.

The look on the faces of the two men was enough to tell them that they had been unsuccessful. Charles relieved them of their hats at the door, lingering as they moved into the salon. Isa, sitting at Amalie's feet, stopped drawing to look up.

"Nothing," Robert said as he advanced into the room and threw himself down on a settee.

"We thought—that is, we hoped that he might have returned while we were gone," George added. He went to draw up a chair beside Chloe, giving her a weary smile as she placed her hand on his arm.

"You looked at—"

"We looked everywhere," Robert interrupted, his tone grating with exhausted patience.

St. Martinville was not a large town, holding less than four hundred people, with a few hundred more scattered up and down the bayou. The number of places Julien could be were limited.

"The drinking houses?" Chloe persisted.

"Yes. He had been seen at a place on the other side of town, near the bayou. That was the only trace we found."

"It's as if he just disappeared," George said.

"His mount?" Chloe turned to the Englishman.

"Now that was an odd thing. It was found outside the livery stable at Broussard's hotel. Whether it was brought there or whether it found its way there because it was often stabled there, no one could say."

Robert sat up, directing his hard gaze toward his aunt, who was staring at George. "If he isn't home by morning, I think we should call in the sheriff."

"No," M'mere said, the word sharp and uncompromising.

In common with most of the planters along the bayou, she had little use for the minions of the law, except to prevent the influx of undesirables into the area, something they had been failing to do of late. Too far from town for active protection, the plantation owners always armed themselves. There were patrols that most men supported, taking turns riding out at night. It was popularly reported in the Northern press that these were solely to apprehend runaways and to suppress public meetings of slaves, and this was done as a means of preventing uprisings, but the patrols afforded many other types of protection. There was a general feeling among many, left over from the area's frontier days, that it was best to shoot at the first sight of suspicious activity and to ask questions afterward. Any interference in this basic principle of defense was fiercely resented. Most attempts by the representatives of the law to help were not appreciated, being considered bungling, if not downright dangerous. The result was self-reliance, but also an aristocratic attitude of being above the law.

"Be reasonable, Tante Sophia. A thorough search up and down the bayou must be made and a great many more questions asked. The first can't be done by two men alone and the second needs greater authority than we possess."

"We can send out the hands, everybody from the quarters. As for the questions, what good will they do? If anyone knew where Julien was, don't you think they would send someone to tell us? And if there is some reason why they will not let us know, then why should they tell the sheriff any sooner."

Robert looked at Amalie. She held his blue glance of appeal for a moment, then rose and went to kneel at her mother-in-law's chair. "Please, M'mere, it must be done. Every moment that passes may mean there is less chance of finding Julien alive. If the sheriff and his men can help, if they can call out a larger search party, then we must let them."

What she did not say, though it lingered at the back of everyone's mind, was that the sheriff could also organize a party to drag the bayou. It was not unknown for a missing man to be recovered from the muddy, slow-moving stream.

"Julien will return," the old lady said, setting her trembling lips. "There is no need for all this fuss."

"We can't be sure of that."

"Think, *chère,* of the great noise everyone will make. The whispers of the duel will become shouts. Everyone will be speculating about us, about the reasons for the meeting. It will be a tremendous, terrible scandal."

Amalie held the thin hands of the older woman. "That may be, but we can't remain silent about Julien's disappearance because of what people will say."

"It may be that he went away. It may be that he did not want to meet Robert and that he did not trust himself to tell him so without becoming angry again. Tomorrow, or the next day, there will be a letter saying where he is, telling us not to worry so."

"Surely he would have told someone before he left— you, me, or at least Tige so that he could pack a bag? He did not do that. He took nothing."

M'mere turned her head from side to side, a low moaning in her throat as tears gathered in her eyes and ran down the lined crêpe of her face. "I don't know, I don't know. Ah, Julien, my son, my son. How can I bear it? How can I?"

It was impossible to press her. The best that they could hope for was that with the morning she would be calmer, more amenable.

Dawn came. Julien's mother did not rise from her bed, nor would she see anyone. She sent her maid Pauline to say that she felt too ill to speak of it and to beg their understanding. Robert swore under his breath, but rode out again with George.

It was the following morning that Lally tapped on the door of Amalie's room. She entered with a coffee tray in her hand, and Isa tagging along behind her.

"*Au café,*" she said, the words serious.

Amalie sat up, pushing her hair behind her shoulders and reaching for her dressing gown. A glance toward the window told her that it was only a little past first light. M'mere always had coffee in bed, as had Julien and Chloe, but Amalie had never gotten into the habit. "To what do I owe this pleasure?"

"I must speak to mam'zelle." The maid set the tray on the bedstand, then poured the coffee from one of the two small silver pots, adding hot milk from the other. She spread a cream-colored linen napkin over Amalie's lap, then carefully handed the cup to her. As Amalie took it, the girl moved to the foot of the bed and folded her hands.

"What is it?" Amalie sipped without taking her gaze from Lally's face.

"It's that Tige. He was sore in his mind about M'sieu Julien. He went to town last night to see what he could find out."

"Without a pass?" Amalie asked, her voice sharp. It could be dangerous for a slave discovered without a piece of paper stating that he was on business for his master. The patrols were not inclined to view clandestine activities lightly.

"He was most careful. But he discovered, him, that M'sieu Julien was at this drinking house that is run by the free man of color, Mulatto Bonhomme. This man is his old uncle, for the mulatto bought his freedom, then make money to buy the freedom of the sister of Tige's mother before he marry her."

"I see."

"Yes. M'sieu Julien goes there often, for he likes Tige's uncle, and because he is most accommodating. It is here that he meets once more the two men."

"Two men?" Amalie asked in sharp tones. "What two men?"

"It was the two men who came from the ship. Hard men, rough men."

"The ship?"

"The men sent to watch over the flower bushes from far-away, the men who were to unload the heavy pots, though they let our people from the quarters do it."

Amalie sat up straighter, her coffee forgotten. "Did Tige speak to these men?"

"*Mais non*, mam'zelle. They have gone. No one has seen them since the night of the Morneys' ball."

"Back to New Orleans, that's where they must have gone," Amalie said, almost to herself. "It may mean nothing, but at least it's a possibility. If only we could find them, but we don't even know what they look like, except for M'mere and George." M'mere could not be depended on, she was in such distress, and George was so wrapped up in his precious plants at the time that she doubted that he remembered them at all.

"I saw them, *petite maîtresse*."

It was Isa. He stepped to the side of the bed and, from behind his back, brought out a roll of drawing paper. He extended it to her and, as she took it, bent his head in such a fine imitation of Julien's slight, graceful bow that she had to clear her throat before she could thank him.

She unrolled the paper and there before her were the two men. They were under a tree, one sitting on the ground with his back against it, the other leaning beside him. They wore no coats and their striped jerseys were rolled to their elbows. The galluses that held up their trousers were twisted and curled at the edges from saltwater. One was bare-headed, with curling hair that merged with a bushy beard, while the other wore a cap pulled low over his forehead, as if to disguise the cast of one of his eyes.

Amalie looked up, smiling at the boy who waited. "This is wonderful, Isa, truly marvelous. I must show it to M'sieu Robert. Bring me a pen and paper and I will write to him at once."

Her note was delivered within the hour and Robert arrived not long after she had completed her toilette. She received him on the front gallery, handing the drawing to him at once and telling him what Tige had discovered as he scanned it. He was not impressed.

"Are you suggesting that Julien made bosom friends of those two and went off with them to New Orleans? It won't hold water. In the first place, Julien was not in the habit of associating with common seamen, and in the second, he would never have failed to show himself on the dueling field."

"What if he were forced? What if he was kidnaped and taken away with them?"

"Why haven't we received some notice, a demand for ransom?"

She shook her head, turning to move away from him. "I don't know, but it seems too much of a coincidence to ignore."

"That's all it is, a coincidence."

Possibly, but it was the only shred of an indication of

what might have happened to Julien that they had discovered. It seemed so obvious to her; why couldn't he see it? She had expected him to be as excited as she was, to spring into action. The way he had brushed her news aside was more of a disappointment than she would have believed possible. For an instant it crossed her mind to wonder if he had any real interest in Julien's whereabouts, then she dismissed it.

"If you say so," she answered finally, her tone dull.

His footsteps grated as he stepped toward her. He reached to place his hand on her shoulders. "Amalie, *chérie,* this is hard for you, I know."

"Do you?"

"I can guess. If there is anything I can do—"

She pulled away from him, moving to one side. Without looking at him, she said, "You can find Julien."

He stood watching her for a long moment, then he turned on his heel and walked away, moving to the salon. After a moment, she heard a knock on the door of M'mere's bedchamber, a murmur of voices, and then the closing of the panel behind him.

Amalie went in search of George. The Englishman, when he had heard her out, was inclined to think there might be something in the presence of the two men. That was until he learned that Robert was not of the same mind. He was able, after that, to see all manner of objections. He remembered the seamen well. They had seemed nice-enough chaps, rather hard-bitten, but that was to be expected, wasn't it? They had served their purpose, seeing to it that none of the shrubs had fallen overboard or been damaged by waves, that they were kept shaded and watered. Their job done, they had returned to New Orleans and their ship as ordered, stopping for a drink in town after being paid off as per the agreement for their extra services. Nothing strange about it, really. It was his opinion that she should stop teasing herself to no end and leave the matter to Robert Farnum. That was his best advice for both Chloe and herself.

In her bedchamber, Amalie paced the floor. If Robert's dismissal of her discovery had disappointed her, George's pompous reception of it had been irritating in the extreme. The more she thought of it, the angrier she got. She had not expected to be congratulated for her brilliance; it was, after all, Tige who deserved the credit. Still, she thought there might have been some consideration of the fact that the men had been the last persons to see Julien. Nothing Robert or George had said had convinced her that it was impossible for the men to be involved in the affair. It certainly seemed to her that it was worth a trip to New Orleans to discover what they might know. It would have to be soon if it wasn't to be too late. Their ship would be sailing before very much longer. If she were a man she would go herself. If only she were a man!

She was not and yet . . . Her husband was gone. She was her own mistress. If she decided to go, who was there to gainsay her? It would be thought shocking, of course, a female traveling alone. However, there were those who did sometimes, of necessity; widows and women whose men were in the army. The latter were sometimes seen on the steamboats, going to join their men in the far western outposts. In such cases, a servant or two for protection was thought sufficient.

She had a black gown left, packed away, that she had not discarded after her marriage. It gave her a peculiar feeling to think of donning it now, when she did not know whether Julien was alive or dead. If a person were superstitious, it could be seen as an ill wish. She was not, of course, she assured herself, and went back to her planning.

A mourning bonnet with heavy black veiling, such as those M'mere sometimes wore, would serve to prevent recognition should anyone she might know be traveling on the steamboat. She could board at New Iberia, rather than at St. Martinville, to decrease that likelihood. It would doubtless be better if she stayed in her cabin and kept to herself, at least until they reached the railroad terminus. She would certainly go by rail; it was much faster and that was important. In widow's weeds, she was unlikely to be molested, but Lally's presence would add respectability and Tige could act as her majordomo.

She had no money. The thought brought her to a halt until she remembered that Julien kept a box in the bottom of his armoire where he tossed the proceeds of his gambling. He was consistently lucky, so there should be sufficient money for the journey.

The worst thing would be the worry to M'mere, but the older woman would only try to stop her if she were told. Nor did Amalie think it wise to inform her just yet of the two men seen with Julien; time enough for that when more was known. She would leave a note in her room explaining, promising to return as soon as possible.

Robert would be angry, even furious. It could not be helped. If he had not wanted her to go, he should have taken the time to look into the matter himself. Besides, having had access to her bed did not give him the right to censure her behavior.

It was easy. Sitting on the train as it hissed and puffed itself away from Bayou Boeuf on its run toward New Orleans Amalie allowed herself to relax for the first time. Leaving the house in the dawn hours dressed in her widow's black, walking to the stables to climb into the carriage instead of chancing waking the others by having it brought around to the front, and boarding the steamboat with Tige going before to make the arrangements and Lally trailing behind with her single portmanteau had been without complications. The hardest part had been leaving Isa behind. Awakened by her early stirring, he had not wanted to believe that she would actually leave him. Wasn't he her page? How would she manage without him? He said nothing of it, but she knew that his greatest disappointment was that he would not see New Orleans. She had felt like an ogre for denying him, especially since she knew it was not the pleasure, but the new experiences, the new sights to record with his pencil, that he craved.

For herself, she was aware of excitement deep inside her. It was caused in part by the satisfaction of doing something instead of sitting around waiting. Still, another part was the thrill of venturing on this journey alone. True, she had Tige and Lally, but they looked to her for direction, not the reverse, and she was accountable to no one. She should not feel like this, not with Julien missing and perhaps being held somewhere, or worse, but she could do nothing about it.

The coach in which she sat was not unlike a large carriage, upon which, in fact, its design was based. The windows had been let down for air, but with it, as the train gathered speed following the curving track, came billows of smoke, the powdering of soot, and an occasional spark. Her veil was helpful in warding off the smoke and ash and was not particularly conspicuous since a number of other women had lowered similar coverings for the same purpose.

Many of the passengers around her had come from Île Dernière. She had watched them getting on: the men rather sunburned, carrying all manner of fishing poles and other sporting gear; the children boisterous and rumpled; the ladies dressed in white and pastels, as was usual with watering places, and in spite of the unsuitability for the journey. From listening to the conversations around her, she understood that they were very nearly all acquainted, a part of the same social round in New Orleans. They had been at the seaside resort for a few weeks, but had decided against staying for the summer because of the mosquitoes and stinging flies. There was a heated debate between a pair of men over whether the presence of the insects was caused by a wind from the wrong quarter or by the various sloughs and ponds of stagnant water on the bay side of the island and the number of straggling animals belonging to the permanent residents. It dwindled away finally without an agreement being reached.

It was fascinating for a time, riding on trestles over the swamps, moving constantly between dry land and stretches of water, watching the turtles slip from their logs and the egrets and cranes rise, flapping, from their perches as the train rumbled past. After a time, however, the clack of the wheels and sway of the coach, combined with her sleepless nights, early rising, and the fanning breeze from the windows, made her drowsy. She closed her eyes.

Whether she slept or not, she didn't know. She was only aware suddenly of a strong sensation of being watched. She opened her eyes, looking around her, her manner as casual as she could make it. Her first thought was of some acquaintance, someone who might believe they had recognized her. She had invented a plausible tale of a cousin dying of a fever and of relatives who would meet the train, thereby giving her countenance. It had seemed necessary to concoct something; so many families were interrelated that a person never knew when a chance-met stranger might turn out to be the connection of a near neighbor. She preferred to be as straightforward as possible, however. She had never been good at deceit.

There was no one paying her any attention. Most of the children had settled down to nap, and many of their fathers had their hats or handkerchiefs over their faces. A woman here and there had succumbed also, though many had taken out needlework or books and periodicals such as *Godey's* and *Harper's* magazine. With a shake of her head, she reached into her own drawstring bag for the embroidery she had brought to relieve the tedium.

It was nearly dark when they reached the station in New Orleans. The twilight rang with shouts and cries and screams of tired children, with the hissing of the engine and the slamming of doors. Amalie, with her portmanteau before her and Lally standing close at her side, stood on the platform. She had sent Tige to find a carriage to take them to the Declouet townhouse. The thought of staying in a hotel, avoiding the gossip of the servants who took care of the house when the family was not in residence, had crossed her mind, but she had decided against it. To put up at a respectable hostelry, such as the St. Charles or the St. Louis, would have taken more money than she cared to spend, but, most of all, would have meant more risk of being recognized. In such a case, the fact that she was not at her own home would have been damning. A lesser hotel or boardinghouse might have been safer in one sense, but was more dangerous to a woman traveling alone.

She had been aware for some time of a man loitering near the door into the station. As the crowd began to disperse, he straightened and moved toward her. He was of medium height, with wide shoulders made wider by the padding in his coat of dark green and a narrow rib cage accented by the high waist of his yellow trousers. His cravat was of green, yellow, and black plaid, his waistcoat of yellow, and his high-crowned hat was shiny black. His face was thin, the upper lip darkened by a narrow mustache, and in his close-set yellow-brown eyes glittered a certain predatory appreciation.

He bowed before her, sweeping the platform with his hat while the cane he held jutted out behind him. "Dear lady," he said, his voice soft and insidious, "is there any way I may be of service to you?"

"Thank you, no," she answered. His hands were long and slim with carefully kept nails. In his cravat was a stickpin in the shape of a die. What he was doing at the station, she had no idea, but she would have wagered a great deal that here before her was a professional gambler.

"Has someone failed to meet you? Most remiss of him, I

do swear. You would not find me so neglectful were you in my keeping."

Her eyes narrowed at the suggestive wording, the elaborate manner that carried its own lash of irony. "Happily," she said in stringent tones, "I am not your concern."

"Can it be that you are suspicious of my overtures? You wound me. My only desire is to make myself useful to you."

"I require nothing. Good evening."

She turned away in dismissal, but he stepped around to face her, placing his hand on her arm. "My carriage awaits. I could take you wherever you wish to go and on the way we could discuss the nice little supper we could share."

Amalie shook him off, looking around, hoping for a sight of Tige. She saw instead a dark carriage waiting at the end of the platform with a driver on the box, undoubtedly the one of which he spoke. Beside her, Lally was staring at the man as if mesmerized. There was something very like a snake about him with his green and yellow coloring, thin features, and insinuating way of speaking.

He caught her wrist. "We could have a most interesting evening. There are many pleasures that you have not sampled, I'll warrant, and may never try now that you are widowed."

"I am not a widow," she said, her tone sharp as she wrenched away from him. "I must ask you to cease annoying me!"

"Ah, forgive me. I saw your ring and your black and there is no man beside you—"

He was moving closer. She said in clear tones, "My manservant will return at any moment."

"Servants," he said with a shrug that was eloquent of the helplessness of such against a determined white man. "He will back away when he sees this."

She watched him twist the head of his cane, pulling it up a scant inch to show her the narrow sword inside the hollow tube.

"A delightful toy for you, I'm sure, but of no interest to me. Will you go away or must I call for help?"

"I think, *chère*," he drawled, staring around the platform that had cleared with amazing speed, "that you have left it too late."

Before she could do more than glance about, he had flung his arm around her waist and was pulling her toward the carriage. Lally screamed. Amalie jerked back away from him, feeling the stitching at the shoulder seam of her gown give. His fingers dug into her side so that she gasped with the pain. She felt herself half lifted, carried. The blood pounded in her ears in the onrush of rage. She kicked at him and heard his grunted curse as her heeled slipper made contact with his shin. She kicked again and felt her foot slip between his legs as he strode toward the carriage. Immediately she hooked her ankle around his knee.

She was thrown forward as he went down. She struck the platform floor with a jar that made her shoulders ache as she caught herself on her palms. She rolled, twisting from him. He grabbed for her once more, his hand closing on her forearm. Across her mind flashed the image of a fight she had once seen between two field hands. In imitation, she drew back her hand and drove the heel of it as hard as she could at the man's nose.

She struck true. The reptilian man gave a screech as

blood poured. Amalie scrambled away from him in a tangle of skirts and got to her feet, backing away with grim satisfaction in her eyes.

The man glared at her above the handkerchief he clamped to his face. "You little bitch," he said thickly. "You are to be congratulated now, but I think you will regret—"

There came the thud of footsteps behind Amalie, slowing as they neared. A deep voice drawled, "I think congratulations will suffice."

"Do you indeed?" The downed man pushed himself up, reaching for his cane as he came erect. The sword blade made a soft, hissing sound as it was drawn.

Amalie called a warning. Only then did she turn to look at the man behind her. The light coming from the station slanted across the bronze planes of his face beneath the hat brim that shadowed his eyes. It was Robert.

He snatched his coat off and whirled it around his wrist. As the other man threw down the useless wooden shaft of the cane, Robert dived for it; rolling out of reach as the sword slashed over his head.

They circled each other then, waiting for an opening. The man in the green coat feinted once, twice; wary, yet in full recognition that he had the upper hand. Amalie, catching a movement at the corner of her eye, saw the Tige had returned. Lally was clinging to him with one hand clapped over her mouth to stifle her cries.

In a sudden flurry of movement, the smaller man lunged. Robert threw up his wrapped arm to deflect the blow, then swung his makeshift cudgel. There was a snapping thud and the sword fell, clattering to the floor. The man stood holding his wrist, the expression on his face one of stunned disbelief. Abruptly he stepped backward, took another step, then whirled and ran, staggering, toward his carriage. He flung himself inside with a shout and the driver whipped up the horse, taking the vehicle careering out of sight.

Robert straightened, turned slowly to Amalie. She stared at him through her black veil as he came toward her. There was suppressed anger in his slow steps, in the way he held the piece of the cane.

"I saw you on the train," he said slowly, "but I couldn't believe it was really you until I met Tige just now. What in the name of hell are you doing here?"

To attack was instinctive. "Are you going to let that man get away?"

"He doesn't matter. I doubt we will be seeing him again. Answer my question."

"What do you think I'm doing here? Meeting Julien? Or maybe bribing his kidnapers to keep him?" It was the scorn for her conduct that she saw in his eyes that drove her, plus the fear that he might in some way blame her for what had just happened.

He looked taken aback for an instant, then his brows came together over his nose. "I never considered either for a moment."

"Then I'll thank you to keep your disapproval to yourself. What I choose to do, where I choose to go, is nothing to do with you!"

"Is that so?" the words were deadly quiet.

"It certainly is. I went to you for help and all I got was a pat on the head. I'm neither a child nor a fool. I know those two seamen had something to do with Julien's disappearance and I intend to find out what it was."

"Masquerading as a widow? Isn't that a bit premature?"

"Widows aren't as likely to be accosted," she flared, then bit her lip.

He jerked a thumb in the direction the carriage had taken. "Someone forgot to tell your friend."

"He wasn't my friend! I never met the man! As for him accosting me, I gave him no encouragement, none!"

A glint of enlightenment appeared in Robert's eyes. "You are young and beautiful and virtually alone. He didn't need encouragement."

She sent him an uncertain glance from under her lashes, all too aware of her relief for his understanding. "I can't imagine what made him think I would go with him."

"He didn't think it, but it seemed too good an opportunity to add to his collection."

"What?"

He smiled into her blank face. "Of women who entertain his friends, those who aren't satisfied with losing their money from his tables."

"You know him?" Her voice was only a thread of sound as she saw his meaning.

"We've met, in a manner of speaking."

She gave a slow nod. "Then I suppose I should be grateful to you for coming when you did."

"I'm not sure it was necessary," he said drily. "In any case, I don't want your gratitude. I never did."

"Good," she said, "because—"

"We can't talk about it here," he said, cutting across her words. He took her arm and turned her toward where Tige and Lally stood with a hired hack waiting beyond. "It will have to wait until we are settled at the townhouse."

"We?" She sent him a startled look.

He lifted a brow, his voice tinged with asperity as he answered. "Oh, yes. We."

Chapter 13

T he light of twelve candles in a pair of silver candelabra gleamed on white-and-gold Old Paris china, coin-silver utensils, and damask linen. It caught the blue sheen in the light brown of Amalie's hair; it glittered on the jet beads that hung from her ears and surrounded the mourning brooch at her throat, while leaving her eyes in mysterious shadow. It flickered on the flat gold studs in Robert's shirtfront and touched his dark lashes as he kept them lowered, his gaze on his fingers as he toyed with his coffee cup. The dining table was long in that large, shadowed room where a silver coffee service shone upon a sideboard and cut-glass decanters sparkled on a side table. In its center was an epergne, its various crystal vases filled with roses and lilies, their scent heavy on the warm air. Amalie sat at the foot of the long table while Robert lounged on her right farther along, with the flowers in front of him.

They had spoken little since leaving the train station. The reason was partially the restraint imposed by the situation in which they found themselves and partially the presence of the servants. The staff left in charge of the Declouet townhouse during the summer had been thrown into an uproar by their arrival. There had been much exclaiming and running here and there to air rooms, heat water for baths, and prepare a meal suited to the *petite maîtresse* and

M'sieu Robert. The activity had not kept them from casting sidelong glances at them, however.

To prevent wild surmises, Robert had told the middle-aged woman who served as housekeeper a portion of the truth. She had gone promptly to a table in the entrance hall where a letter addressed to Julien lay. For an instant, Amalie had felt a surge of hope, but it had only been a note from Chloe, apparently dictated my M'mere, and sent on the chance that Julien might have headed for New Orleans. He had not, for the servants had seen nothing of him and had not heard a word since he had left for his wedding visits with Amalie.

Their dessert dishes were taken away and small glasses of cordial left before them. Lifting his head to catch the eye of the man waiting on the table, Robert made a brief gesture, indicating that they would not need him again. Amalie glanced up, but said nothing. As the man closed the door behind him, she picked up her small glass and sipped at the ruby-red liqueur. Ordinarily it was not served to ladies, but she had felt the need for its stimulating effect.

The silence after the manservant had gone was becoming uncomfortable when Robert broke it. "I didn't ignore your warning about the two seamen," he said, the words abrupt, "it's the reason I'm here."

She sent him a level look. "You don't have to pretend. I'm perfectly willing to admit that I'm glad you followed me."

"I didn't follow you. I was on that train because I took the same steamboat, and I took the same boat because it was the first one going down the Teche after I heard what you had to say. I don't know why I didn't see you embark, but

I didn't, nor did I see you on the trip downriver."

She told him of her ruse of boarding at New Iberia and of keeping to her cabin. Given the circumstances, his presence was reasonable. She was glad of it. She had not liked to think of him behaving in such an underhanded fashion; it gave rise to other, even more disturbing possibilities.

"You might have told me what you meant to do," he commented, his tone neutral.

"You would have tried to stop me," she said, lifting her chin. "Besides, you could have done the same."

"I didn't want to alarm you or M'mere. The fact is, we are chasing only one of the seamen. The other has been found."

"Did he say anything about Julien?" The question was sharp.

"I'm afraid not. The man was dead, found floating in the bayou below the drinking house where he had been seen with Julien."

Her voice was no more than a whisper as she asked, "Dead? How?"

"A blow on the head and a header into the water. The official verdict will be drowning."

"Do you think . . . could it be that Julien—"

"That Julien might have killed him when they tried to take him?" He completed the sentence for her, his tone weary. "It's possible, I suppose. There's no way of knowing."

That was not what she had meant, but she could not bring herself to put the fear into words. She merely nodded, pushing her cordial from her in sudden revulsion. It slopped over the side of the glass, staining the cloth blood-red. Staring at it, she asked in a voice taut with strain, "Where is he? Where can he be?"

"If I knew," Robert said deliberately, "I would be the happiest of men."

She flicked him a quick glance, then looked away again. He had sounded as if he thought she might suspect him of being involved in Julien's disappearance. She didn't, of course, not really. There had been incidences in plenty in the long history of dueling where a man, knowing his opponent to be a superior marksman, had hired thugs to do away with him, but Robert and Julien had been evenly matched. There was also Robert's innate character, which would, she was sure, have scorned such a subterfuge. And yet she would have thought he would never have allowed himself to be persuaded to become her surrogate bridegroom, too.

She moistened her lips. "Now that we are here, what do you intend to do about finding the other man?"

"Go down to the levee where the ship is docked and question the captain of the vessel."

"I have the drawing Isa did."

"There should be no problem as far as the captain is concerned since he will know which men he sent to Belle Grove."

"But if the second man didn't go back to his ship, then—"

"Yes, in that case it should be useful."

It might have been the tone of his voice, reaction from what had happened at the station, or else the news of the death of the seaman, but Amalie was suddenly afraid that they had come on a wild-goose chase. She pushed back her chair and got to her feet. Avoiding his narrowed gaze, she said, "I think I'll go to bed."

"An excellent idea." He stood, draining his glass and setting it on the table before he stepped to join her as she rounded the end.

She sent him a glance from under her lashes as they moved toward the door. He caught it and a smile quirked his mouth as he stood aside, waiting for her to pass through the opening into the hall. She was aware, as she stepped past him with her skirts brushing against his boots, of his dark blue gaze, reserved yet intense, drifting over her. She was glad that she wore the only other gown she had brought with her, a high-necked black crêpe that was brownish-black with long wear and darker in the seams, instead of a more revealing dinner gown. What he had in mind for the night, she was far from certain, and the fact that he knew it did not add to her composure. There were two separate bedchambers made up above stairs. The best thing they could do would be to use them. Whether he would agree was impossible to say.

At the foot of the stairs, she turned. "I will say good night."

"Say anything you please," he answered, his voice quiet, "it will make no difference."

The guttering candlelight falling from the hall chandelier, shining through the brass fixture like an inverted bell, shimmered in the blue-black waves of his hair and wavered across the hard planes of his face. It touched the desire that lay in the depths of his eyes and made it shine. Her uncertainty was at an end. Seeking some shield from her own hunger as much as from his, she said, "Julien—"

"Forget Julien. Where he is, what he is doing, cannot matter to us."

"It seems more of a betrayal somehow." There was a catch in her voice as she spoke.

He reached out to flick her black sleeve. "Don't mourn him yet. Julien is infinitely adaptable. Your scruples, if he knew of them, would make him proud, but would not make him love you."

"He cares for me, in his way. You said it yourself."

Robert sighed, lowering his gaze before he looked up once more. "So he does, but is it the way you want?"

If she said yes with conviction and with compassion, he would leave her to go to bed alone, she was sure of it. She looked at his face, at the sensual molding of his mouth, the jut of his chin, the steady blue fire of his eyes. Her gaze wandered to his shoulders and down to the strong, brown, well-shaped hand that rested on the serpentine coil of the newel post.

She swallowed hard; still, her voice was only a whisper of sound as she answered, "No."

He moved toward her then, the look on his face suspended. He took her hand, placing it on his shoulder as he leaned to slip one arm behind her back and the other under her knees. Her skirts billowed in a froth of springing hoops and petticoats, the extra fullness trailing to the floor as he lifted her high and started up the stairs. She slid her arms around his neck, closing her eyes as she rested her head against the warm side of his jaw. She wanted to protest, knew that she should, but a great lassitude held her in its grasp. His arms were bonds of steel around her; his purpose was steady, as inexorable as his steps as he mounted the stair treads. Her treacherous body recognized his touch and responded to it. How could she resist him?

There was a single lamp burning in the bedchamber that had been prepared for her. The pool of yellow light it cast encompassed the high bed that was turned down for the night with its usual netting in place. Lally started from a stool beside the window as Robert entered. Her eyes widened, then were quickly lowered as she saw her mistress in his arms.

"Bring more candles and lamps, all you can find," Robert said to the girl, "then you can go. And tell Tige that I won't be needing him."

Lally hastened to obey him, slipping from the room. He set Amalie down, but stood with his hands on her forearms as he studied her face. She made no attempt to evade his gaze. A smile began in his eyes and slowly curved his mouth.

The maid slipped back into the room with a lamp in one hand and three candelabra clamped against her chest with the other. She set them down, then left again. She was back in a moment with two more lamps. "Shall I light them, m'sieu?"

"No, I'll do it," he answered over his shoulder.

"Yes, m'sieu," Lally said. With a sidelong glance at Amalie, she bobbed a curtsy and whisked from the room, closing the door behind her.

Amalie watched as Robert moved about, positioning the lamps and candelabra on the various tables of rosewood and mahogany, kindling the wicks by thrusting a candle down the chimney of the burning lamp and moving from one to the other with the flame. Slowly the room, with its jade-green hangings and pale green mosquito baire, brightened until the shadows were gone and the heat from the lamps and candles enveloped them.

Robert replaced the candle he had used in its holder, then turned slowly to face her. His voice quiet, he said, "I have waited a long time for this, dreamed of it both waking and sleeping, of just the two of us, without darkness, without haste."

The deep timbre of his voice was like a caress. The sound, as much as his words, was thrilling, mesmerizing. She stood still watching him, waiting.

The corner of his mouth tugged into a smile and his eyes were cobalt with desire as he held her gaze. Slowly he shrugged from his coat and tossed it onto a slipper chair, then began to tug at the knot of his white silk cravat.

She had never watched a man undress before. Julien had always retreated to his own rooms and Robert had come to her in the dark, except on that day beside the bayou when she had been too close, too involved, to notice or to care how it was accomplished. Now there was a leap in her pulse and she acknowledged a fascination with the process, the slow revelation of his body.

Did he know it? It was possible. He released one end of his cravat and drew it with a silken glide from around the column of his neck. He tossed it toward where his coat lay and did not look when it slithered to the floor. Watching her with a gleam in the depths of his eyes, he slipped the two covered buttons of his pale gray, double-breasted waistcoat from their holes and, with a twist of his shoulders, let it fall down his arms. He flung it toward the chair, then, one by one, began to twist the gold studs from the holes down the front of his shirt.

The lamplight gilded the brown hollow of his throat with its curling black hair at the base and struck tiny gleams from the dark furring lower on his chest. The tips of her fingers tingled with the need to touch, but she clasped them together before her. She drew a deep breath as he removed the last stud, poured those collected in a tinkling shower of gold from his hand onto the bedstand, then pulled the edges of his shirt apart.

His chest was broad and deep, sculpted with muscle and burned by the sun as if he often worked without his shirt in the heat of the day. His paps, like copper coins, were half hidden in the dark triangle of hair that narrowed to a thin line as it skimmed the taut surface of his abdomen and vanished under the waistband of his trousers. So well were those trousers tailored to fit his lean flanks and ridged thighs that he needed no suspenders. As he stripped off the shirt and flipped it aside, Amalie waited with a suspended feeling in her chest for his hands to go to his trouser waistband.

Instead, he moved to lean against the side of the high bed where he released the *sous-pieds,* or small leather bands, that held his close-fitting trousers under the soles of his half boots, then used the toe of one boot to lever off the other. As he did so, his gaze was upon her, faintly mocking yet warm with promise. He surveyed the heart shape of her face, pale yet with hectic color burning on her cheekbones, her softly parted lips, and the quick rise and fall of her bodice. With greater force, he kicked first one piece of footwear aside, then the other. His calf-high, knitted socks were drawn off and dropped into the boots. He straightened.

Amalie felt suffused with heat and liquid anticipation as he caught and held her eyes with his. His assurance, his deliberation were maddening, as was her own reaction to it. She grasped at the shreds of her composure. She had not had much experience of men, it was true, but neither was she a shrinking virgin. If men took pleasure, as she had heard, in the sight of women undressing, then why should a woman not enjoy the same display? Lifting a brow, she gave him a slight smile that trembled around the edges and moved to a nearby chair. She seated herself and, though her nerves fluttered with agitation, leaned forward, propping her chin on her hand as she watched him.

A soft laugh left him, though the burned brownness of his skin took on a darker hue. Supple, unfaltering, his hands went to his waistband, tugging at the buttons of the smooth front flap, moving down to those that closed the lower opening of his trousers. Beneath them he wore linen drawers and these he unfastened, stripping them off with his trousers.

Naked, splendid in the lamplight, he turned from pitching the last of his clothing aside to face her. He tilted his head, his hands falling to his sides. The laughter had vanished from his eyes to be replaced by a waiting stillness.

The muscles of Amalie's abdomen contracted and she felt the involuntary tightening of deeper, more primitive muscles and nerves. Powerful, totally masculine, he was beautiful in the perfect proportion of his limbs, their cording of vein and turning of muscle, the shadowing of hair. There was a sharp demarcation line between the darkness of his upper body and paleness of the lower that gave him the look of a satyr, part lusty being of the sun and part enigmatic inhabitant of the moonlit night. Rampantly male, that organ of his body strutting in arousal seemed silken, enticing, and, at the same time, threatening.

Her throat was dry. The single word she spoke was a soft rustle in the quiet of the room. "Robert . . ."

He moved toward her, dropping to one knee, taking her hand and lifting it to the firm warmth of his lips. Her hoop was pressed against her ankles and her spreading skirt about his thighs, so near was he. The blue flame of his gaze held her soft brown eyes. Turning her hand, he put his mouth to her palm and touched the wet heat of his tongue to that sensitive surface.

A shiver ran over her. She put out her other hand to touch his hair, lifting with her fingertips the crisp waves at his temple, then pressing them to the pulse that throbbed there before tracing along his cheekbone and down his blue-shadowed jaw. The look in his eyes warmed, then he drew back, placing her hand in her lap. He flipped up the black crêpe of her skirt and fullness of her petticoats, his firm grasp upon her ankle. A moment later, he had removed her slipper and was kneading her foot, his fingers strong on the heel and tender instep. Sliding his hand upward over her silk-clad ankle to the calf, finding the narrow leg of her pantaloons and pushing them higher to where her garter held her stocking, he began to roll it down. He bent his head, pressing his lips to her knee as he uncovered it and massaging her calves. His fingers encircled her ankle as he slipped the rolled stocking off and set it aside. Once more he performed the rite before he moved back, pushing her skirts higher, lifting one small foot to his mouth. She felt the warm flick of his tongue between her toes and a low, stifled moan sounded in her throat. She was aware of an ache of emptiness in the center of her being, aware, too, of the open crotch of her pantaloons made for ease in attending to the demands of nature while trussed up in corset and layers of petticoats. It was spread for his sight, and a small smile played about his lips as he allowed his gaze to seek and find that secret, shadowed recess.

She reached for him and he lowered her foot, taking her hand. He placed it on his shoulder, encircling her waist to draw her nearer while his other hand pushed up beneath her skirts, seeking and finding the crotch opening. His finger glided inside, making her gasp as they moved unerringly to the most tender part of her body. His touch was gentle, hypnotic. Her lashes quivered as she closed her eyes. He bent his head to brush his lips along the curve of her cheek to her eyelids, wetting the smooth surface with his tongue, feathering the long lashes. She slid her hand along the muscles of his shoulder to the corded tendons of the back of his neck, while she traced downward with the other, trailing her nails through the hair on his chest and following the narrowing line over his belly to touch the silken, upright thrust of him.

He drew in his breath. His voice was soft, laced with wry humor as he spoke. "I have dreamed so of this night, thought of all the things I longed to do, that now there is so much I hardly know where to begin—or where to stop. Before we go too far, let me see you, all of you."

It was an effort to draw back, to relinquish him. Her eyes were shadowed and luminous as she complied. A blue flame flared in his as he met her gaze, then he took her arms, drawing her to her feet as he stood. His hands went to one ear where, with infinite care, he unhooked the jet earring from the lobe that he massaged for a moment before he turned to the other. With that also in his possession, he moved his fingers to the clasp of the mourning brooch made of her mother's hair, intricately plaited in a willow tree design. A moment later, it, too, was in his grasp. They rattled together as he leaned to place them on the chair behind him. Straightening, his eyes on her face, he slowly turned her with her back to him and began to unloop the long line of buttons that held her gown closed. The scorching heat of his mouth touched the back of her neck as he exposed it, then followed the opening vee.

When the final button was released, she expected him to untie the tapes of her hoop and petticoats. Instead, he caught the waist of the gown of black crêpe and lifted it up, drawing it off over her head with a soft swishing sound. He flung it across the chair and turned to look at her, allowing his gaze to run over the tucked linen and ribbon-shot eyelet of her camisole; to the firm curves of her breasts pushed high by the compression of her corset and the dark circles of her nipples seen through the thin cloth; to scan the slender width of her tightly cinched waist and the mountain of her petticoats.

Her undergarments were white, not the black that would have been required if she had really been in mourning. There had been no time to worry about such details and now she was glad of it as Robert walked slowly around her.

"Has Julien seen you like this?" he asked as he came to stop before her. The question was curious, lacking in heat.

She shook her head. Always, even on the steamboat, there had been someone there—a female steward, a maid—to release her from her imprisoning cocoon and to lace her up again.

"He is a fool, if only because he missed the pleasure of doing this . . ." He reached out to yank on the bow that held her hoop. As it came untied, the heavy garment with its graduated circles of spring steel dropped, caught only by the fullness of petticoats underneath, which prevented it from dipping and swaying. A moment later, these, too, lay in a foam of white around her knees. He offered her his hand and she stepped from the billowing circle, then gave a startled cry that turned to a sigh of pleasure as he pulled her toward him so that she fell against his chest. His arms went around her, holding her pressed to him, while his hands smoothed down her back to test the satin skin and delicate structure of bone, to catch and hold the flair of her hips under the thin linen of her pantaloons.

The press of his maleness against her pelvis and abdomen was hard, exciting. She moved against it, reveling in its heat, aware of the quickening beat of the blood in her veins. Her parted lips were soft and moist, and he lowered his head to take them, plunging his tongue into her mouth to probe the sweetness of her growing arousal in a foretaste of the invasion of her body that was to come.

She felt one hand lift to her head, his fingers pushing into her hair to search for pins. Of carved tortoiseshell, they fell to the floor with a quiet clatter. The soft knot at the nape of her neck loosened, slipped and unrolled down her back, releasing its clean, natural fragrance. He spread the satin cascade, drawing it forward around her cheeks and over his own shoulder, breathing deeply.

"If you were mine," he said against her mouth, "you

would need no maid. I would do this every night or maybe I would keep you like this, always half ready."

The pain threading his voice was a reminder that there might never be another opportunity. The knowledge had been between them all evening, and was, Amalie knew, the impetus that had driven them together despite all prohibitions against their intimacy. If Julien returned, this might be their last night. If Julien returned . . .

"Don't, please don't," she whispered, an ache in her voice. He made no answer, but his kiss grew harder, the grip of his hands more biting. He strained her to him, flattening her breasts against his chest, pressing her stays into her, and constricting her breathing, which was already insufficient. She could not prevent the gasp that escaped her. His hold loosened at once and a deep sigh lifted his chest. Carefully, as if it was a ceremony to be long remembered, he swung her around and began to unlace her corset.

Amalie was so used to the tightness around her that she scarcely noticed it in the ordinary course of events. The quickening of her breathing against it had not seemed at all unusual until the pressure was released. She could not contain the gasp of relief as Robert spread the lacing wide. A soft curse left him, then he was lifting it off over her head, spanning her waist with his hands to rub her rib cage as it lifted with the sudden rush of air into her lungs. She leaned toward him, dizzy with the release.

"God," he said softly, "if you were mine, I might well keep you naked instead of laced up in such a thing."

She managed a low laugh. "And have everyone know me for the wanton I am."

"If you are wanton," he said, turning her and cupping her

face in his hands, his blue gaze holding hers, "then all women would be better so."

He molded her mouth to his own, testing the line of the joining with the tip of his tongue, straining her against him so that the hardening peaks of her breasts dug into his chest. He slid one hand under the lower edge of her camisole, spreading his fingers over the small of her back. Delight ran though Amalie's veins, burning brightly in her blood. With one hand she covered the strong brown fingers on her cheek, while the other smoothed around his waist to his backbone, tracing down it over the lean, hard flesh to clasp his flank. Dimly she was aware of him tugging her camisole higher, drawing it up under her arms. She twisted against him until her breasts were bare, tingling with a swollen feeling as she pressed them to his chest. His hand then trailed to the waist of her pantaloons, untying the bow of the tapes that held them, pushing them down so that the warm air circled around her hips.

He sighed, then with reluctance in his muscles, drew back, sending the pantaloons to the floor and drawing off the camisole. His gaze traveled slowly from the parting of her hair over the shining strands that framed the flushed heart shape of her face and veiled the proud mounds of her breasts, ending at the narrow indentation of her waist. It marked the streaks of red where the excess material of her camisole had been folded, pressed into her skin, and settled lower still to where her hips flared and the white skin of her flat abdomen was shadowed by the triangle of soft brown above the apex of her long, slender legs.

"Beautiful, so beautiful," he murmured and reached to cradle her breasts in his hands, bending his head to taste their apricot-rose nipples. "Like peaches, firm and ripe and sweet, so sweet."

A melting sensation moved through her, settling in the lower part of her body. A secret smile of delight curved her mouth. She touched his hair, smoothing it back from his temple before tracing the convolutions of his ear and dipping the tip of her finger inside.

He made a soft sound in his throat, then bent to take her in his arms, moving toward the bed. Placing a foot on the bottom tread of the bed steps, he mounted to the next, then dented the cotton mattress with one knee before releasing the arm that held her knees. He clasped her to him, pulling her down on top of him as he lowered himself with controlled strength to the soft, resilient surface. He held her, rocking her in his arms with his face buried in her hair, then swung slowly to deposit her on her back beside him.

Levering himself to one elbow, he placed his fingertips on her abdomen, seeking her lips once more. He drew her tongue into his mouth, abrading it with his own that had the rubbed roughness of raw silk and sending delicious prickles over her skin at the gentle suction. His hand was upon her, the spread fingers brushing the arching curves and moist hollows of her body, testing, probing, bringing her senses to such a vibrant pitch that she writhed, moaning. He did not stop, but found the center of her being, touching it with tender magic as, with mind-stopping deliberation, he began to follow the path his hand had taken with lips and gently nipping teeth.

Her blood pounded in her veins and she could hear its thunder in her ears. Her chest rose and fell with the force of her breathing. She felt as if her skin was glowing with heat, while the muscles of her abdomen and her thighs tightened, quivering. She turned her head from side to side, her hands trembling as she clutched at his shoulder. Inside, she was hot and liquid, waiting, suspended.

He lifted his head, lying back, turning her toward him. She moved to press herself to the muscular strength of his body, reveling in the heat and power of him, the glistening of his muscles with perspiration in the lamplight, the faint tremor of his hand upon her as it closed over her hip. At his guidance, she parted her thighs, lifting one over his taut flank. A small cry left her as she felt his sure, sliding entry, then she reached to draw him close, taking him deep, embracing him with slow internal contractions.

"Look at me," he said, tilting her chin with his knuckle, the words a husky command.

She obeyed, her eyes liquid with the desire that suffused her, her soft lips open. His own gaze was blue-black, devouring. His chest lifted with a long, difficult breath.

"I love you, Amalie."

"And I, you," she answered.

A fierce joy sprang to his features and he snatched her close, plunging into her. Together in a frenzy of pleasure and gladness and desperate longing they moved, surging upon each other with panting breaths and tender, engorged flesh, seeking to deny the undercurrent of pain that haunted them. He rolled to his back, taking her with him, holding her as she moved upon him, then heaving over with her hair coiling around them as they tumbled about the mattress.

It was vivid ecstasy, a pulsating and sensual indulgence that stretched time and pleasure beyond reckoning. They hovered, striving, enraptured mouth to mouth, their limbs locked. Then inside her grew a suspended, ballooning sensation. Her hold grew rigid. A soft sound escaped her.

Robert rose above her, thrusting strong and steady with the tempo of a heartbeat. She raised her eyelids to see him, golden and powerful, above her, gleaming with the perspiration that dewed them both, his eyes blazing.

"Robert," she breathed, the word ending in a soft cry as she arched upward in an explosion of bliss. He drove into her with shuddering impacts that lifted her so that she clung to him to keep from being driven over the mattress. She reveled in the violent strokes, wanting, needing them to send her soaring higher and higher still. He throbbed inside her, stretching, filling, pounding, his fingers sinking deep into her hips, his every movement fueling the wondrous rush that swept through her.

It was a miracle, untainted and glorious, an upheaval of the senses that transcended the puny bonds of earth. Stunning, brilliant, it held her, and then with a final wrenching plunge, he was joined with her in its enchanted magic. Clinging in enthrallment, they drifted, surrendering, and hardly knew when he collapsed upon her, drawing her against him as they slept in the blaze of lamplight.

There was the smell of burned candlewax and hot oil in the room when they awoke. The bright daylight beyond the windows caused the flames of the two lamps that still burned to fade to only a yellow flicker. A fresh breeze stirred the curtains, causing them to billow. It smelled of flowers and mud and the aroma of frying onions and boiling shellfish.

Amalie opened her eyes. The day was far gone; she realized that at once. Clenching her teeth against the protest of sore, cramped muscles, she tried to move. There was a heavy weight across her midsection. Looking down, she found that she had lain the night through without a covering. There was a hard arm across her, the fingers lightly holding a breast for purchase. Robert was lying against her back, his long limbs curving around her like a spoon nestled against another. She started, then a slow smile tilted her mouth.

"Lie still." Robert's voice was a rustle of sound against the top of her head.

She complied readily enough, intrigued by the feel of his thighs with their light covering of hair against the backs of her own and something that was smoother, and at the same time harder, at their juncture. He shifted and his manhood pressed between her legs, seeking the still-moist entrance of her femininity while his thumb caressed the nipple of her breast, sending exquisite shivers along her nerves.

A knock sounded on the door. "Mam'zelle?"

It was Lally. Robert kicked at the covers, lunging to draw the sheet and coverlet up over them, though without dislodging their position overmuch. Amalie cleared her throat, calling, "Yes?"

The maid opened the door, though she came no farther into the room, nor did she allow her gaze to rest on their clothing scattered over the floor. Her voice soft, she said, "Will you and M'sieu Robert have your breakfast downstairs or shall I bring it?"

"We'll have it here," Robert answered.

"The other servants—" The maid trailed off, as if uncertain how to voice her objection.

"Tell them I am still abed and am such a light sleeper that I will have no one above stairs until I ring."

The girl gave a nod. "Yes, m'sieu."

"And Lally?"

She turned back. "Yes, m'sieu?"

"Mam'zelle is ravenous, amazingly so."

She flashed him a quick grin of understanding and went out, closing the door smartly behind her. As the latch clicked, Robert leaned over Amalie, his breath warm at the shell-like turnings of her ear and his hand closing once more on her breast. "Now," he asked, lazy anticipation threading his tone, "where were we?"

By the time Lally returned, Amalie, flushed from love-making, had had recourse to the pitcher of water that sat on the washstand and located her nightgown caught between the mattress and one of the bedposts, where it had slipped after being laid out the night before. Robert lunged across the bed for it, tugging it out of her hands, coaxing her to return to lie beside him without it. Shaking her head, she looked around, then scooped up her pantaloons and camisole instead. Instantly he leaped from the bed to catch hold of them. They were wrangling over them in mock anger when another knock came. Amalie gasped and dived for the bed. Robert followed close behind her, her undergarments dangling from one brown hand. He flung the sheet up so that it billowed as he slid under it. He stuffed the camisole and pantaloons under the pillow before he lay back, clasping his hands behind his head. Amalie sent him a glance of exasperation, though her eyes were dancing with amusement as she called for Lally to come in.

The breakfast brought to them was light: *café au lait* and

a generous basket of warm rolls. To go with them was a molded round of pure butter and a small pot of wild honey. The honey pot was of china and painted with a design of clover, apple blossoms, and honey bees, and had its own small china ladle that stuck up through a notch in the lid. There was a single cup and saucer of white china banded in apple blossom pink and rimmed with gold. The heavy linen napkin was pink with a damask design of apple blossoms, and the small pitchers of coffee and hot milk were of silver. Setting the tray bearing the repast on the bed between Amalie and Robert, Lally brought out a second cup and saucer from her apron pocket with the air of a conjurer and placed it before him. Assured that there was nothing else they needed, she went quickly from the room.

Robert watched the door close upon her. "That girl is devoted to you."

"You exaggerate," Amalie answered. She sat up higher in the bed, pulling a pillow behind her and drawing the sheet up to cover her breasts before reaching for the pot of coffee.

"I don't think so. She would do anything for you. Most of your people at Belle Grove seem to feel that way, I've noticed."

"No more than on any plantation," she protested. "It's perfectly normal since I feed them and take care of them."

"But you care about them. You see them as people with feelings and needs and treat them in that way, instead of like valuable animals."

Amalie shook her head, then flung her hair back over her shoulder out of the way. She poured the coffee and set down the pot before taking up the milk, filling the cup the rest of the way with the hot foaming liquid. She handed him the cup, frowning a little. She was well aware that most plantation mistresses preferred not to become closely involved with the people in their care. Attachments could not only be hurtful, since a mere wife was powerless to control the fates of those around her, but could interfere with discipline, and so it was better not to allow them to develop. Amalie was often troubled that she could not seem to keep a proper distance.

"I suppose I shouldn't."

"Not at all. I'm glad to think that the people at Belle Grove are fairly content, though Dye certainly does nothing to help matters."

"What do you mean?" She paused with her own cup in her hand as she waited for his answer.

"There is such unrest now with the abolitionists at work and the constant bandying about the idea of secession. We have all of us lived on the lid of a powder keg for years. So far there has been amazingly little repercussion, if you will pardon the analogy. That doesn't mean it will always be that way."

She offered him the roll basket, then took one herself, buttering it, taking honey, and putting it on her plate before scooping a generous amount onto the warm, yeast-scented bread. Before she bit into it, she asked in a contemplative tone, "You think there may be trouble?"

"Who can say?" He disposed of a roll in two bites, then swallowed a mouthful of coffee. "The abolitionists certainly hope that there will be an uprising of the slaves, if the South tries to go its own way, and that the government in Washington will prevent us from breaking away from the

Union. I keep telling myself that it won't come to that, that the sane and intelligent men we have chosen to represent us will find a way out of this dilemma. In the meantime, we all have to worry that the trouble fomenting may affect our people to the point of endangering those we love."

Amalie thought of Isa and Lally, of Tige and Marthe and Sir Bent, and all the others at Belle Grove who had become so familiar to her. There were those among their people who were slackers, whiners, and troublemakers, but they were far outnumbered by those who lived decent, helpful, God-fearing lives, making the best of the situation in which they had been born. "I sometimes think how much easier it would be if the slaves were freed, if they could be paid a wage for their labors."

"An impractical dream, I'm afraid. Planters all over the South have too much money tied up in them, not only for the prices paid, but for the food, shelter, and clothing provided, in most cases for years, even generations. There is no one who will reimburse the owners for these expenses and most can't afford to take the loss."

"Some argue that the planters have recouped their outlay by the crops harvested."

He nodded. "But what of the years when weather and disease cause the harvest to fail while the bills for the care of the people in the quarters mount up? The major problem, however, is not the men who have gained some material advantage in life using slave labor; it's the small farmers out there who are still scratching out a living. They look around and see how they can make their acres pay if they can manage to buy a slave or two, gradually increasing the number and using the labor of other men, until they have gained the leisure and status of the big planters. It's this promise, for men who have come from the distant countries where there was never such a chance, that will prevent the slavery system from changing. They are the ones who will fight hardest to keep the institution."

It made sense. She nodded as she reached for another roll. "And so we have to worry and watch and wonder if men like Patrick Dye are jeopardizing our very lives. I despise the man and have the feeling he feels much the same about me, but can't make Julien see it."

"Julien sees results, and admittedly, they are good," he answered, the words serious though his gaze wandered to the upper part of her body that was bared as the sheet slipped down around her waist. "As for Dye, you thwarted him, and that never sits well with a man of his stripe, especially coming from a woman. There's another thing, I think. You treat him as the overseer he is, nothing more, and he is used to some success with women, even the wives and daughters of his employers."

"You must be joking!"

He sent her a crooked smile. "Not everyone has your excellent taste in men, my love."

Her own lips turned up in answer, but a moment later, she looked away, hiding her face in her coffee cup as she sipped at the brew that had suddenly turned bitter.

"What is it?" he asked.

"Nothing."

"I don't believe it. For a moment there I had the feeling I was not much higher in your estimation than Patrick Dye, and I want to know why."

The demanding tone caught her on the raw. "Very well,"

she said, rounding on him. "I understand that you are also supposed to be a man who enjoys considerable success with women."

"Who told you that?"

"Do you deny that you have been the object of a great deal of female devotion, particularly one married lady who tried to end it all for your sake?" Jealousy in a woman had always seemed an unpleasant trait to her, but she could not prevent the words that tumbled from her lips.

"Chloe," he said, disgust in his voice.

"What of it?"

"I might have known I could depend on her to dredge up all the most sensational tittletattle for you."

"What does it matter, if it's true?"

"It isn't true," he said, setting his coffee cup on the tray so hard that the coffee and milk splashed out to make a brown pool. "At least not entirely. I haven't been a monk. I've enjoyed my share of light flirtations, but I've never encouraged a young unmarried girl to hope I would wed her nor set out to destroy another man's marriage."

"Very commendable, I'm sure," she said, her voice cool. He sent her a dark look that spoke plainly of his dislike for her sarcasm. "The incident that Chloe told you about happened years ago. I was just back from attending Jefferson College at Natchez, at loose ends, a young man on the town. The new wife of one of my father's friends, a girl half his age, took an interest in me. She was intelligent but high-strung, romantic, and dissatisfied with her life and her marriage. The problem was that she read more into my courtesy toward her than was there."

"Your courtesy," she said. What did that entail? she wondered. A kiss on the hand, polite conversation, or perhaps an evening or two in bed? Was it mere courtesy for a man to speak words of love to the woman he is bedding, if he thought that was what she expected to hear at that moment?

"For lack of a better word. I spoke to her, escorted her at her husband's request when he was busy. Then one day she began to send me notes that were rather, well, passionate. She invited me to ride with her, to come to her house when her husband was away, even arranged for us to be alone in her box at the opera without my knowledge or her husband's. I was young enough to be flattered, but uncomfortable. I didn't know what to do to discourage her without creating a scene. Finally, her husband confronted her. She came to me, crying, begging me to take her away, to pack that night and go away with her to relatives in South Carolina. I was dumbfounded and certainly had no thought of agreeing. I said so rather bluntly, I'm afraid, when she wouldn't understand. She went home and drank a bottle of laudanum."

"Did you ever make love to her?"

"It was years ago, before I met you. Why go into it?"

"Did you?"

He ran his fingers through his hair. "All right, yes, once. I came home to find her in my rooms, naked in my bed, shaking like a leaf. What was I supposed to do? Throw her out? The humiliation would have destroyed her."

"I see." He had made love to her out of compassion. Amalie, buttering another roll that she did not want and adding honey, felt a chill move over her at the thought. She was forced to wonder if, having begun his affair with her at M'mere's suggestion, he was continuing it now because he feared what would happen, how it would affect her, if he ended it.

He watched her, a suspended look on his face. "Do you? Let me repeat: It has nothing to do with you or with how I feel about you. You are a fire in my blood, the woman I would pursue to the ends of the earth, or would take there this moment if you would come with me. What I feel for you makes the past as if it had never been and does not look toward the future. It is here, now, a part of every passing moment, every breath, every heartbeat. All I ask, all I have the right to ask, is that you share it, just for today, with me."

She wanted to believe him and that was the important thing. She stared at him, lost in the vivid blue of his eyes, feeling the slow heat of a flush that had nothing to do with embarrassment rising to her hairline. The roll she held in her hand shifted and a golden drop of honey and melted butter fell onto her breast. With an exclamation, she reached for a napkin.

Robert shot out his hand to capture her wrist. Leaning toward her, he said, his voice deep, "Allow me."

He leaned to press his mouth to her skin and she felt the velvet lick of his tongue where the honey and butter had been. He lifted his head to meet her brown gaze, the pupils of his eyes dark and expanding with desire as he murmured, "Delicious."

"I—I'm still sticky," she said and immediately sank her teeth into her lip as she realized the connotation that could be placed on the words.

"So you are. You'll have to have a bath." His silken tone might have warned her, even if he had not reached at that moment for the china spoon in the honey pot, turning it so that only a fine drizzle streamed from the tip.

"Robert, what are you doing?" she gasped as he began to make a delicate pattern in honey over her breasts and down her abdomen, pushing aside the sheet to allow the fine stream to reach the apex of her thighs.

"Guess," he said.

Chapter 14

It was after the noon hour before Amalie and Robert left the house. With Robert handling the reins himself, the phaeton carriage made slow, clip-clopping progress through the hot streets. They were nearly deserted at that hour as New Orleans, in keeping with its long Spanish heritage, rested after the heavy midday meal. A few servants moved with languid strides about their errands, and in a side street a group of young boys yelled as they chased a dog with a leather ball in its mouth. It had rained recently and the gutters in the center of the street were fairly clean, but still the stench as they neared the narrow streets of the French Quarter was so overpowering that Amalie raised a handkerchief scented with violet water to her nose.

They were heading toward the levee where every kind of vessel from flatboats to oceangoing ships docked. They passed the square before the cathedral, recently improved by the Baroness de Pontalba, set with a bronze statue of General Andrew Jackson, hero of the Battle of New Orleans, and encircled by a new iron fence. The massive apartment buildings that flanked it, said to be the first built especially for that purpose in the country, made a fine show on either side with their soft red brick and iron work. Even the cathedral itself had been refurbished, with a rather imposing set of steeples added, while the old Presbytery to the right had been rebuilt to balance with the fine lines of the Cabildo on the left. The construction work had gone on through the previous winter and was basically completed. The square was now an attractive promenade, but there was no time for them to enjoy it.

Near the square was the long colonnade of the French Market, quiet at this time of day since most had already bought their meats and seafood, fruits and vegetables for the day's meals while everything was fresh. Some of the stalls were empty, though there were others with tables still laden with wilting greens, ears of corn, baskets of potatoes, and stacks of cabbage and carrots, and long shriveling beans, with fly-blown carcasses of meat and barrels of fish in slimy water. There were times when the market could be enjoyable, a place for meeting friends and acquaintances, of rivalry, bartering, and friendly commerce among fresh flowers and comestibles. This was not one of them.

They passed the section of the levee where the steamboats docked. There were a number of packets lined up at the wharf, their bows facing straight in as they dipped and swung with the river's current. The hot sun shone on their paint and brightwork. Here and there on their decks passengers stood in idle conversation or sat back in the shade of awnings. A few of the packets had steam up, their stacks trailing gray smoke against the clear blue of the sky. Beyond them, with their masts like outstretched arms, were the oceangoing steamers.

There were five of the large ships in, two at the wharf for loading and three standing out at anchor in the river. Neither of the two close at hand was the one they were seeking. Leaving Amalie in the carriage with the top up as protection against the sun, Robert got down and went into the steamship office to check on the china clipper they were searching for.

Amalie sat fanning herself, now and then plucking at her skirts where the sun, angling into the carriage, heated them. Beads of perspiration formed on her lip. To distract herself, she looked around at the stevedores on the wharves, many lying asleep in the shade of bales of cotton, but most at work, stripped to the waist, their torsos glistening as they carried kegs and crates and rolled barrels on board the steamships. From down the street came a praline seller, a middle-aged Negro woman with a spotless white apron over her dress of denim material and a white kerchief about her head. She carried a straw tray that rested on her hip with the sweet confection of milk and sugar and pecans spread upon it, covered by a tea cloth against flies. The stevedores gathered around her, digging into their pockets for coins even as their overseer cursed. Finally the last man paid and wandered away chewing his praline.

The woman had been eyeing Amalie sitting there in the carriage. Now she came toward her. As she stopped beside the vehicle, she lifted the cloth of her tray enticingly. "Buy a praline, mam'zelle? The best in N'Orleans."

The milky-sweet smell reached Amalie and a wave of nausea struck her. She plied her fan faster, turning her head away. "Thank you, no," she gasped, "I—I'm not well."

The woman covered her candy, studying Amalie with wise eyes. "A bit of dry bread is what you need, mam'zelle. Shall I fetch it?"

"It's very kind of you, but I will be all right in a moment."

"Or in a few months, hein? Don't fret, *pauvre petite,* it comes to all of us."

Amalie smiled a bit weakly, and with a nod, the woman went on. Amalie closed her eyes. She had not been much troubled by morning sickness. Her illness came later in the day and was usually triggered by odors. They need not be unpleasant ones, or particularly strong, and the same ones might not bother her at all at other times. She had not yet been really ill. It was most peculiar. Other than that, and a bit of soreness in her breasts, there was little sign of her pregnancy. Most women would consider that she was to be congratulated, but under the circumstances she could not think so.

She looked up to see Robert coming toward her. There was a grim look on his face. He stopped beside the carriage, bracing his hands on the frame. Without waiting for him to speak, she asked, "What is it?"

"We are too late. The clipper has sailed."

"When?" She could hardly form the question so fearful was she of the answer.

"Yesterday morning."

"I see."

"Don't berate yourself," he said, his voice rough. "If you had come the minute you stepped off the train, it would still have been too late."

Relief crept in upon her. She managed a smile and a slow nod.

"I inquired about the seaman, but they could tell me nothing," he went on, his frown deepening. "The captain of the ship doesn't appear to have mentioned the fact that he had a missing man. I suppose it's too common an occurrence to bear comment."

"What shall we do now?"

He sent her a straight glance. "What would you have done if I had not come?"

"I don't know; I hadn't thought beyond seeing the ship's captain." She stared into space, considering for a moment, then said doubtfully, "I suppose we have to conclude that the second man of the pair returned to the ship and is now on it sailing for parts unknown."

"It's the logical deduction."

"Then we may as well go home."

"Yes."

He climbed into the carriage and unwound the reins from the whipstock, then sat still for a moment. "We could make a few inquiries at boardinghouses and beer halls, just in case the man failed to make the sailing or had his own reasons for letting the ship go without him. It's worth a try, at least, since we have a likeness of him."

For an answer, Amalie reached for Isa's drawing that was rolled up on the seat beside her, sitting back in the seat and opening it as Robert set the carriage in motion. She was still studying the pencil drawing when the glimpse of a building from the corner of her eye made her look up. "This isn't the section we want."

"Yes, it is. I'm taking you back home."

"But I don't want to go."

"This man wouldn't be likely to stay at the St. Louis Hotel or St. Charles. He would hole up in the dives in the roughest part of town, where they have seldom seen a lady, much less know how to behave around one."

"I know that as well as you and I don't care! I won't sit at home waiting for news; I've done enough of that. I want to come with you."

"I can't allow it."

"Can't you? I'm a woman, not some fragile flower that must be protected. I have a right to know what is happening, to do something instead of sitting like a statue!"

His blue gaze was direct as he turned to look at her. "I know it isn't a question of will or courage or ability, but Amalie, you are a respectable female and you can't get away from that fact."

"Am I indeed? I very much doubt it, after this past week!" There was heat and frustration in her eyes as she glared at him.

"I don't. It doesn't depend on a spotless reputation, but on your personal integrity. If you go with me into the kind of dive where we might find our seaman, there is little doubt that you will attract the sort of attention you won't like and that I will be forced to act as your shield against it. If you stay outside, you will be even less protected. A woman in low surroundings is seen as fair prey; it's as simple as that."

"I cannot believe I would be molested if I were with you."

A wry grin curved his mouth. "I appreciate your confidence, but I couldn't guarantee it. Besides, if we went together, it would seem too much a demand for answers. In that part of town, such a thing can get you a knife in the ribs. If I change my clothes to something rougher, go alone, order a drink—"

"I see," she said, cutting him short. What he said was perfectly reasonable, but that did not make it any easier to bear. "Take me home then."

The hours passed slowly after Robert left her at the town-house. Amalie paced, moving from window to window of the house, staring out at the other houses and lawns, at the fine horses and elegant equipages that passed carrying ladies in lightweight summer silks with bead-and-lace-decorated parasols over their heads and gentlemen sweltering in coats and cravats beside them.

She railed at convention. It was that, not weakness or an inability to protect herself, that held her imprisoned once more. So long as men made it a point of honor to guard women, then those who went unguarded must be considered open to insult. And so long as a gentleman must risk his life to shield a lady, then that lady was honor bound to behave in a way that would prevent any unnecessary hazard for him for her sake. It was a grim trap, a double bind. She wished that it could be done away with on the instant.

Still, if that convention were removed, what was to restrain those men who recognized only fear of their own lives as a deterrent to their base desires? For one class of man there was fists, the flat of a sword, the horsewhip; for the other there was the duello. The last was carried to extremes, with meetings for the slightest jostle or inadvertent word; many were the young men who had died for no cause. And yet, due to its threat, men walked softly and were punctilious in their dealings with others, both men and women.

Frowning, Amalie stood still. How much simpler it would be if there was only one side to a problem. Or if she could at least acquire the comforting facility of being able to ignore any aspect that did not concern herself.

Dinnertime came and Robert had not returned. She tried to eat, but only succeeded in pushing a portion of each course from one side of her plate to the other. The two glasses of wine she drank were reviving, but their effect had worn away by the time she finally made ready for bed.

She was sitting up against her pillows with a book open to the first page on her lap, where it had been for two hours, when she heard a noise downstairs. Reaching for her wrapper, she slid off the bed and went swiftly from the bedchamber. She was still pushing her arms into her wrapper sleeves when she reached the top of the stairs.

Robert stood below, his legs firmly planted in a spread stance. His hair was tousled, his open-necked shirt grubby, the sleeves rolled to the elbows. His trousers were a coarse twill and had been tucked into boots that looked as if they had been deliberately scuffed to remove the shine. He held a bed candle in a silver holder in one hand, and she thought she could hear the retreating footsteps of the servant who had let him in. She must have made some slight sound, for he turned with infinite care to squint up at her.

"Robert," she breathed, "are you all right?"

" 'S a matter of 'pinion."

"You've been drinking!" She kept her voice low, moving a few steps down the stairs. The candle he held was the only light other than the one that fell from her bedchamber behind her. The single flame flickered over his face, highlighting his cheekbones and his mouth, leaving his eyes in shadowed hollows.

"I foun' it ne'ssary to buy roun' or two." He articulated

each word with extreme care, but even so the syllables were slurred.

"Did you find anything of the man?"

"'Fraid I mus' report failure." He started to spread his free hand, then thought better of it as he wavered on his feet.

"No sign at all?"

"Non'," he answered, then went on without a pause. "*Mon dieu,* bu' you are beau'iful like that."

She glanced down and saw that the light behind her was shining through her nightgown and wrapper, which had fallen open, silhouetting her form against the soft, gauzy cloth. Color rose to her cheeks and she descended a few more steps to remove herself from the light, still there was amusement tracing her tone as she said, "I'm surprised you can see me."

"I'm no' blin', only drunk."

"Then come to bed."

A raffish grin lit his face. "Such im'odesty. Are y' sure?"

"I was never more certain in my life."

"In tha' case, I 'cept with all m' soul, for I neve' thought y'd ask."

He started toward the stairs, swaying. He went to put his hand on the bannister and finding the burning candle in his hand, stared at it as if he wondered how it had gotten there. Amalie hurried down to him, taking the candle and putting her hand under his arm as he mounted the stairs. Their progress was slow, but finally they reached the top. Together they moved along the hallway to her bedchamber and stumbled inside.

She cast an appraising eye at a slipper chair, then decided

it was too low, that she might not be able to get him out of it again if he sat down. Instead, she guided him toward the bed. He leaned against it, his expression bemused yet warm as she unbuttoned his shirt and trousers, then slipped them from him. When she gave him a push toward the mattress, he had the presence of mind to step up onto the bed step before trying to sit down. Leaning back on his braced arms, he made no attempt to help her as she tugged at his boots.

They did not come off without a struggle. When she stood up with the second one in her hands, he leaned forward, reaching out to take a strand of her hair that lay over her breast. Rubbing it gently between his fingers, he said quite plainly, "Lovely Amalie, sweet Amalie."

She gave him a tremulous smile. On impulse, she dropped the boot and moved to take his face between her hands, pressing her lips to his. His mouth tasted of cheap whisky and there was the smell of stale cigar smoke about him, but she did not mind. His arms came up, closing around her, and he fell back on the bed with her clasped to him.

A laugh bubbled up inside her, for she was draped over the edge of the bed in an impossible position between his legs. She pushed at him and he released her, letting his arms fall back so that he was spread-eagled on the mattress with his feet dangling from the side. She raised herself, sliding backward until her feet touched the floor. Standing, she moved to lift his legs, grunting in a most unladylike way as she heaved them up to shove them onto the bed.

As she moved around to the other side, he craned his neck to watch her, his eyes kindling as she slipped from her wrapper and climbed to the bed to kneel over him. Pulling at him, she got him turned in the right direction with his head on the pillow. She started to lie down beside him, then remembered that she had not lowered her lamp. Twisting around, she got up to do it, also blowing out the bed candle, then feeling her way in the darkness, got back into bed and drew up the covers.

Strong arms reached for her. She moved closer, settling against Robert's long form. He stroked her hair with tender care, brushing it back behind her ears and over her shoulders. His finger, none too steady, traced the outline of her face, following its heart shape, moving from the center of her forehead down the slope of her nose to her lips, brushing them as a deep sigh lifted his chest.

"Am'lie, love, I don't wan' to go home," he said.

Staring into the darkness, feeling the steady and vital beat of his pulse in the arm on which her head rested, her reply was a whisper of sound. "Neither do I."

They did, of course, because in the end there was nothing else to be done. The return trip was much like the one on which they had come, except that Robert sat beside her on the train, only leaving her for his own cabin as they took the steamboat up the Teche.

At Belle Grove, nothing had changed; the sun still shone down upon the old house and its new gardens, the Teche still ran in its deep channel, the hands still sang their work songs as they toiled in the fields. The only difference was that Chloe was sulkier and M'mere thinner and quieter, while Isa had used up all of his drawing paper in his idle time during her absence and had been banished temporarily from the house for drawing on the gallery floor.

George welcomed them with touching relief, since he had the responsibility of the two women, and the placating of them, on his shoulders during their absence. M'mere had come to her feet at their entrance, her hands clasped together until the knuckles were white, and Chloe had jumped up and run forward, demanding their news. One look at their faces had been answer enough for both, however, though there was still the tale of their efforts to be told before Amalie and Robert could rest.

It was the next morning that the situation began, inevitably, to alter. Robert had spent the night in the *garçonnière,* at M'mere's insistence. At the breakfast table, he set out, with great tact, the known circumstances of Julien's disappearance, including the discovery of the body of the seaman. At the end of it, he recommended once more that the sheriff be called in. M'mere was still reluctant, but in the end she agreed. A groom was sent into town with the polite message that Robert had drafted requesting the sheriff's presence at Belle Grove. Two hours later, the man's buggy was bowling around the drive in a fog of dust, pulling up at the front door.

Robert met him on the front gallery and ushered him up to the salon. The sheriff entered with a certain diffidence, removing his hat as he came forward. Of medium height and in his late fifties, he had straight brows touched with gray over shrewd gray eyes and a square jaw. Across his head was a red line where his hat sat on the high forehead left by a receding hairline. His bow was brief, respectful without being in any way servile.

"I regret to hear of your trouble, Madame Declouet," he said. "Please believe that my office will do everything in its power to discover the whereabouts of your son."

"Pray be seated, sir," M'mere said and signaled for Charles, who hovered near the rear door, to bring refreshments. "I don't believe you have met my son's wife, Amalie Declouet, née Peschier? My goddaughter Chloe, you know, however, and you may have heard of our guest from England, Mr. George Parkman."

The sheriff looked around, nodding to each in turn, before he selected a chair and lowered himself into it. There was an awkward pause until George filled it by commenting on the heat, comparing it to the damp coolness of England. Chloe and Amalie came to his aid, helping to fill the silence until the butler arrived with the coffee, tea, wine, and cakes. Charles placed the heavily laden tray before M'mere, who, with a wave, indicated that Amalie must be the one to pour. His face impassive, he moved the tray, then went out, closing the door behind him.

Robert came forward to help, filling glasses with wine for George and himself since the sheriff had refused, preferring coffee instead. Robert handed around the cake as Amalie placed it on serving dishes and passed the cups as she filled them. M'mere sat with her chin high, staring into space. Chloe and George spoke quietly together.

The sheriff took a sip of his hot, dark coffee, then cleared his throat. "I don't mean to be abrupt or to disturb the sensibilities of the ladies, but I would like to know exactly when Julien Declouet was last seen and what were the circumstances."

Robert glanced at M'mere and, at her nod, took upon himself the role of narrator. As the tale unfolded, they each added small details, but in the main it was a straightforward recital of facts. Robert spoke openly enough of a disagreement with his cousin leading to the proposed duel, but did not elaborate on the cause, nor was there any suggestion as to the reason Julien might have felt the need to get away from the Morneys' ball that night. Robert suggested a connection between the seaman pulled from the bayou and his cousin's failure to return home, but could offer no reason for it other than the fact that they had both been seen in the same drinking house.

The sheriff had pulled out a small notebook and made several notations as he listened. When Robert ceased speaking, he looked up. "Peculiar, most peculiar. You will forgive me, I trust, if I point out that there have been rumors concerning this duel?"

"I am aware," Robert said, his tone cool.

"You will not object if I ask you a few questions about it, in private, if you wish."

The man had not once looked in Amalie's direction, but since he had glanced at the others quite normally, that in itself was significant. She lowered her gaze to the tray in front of her. Her own cup sat untouched. She reached out to pick it up, but her fingers were so unsteady that she changed her mind, taking a finger of sponge cake instead. She put it into her mouth and began to chew it, but her tongue was so dry that she could scarcely swallow. The rattle of her cup was loud as she was forced to take it up. The sheriff turned his head, his gray eyes cool as he stared at her.

Robert's voice was a trifle loud as he answered. "You must hold me excused, m'sieu. I can tell you no more."

"Can't or won't?" the sheriff asked bluntly as he turned back.

"I must ask you not to press me."

"Indeed. You realize how such a stand must appear?"

Robert inclined his head.

"I believe you must give me a reason for your refusal, nonetheless."

"I fear I cannot."

"Can it be, then," the sheriff asked softly, "that the reputation of a lady is at stake?"

Robert's answer was swift. "You must think what you like."

"Very well." The man set his empty cup aside and rose to his feet. He inclined his head to M'mere, then nodded to all around once more. "I will begin my investigations. You will receive a full report of anything we may discover. If there is anything more you may think of to add, any of you, you may send it in writing to me at my office."

"Ring for Charles, if you will, Robert, to see the sheriff out," M'mere said quietly.

"Thank you, Madame Declouet; I can find my own way."

They sat without speaking until his footsteps had echoed down the outside stairs and his buggy could be heard rattling away. "I do believe," Chloe said, her eyes narrowed, "that if Julien can be found, that man will find him."

"Yes, so do I," Amalie said, her voice strained.

"Yes," M'mere agreed and sighed.

Robert left before noon for The Willows. The waiting began again. It was two interminable days later that Amalie, coming down for breakfast with Isa at her heels, found Patrick Dye at the table in the dining room.

She came to a halt in the doorway, stopping so abruptly

that Isa stepped on the hem of her gown of rose-pink gingham. Though she turned her head to give the boy a mechanical smile, she hardly heard his soft apology.

The overseer looked up from the plate he was hunkered over. He paused in his eating, his fork loaded with fluffy golden omelet halfway to his mouth. A smile curled his far too sensual lower lip, but did not reach his eyes. "You look surprised to see me, Mam'zelle Amalie. I have the permission of the big mistress, I do assure you. I happened to mention I was peckish, and like the dear sweet lady she is, she told me to help myself."

The insolence of his tone was an affront. She made as if to turn away.

"Don't go. I like company while I eat." The words were mocking, as if he thought her flight was out of fear instead of repugnance.

"Where is M'mere?" Amalie asked, pausing. It went against the grain to have him think she was afraid of him. She turned back, her brown gaze level.

"She found she had no appetite. Guess she hadn't been up since daybreak. Me, I've been out so long this is a second breakfast."

"I rather thought you had a woman to cook for you." There was acid in Amalie's voice as she advanced into the room. Isa skipped around her to draw out her chair for her and she sat down.

"Right you are, but her real talents don't lie in the kitchen," the overseer answered with a leer in the back of his eyes, his gaze roving over the fashionably tight bodice of her gown.

She did not honor his crude comment with an answer.

The urge to leave him was so strong that she had to force herself to accept the coffee and pair of warm rolls that Isa brought. Her words of thanks were strained due to the tightness in her throat.

"This is all right, though," Patrick went on expansively. "I like doing things like a sugarcane nabob, having my coffee at first light and my real breakfast in the middle of the morning after riding over the fields."

"Borrowed glory?" Amalie asked before she could stop herself, her temper exacerbated by his self-satisfied tone and the proprietorial way he looked around him, allowing his gaze, finally, to rest upon herself.

A dull flush rose to his face. "Could be," he sneered. "I hope eating with the hired help for one morning won't be too much for you."

"I believe I will survive it."

"I'd say so. You, and the big mistress too, have been eating with that English gardener for weeks."

"Do you think that M'mere made her very natural weakness at this time an excuse to leave the table?" Amalie kept her gaze on a roll she was buttering. A vagrant memory assailed her, of another morning, another roll dripping with butter and honey. Heat curled in her stomach, spreading through the lower part of her body, but she closed her mind against it.

He grunted. "Are you saying she didn't?"

"I wouldn't think so, but even if she did, I see no reason for you to resent it. It isn't customary for someone in your position to eat with the family."

"No matter how many other chance-met strangers partake of every meal? Oh, yes, I know that well enough," he said, his tone bitter, though it did not appear to put him off his food.

"If you dislike your place as overseer here so much, why do you stay?"

"What else would I do? Besides, I don't dislike it, not one bit."

"If you say so, though it seemed to me quite otherwise." She deplored the superior tone she heard in her own voice. It was a form of defense, one his arrogance and lack of manners drew from her.

Behind her, she heard the soft rustle of Isa's clothes as he shifted. He was no more fond of the overseer than she and was nervous in his presence. If she were considerate, she would send him from the room on some trifling errand to allow him to escape, but she needed his unspoken support too much to release him. She wished that Chloe or George would come. She could not imagine what was keeping them, unless they had already eaten. The movement casual, she lifted her head to look at the stack of plates on the sideboard. No, theirs were still there, if one counted the fact that Patrick was undoubtedly using the one set out for M'mere. The extra set always left for Robert, just in case, was also unused. She gathered her attention once more as she realized Patrick was speaking.

"You can't go by the way things seem. You of all people ought to know that."

She sent him a glance of inquiry. "I'm afraid I don't know what you mean."

"Oh, come on. Why pretend anymore? That husband of yours is gone and you must be happy."

"I beg your pardon!"

He laughed. "You should take to the stage, sure and you should. The deserted wife, loyal, bewildered; you play the part to the hilt, I'll have to give you that."

She pushed her plate from her, touched her lips with her napkin, and dropped it beside her plate. "I find your language and your suggestion offensive, M'sieu Dye. You will not be surprised, I trust, if I, too, leave you."

"Really, Mam'zelle Amalie, you needn't keep it up, not with me. I'm one of the ones who knows exactly what Julien Declouet is."

Something in his manner, some assurance, some gloating intimation of having the upper hand, prevented her from getting up and sweeping away from him. "What do you mean?"

"Don't fence with me. We're all friends here, and just might get to be something closer. But if you want it in plain words, you and I both know that your precious husband had little use for a woman, any woman, even one who looks like you."

"I believe I once indicated to you—"

"It's no use pretending he got it up for you because I don't believe it, not anymore, not after seeing him out till all hours, not after drinking with him a time or two a couple weeks back. It might have been different if you'd been shaped like a boy."

The blood left Amalie's face. Her eyes were deeply shadowed as she whispered, "What?"

"Don't tell me you didn't know Julien likes boys," he said, though there was a cruel light in his eyes that belied his words. "I'd never have thought it after all the talk. But since I've gone this far, I can't stop now, can I?"

He continued, the words crude but graphically descriptive. For all her twenty-four years, Amalie had scarcely known such an aberration could exist. Sickness moved over her and a terrible pity, only to be routed by swift anger.

"You lie!" she cried, surging to her feet. "Julien wasn't like that!"

"No? Would you say that he was a loving husband to you?"

"You can know nothing of the matter!"

"Can't I?" he said, his tone laden with purring sarcasm. "I've been around here longer than you have, been off with Julien where he was drinking, talking, looking for boys who wanted to make a little silver. Why, hell, I've even joined him when he found more than one, though I'd sooner have a soft woman under me."

She sent him a look of loathing, pushing back her chair and swinging from him toward the door.

"Why do you think he married you?" the overseer called after her. "Why do you think a good-looking man like that, with a fortune behind him, had to let his mother arrange his marriage? I'll tell you. You were picked because you lived too far away to have heard the rumors about Julien, because you didn't have a father or brother who might have heard. And the big mistress went about the business for him because he didn't have the stomach to do it himself!"

The things he was saying answered so many questions that had plagued her. She stopped, her skirts swinging like a bell. Over her shoulder she said, "He need not have married at all."

"In a pig's eye. The old lady wanted an heir for Belle Grove, was always after him to provide one to inherit everything she and her dead husband had worked for all these years. For some, some men like Julien, I mean, it wouldn't have been impossible. They may not prefer women, but they can shut their eyes and do the job."

She clenched her jaws together, a tight feeling in her brain as she tried to think. Suddenly she remembered something. She whirled around, almost giddy with relief. "What of his quadroon mistress then? Haven't you left her out of your sordid little story?"

"Not at all. She was set up to scotch the rumors, the typical plaything of a spoiled young Creole buck. Actually, it was her young brother, about fifteen when it started, that Julien was interested in all the time. And it was because of that boy that you were brought off the shelf to be Julien's bride."

"I don't—"

"No, I'm sure you don't. The boy killed himself after so many years, see. The poor kid couldn't take the idea of what he had become, what a rich man like Julien had made him see that he was. It happens. But scandal threatened Madame Declouet's darling boy again, and so she looked around her quick for a wife for him. The idea was to stop the gossiping tongues, but I guess the old lady thought he might change, settle down. Maybe he even thought so himself, I don't know. But it didn't work, did it?"

No, it hadn't worked. In a daze, Amalie recalled those nights when Julien had come to her, his tenderness, the way he had cried at his failure, lying so still and holding the pain inside him. If only she had known, she might have helped him. She had seen a part of his torment, but how much more he must have endured, knowing himself to be different from the other men around him, suspecting their intolerance if it was discovered. He had striven so to project the image of strength and ability with weapons required in their society where manliness, the celebration of courage, honor, and prowess with the opposite sex, was everything. He had tried, too, to appear the possessive, jealous husband. What must it have cost him?

And where was he now? Had he decided the game was not worth the candle any longer? Had he gone away in order not to have to fight his cousin over a woman and a situation that had no meaning for him in any case? Or had he taken a more permanent means of ending his pain?

There came the scrape of a chair as Patrick got to his feet. He moved around the table toward her. "Don't take it so hard. What's the difference? They're saying in the quarters that you found yourself a man, anyway. I've lain awake many a night thinking of you saying I was mistaken about you as the virgin wife. I was pretty sure Julien wasn't the cause, and after a bit of snooping, I think I know who was. That's all right; it's no soup out of my pot."

"Very obliging of you, I'm sure," she said coldly and turned toward the door where Isa waited, his eyes wide.

Patrick reached out to clamp his hand on her arm. "Not so fast. We still have some talking to do."

"Let go of me!" she said, twisting from his grasp.

He held up his hands, smiling with such sureness of his power over her and his own attraction that it set her teeth on edge.

"Sure, sure, but you stand there and hear me out. Like I said, I've thought of you a lot of nights, thought of you being the soft woman moaning under me. You do that, you be nice to me, and I'll forget what I know about your husband."

Her hands trembled with the need to slap him across the mouth. Her position was not strong enough at this moment to do that. Her rage grated in her tone as she spoke, however. "I am neither a loose woman, nor a stupid one. If I hear one word you have spoken to defame Julien's character, you will be off this plantation within the hour. This I promise."

"You tried that once before."

"It was Julien who stopped me that day, but he isn't here. M'mere is ill and has turned the responsibility of running this place over to me. The hands will, I believe, obey me if I order them to remove you and your possessions bodily. Moreover, I think you know that Robert Farnum will support me if there is a need. If you truly like your job, you will never touch me again, but will treat me with the degree of respect you would accord your own mother. Good day, M'sieu Dye!"

She left him standing there, sailing out onto the gallery with her head high and bright spots of anger burning on her cheeks. She climbed the stairs to her bedchamber and, leaving Isa in the salon, closed herself inside. She did not come out again until midafternoon and only then because Charles knocked on the door, informing her that she had a visitor.

It was Sheriff Tatum. Because of the heat, he had been shown to the front gallery. The only other occupant was Isa, lying half asleep with his back to a colonette and the new sketch pad Amalie had brought him on his knee.

The sheriff came to his feet as she stepped out of the

house and moved toward him. He took the hand she offered, returning her greeting, but refused her offer of refreshment. Instead, he took his handkerchief from his pocket and began to unroll it, carefully drawing out the items it contained.

"I am sorry to disturb you, Madame Declouet," he said, "but it is imperative that someone identify these."

As he held them out toward her, Amalie automatically took the long strips of waterlogged leather. Blackened, half-decayed, they were not the sort of thing a gentleman ordinarily gave into a lady's hand. She stared down at them; it was a moment before she saw the circles of gold with their distinctive scrolled designs. She drew in her breath in a sharp gasp.

What she held in her hand, stained from long submersion in water, were the decorative initial buckles from Julien's shoes.

Chapter 15

I can identify them for you, Sheriff Tatum," she said, her tone quiet, as if a lack of emotion would ward off the blow that must come. "They belong to my husband."

"So I thought. I regret to have to inform you, Madame Declouet, that your husband's body was found in Bayou Teche this noon, snagged on a stump. He had been killed by a blow to the head."

He did not sound as if he regretted it. She moistened her lips, which were dry with shock, staring into his hard eyes. "How long—"

When she stopped short, unable to continue, he gave a

grudging answer. "Since the night he disappeared, at a guess."

She turned from him, moving to a chair where she sat down. Isa put down his pad and crawled to kneel at her feet, one hand on her knee, though he said nothing. Her frozen gaze rested in his drawing, a scene with Robert with a shovel in his hand, helping to clear one of the drainage ditches at the edge of a field near the house.

She looked away, taking a deep breath. It was this second shock this day that made her feel stunned into dullness. "Where is his body now?"

"In town with the coroner. It will be brought out to Belle Grove in due course, though I would advise you not to let his mother see him."

"Yes." The bloated bodies of drowning victims long in the water were never a pleasant sight, or so she had been told. The sheriff's concern, however, was all for M'mere, with none for herself, the widow not long a bride. It was odd how that made her feel, as though she were guilty in some way.

"Our investigation into the murder has been as thorough as possible, given the time lapse between your husband's disappearance and the discovery of the body. Perhaps you would be interested in the results."

She lifted her blue-shadowed brown gaze to the man standing over her. "Yes, certainly."

"My men questioned every man known to frequent the drinking house where he was last seen. They turned up the information that, as had been said, your husband talked with the two seamen who had been working at Belle Grove earlier in the day. They also discovered that these men, moments earlier, had been seen outside this establishment in close conversation with a woman in a long black cloak. I would be interested to know, Madame Declouet, if you own such a garment."

Beside her, Isa scooted backward, then got to his feet. He inched away in the direction of the stairs, then whirled and pelted down them. Amalie heard his bare feet pound across the lower gallery, then nothing else as he struck the grassy lawn beyond the front steps. His behavior was puzzling, but she did not have the time to consider it.

"No, Sheriff," she said steadily, "I do not." Hers was of dark gray stuff, but she need not point that out, surely.

"You will forgive me if I say that you do not seem to be heartbroken by the news I have brought."

Did he expect her to weep and wail and tear her hair in her grief? That had never been her way. There was a great desolation inside her and the press of unshed tears in her throat, but she kept her composure. "I . . . It's such a shock. I can't believe it."

"The answer might also be that you have been expecting the news any time these past several days."

She looked at him squarely. "You have no right to say such a thing."

"Perhaps I should tell you that my men and I have collected a number of rumors joining your name with that of your husband's cousin, Robert Farnum. They all bear out the fact that you were the cause of the duel that was to have been fought by the two men, a fact confirmed by Mr. Farnum's refusal to answer my questions concerning the proposed meeting."

She looked away out over the railing at the placid bayou. After a moment, she lifted her hand in a futile gesture.

"You don't know, you don't understand."

"I understand more than you think, madame. I have discovered that on the night that your husband disappeared, you attended a ball at the house of M'sieu Morney in company with your husband, his mother, her goddaughter, one George Parkman, and Mr. Farnum. I am also reliably informed that you excused yourself to your hostess with the tale of a headache and left the festivities early in the evening."

"That may be true, but I did not kill my husband!"

"Oh, I'm not saying you did, but it's a cardinal rule to look to the surviving spouse whenever a husband or wife meets an unnatural death, and in this case, I think it a wise one. What I believe happened, Madame Declouet, is that, knowing your husband's reputation in the duello, you feared for the life of your lover. Rather than leave matters to chance, you hired the two seamen who were here that day to do away with your husband, then you left the Morneys' ball to pay them for that job of work. Your husband, being a man of some spirit, dispatched one of his assailants before he was foully murdered by the other. Both bodies were then thrown into the bayou to hide the crime."

The news of Julien's death coming on top of Patrick's revelations was bad enough, but to have this accusation added to it was devastating. She could not think what to say to refute the charge. All that came to mind was how very glad she was that the sheriff had not, apparently, discovered Julien's secret.

"That will do!"

The words came from the door to the salon. As Amalie turned, she saw Robert in the opening with Isa hovering behind him. They had come from behind the house, entering from the back, the fastest way to reach the front gallery. The two came forward, Robert just shrugging into his coat, regardless that his sleeves were rolled to his elbows and perspiration glistened on his forehead from his recent exertion.

"Mr. Farnum, I'm happy to see you. I have a few questions to ask you, too."

"Ask anything you like, only you will cease browbeating my cousin's wife."

"Your cousin's widow."

"So I understand," Robert said, the words short. There was a pale line around his mouth, but his dark blue eyes were hard.

"I was merely questioning the lady about her actions on the night of the Morneys' ball."

"I heard."

"Then you will understand my anxiety to know where she went and what she did after her departure?"

There was in the man's words a suggestion that they were two men together discussing the whimsical conduct of a flighty and possibly hysterical female. Robert repudiated it with a flat gesture of one hand. His voice without expression, he said, "She was with me."

"What?" The sheriff stared at Robert, his brows drawing together over his nose.

"I escorted Amalie directly from the ball here to Belle Grove, then returned for M'mere and Chloe, with George, Mr. Parkman, of course. There was never an opportunity for her to arrange Julien's death. She was here at the house when I returned with the others and here she remained through the night."

"You are saying, Mr. Farnum, that you were with her all that time, from midnight until dawn?"

"Exactly. There is no way she could have left this house, ridden into town to meet the two seamen as you suggest, and returned before I was back again with the rest of the party. It seems, therefore, that she cannot be your woman in the black cloak."

It was a lie. Moreover, it was one that condemned them both. He had branded her an adulteress and himself a traitor to his cousin. She was grateful for the impulse that had caused him to want to protect her, but surely it could have been done in some other way? It was not for herself that she cared, though she was no braver when it came to social stigma than most, but she did not dare think what having the information become public knowledge instead of private whispers would do to M'mere.

As if her thoughts had conjured her up, there was a movement at the doorway leading from the salon out onto the gallery. M'mere paused with one hand clinging to the frame. The two men did not see her, however, so engrossed were they in their altercation.

"What you have just done, Mr. Farnum," Sheriff Tatum said, his voice grim, "may seem commendable to some, but not to me. You should remember that you are not above suspicion yourself. It may be true that you were to have your opportunity, given time, of ridding yourself of your cousin by so-called honorable means, but that doesn't exempt you from a charge of accessory in the murder of Julien Declouet."

"Murder?" M'mere cried, tottering forward. "Not Julien,

no, no, no, not Julien."

With a soft imprecation, Robert spun around, reaching his aunt in a single stride and catching her in his arms. She stared up at him, her lips blue in the parchment color of her face, her eyes staring as her hands worked, clutching at his arms.

"It cannot be," she whispered. "Tell me—tell me it isn't so."

"Ah, Tante Sophia," he said, an aching sound in his voice.

"Tell me!" Her dark eyes were wild in the skeletal hollows of her face.

"They found him in the bayou. They have the gold initials taken from his shoes."

"No! No—oh, no."

"I'm afraid it's so." He turned and reached out for the sodden pieces of leather with their gleam of gold.

M'mere stared at them with horror and agony stark on her features. "Oh, Robert," she whispered.

"It's true."

She closed her eyes as a moan was torn from her. "My son, my beloved son."

Robert held her and after a brief moment her lashes flickered upward. "Did I understand? They think it was you who killed him—and Amalie?" There were tears standing in her eyes, running, catching in the hollows beneath her eyes and the fine wrinkles of her face.

"No, no, they are only guessing," he said softly, rocking her with a gentle motion.

"The disgrace, the scandal," she murmured, her face twisting. If she heard his reassurance, she gave no sign.

Abruptly she stiffened, her hand going to her heart. A low cry of pain and horror and grief came from her throat, then she sagged, bonelessly, against him.

So at Belle Grove the clocks were stopped and the mirrors turned to the wall. The black garments owned by all Creoles, who were said to go into mourning upon the death of the family cat, were brought out of the armoires and trunks. Yard upon yard of crêpe material left from the death of Julien's father, stored in the attic against need, was brought down and aired on the galleries before being hung at the windows. The bunting of black draped over the railings in the summer air was a signal to anyone passing that there was a death in the house. Then the condolence calls began.

Amalie was so busy in the sickroom with M'mere that she seldom saw those who came, either the ones who left cards or that remained to drink a cup of coffee, a glass of orange flower water, or something stronger. It was Chloe who sat in the darkened salon murmuring the proper responses, turning aside the curious questions, and giving the latest reports on M'mere's condition. It was the young girl, too, who saw to it that the black-bordered notices of the funeral were posted in town, that the invitations to the obsequies were written and delivered, and that notes were sent to those relatives too far away to attend.

Those uncles and aunts and cousins within twenty-five or thirty miles began to gather for the death vigil. Since they must be put up, the sleeping loft and *garçonnières* were soon filled to bursting. Julien's room was hastily turned out to accommodate them, and extra mattresses were put down in every bedchamber except that where M'mere lay. The cabins in the quarters were also strained to capacity with the numerous servants that had been brought in to serve the needs of masters and mistresses or to watch rowdy children.

There was a constant coming and going so that dust hung in a cloud over the drive and the dark green live oaks appeared powdered with gray. People tried to keep their voices muted, as befitted a house of mourning, but still there were shouts and yells from the children, the servants outside, and the forgetful few. Just as bad was the noise from the tramping up and down the stairs and the drone of conversation in the salon like the buzzing of persistent flies.

The Belle Grove house servants were run off their feet, and several extra men and women were brought in from the quarters to fetch and carry and help Marthe prepare the enormous quantities of food that issued from the kitchen. Amalie, often annoyed at being forced to wait for those few things she requested for M'mere's comfort, and distressed over the frequent interruptions to the ill woman's rest, found herself thinking with weary and guilt-ridden relief what a blessing it was that, due to the heat and length of time before the body had been found, the funeral could not be long delayed.

The smell of death was in the air: the odor of old crêpe, vetiver, and tobacco used to prevent moth damage; the massed roses and daisies and cape jasmine in vases around the casket of cedar wood; and yes, the whiff of corruption in the passageway where the casket stood between the dining room and the lower gallery. In the air, too, was the hint of scandal, avidly pursued behind hands in odd corners.

Amalie, sitting one night beside M'mere's bed and watching the slight form beneath the sheet, swathed around with the filmy mosquito baire, heard a sound at the door. She looked up, discovering M'mere's old friends, the Oudry sisters, peering in at the door, holding it open the merest crack. Thinking they might be comforted by looking in on the elderly woman who had been their companion for so many years, she beckoned them forward. They had stiffened, as if in insult, and retreated immediately. The only conclusion Amalie could draw was that it was she who had been the object of their surreptitious regard.

Robert was a bulwark of strength during that trying time, though she was never alone with him and they seldom spoke. He was constantly moving about the house, filling the role of host. His manner was confident and calm, defying anyone to speak openly of what was being whispered everywhere and discouraging the defamation of the roof that sheltered them even as he dampened rude conjecture. He visited M'mere often, but usually when Amalie was resting from her self-imposed task. For news of his aunt's condition, he depended primarily on the doctor who had been called into attendance.

The physician, portly and gray-haired with a brusque habit of speech, was of the opinion that M'mere had suffered a stroke. She would recover partially, with time, but had lost some of the use of her left arm and had a degree of paralysis in the left side of her face, resulting in garbled speech. There was a possibility that she would regain what she had lost; then again, she might not. It would depend on the will and strength of the patient and the quality of the attention she received.

Amalie had no objection whatever to seeing to the needs of her mother-in-law. She had a genuine fondness for M'mere in spite of what she had done. There had been no malice in the older woman's machinations. It could be argued that she had cared little for Amalie's feelings in the matter, but it was not to be expected that she should. If her love for her son had been excessive, then so had been her suffering at his weakness.

Still, it was as a refuge that the sickroom had its greatest appeal to Amalie. She was glad to be needed at this time, to have a reason for avoiding the gathered family members and for relegating thought and feeling to the deepest recesses of her mind while she gave her strength and energy to the task at hand. This feeling was never more pronounced as on the day of the funeral itself.

Women in the Creole portion of Louisiana did not attend burials, though they might be present at the mass for the soul of the dead. They could give birth in a welter of gore, tend the incontinent elderly in their last days, and witness, not to mention clean up after, the bodily degradation caused by most illnesses; but they were, of course, far too delicate to sustain the sight of their loved ones being lowered into the grave. It was an incomprehensible custom, still it spared females something. For this, too, Amalie was grateful as she watched the hearse, with its glass sides and bobbing black plumes on the four ornate corners of its roof, being pulled away along the drive by four black horses with plumed headgear. She had said her good-byes to Julien in the early hours of the morning and saw no reason to prolong them.

During that time while everyone was asleep except for the few left to watch through the night, she had gone to kneel beside the casket. She had prayed for peace and repose for Julien and had shed her tears. She had thought of him as he was on the day they had first met, dark and debonair and kind, and of the pleasant times they had had in New Orleans, especially the day he had helped her to complete her wardrobe. She had remembered his consideration on their wedding journey, his pride the first time he had sat down to dinner at Belle Grove with her at the foot of his table. She recalled the quiet timbre of his voice as he read the poetry he had so enjoyed, the brilliance of the productions of plays he had conceived. Instead of the violence of their quarrel on the day she and Robert had returned from The Willows, she brought to mind the gentleness of Julien's apology and his concern for her. Deliberately she refused to remember Patrick's accusation.

It would not go away, however.

If it was true, then Julien's secret was at the base of everything: her marriage, her adultery, the challenge to a duel, even most probably his death. Because of it, she had become intimate and fallen in love with his cousin; because of it she was afraid of Robert.

He had lied.

Robert had not been with her the night of the Morneys' ball. She had taken a few drops of laudanum for her headache and had gone to bed with a cloth soaked in cologne on her forehead. So far as she knew, he had spent the night in the *garçonnière*. It might just as easily have been otherwise, but the fact remained that she had slept alone.

The question that plagued her was: Had Robert lied to protect her or to protect himself?

Had Robert, perhaps, gone to Julien to try to talk to him about the meeting between them, become angry and a little apprehensive about his cousin's skill with a pistol and struck him down? Had Robert gone to the dueling ground at dawn the next morning knowing he was in no danger?

She could not believe it, not entirely. Robert's reaction to Julien's failure to appear, his attempts to find him, his repeated pleas to call in the sheriff, his tracking down of every lead, such as the one that had taken them both to New Orleans, were normal. And yet there had been times when she had thought he knew more than he would admit. Doubtless a part of it was Julien's secret. Still, the possibility remained.

At the same time, she was aware of a certain coolness in Robert's demeanor toward her. There was also the fact that he had not tried to seek her out, had hardly spoken to her. There was a need for the utmost propriety in their present situation, of course, but it was hardly the conduct of the ardent lover she had known. Could it be that, despite his defense and the lie he had told to save her, he was not sure in his own mind that she was not the lady in the black cloak? She could think of no other explanation.

A light tap came at the door. Amalie glanced at M'mere sleeping quietly as she did so much these days. Not wanting to risk waking her, she moved to open the panel door.

It was Chloe who stood on the other side. With a finger to her lips and her black eyes dancing with excitement, she motioned for Amalie to step out into the salon. Smiling a little, though her brown eyes remained somber, Amalie complied.

"You'll never guess what has happened," the girl began at once.

"No, tell me."

"George has agreed that we marry without delay! Well, I pointed out that since the household is involved in this terrible scandal he can hardly say that I am above his touch any longer, but he needed only the slightest bit of urging."

"How marvelous. I'm very happy for you."

"Yes. It is the luckiest thing. Even if Julien were alive, he could hardly refuse his permission, but since he is dead there is no problem whatever."

"Chloe!"

"Oh, I'm sorry! You know I do not mean it that way. But you have no idea how maddening it has been to have him stand in the way. He did not want me for his bride, but neither would he let another man have me, and all out of pride, stupid pride."

"He wanted you to be sure."

"I am sure. George and I will be made man and wife as soon as possible."

Amalie put her hand on the other girl's arm. "I understand how you feel, but this is a period of mourning. You will have to wait."

"Why? I was related to Julien only the least little bit."

"But you have been treated more as his sister than simply as M'mere's goddaughter," Amalie pointed out as gently as she could. "If you are not to cause more talk, you must recognize some degree of obligation."

"Really, Amalie, if people had considered me Julien's

sister, the prospect of our marrying would have caused much more talk than mine to George now. Besides, you are hardly the one to instruct me in conduct!"

Amalie's eyes darkened. "I am only trying to keep you from making a mistake."

The other girl's face crumpled. "Ah, forgive me," she cried, throwing her arms around Amalie. "I could bite out my tongue. I don't really believe it, any more than I believe all these silly rumors and gossip. People will say the most vile things and without caring at all who they may hurt."

Amalie withstood the onslaught well enough, warmed by Chloe's expression of faith. "It's all right. I understand."

"Do you really?" Chloe asked, standing back. "Everything has been so terrible with Julien dead and M'mere sick and all the old tabbies warning me against associating with you. It sometimes seems that nothing is the same, except George. All I want is to get away, just go away somewhere and never come back."

The feeling Chloe expressed was one Amalie came to know well in the days that passed. The investigation into Julien's death did not progress. With no additional evidence, no insights into the events of that final night of his life, the feeling in the community that Amalie had had something to do with it intensified. Sentiment was divided fairly equally between those who thought that she had acted alone and those who were certain Robert had been her accomplice as well as her lover. Several times the sheriff returned to question her, but he always went away again in disappointment.

M'mere improved by degrees. She sat up in bed and began to eat, but did not try to talk. Finally after a week the day came when she no longer needed constant attention. Amalie sat with her, anyway, through the morning, finishing a book that she had begun to read two days before called *Jane Eyre*. When after a light noon repast M'mere fell into an easy, natural sleep, Amalie went to her room, put on her bonnet with its trailing black veil, and sent Isa to the stables to order a carriage brought around to the door.

She was waiting on the lower gallery when the carriage appeared. She had started forward, pulling on her gloves, when Charles emerged from the lower rooms. He looked as if he would have liked to ask where she was going, but contented himself with requesting to know when she would return. "I'm not certain, a few hours," she answered, smoothing the wrinkles from the kid leather that covered her hands.

"If you have shopping, mam'zelle, maybe Lally could go with you, to go into the stores and bring out whatever is needed." He was afraid of how she might be received in town. She was touched by his concern, enough to seek to allay it. "I will not be going shopping."

"You have your visiting-card case, then, mam'zelle?"

She smiled with a shake of her head before moving away. "I won't be needing it."

She felt lucky to have gotten off with so little commotion. Isa would ordinarily have had to be placated, but he had gotten out of the habit of remaining near during M'mere's illness. It was not possible for him to stay in the sickroom and he had become bored with hanging about the door. When Robert was on the premises, he trailed after him, but when he was not, the boy played with the other children, who had now come to accept him as someone with a special place in the servant hierarchy.

Amalie directed the driver to take her into St. Martinville, then leaned back on the gray velvet seat. What she was going to do was foolhardy and probably useless, but she had to do something. She could not just sit and wonder about Julien's death, letting herself be slandered without mercy. It was asking too much to expect it of her.

The lady in the black cloak. That figure had become an obsession with her. The entire incident seemed to hang upon it. Most of the community had seemingly come to the comfortable conclusion that it was her. Only she herself knew better.

But who was the woman? The most likely answer was that she was some lady of the evening, an innocent person, if such could be so classified. The other possibilities were less strong.

It might have been Chloe. The girl had cordially disliked Julien, or claimed to, and had been upset with him for preventing her marriage. She was temperamental and flighty, but her very volatility might have led her to hire men to do away with the one person who was an obstacle to her happiness.

It might not have been a woman at all, but a man in a cloak. Some men wore garments much like an Arabian's burnoose, and wearing a hood could have made him look like a woman. Perhaps some man with similar tastes to Julien's had paid to have him killed?

There was, however, a more likely suspect. The quadroon who had been under Julien's protection had more than one reason to wish him dead. He had paid her off before his wedding, after an association of years, when she must have thought that she could rely on him for her security for all time. He had ignored her in favor of her younger brother, something few women could understand, much less forgive. But more than that he had been the cause of her brother's suicide. The grudge the woman must have against Julien Declouet was immense.

Amalie was not sure when the idea of visiting the quadroon had come to her. It had just seemed one morning that the woman was a possibility that everyone was overlooking or else ignoring. Such women were negligible in the eyes of most men, women of the shadows. From her experience with such in the quarters, Amalie could not view them in that light. She knew them to be tempestuous creatures, warm of heart but quick to anger, proud of their mixed blood and the attention it brought them, and ready to protect themselves against insult. As for the woman who had enjoyed Julien's protection, Amalie might learn nothing from her, but it could not hurt to try.

There was still that quiet, closed-in look about the Acadian-style house with its narrow porch and loft stairs. Amalie sat for a moment in the carriage, thinking of the day she and Chloe had driven past it. It was as if this visit had been preordained, or maybe she only preferred to think so to strengthen her resolve. A flutter of movement at one of the front windows caught her eye. At that instant, the groom, who had been riding beside the driver, opened the carriage door and there was nothing to do except step down.

The front door of the house, of whitewashed cypress, opened only a crack at her knock. A light and breathless voice came from inside. "Yes, madame?"

"I would like to speak to the lady of the house." Amalie was gratified to find that her tone was firm.

"Yes?"

"You are she?"

"Yes, mam'zelle."

"What is your name?"

"Violet, mam'zelle."

"Well, Violet, may I come in?"

"Who are you?" The girl's words quavered with nervousness. It was not to be wondered at, of course.

"I am Madame Julien Declouet. I would like to speak to you about my husband."

There was a gasp from within, then the door slammed shut. Before it could be latched, Amalie drove her hand against it, pushing inside. The girl backed away, her eyes wide. Swinging her head, the quadroon sent a frightened look toward the door of the small, two-room house that led into the sleeping chamber.

Julien's former *placée* was not large, but was beautifully formed in an opulent fashion. Her hair waved back from her face and was caught in a blue chenille snood. Her skin was the color of *café au lait* and touched with rose on the cheekbones. Her hands were long-fingered and carefully tended, with smooth almond nails. She wore a gown of muslin with a pattern of yellow daisies on a blue background, but, as a concession to the heat, was without a hoop or more than one petticoat. Her age was perhaps twenty, which would have made her scarcely sixteen when she became Julien's supposed mistress, and she still seemed little more than a child.

There was a long moment of silence while the girl stared

at Amalie and Amalie studied her. Finally, Amalie spoke. "I am sorry to intrude upon you, but I really must speak to you about my husband's death."

The girl backed away, her eyes growing wider. "I know nothing, I swear. Nothing."

"I don't believe you. A woman was seen talking to the men believed to be responsible. I think it may well have been you."

"No! Oh, no, Madame Declouet."

"Why not? You must have wanted him dead for a half-dozen reasons."

"Never, oh, please." Again she glanced toward the partially opened door.

A sense of disquiet seized Amalie. The girl was not as she had expected. She was obviously frightened, and it was not entirely due to her presence. "Is there someone here with you?"

"Please, mam'zelle, you must go. I can tell you nothing."

It would be wise of her to accept the suggestion, to forget this wild idea. She no longer thought the quadroon might be guilty; she was too young, too timid. Still, she hated to give up. Setting her chin, Amalie said, "I think you should come with me to see the sheriff."

"No! Please, no."

The door of the sleeping chamber opened. Amalie turned her head sharply, expecting to see a dark man of the girl's race. But the man who stepped into the room was white. He reached for the girl, holding her against him with one arm encircling her so that his hand closed over her ripe breast.

"I don't think this little pigeon will be going anywhere, Mam'zelle Amalie," Patrick Dye said.

Chapter 16

hat are you doing here?" Surprise made Amalie's voice sharp.

"I might ask you the same—and you without an escort, too." The overseer squeezed the girl in his arm, smiling into Amalie's eyes as if enjoying her discomfiture.

"Where I go and how is no business of yours. While on the other hand—"

"On the other hand I'm not to forget that I am in your employ, is that it? I answer to Farnum, you know, as executor of the estate, not to you personally, Mam'zelle Amalie."

It was true, she supposed. She had not considered it, but in all likelihood Patrick was sure of what he was saying since he would not care to feel himself under the authority of a woman. A piece of ridiculous male pride, of course, but there it was. "It makes no difference."

"Oh, you're wrong there. You may care little for family honor, but our Robert knows how to value it. He'll no more turn me out than your dear departed husband, regardless of how he may wish to do it."

She gave him a hard stare. "I wouldn't be too sure."

"But I am."

"If that's so, then I believe I know the reason for their forbearance."

"I expect you do; you're a bright girl."

"And you are a blackmailer."

"Enterprising of me, isn't it?"

"That isn't the word I had in mind."

"Isn't it now?" Patrick released Violet. The girl stumbled as he pushed her from him and a soft whimper of despair came from her throat. She collapsed onto the faded settee that sat against one wall, her hands over her eyes as if to shut out the sight of Patrick stalking toward Amalie.

The urge to retreat was strong, but Amalie stood her ground. "I prefer to say devious, underhanded, conniving; any one of those."

"You are a rare judge of character, but something of a fool for coming here alone. What did you hope to find out?"

She brought up the parasol she held in her hand so that the point touched his chest. "The identity of the woman in the cloak, for a start."

He laughed, catching the parasol tip and pushing it aside. "Oh, that."

"Why do you say it that way?" She stepped back, bringing the parasol up again.

"Sheriff Tatum is trying to make such a mystery of her when all the time it was probably nothing more than some whore trying to interest those two in her wares. Now if she had been anything like you, the whole thing might have turned out different."

"What?"

"Those two sailing men would have been too busy taking off that cloak to worry about Julien Declouet—that's if they had anything to do with him turning up in the bayou."

"You think they didn't?" He was deliberately moving as he talked, pressing against the tip of her parasol as if he would impale himself upon it. Her hand began to feel the strain as she kept her grip tight.

He shrugged, spreading his hands wide. "I don't know, but just because a seaman is found floating belly up, shoved in on the same night as another man, is no reason to think there's a connection between the two."

"It seems unlikely that there wasn't, given the small size of St. Martinville."

"And there might have been. All I'm saying is, it doesn't necessarily follow." He reached over the parasol and grabbed her arm.

He was right, as much as she hated to admit it. Still, this was neither the time nor the place to discuss it. She wrenched her arm free. "I'll thank you to keep your hands off me. You seem to have taken Julien's place here and that should be enough for you."

"Julien's place?" he queried, a grating note in his voice that also revealed an increase in its Irish brogue. "I thought I told you he had no interest in women. Violet here, she's mine; I had her first and I'm the only man who's had her. That doesn't mean I'm not interested in a bit more variety."

"I'm surprised you could afford the upkeep of a quadroon, or was she just another part of the price for your silence?"

"You do have a vicious tongue in your head, but I can think of several other uses to put it to besides flaying me."

The flush that rose to her face was as much from rage and the effort to keep him from forcing her backward while he leaned against her parasol as from his suggestive words. Her tone waspish, she said, "As much as I dislike to disturb your peculiar little Eden here, I must point out that now Julien is dead, there will no longer be any payments for his quadroon, pensioned off or not. There was no provision for her, as I remember, in his will, though you can, of course, consult with M'sieu Farnum. What will you do?"

He stared at her with a glint of dismay in his eyes. In that instant, she stepped back quickly so that he plunged forward as the support of her parasol was taken away. Before he could recover, she spun toward the door, jerked it open, and dashed out onto the porch. She did not think he would pursue her, not in plain sight of the driver on her carriage box, but neither did she look back to make sure. With as much dignity as her haste allowed, she moved down the walk to the vehicle, climbed in at the door held open for her, and gave the order to return to Belle Grove.

Robert was waiting for her when she reached the house. He stood leaning with his hands braced on the railing of the upper gallery as she climbed down from the carriage. He did not move as she came toward the house, crossed the lower gallery, and mounted the outside stairs. Only as she reached the upper landing did he turn toward her. He stood so tall and straight and broad, with the light of late afternoon slanting across his well-molded features and glinting with a blue sheen on his hair, that she felt a familiar tightening inside her chest.

"Where have you been?"

The question was quiet, freighted with concern, but carrying also a lash of suspicion. She paused in the act of drawing off her gloves, then continued, dropping them with her parasol and drawstring purse onto the seat of a wicker chair. She reached up and removed her bonnet with its swath of veiling before she spoke.

"I went into town."

"I know that. I was also told that you went alone and

refused to say where you were going."

"I didn't refuse, but neither did I volunteer it."

"A fine distinction," he said, his handsome mouth grim, "but you will forgive me if I don't appreciate it."

She flung down her bonnet and swung toward him, her nerves jangling from her recent quarrel with Patrick. "If you must know, I have been to see Violet."

"Violet?" His tone was blank, then abruptly he gave a nod of recognition. "Why?"

The judgmental look in his dark blue eyes touched her on the raw. "Why do you think? To conspire with her and congratulate her in our murder of Julien, what else?"

His face went expressionless with shock, then his brows drew together. "What kind of thing is that to say?"

"It's what you were thinking, isn't it?"

"Don't be ridiculous!"

"Oh, come, you have been tiptoeing around me for days as if you were certain I was the woman in the cloak. Why deny it now?"

He met her gaze for a moment, then looked away over her shoulder. "I am well aware that you couldn't have been. I saw you home myself remember?"

"But you don't know that I stayed there!" She could not prevent herself from goading him, or from giving herself the pain of putting all the suspicions she had accredited to him into words.

"If I had thought you hadn't, I could have let Sheriff Tatum bring you up before the grand jury."

"Why didn't you? Why did you lie to prevent him?" Her face was pale, but her eyes were brilliant with fury and pride. The black she wore was a startling contrast to the clarity of her skin, the pure lines of her still-slender shape. She stood with her back stiff, though her hands were trembling so that she folded her arms, tucking them out of sight.

"Because I—" he began in hard tones, then stopped. He stared at her for a long moment, then began again. "I couldn't stand the thought of you being humiliated that way, because I felt to blame."

"Or maybe because you needed an alibi?"

A pulse beat in his temple. His voice was soft and yet deadly as he said, "So that's it."

"You haven't answered me."

"Such a charge doesn't deserve an answer."

"Oh?" She lifted a brow, though her heart was beating with suffocating strokes. "You are free to think all manner of evil of me and it's all right because I must have done the deed for your sake, but I am not to think it of you because your motives would, of necessity, have been more base?"

"I am not a coward. I had no desire to meet Julien, but I didn't have him killed to avoid it."

"You expect me to accept your word?"

"Sheriff Tatum had no objection to it," he said, "when I lied to save you."

"Everything done in the honorable way, naturally! The sheriff took you for a man of honor, not to say one of position and community standing, and you pledged your word falsely only for the sake of a lady. How can anything be wrong with that?"

He took a deep breath and let it out slowly. "Listen, Amalie, I am more sorry than I can say for the infamy that I have brought to you. I would do anything to be able to go back and do it all over again, to arrange matters so that you need not be placed in this terrible position. But it isn't going to happen. The thing is done and we are going to have to live with it. I have tried to make it as easy as possible for you by staying away, by letting the talk die down. Trips like the one you made today won't help matters; someone will have seen you, they always do, and there will be more discussion, more gossip. I understand that it has been a strain living in such a situation, just as the hours you have given to M'mere have been a drain on your strength; still, there is no point in quarreling."

"You don't understand anything," she said, hardly giving him the time to finish. "I don't want you to shield me because of what has been between us, but because you believe in me. I don't want you to worry about what I might be doing to bring more shame upon myself, but to help me find out who killed Julien!"

"Not shame, Amalie—unless—"

"Unless I feel ashamed? Why should I not, if you can think I would—I would do away with my husband for you!"

"Why shouldn't I think it, when you are all too ready to think that and worse of me?"

They were back to where they had started. Amalie swung away from him with a small gesture of futility. "I don't think it—not really."

He put his hands on his hips. "I think you do. I think that somewhere deep inside you are afraid I did have Julien killed, though how you could, knowing how close we always were, is more than I can see."

"Maybe that's why." Her voice was so quiet that it barely made a rustle of sound.

"What do you mean?"

Her mouth was dry, so dry she could not speak. She wished that she had said nothing, that she could take back the words, but it was too late.

He stepped closer, placing his hand on her arm and drawing her around to face him. "What are you saying?"

She moistened her lips. "Patrick—Patrick told me about Julien."

His dark blue gaze moved over her stricken face, coming to rest on her clouded brown eyes. After an eternity, he dropped her arm, turning. "Why did he do that? There wasn't a reason in the world that you should know, not now."

"I think there was. After all, I was his wife."

"But what good is served by it?"

"For one, I need no longer be afraid that I was to blame for his—his lack of interest in me." She had not meant to say it; it seemed to come from some hidden store of fears.

He slanted her an odd glance. "You must have known that was not true."

"Because you desired me? What has that to do with anything? You don't know—"

"Nor do I want to," he said savagely. "What you were to Julien, or he to you, is nothing to do with me. I am more interested in learning just what there is about my friendship with Julien to disturb you."

"I can't tell you."

"You have to. You began it, now finish it."

Had she ever thought she loved this man with his harsh words and iron will who sought to force her to reveal herself? It did not seem possible. She swallowed, looking out over the bayou now running low and sluggish in its banks, so slowly that it appeared not to be moving at all.

Still he waited. She swallowed. "We are agreed that Julien loved me, in some manner."

"Yes." The word was clipped, uncompromising.

"That may be true, I don't know. But what I need to know now is, did he also love you, in yet another, peculiar fashion? And was the jealousy that brought on the duel over me, as it seemed, or was it over you and what had been between the two of you all the time?"

"*Dieu,*" he breathed, stepping away from her, his hands clenching and unclenching at his sides. He stared at her as if he had never seen her before, with sick rage in his eyes. Abruptly he lunged past her, striding toward stairs, pounding down them.

Amalie stood where she was until the sound of his leaving had died away on the still, hot air. She breathed slowly and not very deeply against the pressing ache in her chest. Her eyes burned from staring without blinking. Her hands gripping the railing were numb to the fingertips, a bloodless gray. Abruptly she gasped, and the warm, salty tears filled her eyes, overflowing, tracking down her cheeks.

The days crept by, each hotter and more humid than the previous one as the summer closed in upon them. There were reports of fever, cholera as well as "bronze John," in New Orleans, but no cases had been heard of along the Teche as yet. It was a time of political rallies, including barbecues, torchlight processions, flag-raisings, and glee clubs, since it was an election year with the South's candidate, James

Buchanan, running against the Republican J. C. Fremont and Millard Filmore of the "Know-Nothing" party. There was some support for the "Know-Nothings" locally, but it was expected that Buchanan would be victorious. In Europe, the last of the soldiers who had fought in the bloody Crimean War were returning home. Many of the English regiments were being sent to India where the British regime had recently annexed another Indian state and there were rumors of unrest.

There was peace of a sort at Belle Grove. They were not troubled by callers. The whispers had become less virulent, finally dying away. The scandal had not been forgotten, but had been discussed until there was no longer any possible interest in it. No new facts about Julien's death had come to light. The sheriff's preoccupation with the incident had waned as the days grew more sultry and the evidence dimmer. He ceased to come to the house and was heard to rail against the murderous riffraff passing through his parish before he turned his attention elsewhere.

M'mere had regained the use of her limbs and was able to get about on her own, though she seldom left her rooms. There was only a slight stiffness in her face, but she talked little due to the slur in her speech. Her prayers were silent ones, though constant; she spent more time than she should at her prie-dieu. The dreams of the older woman were disturbed; often Amalie was awakened by her cries and would go and sit with her until daylight came. Still, Julien's mother was slowly recovering from the shock she had suffered.

Or so Amalie thought until the night when, entering her mother-in-law's bedchamber, she found her tossing, tangled in the sheets and bathed in perspiration. Every window in the room was shut tight against the noxious night air and the older woman was wearing a nightgown of cotton flannelette with a high neck and sleeves to the wrists. Her hair was matted and wet and her face was flushed with the heat in that stuffy, airless room. Great beads of sweat stood out on her forehead and upper lip, trickling down her cheeks.

Amalie set down her bed candle and moved to the French windows, pushing them open and setting them wide, then went to do the same with the side windows. Turning back to M'mere, she drew up the mosquito baire, draping it to one side, then caught the covers, flinging them back. As she leaned over the side of the bed to catch the older woman's shoulder and give her a shake, M'mere woke.

She gave a violent start, then sank back, closing her eyes. "Oh, it's . . . you, *chère*."

"Yes, it's I. What are you trying to do," Amalie scolded, "scald yourself alive? You should know better."

"You don't . . . understand. It's better this way."

"I refuse to believe it. Anything so uncomfortable can't be healthy," Amalie said, reaching to push up the sleeves of M'mere's gown, then beginning to unbutton the neckline. "Don't!"

The sharpness of M'mere's tone was so unusual a sound since she had been ill that Amalie looked at her in surprise. "I'm only trying to help."

"Permit me . . . to know what I want . . . if you please." The words were halting, with a drunken sound, but were plain enough to be understood.

"Yes, of course, I'm sorry," Amalie said, letting her

hands fall. As she moved back, however, her knuckles brushed something stiff, unyielding under the soft flannelette of M'mere's nightgown. Deliberately she allowed her hand to trail across the older woman's chest.

"What is this?" she asked, turning her hand to pinch at the material. "What are you wearing?"

"Nothing, nothing." The older woman's voice was querulous.

"It can't be—it is, it's a hair shirt! Oh, M'mere, why?"

The hair shirt was a garment lined with harsh, itching, stinging hair, worn as a penance, though most often by those of the religious orders. Hideously uncomfortable in mild weather, in the heat of summer it could be a torment. To find one on a woman who had been as ill as M'mere was amazing, beyond belief.

"That does not . . . concern you. You will speak of this to . . . no one."

"But you can't do this, it's—it's mad."

"Don't say that!"

"What do you expect me to say?"

"I didn't," the older woman said unanswerably, "expect you . . . to find it."

Amalie was silent for a moment, then her lips tightened "Well, I did, and now that I have I can't keep quiet. No wonder you can't sleep! I'm surprised you haven't driven yourself into a fever. Whatever will the doctor say."

"Nothing, for you . . . will not tell him."

The implacability of M'mere's words, despite the trouble she had with sounds, was daunting, but Amalie had become used to asserting herself in the sickroom. "I must. If you should fall ill again, I would feel responsible. More than that, it would be my fault for letting you continue with this barbaric practice."

"I have my . . . reasons."

"As with many other things you have done, that doesn't make it right. Now, sit up, if you please, and let me remove it."

"I think not."

Amalie drew back. "I can't force you, of course, but I'm sure you would you not like me to send for Robert to persuade you."

"Why not, if it would . . . bring him here. We . . . see so little of him of late." The older woman's shrewd old eyes turned to Amalie, raking over the composed heart shape of her face.

"It's the busy season."

"Humph. Not so busy . . . now that the cane is high enough to . . . shade the grass."

It was true enough. "I'm sure he has other concerns more important."

"No. The two of you have . . . had words, haven't you?"

"It doesn't matter," she said with a shrug.

"It matters, and well you know it."

The past lay between them, a vast gulf they had never discussed. At first it had been too personal, too painful, then concern for the outcome of the duel, for Julien's disappearance, had driven it from Amalie's mind. More lately, the elderly woman's health would not permit it. Amalie had never charged M'mere with her meddling in her life, had never spoken of the joy and pleasure she had found with Robert. She sometimes thought the old lady knew it, anyway, had guessed from watching them together perhaps, or maybe even questioned her nephew. Even in M'mere's concern for the scandal, she had never acknowledged exactly what form it took or her own part in it.

Was that guilt the reason for the hair shirt? Did she blame herself for the rupture between Robert and Julien that had resulted, indirectly or not, in her son's death? There was nothing that could remove such a burden, but it might be possible to ease it.

Amalie looked down at her hands that had become gripped together at her waist. "If I tell you something that—that will please you, will you take off the shirt?"

M'mere turned to look at her, her eyes narrowing, becoming brighter as they moved to the waist of Amalie's wrapper and back up again. "Tell me."

"First you must promise."

The thin crêpelike eyelids came down. "You understand that I do what I do for the good of my soul?"

It would be useless to point out that too much suffering might separate the fragile hold of the body from that soul. "This will be good for your spirit, at least I hope so."

"If it is what I . . . pray it may be, then . . . yes, I will give it to you."

Amalie moistened her lips. "It is sure now; I am to have a baby."

The joy that blazed in the fine old eyes was so fierce that it brought a hard knot of tears to Amalie's throat. She hurried on.

"Because of the talk that has been bandied about, there may be those who say it is not Julien's."

"Never mind. It cannot be proven," M'mere said.

"I wish that—"

The elderly woman stopped Amalie with an upraised hand. "There is no need to . . . say it, for I know . . . well your innocence. The fact remains that . . . this child will be born within . . . nine months of my son's death. It will, won't it?"

There was a sudden anxiety in her face and Amalie hurried to reassure her. "Yes, it will."

"In that case, it will . . . indeed be . . . his posthumous child, his heir by right of law . . . because you are his legal wife. This much . . . cannot be taken from him." M'mere lay back, closing her eyes as if suddenly exhausted by her attempt to be understood.

"Yes," Amalie murmured. She moved to the wardrobe where a gown of light and cool white batiste lay on a shelf. She shook out its folds as she returned to the bed, then placed it across the mattress. Turning once more, she went to the washstand and poured water from the pitcher there into the bowl in which it sat. She found a linen cloth and dropped it into the water, then carried the bowl to the bedstand. Ready at last, she leaned over the older woman and began to unbutton the flannelette gown. M'mere made no move to stop her. Her breathing rose and fell with an even, steady rhythm, while her hands were relaxed on the coverlet beside her. She was already asleep.

Amalie did not mention the hair shirt to Robert; there was little opportunity since he was never alone with her, but she saw no real need to mention it once it was removed. She did speak with the doctor about it. That gentleman shook his head, scratching absently at his side-whiskers. He had been agreeably surprised by the improvement in his patient over the last visit, but was not satisfied with her overall progress. The heat, the appalling humidity with its attendant mosquitoes and flies and noxious vapors was impeding her recovery. It would be better for her to have fresh air, a change of climate. It might also be better if she could be removed from the scene of so much grief. Among other views, other people, she might free herself from the preying questions concerning her son's death and the memories that it evoked.

It was Charles, coming into the room with a glass of wine for the good doctor, who suggested Île Dernière. The *grande maîtresse* had always been happy there. It might also be good if she could feel that she was well enough to go, as in all the years before, removing only slightly behind their usual time for the seaside. The doctor declared it an inspired suggestion and so it was adopted.

To transport a semi-invalid so far would not be an easy undertaking. The list comprising the items they would need would amount to several pages. There was one basic requirement that must be met before pen could be put to paper, however. There must be a male escort for the party.

"I couldn't possibly," George said.

They were sitting on the gallery before dinner, in the time when the furnacelike heat was dying slowly out of the day, leaving only a soft, tired warmth stirred by a languid breeze and the vagrant singing of a mosquito. "But I thought you might quite like to visit our seashore," Amalie said in surprise. "It will be different from those of England."

"I would be delighted under most circumstances, but as I understand it, you would be gone for some weeks. You must know that I can't leave my shrubs, not for so long. They must be watered constantly and there is no one I can trust to do it, not in weather like this."

She had been aware of George's diligent efforts in that direction. He watered a section of the plants every day, rotating the sections so that each one was soaked every five days when there was no rain. Earlier, there had been frequent evening showers that had been more than adequate; still, in these past two weeks little moisture had fallen.

"Surely Sir Bent could see to it," she answered finally.

"He would try, I'm sure. But he's really too old to look after the task properly, and I can't depend on him being able to get some of the younger ones to help him."

"If George isn't going, then neither am I," Chloe said, putting down her needlework and tilting her head at a challenging angle.

Amalie turned to her. "You can't stay, not without a chaperone."

"I don't see why not."

"Then you are entirely too young to be married," Amalie snapped, then put a hand to her head. "I'm sorry, Chloe, I don't know what's gotten into me lately."

"It's my opinion you need to get away as much as M'mere," Chloe returned and slapped with unnecessary force at a mosquito that was buzzing around her arm.

"You could be right, and of course I must go with her in any case, which means there will be no one here to act as your duenna. You'll have to go."

"I wouldn't," the girl said, sending Amalie a quick glance, "if George and I were married before you left."

George made a slight, choking sound, but offered no objections. Amalie, grasping at excuses, said, "But there is no time."

"How much is needed for Père Jan to give us his blessing? I'm sure he would come out to the chapel here, which is what I would prefer, or we could go to the church in town."

"Your trousseau—"

"Has been ready any time these three years, complete to nightgowns embroidered in France, now probably a bit small, but nicely so, for George at least. M'mere saw to all that when she expected me to marry Julien."

Amalie wondered why the girl had been so against the marriage to her distant cousin. Had she guessed something or merely sensed it? To ask would leave her open to all manner of questions that she did not care to answer.

"I won't mention again the fact that this is a house of mourning."

"No, please do not. That is the reason it will be such a quiet ceremony."

That the vivacious, pleasure-loving Chloe was willing to forego the pomp and luxury that a wedding usually entailed was telling. Amalie sighed. "I am not the one whose permission you must have, you know. If M'mere agrees, I will help you any way I can on one condition."

The girl sprang from her chair, going to her knees beside Amalie's chair. "Anything! What would you have me do?"

It was a moment before Amalie could bring herself to speak, then her voice was low. "Write a note to Robert. Tell him M'mere and I will be grateful for his escort to Île Derrière, if he can spare the time."

Chapter 17

T he seaside spa of Île Dernière, called Last Island by its American visitors, was located on one of the barrier islands that protected the shoreline of Louisiana from the ravages of the waves from the Gulf of Mexico. It was the westernmost, or last, island in a chain that encircled the deltaic plain of the state and included on the east the Chandeleur Islands, and on the west, the low-lying masses of Grande Terre, Grand Isle, and Cheniere Caminada. To one side of them was the sea; on the other a series of shallow bays and lakes that turned into marshlands and swamps cut by bayous and rivers, slowly rising to become the richest farmland in the world.

It was among these islands that Jean Lafitte had found sanctuary while plying his trade as the scourge of the gulf, both before and after the War of 1812 when his cutthroats had come to the aid of New Orleans. The refuge also of outcasts and smugglers from the earliest days of colonial Louisiana, the islands had been discovered by the elite of the state only some eight or nine years earlier.

The island's main attraction in the beginning had been the fishing to be had, both in the gulf and in the freshwater bays. Steamboat excursions for that purpose had been a regular feature for some years, with the passengers eating and sleeping on the boat, only using the island as a convenient fishing platform and for picnics, sea bathing, and walking on the beaches. Then the healthful benefits of the salt air had been discovered; it appeared to be a fact that yellow fever was seldom epidemic on small islands bordered by the seashore.

There had been a respectable number of regular summer visitors to Île Dernière before the terrible disease-ridden summer of fifty-three, but since that time, and with the completion of the railroad from New Orleans to Bayou Boeuf, the arrivals had doubled and tripled. There was a decent hostelry called Muggah's Hotel, formerly owned by Madame Pecot, in place at present, as well as several boardinghouses among the cluster of dwellings belonging to the permanent residents, and some thirty or forty privately owned summer cottages. These accommodations were becoming inadequate, however, and there were plans for a huge hotel to be constructed by the same group of investors who had built the St. Charles in New Orleans. To be called the Trade Wind Hotel, it would be a building designed on the same grand scale and was expected to house over five hundred guests when completed.

Most of the main buildings on the island were located on the west end of the long, narrow spit of land. They straggled in no particular order, fronting on the gulf for the spectacular view and access to the water, and with their backs to the small stream that opened onto the bay called Village Bayou. There were a few palm and banana trees, with here and there a small grove of oaks with limbs stunted and twisted by the wind, but other vegetation was sparse, confined mostly to prickly pear, palmetto, and a coarse yellow grass.

Everywhere there was the cream-colored sand, with a buried timber or piece of driftwood here and there to indicate that the waves sometimes drove over the island during winter storms.

There was regular twice-weekly steamship service to the island, arriving on Thursday and Saturday, with alternate service by the steamships *Star* and *Major Aubrey*. The approach was through Caillou Bay, then up Village Bayou to the landing directly behind Muggah's Hotel.

Amalie, arriving on the *Star* late on a Saturday afternoon during the third week in July, leaned on the ship's rail and scanned the scene with bright eyes. Île Dernière at last. She had heard so much about it and finally she was here.

Before her was the hotel, a two-story structure built up on square pillars with a high-pitched, gabled roof containing dormer rooms, chimneys at each end, and square columns supporting both front and rear galleries on both floors. Jalousie blinds covered the windows and had been used to form a secluded retreat at one end of the upper galleries on both the gulf and bay sides, while a large set of steps, wide and outward curving at the bottom in the style known as welcoming arms, led up from the ground at the front and back. People sat about in congenial groups along the airy galleries, like outdoor living rooms, talking, enjoying the evening air, most of the men with a drink in their hands. The slanting pink light of sunset cast peculiar shadows across their faces and turned the fading whitewash of the hotel to a muted lavender-gray. Behind the building was a great bell on a post of the kind used on plantations to call in the hands and to signal emergencies, but here on the island seemed most likely to be used for the purpose of announcing meals.

On the bayou around the slow-moving steamer were sailboats of all sizes and shapes, along with pirogues of hollowed-out logs. Young men and half-grown boys sprawled aboard them, some trying to use the constant breeze to race the steamboat. On the dock sat a row of small boys, each with fishing pole in hand and their attention divided between the approaching boat and their makeshift corks bobbing on their lines in the water.

Beyond the hotel, the turquoise waters of the gulf rolled toward the beach, touched here and there with white froth, tinted purple by the fading light. A few people strolled along the edge of the foaming surf, the skirts of the ladies and the coattails of the gentlemen fluttering in the wind. Down the island road that paralleled the bayou came a quartet of young people on horseback, the two ladies in well-cut habits and jaunty hats with flaming veils and feathers in the lead. They thundered past a group of turtle pens, great enclosures built of timbers sunk into the ground, set close together, and extending out into the water where the humpbacked beasts were kept waiting to be turned into soup. The turtles did not even look up.

The salty wind blowing across the island was fresh, invigorating. It carried the smell of the sea, of fresh-caught fish, of baking bread and cooking seafood, of ripe fruit from a small open-air market, and the taint of privies and pigpens from further along the bayou. It was a ripe smell, redolent of the subtropical clime, just foreign enough to be intriguing.

Amalie smiled, turned to look at the man beside her. He stood frowning at his hands as he leaned on the railing, a withdrawn look upon his face. She felt her own enthusiasm wane, pushed aside by a too-familiar depression of the spirits. Her smile faded. Robert had been like this, lending his presence but not his companionship, since they had left

St. Martinville. She could not decide whether his grimness was deliberate or an expression of his mood. If it was the last, she could endure it, but if he gave her the least hint that it was the first, then she had a few things she intended to say to him. Their situation was a strain, but it was no less so for her than for him. It was not she who had demanded his escort, but custom, propriety. She would have been just as happy, perhaps happier, alone.

She turned to look toward where M'mere was seated in a chair under an awning. The older woman's face was calm, her eyes interested as she gazed once more on familiar sights. Her maid Pauline was beside her, a concession to her infirmity, since most of the other servants who had been brought along were on the lower deck, including Marthe, Lally, Tige, and even Isa. They would wait until the upper-deck passengers had disembarked, then see to getting the mountains of baggage off the steamer.

Isa had been no trouble on the trip down the Teche, into the Atchafalaya, and then out into the gulf for the nine-hour run to the island. He had sat for nearly the whole time with his drawing pad in his hand and his back to a keg of nails, trying to capture the scenes that had eased past. He was there even now; Amalie could just see the top of his head by leaning out over the railing.

The journey had been uneventful, an endless parade on the bayou of fair skies, still, dark waters, stretching plantation lands, and graceful houses surrounded by orange trees, magnolias, chinaberry trees, and jasmine. There had been forests that brought to mind the lines from Longfellow's poem of a "forest primeval": huge cypresses and sometimes a cathedral of oaks, ancient trees holding their mighty arms out over the water for them to pass under. Sometimes the men had fired off their guns at alligators lying in the water or at great white cranes standing on logs. Once they reached the gulf, they had tried their aim at the gulls that followed them, but due to the pitching of the boat, were seldom able to hit anything. For the most part, the time had been passed with cards, books, conversation, and eating, the last due to appetites sharpened by the sea breezes. Some of the younger people had even got up an impromptu dance when a fiddler was discovered on board.

Amalie had not kept to her cabin, but neither had she attempted to join any of the congenial groups on the decks. It had been fear of her reception, as much as the rigors of mourning, that had held her back. She had read to M'mere, played a game of two of piquet with her, and strolled in company with Robert. The last might have been pleasant if things between them had been different; as it was, she vacillated between the urge to share her feeling of ebullient release with him and a grinding awareness of the suspicions that lay between them.

Her voice subdued, Amalie said, "I had better see to M'mere."

"Yes," he said and straightened to move beside her as she turned toward the older woman.

For an instant, Amalie wondered if his short answer indicated that he thought she had been neglecting his aunt, then she dismissed the idea. She was being foolish, reading meaning into every word and glance. What did it matter what he thought, anyway, so long as she was easy in her own mind?

The truth was, she could not be easy. The things she had

said to him echoed in her memory, standing between them. She could not retract them so long as there was the chance that they might be true, nor could she dismiss the accusations he had made in return though she was able to forget them for brief moments.

He had been of invaluable help with M'mere, that much she had to admit; always there to support the older woman's unsteady footsteps on the moving deck, to talk to her, and to bolster her with teasing comments. It was only to Amalie that he displayed reserve.

The boat nosed into the landing. The hawsers were secured and the gangplank run out. As the people began to move off the steamer, the small crowd that had gathered to meet it surrounded them. There were hugs and slaps on the back, cries of greeting and exclamation as friends and relatives were discovered.

No one had been informed that they would be arriving. Amalie hardly looked around as she moved at M'mere's side to the planking of the dock. Her first warning was when a girlish voice cried, "Oh, look there; it's the Declouets, Maman, and M'sieu Far—"

Amalie raised her head to see Louise Callot standing with her mouth open. She had broken off because her mother had grasped her arm in a tight hold, giving her a shake. The cotton factor's wife sent Amalie a chilly stare, gave a slight nod to M'mere, and ignored Robert. Retaining her grip on her daughter, she swung around in a swirl of tan drab skirts and marched away in the opposite direction.

It was over as abruptly as it had begun. Most of those around them had noticed nothing amiss, but there were a few who had, a few who whispered behind their hands, their eyes avid. M'mere's footsteps faltered. Robert swore under his breath and looked around for a carriage, pushing with his broad shoulders toward the single dilapidated vehicle, waiting to one side, that appeared to be for hire. He helped his aunt in, then stood aside for Amalie and M'mere's maid to enter before giving their direction to the driver and climbing in after them.

"What about Isa and the others and the baggage?" Amalie objected.

"This excuse for a carriage can return for them."

She said nothing more, though she knew the cottage would be closed when they got there, with everything in dust sheets more than likely and not a piece of clean linen to put on a bed, a glass to drink from that was not full of spiders and dust, or a drop of water to be had, much less anything stronger. She was glad to get away from the scene on the dock, the staring eyes and condemning faces. Somehow she had thought that once on Île Dernière things would be different. She should have known better.

The cottage, like every other building on the island, was raised on pillars. It was a comfortable size, but far from ostentatious, with a single story divided into six large rooms, front and rear galleries, and a sleeping loft for the servants that was reached by an outside stair in the Cajun style located on the rear gallery. There was a wide hall through the center that served also as a sitting area since the sea breezes funneled through it, and a small, enclosed garden at the back that was laid with brick and flanked on one side by the combination outdoor kitchen and laundry room.

Robert occupied himself with opening the house. He unbarred the heavy jalousies that also served as storm shutters, flinging them wide and latching them open, and brought out the rocking chairs that belonged on the gallery. He found and filled a few lamps against the gathering darkness, then checked the cistern and the system of gutters that led from the gray, cypress shingle roof to be certain they would have a good supply of water. His lack of need for instructions made it obvious that he was no stranger to the cottage, that he must have come here often with Julien and M'mere.

Amalie settled M'mere in one of the chairs on the gallery, then wandered back into the house, throwing windows up to dispel the closed, airless smell of mildew and old dust, inspecting the rooms. At the front on one side of the hall was a formal salon for receiving visitors that had a fireplace, the only one in the house. Beyond it was a small library and cardroom, with the dining room and its connecting pantry on the rear. On the opposite side were three more bedchambers, each opening into the other for cross-ventilation. The arrangement was going to be a little awkward, Amalie thought. She was not certain she could sleep knowing Robert was so near, with not even a door to close between them, knowing that if he woke early as was his habit he could look in upon her as she slept.

M'mere solved the problem in some part by claiming the middle bedroom, directing Amalie's belongings be placed in the one on the front or gulf side. The sound of the waves disturbed her, the older woman said, and she could not abide the dampness of the salty spray that came into the room at night.

The carriage returned with Marthe, Lally, Tige, and Isa. They settled in with a great deal of sneezing and coughing and flapping of dustcloths. A sketchy meal was prepared and eaten. Amalie, with Isa at her feet, sat for some time on the gallery, listening to the constant murmur of the water washing onto the sand in the darkness, to the faint sound of a violin singing sweetly on the air from the direction of the hotel as the nightly dancing progressed. The moon came up, striking a bright path across the water that heaved restlessly in its light. One by one the lights in the cottages up and down the beach were extinguished, and still Amalie was alone. Finally, she stood, sighed, stretched, ruffled her hand over Isa's tightly curled hair, and went to bed.

It had been understood that Robert would see them to the island, then return home. There was very little danger for two women in that small resort, where most people were known to each other and there was limited access. They had Tige to act as majordomo, to procure anything they might not have brought with them and to supervise the buying of fresh vegetables, meat, and seafood if Amalie did not feel like undertaking the task.

Still, the *Star* departed and Robert was not on it. Thursday of the following week brought the second mail boat and he made no move to pack and be gone. Instead, he spent his time fishing from a rented pirogue in the bay or sailing one of the small boats along the coastline. He brought home whitefish, pompano, flounder, sheepshead, red fish, mullet, and succulent green turtles that were quickly turned into delicious meals by Marthe.

He grew darker, burned by the sun, and almost piratical with his shirt hanging open without studs and his sleeves rolled up to the corded muscles of his forearms. Some days his hair was dull with salt and wildly tangled from where he had been swimming in the sea, though it was easy to see that he had run his fingers through it in an attempt at order.

By degrees, he lost some of his reserve, though he was still distant with Amalie. At times she looked up to find him watching her, a brooding expression on his face though there was a sapphire glint in the dark depths of his eyes. On such occasions she could not control the feeling of being drawn to him. She often found herself remembering his kisses, his touch, the flick of his warm tongue upon her swollen breasts, the prolonged pleasures they had enjoyed. Her face would grow warm and her clothing tight; she would wave her palmetto fan at a faster pace. Nothing helped.

Sometimes in the night she would lie awake, listening to his footsteps moving through the house. She would think of rising, of going to him and slipping into his arms, of lifting her mouth for his kiss. She longed for the secure feel of him against her, around her, inside her. As Julien's widow, she was so alone, so very alone, and in need of love. She did not want to feel that way. Flinging herself over in the bed, she would bury her head in her pillow, shutting her eyes tightly and holding her arm over her ears so that she could not hear his pacing.

At breakfast one morning it was M'mere who said, her speech fluent if rather endearingly tipsy sounding, "Shall we take a picnic to the oaks today?"

The place she spoke of was the thick stand of live oaks a short distance down the island. They were a popular spot since they provided some protection from the brilliant sun, a shady retreat after the drive along the blinding sand of the beach. Robert had no objections, no other plans, and so a basket was packed. Tige was sent to procure a carriage for M'mere and mounts for Robert and Amalie, and they set out.

Isa had joined the expedition at the last moment, piling into the carriage beside M'mere with his pencil in his mouth and his pad under his arm, as if he had every right in the world. Amalie had laughed, holding her mare in as the animal curvetted, but she had known without looking at Robert that he thought her irresponsible. Something would have to be done about Isa, but she could not bring herself to curb his encroachment, could not bear the look in his eyes when others did.

Still, the day was glorious, hot but exhilarating with the cooling sea breeze in their faces and the crash and hiss of the aquamarine sea at their feet. The carriage rolled along over the hard sand left by the retreating tide, with M'mere sitting ramrod straight while the fringe of her parasol fluttered over her head, Isa hanging over the side, and Tige sawing on the reins. Amalie and Robert rode on either side, the hooves of their mounts throwing up showers of damp sand. They nodded, politely smiling, to a foursome they met on horseback, the same group they had seen the day they arrived. In return they received smiles and a lifted hand, though they were aware that at least one of the riders turned in the saddle to stare after them when they had passed.

The shade of the oaks was welcome, as was the grass that carpeted the ground beneath them; already they were growing disenchanted with the sand that stuck to their shoes, clung to their faces, and was blown into the house so that it infiltrated every corner causing endless sweeping. Tige took a packet of sandwiches and a mug of home-brewed beer and went to walk the horses, cooling them down. Isa threw himself full-length on the grass, licking the end of his pencil before putting it to paper. Robert helped M'mere down and saw her into the chair that had been brought for her comfort, then returned in time to help Amalie with the basket she was lifting down from the carriage.

His hand touched hers on the handle and her stomach lurched. She knew she should relinquish the basket, allow him to take it, but she stood still with her fingers tight on it. She could smell the scent of starched linen and his own warm male tang. His coat hung open and, at M'mere's insistence, he wore no cravat, only an open-necked shirt. The brown column of his neck rose from the soft linen collar, showing a curling tuft of black hair at the base of his throat. The impulse to reach out, to touch that hair and trace the outline of the hollow where it grew before winding her way lower was so strong that Amalie felt faint.

"Permit me," he murmured.

"Thank you," she answered in breathless tones, releasing her grasp and turning sharply away. By mere accident, her shadowed gaze met that of M'mere. The older woman was watching them, a troubled look in her fine eyes.

When the picnic was spread and everyone had indicated their preference and received a heaped plate, a small silence fell. Isa chewed on a chicken leg that he held in one hand while he drew with the other. Robert sat on a corner of the cloth-covered quilt that was their table with one knee drawn up and his wrist resting across it, thoughtfully eating a ham sandwich. Amalie, at right angles to him, picked at her potato salad, while across the way M'mere ate cold shrimp with dainty care, watching them both from under her lashes.

"My dear Amalie, you look to be sweltering in your black," the older woman said finally. "How nice it would be for you if you could bathe in the sea like Robert. I believe you mentioned once something about having one of those bathing costumes made up?"

"Yes. Somehow I never found the time."

"That should not be a problem now."

The costumes worn on the island by most young women were of red, green, or blue bombazet and were constructed in the style of the garment made famous by Mrs. Amelia Bloomer, with voluminous pantaloons topped by a slightly shorter skirt and a close-fitting blouse with a round neck and elbow-length sleeves. There was a woman in the village who made pin money by sewing them up to order from her own stuffs.

"I'm not sure there would be black available," Amalie said, resolutely keeping the temptation she felt from her voice. "Besides, sea bathing is hardly a pastime for a widow."

"So long as you remain in the privacy of the beach before the cottage, I see no objection," her mother-in-law said.

"But the black—"

"Surely the woman in the village will be able to dye a piece of blue? Everyone has black dye for just such occasions."

"No, really, I don't think—"

"If you are afraid of the water, I'm sure Robert would bear your company."

"It isn't that," she said hastily.

"Of course," Robert said at the same time.

"That's settled then," M'mere announced triumphantly. Torn between desire and duty, Amalie said no more. After a moment, M'mere went on. "It is kind of you to give us so much of your time, Robert. We both appreciate it, I'm sure."

"It's been my pleasure."

The sincerity in his voice could not be mistaken. Listening to it, Amalie waited a moment too long to add her own assurances. M'mere frowned at her before she spoke again.

"I would not like to think, however, *mon cher,* that you are neglecting your own affairs simply because of—of that unfortunate incident at the landing."

He looked up, summoning a smile for his aunt. "Don't let it trouble you; I do only what pleases me."

The elderly woman pursed her lips. "I am happy to think so, indeed, as it turns out."

Was it a double entendre? Amalie could not be certain. Robert seemed to have no such difficulty. He stared at his aunt, a frown between his brows. After a moment, he said softly, "Don't."

"What?" M'mere asked, her own gaze limpid.

"You have done enough."

A spasm crossed M'mere's face. She dropped her fork and lay back in her chair, closing her eyes.

"M'mere?" Amalie said urgently, reaching out to touch the older woman's arm.

Robert levered himself to one knee. "Tante Sophia?"

The older woman opened her eyes with what appeared to be a considerable effort, then raised one hand in a calming gesture. "How you two worry; I'm sure I don't deserve such devotion. But come here, if you please, both of you."

They drew near, kneeling on either side of her. The elderly woman took one of Amalie's hands in her right and one of Robert's in her left. Carefully she drew them together, clasping their entwined fingers with her own so that they could not draw apart.

Her tone pensive and low, she said, "I owe the two of you a debt beyond—beyond calculation. I have wronged you, hurt you, though I trust the damage is not beyond repair. My only excuse is that I have grown old and so forgot the enormity of what I asked. I wish to say something to you and then we will never speak of it again. My regret and my gratitude is a part of my every breath, my every prayer. That is all."

Amalie looked across their joined hands to Robert. He was watching her, his face still, his eyes dark with pain. Then his lashes came down. Gently he disengaged his hands and leaned over M'mere to touch his lips to her forehead.

"There is no need for either," he said.

Amalie, retaining the older woman's hands, holding both between her own, said quietly, "No, none."

Three days later, the bathing costume was completed and ready to be worn. Trying it on in her bedchamber, Amalie was struck by its practicality, the ease of movement in it. No doubt Mrs. Bloomer was right. Wearing such a costume without stays or cumbersome petticoats would be much healthier for females, if only because it made them less likely to catch their skirts on fire around open flames. The style was also flattering to the slenderness of her shape, though she was somewhat dubious of the effects of water on the inexpensive material. Once wet, it might well show more of her form underneath it than was seemly.

It was a little annoying, after her worries, to see the costume Robert intended to wear for going into the sea. It consisted of only an old pair of trousers rather inexpertly cut off above the knee. He stood waiting on the gallery for her, carrying a length of toweling slung over one shoulder that did nothing to obscure the view of his deep, sculpted chest, naked as she had not seen it since that night in New Orleans. There was a catch in her breathing as she stared at him. Glancing up at his face to see if he had noticed, she found him watching her, his dark gaze moving slowly over the outline of her breasts under the thin, dark bombazet, the narrow tapering of her waist that flared into the curves of her hips under the limp skirt over the full bloomers.

"Are—are you ready?" she asked.

His eyes met hers briefly. "If you are."

He did not touch her as they left the house, not even as they descended the steps. It wasn't necessary, of course, without the long, full skirts that might trip her; still, the omission was telling. The tension of unwanted desire was stretched taut between them as they moved toward the sparkling water. Never had Amalie been so aware of such an emotion, such a primitive, galling need, in her life.

At the edge of the sea, she tucked her hair more securely under the black bombazet cap edged with a ruffle that protected it. She kicked off her slippers and walked in her black knit stockings, which protected her ankles from view, into the waves.

The coolness of the water and the strength of the washing surf brought a cry of pleasure to her lips. She stood for a moment with the clear, turquoise water flecked with foam swirling around her knees, playing with her skirt. The breeze blowing across the water, coming from the faraway Yucatán, was in her face, the sun warm on the top of her head. The ceaseless sweep of the waves toward her was like the throb of the blood in her veins. The taste of salt was on her mouth. Under her feet, she could feel the sand shift to the rhythm of the surf. She began to wade deeper.

Buoyant, caressing, the embrace of the gulf waters was unlike anything she had ever known. She was enthralled, reaching out to the waves that rolled in upon her, moving farther and farther out toward where they heaved into crests before riding toward the sands. So strong was their surge that she staggered, but she righted herself each time, laughing. The water grew deeper, coming to her shoulders in the troughs, well above her head at the crests so that she had to jump to stay above them. That instant when the water took her, carrying her shoreward, was pure joy.

A shadow fell across her and Robert was at her side. "This is far enough," he shouted above the crash of the water.

She turned to look at him, at his wet hair glinting in the sun and the droplets of water shimmering on his brows and lashes, and beading on the skin of his shoulders. A great wave caught her by surprise, lifting her from her feet. It poured over her head, driving her toward the bottom, crushing her with its weight as it ground her in the sand. She pushed upright, her head breaking water as she gained a precarious foothold, though her cap was gone and her hair streamed over her face. She coughed, brushing the wet, clinging strands back. Then as another wave came down upon her, she was caught in an iron grasp that sent her surging up, riding the wave with her hair swirling in the water, tangling, wrapping itself around both her and Robert like seaweed.

They regained their footing in water no higher than her breasts, still he did not release her. The waves pushed at them, moving their bodies together with soft, insinuating motions. Amalie's eyes burned from the saltwater and there was a harsh stinging in the back of her nose, but she managed a laugh as she looked up at the man who held her.

His face held no answering amusement. He was staring at the soft, pearllike sheen of her face and shoulders in the molten sunlight, at the sweet rise and fall of her breasts, outlined in startling perfection by the wet bombazet. His thighs against her were ridged and she could feel the strutted shape and heat of his need. His grip tightened, biting into her arms. On his features was mirrored haunted desire and twisted self-condemnation.

She winced, pulling away from him. He let her go without a struggle; then with one last searing glance at her body in its wet, clinging garments, he plunged away from her, diving into the waves and swimming strongly for the shore. He rose from the water and walked up on the sand, then flung himself onto the beach facedown with his face buried in his arms.

The wash of the waves was soothing, pleasurable, but it

had lost its power to excite. Amalie played for a little longer in the water, then moved against its determined back surge toward the beach. She stood for a moment wringing out her skirt and bloomers, flapping them around her so that they would not cling, squeezing the water from her hair. Finally she made her way to where Robert lay. The towel was beside him. She went to her knees, picking it up to dry her face.

"You had better go into the house before you burn your skin," he said without moving.

The taut, hard sound of his voice was like a blow. "Yes," she said with quiet emphasis, "I expect that would be best."

She did not see him for the rest of the day, though she heard him come in, heard the preparation for his bath, as the sun was going down beyond the bay. She had been hoping that he would not return until after dinner. M'mere was feeling rather tired and intended to have a light repast in her bedchamber, so they must face each other over the table without her presence as a buffer.

Amalie, seeing the way the older woman had studied her as she read to her earlier during the afternoon, had not been able to help wondering if M'mere had watched Robert and her that morning. What was it she hoped to accomplish with her attempts to bring them together? Would it ease her conscience if they were to wed? She could not know how useless her efforts were. She was not aware that Robert's claim to have spent the night Julien died with Amalie was a lie. She could not guess that her son's tragic secret was a canker between the two of them.

To counteract the trepidation she felt and to boost her spirits, Amalie dressed carefully for dinner. She wore black silk with a small edging of white lace at the low décolletage and at the elbow band of the pouffed sleeves. The skirt was looped in the Austrian style and finished with a flounce, a creation that would have done credit to a ballroom. The work of a New Orleans dressmaker who had come to stay at Belle Grove while she outfitted both Chloe and Amalie in the weeks immediately following the funeral, it would also not have looked out of place in Paris, though it might be a trifle *outré* for a cottage by the sea.

Still, Amalie was glad she had worn it, glad she had had Lally put her hair up in a waterfall cascade of curls, as she sat with Robert at the table. He seemed determined to stare her out of countenance. He gave only the most cursory answers to her efforts at conversation and volunteered nothing of his own. He had gone fishing, caught nothing, seen no one, talked to no one. He had no idea who else was on the island and his tone suggested that he did not care. Yes, the day had been hot. No, he had not collected seashells as a boy and knew nothing about them.

Finally Amalie said in exasperation, "If you are so intolerably bored with the island and my company, I fail to see why you stay."

"Do you?" he inquired, a light kindling in his blue eyes. "I stay because I am compelled. Because having tarnished your name beyond repair, I would feel responsible if any man with dishonorable intentions sought out the beautiful young widow of Julien Declouet because of it."

She felt the color leave her face. "So that's it."

"That's it."

"I'll have you know I am quite capable of discouraging unwanted advances."

"Are you indeed?"

"If you think that because I allowed you to—to touch me that I would not repulse any other, then you are much mistaken!" Her paleness was replaced by a fiery flush of rage and pain and chagrin.

He made a sharp gesture with one hand. "I meant no such thing. I only suggest that you would be unprotected and some men are without scruples in such cases, particularly if they have reason to think their advances would be welcome."

"I am much obliged to you for the lesson in the perfidy of the male species, but I would remind you that I have Tige and Isa."

"Both of whom could be brought up before the sheriff for striking a white man."

"It would be a most daring official who would charge them for protecting their mistress."

"Your testimony would be required and the gentleman in question would see to it that all involved realized he thought you less than a lady."

She stared at him in anger for leaving her no answer. "The question is hypothetical. I have never felt safer than on Île Dernière."

"Feeling safe and being safe are two different things."

They were interrupted by Tige who, since Charles had been left behind at Belle Grove, had taken on the role of waiter. He began to remove their plates. If he had heard their raised voices, he gave no sign of it. His face was smooth as he spoke. "It is such a pleasant night. Perhaps mam'zelle would like coffee served on the gallery?"

The shift of location would free the dining room so that

it could be put back into order, leaving more time for Tige to walk along the shore in the dark with Lally before the maid was called to undress her for bed. This knowledge was in the back of Amalie's mind as she summoned a smile, saying, "That would be nice."

Outside, Robert walked to the end of the gallery while Tige placed the coffee tray on a wicker table. He stood with one hand clasping the back of his neck, staring up the beach in the direction of the hotel that was lighted at every window, before turning to his left to look back toward the bay.

"The *Star* is running a little late," he said over his shoulder.

Could it be Saturday again? It didn't seem possible. Amalie moved to join him, her silk skirts making a soft swishing sound that was echoed by the waves on the gulf, dimly seen as the foam of their breaking caught the light from the house.

The *Star* was racing toward the opening into Village Bayou with her paddle wheels churning and light streaming from her decks. People lined the rails, ready to disembark, while the tall smokestacks raking the night sky spewed smoke that was shot with orange sparks. Faintly they could hear the thudding beat of her beam and the throb of her engines.

"What could have been the delay?"

"Probably engine trouble," he answered, "or who knows? Maybe the train from New Orleans was running late."

Anything was possible, and at least the steamer had made it; not all of them did. Steamboat accidents were a common occurrence. Amalie turned away. "The coffee is getting cold."

They sipped the hot, aromatic brew in silence. The night drew in. The other cottages grew dark, though rich lamplight still beamed from the hotel. Amalie saw Tige and Lally come from behind the house and cross to walk along the sand, passing in front of the hotel and continuing up the beach. She watched them go out of sight, then closed her eyes. The feel of the sea wind in her face, the sound of the waves, filled her with a curious yearning languor. She wondered if it affected the man sitting so still in the chair across from her in the same way.

Music played at the hotel, the vigorous refrain of a polka, as the dancing began. There across the way, the guests would be gathered in the new ballroom wing and everything would be light and gay. It was said that the German violinist who played for the affairs had no equal when it came to the romantic rendition of Strauss waltzes; that he was quite a celebrity about the place during the day, as popular with the guests as Mr. Muggah himself.

There was a moment of silence, then soft on the night air came the strains from the German's instrument. So lilting, so sweetly nostalgic were they that Amalie felt the rise of an obstruction in her throat. Against her will, she remembered the last dance she had had with Julien at the Morneys' ball, his fluid grace and timing, the gentle possessiveness that had been in his eyes. Julien, who had been struck down that night, thrown like a piece of refuse into the bayou. Had he been alive then? Had he died by drowning? Or had he been lifeless already, his handsome face pale and blood-streaked?

She came to her feet and, picking up her skirts, crossed the gallery, running down the steps. Behind her, she heard Robert call her name, but she did not answer, nor did she stop. She moved out over the sand, indifferent to the grains that found their way into her slippers and clung to her skirts. Unconsciously she went toward the water, though she had no real intention of doing so when she set out.

The sand crunched as Robert gained on her with his long strides. He made no attempt to stop her, but matched his pace to hers, walking beside her. Amalie glanced at him, slowed, then came to a halt. He was a dark shape before her, a faceless figure, and yet she could feel the warmth emanating from him and the restraint he held in leash. Her heart began to pound, jarring in her chest. She clenched her teeth to keep them from chattering. She wanted to ward him off, but could not move. From the hotel, the music played on.

"May I?" he inquired, his voice soft.

He encircled her waist with his arm, drawing her near, then began to move in the flowing steps of the waltz that drifted on the night. She let out her breath, melting into the rhythm, feeling it singing in her veins. Over the sands they whirled, round and round in a dreamlike trance, with the sea breeze billowing her skirts around them and the waves at their feet. Caressed by the salty breeze and the night, they drifted, their bodies meshed and moving, without past or future, beyond memory. Until the music stopped.

Chapter 18

Robert did not release her. He stood still, then slowly lowered his arm, relinquishing her hand so that he could place both of his at her waist. "Amalie, *mon coeur,*" he said, his voice rough, a husk of sound, "repulse my advances if you can, for I fear I am your worst danger."

He was going to kiss her and more, she knew, but made no move to stop him. She wanted his touch with a fierce longing that gave no heed to propriety, nor ever had, that cared nothing for what he was nor what he might have done. It didn't matter. Nothing mattered except for the fire in her blood and the ache in her heart that only he could ease.

His mouth was warm and firm and tasted of salt from the wind-blown spray. She reveled in the burning pressure, lifting her arms to twine them around his neck, pressing against him. She heard his indrawn breath, felt the hot flick of his tongue upon the sensitive surfaces of her lips. She opened her mouth, inviting his entrance, drowning in the sensations that crowded in upon her and the gratification of senses long denied.

His arms caught her closer, like steel bonds as they tightened around her. She stood on tiptoe, arching against him, wanting to be closer still, though his shirt studs ground into her and she could not breathe for the constriction of her stays. Reality faded. There was nothing except the two of them, the night, and the sea.

He shifted slightly and she felt his hand at her breast. He cupped the ripe globe pressed upward by her corset, brushing the peak with his thumb. Tiny prickles of pleasure radiated through her, converging in the lower part of her body. She made a low sound in her throat, pushing her fingers into the thick hair at the back of his neck, twisting them into the coarse silk.

He drew her down to her knees in the sand, kneeling before her as he slipped the buttons of her bodice free and pushed it back from her shoulders. He bent his head to taste the pale skin of her breasts as he lowered the small cap sleeves of her camisole. The night air was soft upon her and his breath, his lips were warm. She offered herself, guiding his mouth to her strutted nipple in wanton abandon, and sighed as she felt the wet heat, the suction that she craved. Her hands went to his waist to steady herself, then since she had gone so far, she allowed her fingers to smooth the front of his trousers, to find the long ridge of him beneath them. She outlined it, pressed her palm upon it, stroking.

He pressed toward her and she toppled backward. He lunged, reaching for her, twisting, catching his weight on his elbow an instant before she fell against his chest. He lowered her to the fanned-out expanse of her skirt and leaned to take her lips that were parted in surprise even as he reached to draw the front of her skirts higher.

She was trembling so that the shudder which ran over her as he found the open crotch of her pantaloons was scarcely discernible. Her flesh was moist and heated, swollen there, too, growing moister still to his probing. She stretched out her hand, gripping the hard, muscled length of his flank.

"*Dieu* protect us," he whispered and rolled away. There came the rustle of his trousers as he lowered them, and then he was above her, his mouth burning upon her breasts as he fitted his body to hers.

Delight exploded inside her and she arched against him with her eyes tightly shut and her hands clenched upon his shoulders. He sank into her again and again and she met each hard thrust with her own force, as if the violent union of their bodies would relieve the ache of sorrow inside her, as if in the give and take of this desperate act of love surcease would be the reward.

They sought each other, while the sea pounded in their ears and the reaching waves of the incoming tide edged closer. Blind and deaf and uncaring to anything except the white-hot ecstasy of the moment, they strained together, a part of the force of life and death because they could feel and knew the pain of caring.

And because the source of life is benign, they found what they sought, felt the joy of its release enfold them in a silent explosion of intolerable bliss, saw the darkness that engulfed them in its sweet and gentle quietude.

Amalie lay still. How long it was before she felt Robert stir, felt him withdraw from her, she could not have said. She felt rather than saw him lean above her, felt the touch of his fingers on her face in the darkness.

"Are you all right?"

Her lips curved in a slight smile, though he could not see it. "Yes, I'm fine."

"We had better go back."

It was a great effort to push herself erect and do up the buttons of her bodice, but she managed it with the aid of his knee to lean on. He helped her to her feet and shook the sand from her skirts. She took his arm as they turned back toward the cottage since she was not certain he meant to offer it. As they walked she sent him an upward glance once or twice, but could tell nothing of what he was thinking in the darkness, though she was aware of the drag of tiredness in his step.

At the door into the cottage, he stopped. He tipped her chin with his knuckle and pressed his lips to hers for a long moment before he let her go and stepped back. "Good night, Amalie."

"Aren't you coming in?" A flicker of disturbance crossed her mind. His kiss had seemed too gentle, almost like a farewell, a renunciation.

"Not just yet."

What could she say? The moment when she could have asked him boldly if he meant to share her bed now was gone. "Good night, then."

She waited an instant, but when he made no other reply, she moved into the house.

Lally had not returned. Amalie undressed herself with some difficulty, then rather guiltily left her gown lying on the floor, hoping that bit of apparent carelessness would appear to be the cause of the wrinkles that marred the front of the silk. She used the tepid water in her pitcher to bathe, splashing in it as she knelt in the hat tub, then dried herself and donned her gown. She yawned as she climbed into bed, still she lay awake for some time, listening for Robert to return to his room.

She did not hear him. Tired, replete, she finally fell into dreamless and deep slumber. When she awoke at mid-morning, Robert had been to his room and gone again. His trunk had been packed and sent to the landing. He had said his good-byes to M'mere, but had not wanted to disturb Amalie. The *Star* would be leaving at noon, in little more than an hour, heading back to the Teche country.

Robert was already on it.

The days were long after that. M'mere, as if to distract Amalie's mind, made a great effort to get out more, to explore the amenities of this "Little Deauville" of the South as the resort was being called after the seaside watering place of that name on the coast of France. The older woman introduced Amalie to her old friend, the owner of the hotel, Dave Muggah, who most gallantly insisted that they take afternoon tea there on the gallery with him. They spent an enjoyable half hour that turned out to be the beginning of more social contact for them.

The cause was aided by an incident two days later. Amalie was walking with Isa along the beach. They were passing an area between the cottage and the hotel that was given over to a playground for the children. There were three or four youngsters on the whirligig, a large merry-go-round with a steel shaft sunk into the sand and crossbars stabilized with wires. High enough off the ground so that smaller children would not be hit by it as it revolved, it was a vehicle for the older ones. At each of the four bars there was a stirrup-step so that the rider could mount, then stand on the lower crossbars while reaching up to hold on to the upper ones. The thing was propelled by taller children pushing at the lower bars, who, as the contraption began to whirl, could hang on and lift their feet for the ride.

Once or twice, when no one was about, Amalie had given Isa a ride, pushing at a bar herself. He had crowed with delight then, but showed no sign now of wishing to join the others, seeming content to shuffle along beside her with his pad under his arm.

Beyond the whirligig was an oak tree where two women sat, one with a baby on her lap, the other, dressed in black, with a young girl at her side who was also wearing black under a white pinafore apron. Amalie smiled and inclined her head in their direction and received a civil greeting in return. She expected nothing more and had faced forward again when there came a cry from the direction of the spinning, squeaking whirligig.

A boy had lost his footing on the crossbar and was hanging from one hand. Even as Amalie looked up, his grasp broke and he fell. He thudded to the sand and rolled, coming to a stop facedown. The women screamed and the children yelled as they clung to their own handholds. Amalie picked up her skirts and began to run. Being closer than the others, she reached the boy first and turned him over with careful, gentle hands.

He had a cut on his forehead that was streaming blood, but he opened his eyes at once. "Fell. Can't . . . get . . . breath."

"You've just had a hard knock. It will come back," Amalie said. Her calm certainty seemed to relieve him, for he closed his eyes again, relaxing, and his chest lifted sharply, then began to rise and fall in a natural, if quick, rhythm. She took out her handkerchief from where it was tucked into her sleeve and pressed it to the cut on his head.

At that moment the woman in mourning dropped to her knees beside Amalie. Behind her came the young girl with tears streaming down her face. The woman, her voice hushed, said, "Is he—is he—"

"Heavens, no," Amalie said, her tone brisk.

"Thank God," came the fervent reply. "Oh, I should not have let him ride, he's still so small, though he did beg so. But there's such a lot of blood."

"Head wounds always bleed a great deal, I believe." Amalie looked up to find the other woman beside her, too, with Isa squatting just beyond, furiously sketching. She turned back to the woman who, from her resemblance, must be the boy's mother. "If someone has another handkerchief, perhaps I could fashion a makeshift bandage—unless you prefer to do it?"

"No—no, you go ahead." The woman in black drew out a black-bordered handkerchief of some size from a drawstring bag at her wrist and handed it over.

In a moment, Amalie had the boy sitting up with the bandage in place. He was a little pale, but gave her a manly smile and a polite thank you.

"Oh, yes," his mother said, "we both thank you most sincerely. But permit me to introduce myself. I am Frances Prewett, and this is my son Augustine and my daughter Mary Ida." She drew the young girl forward as she finished speaking. The girl was still crying, screwing up a small fist into one eye while her mother patted her with soothing murmurs.

Amalie looked at the trio with interest. This was the young woman and her children whom she had heard mentioned at the Morneys' ball, so long ago now, a connection of the Weeks family of the Shadows in New Iberia. There had been some mention of her being widowed, not once but twice. Amalie gave her name. If it was familiar to the other woman in black, she gave no sign. She turned to introduce her friend and it seemed, however, that the other woman stiffened, holding her baby closer.

Frances Prewett opened her mouth once more to speak, but so loud was the crying of her daughter that her soft voice could scarcely be heard. She and Amalie looked at each other helplessly. At that moment, Isa edged forward, holding out his pad. Amalie took it, but with only half her attention. The little girl saw it and abruptly stopped crying.

"It's Tin-Tin," she said in wonder, giving her brother the diminutive that was the universal custom among the Creole families and those who lived in close contact with them.

Isa had drawn the whirligig with Augustine holding on with one hand, his eyes wide and his mouth pressed in a tight line as he fought to keep his grip. The contrast with the excitement and joy on the faces of the other children was striking, but it was also a reminder that the whirligig was meant for fun and brought more of that commodity than of grief.

Now the other children had jumped from the crossbars as the whirligig slowed to a stop. They came to stand around Augustine, craning to see the drawing. The boy stretched to see it also, and Amalie handed the pad to him.

"How very clever," Frances Prewett said.

"Yes, Isa is most talented," Amalie agreed.

"And you are good to encourage him."

"It's entirely selfish, I assure you. It gives me pleasure to watch him."

"I trust you will give me the pleasure of your company for tea this afternoon? I would like so much to show my appreciation for what you have done in more congenial surroundings."

"It is kind of you, but in truth I did little, and I am here on the island with my mother-in-law, Madame Declouet."

"Then she must come, too, and I hope you will bring your young artist, also. I believe he will make a fine addition." She nodded to where Isa was signing his drawing with a fine flourish, the last something he owed to Amalie's instruction of the simple letters of his name.

"If you are sure," Amalie agreed after a moment's hesitation. It seemed there should be some way to warn people that one was not considered a proper acquaintance, but it was not possible. Amalie did the next best thing. "But if— if something should occur to prevent it, you may send word to our cottage."

Nothing did occur, however. They went, she and M'mere and Isa, and were seen to be accepted by Mrs. Prewett of the Shadows. Frances had heard Amalie's tale by the time they arrived at the hotel, but was kind enough to say she believed not a word. She had known Robert and Julien for years and any fool could see that they were too fond of each other for there to be bloodshed between them. With quiet good manners, she passed on to other subjects. She had once had a connection in the Florida Parishes, a half sister of her grandfather's by the name of O'Connor; had Amalie ever heard of her? She had. The lady had been a dear friend of her aunt, though she had been dead for a good many years. But everyone knew that the plantation Madame Rachel O'Connor had owned had become a part of the Weeks estate.

The ages of Amalie and Frances were nearly the same and they were both widows, though it was the second time for Frances. The other woman seemed to feel that the two of them had much in common, and in truth, Amalie felt it also. Frances had her children from her first marriage; so would Amalie soon. The other woman was now dependent once more on her mother, without a home of her own despite two marriages, while Amalie was in much the same case. With such similarities to be discovered and so much to discuss, the time passed swiftly.

Afterward, there were many more friendly glances cast in Amalie's direction. They received calls the next day from several of their neighbors, including Mr. W. W. Pugh, who was the speaker of the state's House of Representatives, with his wife Josephine and several of their children, and also Monsieur and Madame Michael Schlatre. M'mere greeted them all with bountiful hospitality, but a shade of coolness. It would not be good, she maintained, to seem too eager to be accepted once more.

The intricacies of such matters concerned Amalie not at all. She smiled and chatted with politeness, moving through the slow-moving days with outward serenity. But at the back of her mind there loomed a single question: Why had he gone?

The quest for the answer absorbed Amalie's thoughts. It was there as she walked the beach kicking at broken seashells, dead seaweed, and bits of flotsam. It hammered at her as she rode with the warm wind in her face and the beating wings and shrieking cries of gulls about her head. It was there when she finally slept in the small hours of the night and was still with her when she awoke.

Had he felt that his duty toward M'mere and herself was at an end at last? Had he been disgusted by her uncontrolled behavior, afraid she would bring down more disapprobation upon them by her weakness? Or had he perhaps been afraid that, after that night on the beach, she would expect him to resume their close contact, something he was reluctant to do for the sake of his cousin?

Could it be that, having made use of her, he had discovered that she no longer attracted him as she once had, that with Julien gone, so was the spice of danger that had whetted his appetite for her favors?

Had he discovered that the memory of Julien intruded when he was with her, that his desire for her had been twisted and tainted by guilt? Had he discovered that making love to her was more pain than pleasure?

Or was it that having killed Julien, or caused his death, because of her, he found that the prize was not worth the cost?

The ideas her brain could supply to torment her were endless. The charm had gone out of the island for her and she could take little interest in whether or not she was included in the activities of it. They were meaningless, the teas, the parties, the whole round of petty entertainments sponsored and attended by people who in their stiff propriety seemed hardly to be alive at all. If they had ever felt passion or the supreme ecstasy of love, they concealed the fact well. So stiff and proper and pompous were they with their canes and stiff cravats, parasols and confining petticoats, that it seemed miraculous there were so many children running here and there over the island.

The babe that was growing inside her was also a miracle. She had been half afraid that the fury of her encounter with Robert might have been harmful to it, but no. Neither she nor it had taken any hurt. Such accommodations were natural, she supposed.

She would be glad when the child was born. She would have something, someone, of her own then, someone to love without reservation, someone to play with and help to grow. Would it be a boy like Frances's Augustine, or a girl like her Mary Ida? It did not matter; she was only curious to see.

Robert had not minded the idea of becoming a father, she thought. If the situation were different, he would have been a good one. Perhaps in time he would be able, as a near relative, to help her raise the child as it should be. Whether boy or girl, it would have need of a father.

Robert.

"I am your greatest danger."

It would be better if she could teach herself not to think of him at all. And not to cry. Unless it was for Julien. That would be all right. That would be expected. And he deserved her tears.

It was on one of her rides, when she had taken the road that led down into the village, past the handful of shops and the straggling market, past the seedier boardinghouses and the shanties where the island's residents who stayed through the winter lived, that she saw Patrick Dye. She could not be certain it was him, for she had no more than a quick glimpse. He was standing in a doorway, talking to a balding, potbellied, unshaven man wearing only a pair of sea-stained trousers held up by a single gallus over a set of faded red underwear marked with sweat rings under the armpits. The Belle Grove overseer did not look much better, except that his hair was covered by a battered, stained hat with a band made of seashells. Patrick, if it was he, straightened at the sight of her and stepped back into the drinking house where he stood, disappearing from sight. Still, Amalie had a prickling sensation between her shoulderblades for some yards, until she had put the drinking house behind her. So certain was she of whom she had seen that she spoke of the incident to M'mere that night at dinner.

"Oh, no, surely not, *ma chère* Amalie. Indeed if it was him that you saw, then the man would most assuredly have come to us. What reason could he have for being here except to consult us on the business of the plantation? Overseers do not take pleasure trips."

"You are right, I expect, but the man was so very like him."

"He did not recognize you?"

Amalie shook her head. "He went to great lengths to avoid me."

"I'm sure you exaggerate. It was some fisherman, no doubt. I'm told some of them are no better than common criminals, who came here years ago to escape the law, and that they resent visitors for fear of recognition."

"Yes, the last of the pirates," Amalie said with dry humor, "though this man was hardly old enough for that."

"There are other crimes that a man may wish to escape, other weaknesses," M'mere said, her old eyes desolate.

"Yes," Amalie murmured and said no more, letting the matter drop.

They were eating oysters topped with spinach sauce and baked in their shells on a bed of salt. The oysters were harvested near the island and brought in fresh to the market every morning. They were delicious, with a delicate and mellow flavor. After them came roast chicken, a fairly light meal that was finished off by a custard with caramel sauce flavored with brandy. M'mere waited until coffee had been served, talking idly of this and that, before she reverted to the subject of Patrick.

"This man, our overseer, you do not like him, I think?"

Amalie looked up in surprise. "No, I don't."

"I have been used to thinking him a species of vermin," the old lady said frankly, "annoying, like the rats that get into the corn, but not dangerous. How do you find him?"

"I don't know," she said slowly. "Crude, ill-mannered, conceited, not a man to trust."

"You fear him?"

"I think I would, if I were unprotected."

"Yes," M'mere said slowly, "or were in his debt, or in some other way in his power."

Amalie leaned across the table to touch her mother-in-law's hand. "Is this the case with you, M'mere?"

"Ah, do not worry, *chère*. I may be old, but I can still face down a *parvenu*."

Amalie hesitated, but finally she sat back. She could not press the other woman; her pride, the pride of the Declouets, would not allow it. "If you need me," she said quietly, "I am here."

M'mere nodded, a slow and measured movement. "So you are, this I know and I am grateful. You have been as a daughter to me in my illness, an angel, when I deserved only your reproach. It pains me to see you as you are now, troubled in mind and heart. May I say something to you?"

"Yes, of course."

"I have no right to interfere, but that has never stopped

me in the past, so why should I trouble with such scruples now? It is Robert, my dear nephew. He did not leave you of his own will, *ma chère.*"

"Please, don't," Amalie said, her own pride bringing her upright in her chair.

"No, let me finish. He left because of his fear for you and his desire. He left because he was certain that he could not restrain himself where you are concerned; it has been so from the beginning and so it is now. He did not want to bring you more grief, more shame, and so he did the only thing he could do. He went away."

It was a comforting explanation. Amalie wished that she could believe it. "I see. It was kind of you to tell me."

M'mere's face crinkled in a sad smile. She gave a small shake of her head. "It is only right that you should know."

Later, as she lay on the edge of sleep, Amalie found the words M'mere had spoken running through her head. How could Julien's mother know what Robert thought, how he felt, when she did not herself? And yet there was a certain peace, enough to bring repose in the thought that she might.

In the early hours of the morning, the wind shifted, swinging around the compass to blow from the north across the bay, ruffling the water into whitecaps and pushing it high onto the sand of the island. It sucked and billowed the curtains at the side windows of Amalie's bed-chambers, sending a cool draft into the room.

Amalie shivered, but did not awaken.

Chapter 19

I t was fascinating. The dark blue waves began to heave far out on the horizon, great, erect breakers that stretched as far as the eye could see, racing down onto the beach, one behind the other. They grew bigger as they came, flat on top as if they had been sheared off, until they reached halfway when they began to curl in upon themselves with heads of foam. They crashed upon the sand of the beach with a furious roar that dashed the now pale green water into a boiling froth. On and on they came in endless procession, those in the rear chasing those before them. It was as though each wave had taken on life and, knowing the short span of its existence, meant to display its majesty for those on the beach before smashing itself to pieces at their feet.

The shore was lined with people. A few had on their bathing costumes, but after one or two had been hurled back to the surf line by the waves and ground into the sand, the others had backed away in distrust. Still, no one left. They all stood staring at the spectacle as if in thrall, talking among themselves in low voices. And all the time the wind was at their backs, coming from the north and blowing into the faces of the waves, sending their spume flying back out over the gulf.

Amalie and M'mere sat on the gallery of the cottage, watching with the rest. M'mere, despite the time of year, was huddled in a shawl. It was not so much that it was cool as that the drop in temperature was so drastic after the earlier heat. Amalie was not at all chilly. There was a peculiar exhilaration running with the blood in her veins. The turbulence of the sea seemed to echo some turbulence within herself. She watched it with concentration, her head resting against the back of a wicker chair and her hands lying still along its arms.

"Ah, *chère,* I don't like it, I don't like it at all," M'mere said, slurring the words more than usual. "I see M'sieu Muggah along the beach there. He must have studied the gulf here in many moods. If you don't mind, will you not go and see what he thinks."

Amalie was glad of the chance to walk along the sand. She had been longing to get out into the wind, though she had not liked to leave the older woman while she was disturbed. She descended the steps and moved down the beach where the portly owner of the hotel could be seen talking to his guests, gesticulating toward the water.

He turned to give Amalie a slight bow at her approach. "Good afternoon, Madame Declouet," he said. "What do you think of the display I have arranged for the entertainment of the visitors to our fair island?"

"Magnificent, sir," she answered, "but my mother-in-law finds it unsettling. She fears it means a storm in the gulf, one that may come our way, and she wishes to know your opinion."

"She is a wise woman. Undoubtedly there is a disturbance, though she may put her mind at ease. It is some distance away yet, a tropical storm from the far Caribbean. We may get some rain from it eventually, which would not come amiss since the cisterns are always low from bathing to rid the skin of salt and sand, but we have weathered many a storm here, and will weather many more."

"Do you think—that is, could it be a hurricane?" Hurricanes, the dread storms of September, were greatly to be feared. Dave Muggah glanced about him quickly before he answered. "Who can say? It's only the ninth day of August and yet I've seen them come earlier. We won't really know until it gets here."

"This north wind is rather peculiar for this time of year."

His smile was genial. "I'll grant you that, but it makes a most pleasant change, don't you think?"

She had to agree. At that moment, a young woman, one of the riders that had been seen everywhere about the island, came strolling up within earshot. "Are you talking about the storm? For myself, I will be disappointed if we don't have one. I have never seen a real gale and look forward to the prospect."

"You don't know what you are saying, my dear girl," another man spoke up. "I have been on a ship at sea during only a minor blow and it is not an experience I wish to endure again."

"Nor I," said the woman at his side, obviously his wife. "I cannot like the thought of being on this low piece of land should the sea become even rougher. If the weather is not more calm by tomorrow noon, I am thinking of leaving on the *Star* when she comes in."

"Oh, there can be no need for such alarm, can there, Mr. Muggah?" the equestrienne asked, turning to the hotel proprietor.

"I sincerely trust not. There have been people living here for seventy years and more, generations of them now, and you don't see them packing to leave. The hotel has stood many a blow; she's a stout building, built strong and steady, as are most here. I see no danger."

His words were reassuring, but Amalie saw the glance he cast at the high, roiling clouds overhead. They were scudding, ever changing, pale gray and white shot now and then with silver gleams of sun. She watched them as she moved back toward the cottage. They were as interesting, as disturbing in their way, as the sea.

The next morning, a Saturday, the wind had swung around to the northeast. The clouds were dark, casting a gray pall over the island, taking the color from the waves that had turned angry, threatening, as they rolled down to smash upon the beach. On the bay side, the waves were crowding onto the shore, driven by the wind, lapping higher and higher. There was a faint roaring noise that was neither the wind nor the sea hovering in the air.

Amalie rose early, walking along the beach, cutting across the narrow neck of land to look also at the bay. As she passed the penned cattle belonging to the hotel, the beasts were crowding together with their heads, lowing. The sound followed her as she walked with her head down and her skirts whipping in the wind.

At the bay side, she stood, looking out over the water toward where the mainland lay some twelve or fifteen miles away. The brown waters of the bay heaved and rolled, slapping at the mud verge at her feet. From it came a fishy, muddy smell, as if it were being stirred to its depths. At the sound of screaming cries overhead, she looked up to see a flight of gulls flying into the wind, dipping and swinging in formation, but winging out over the bay toward the marshland of the Louisiana coast.

She walked back in the direction of the cottage with her

arms hugging her chest. The wind that pushed her along was strong, making her stumble forward now and then. It picked up the sand disturbed by her footsteps, sending it flying ahead of her. Now and then, as she turned her head, she could feel the sting of more sand on her face along with a fine mist from the tops of the waves on the bay, could hear it peppering against the bombazine of her gown.

When she arrived at the cottage, she found a note had been delivered inviting M'mere and herself to the cotillion ball to be held that evening at the hotel. With it was another from Frances Prewett urging them to attend. They must all stick together against the forces of nature, the young widow said, drawing strength and comfort from one another. It was not usual for ladies in their situation to put in an appearance at such festivities, but it would be acceptable this once under the circumstances. Since they would not be dancing, of course, she and Amalie could keep each other company.

M'mere dithered all day about whether they should attend. It was her own fears, allied to the deepening gloom of the evening, that decided her. It would be less nervewracking to go into company that might possibly spurn Amalie than to sit in the unnaturally dark cottage with the wind tearing at the storm shutters that had been fastened and barred over the windows.

It was definite now that they were in for a storm, and the day had been spent in preparing for it, closing the shutters, bringing in the chairs and cushions from the gallery, cooking extra food and bringing it into the house, collecting extra candles and lamp oil to have handy at need without having to search them out. The same thing had been happening up and down the beach, and even at the hotel, in spite of the owner's optimism.

Tige took a lantern to guide them across the sand to the hotel. M'mere clung to Amalie, regretting with every step that she had not elected to stay at home. Off on their right, they could hear the rushing rage of the sea, catch the drift of its spume. They could also hear, however, the strains of the cotillion band in a polka that was brisk and carefree, a challenge to the elements that poured from the open windows of the ballroom wing with the soft yellow light of hundreds of candles. That light, the only glow to be seen on the island battened down for the storm, was a beacon and a promise.

The ballroom, a recent addition, was done up in the latest style with brass and crystal chandeliers, parquet floors polished with beeswax to a brilliant sheen, and sea-green wallpaper. There were a few tables left around the edges of the room, since it was the dining room when not in use for the cotillion balls. Contrary to Amalie's expectations, there was a large crowd gathered. It appeared that everyone felt the need for the close proximity of other human beings.

The atmosphere was cheerful, with much talking and laughing above the sound of the music. There was, too, an undercurrent of excitement, closely held, almost an exhilaration. It was the effect of the danger that everyone sensed, though most denied. Voices were higher pitched, men talking together in corners made quick, animated gestures, and the dancers on the floor swung through the movements with verve, watching each other with brilliant eyes. There was a great deal of discussion about what should be done if the water swept over the island. One wag, a young man from New Orleans with dark eyes and a dashing mustache who was causing havoc among the ladies, suggested that the only thing left to do would be to simply dance on the tables until they were swept out to sea.

Not everyone was so sanguine. There was any number who stood at the windows looking out over the bay. They were watching for the arrival of the *Star*, and intended to go aboard her the moment she hove-to at the landing rather than run the risk of being swamped by rising water. The steamer was late again, but it was not to be wondered at. Some suggested that Captain Smith might not have set out to sea because of the weather or that he had put into some sheltered cove or bay to ride out the storm. If that was true, then they would be trapped on the island and must turn and face what was coming.

Frances Prewett was calm enough, greeting Amalie with pleasure and finding a seat for M'mere with ladies who might be congenial. She had quite enjoyed watching the waves, she said, though they made her nervous, her trust was in her maker. She would have been happier if Augustine and Mary Ida had stayed at the Shadows with her mother, but her young son was enjoying the whole thing immensely, especially since some kind gentleman had told him the waves were horses of the sea and the foam their manes.

To aid the high spirits, Dave Muggah brought out champagne as the evening advanced; the *Star* was bringing a new supply so they might as well make use of the last bottles in the house. The music became even livelier after that since the band had been included in the round of drinks. The pianist beat upon the keys to make their sound heard above the noise of wind and surf and shuffling feet, the man with the French horn blew until his eyes watered, and the German violinist sawed away until the handkerchief he had tucked under his chin was damp.

During the lulls in the music, the click of billiard balls issued from a room not far away, along with blue curls of smoke rich and aromatic with the smell of Louisiana Perique tobacco. There could also be heard the slap of cards from the cardroom as each tried to forget his fears in his own way.

Champagne was also served with the supper that was laid out. The late repast was a delightful banquet that included every type of seafood that could be imagined, both in hot dishes and in cold, in sauces and mayonnaises, in pastry shells and delectably alone. People crowded around the laden tables as if they were famished and might never have another meal. Within half an hour, not a morsel or a sip of the bubbling wine was left.

It was a turning point. Soon afterward, someone remarked on the fact that the *Star* had still not put in an appearance. It was unlikely that it would make it, in that case. They were, in reality, trapped, stranded on a low sand spit with a storm bearing down upon them and no way to get off.

By degrees the gaiety went out of the evening. The guests began to leave. Tige was sent for in the kitchen where the servants were having their own party, and, with Lally who had joined him, he lighted the way back toward the cottage once more for Amalie and M'mere.

They were nearly to the door when Tige stiffened, coming to a halt.

"What is it?" Amalie asked, keeping her voice low by instinct.

"I don't know, mam'zelle. I thought I saw something move behind the kitchen."

Amalie strained her eyes, but all she could see was the bulk of the small kitchen building in the lantern's rays. So overcast was the sky that everything else was black in the moving gloom of the windswept night. "Could it have been something blowing in the wind?"

"I thought it looked like a man."

M'mere made a soft sound. "Let us get into the house."

They began to move forward again, though their steps were more wary. Amalie did not take her gaze from the space behind the kitchen. The movement Tige had seen might have been a servant absent without permission who did not want to be seen or a man bent on some clandestine errand. It was always possible, too, that it was a horse or cow that had gotten loose from its pen to wander in the dark, and in the dimness its partial outline had only looked human. If it was none of those things, then it would be as well if they put themselves behind a locked door as soon as possible. There had never been any danger on the island, any disturbance to the possessions in the summer cottages during the winter season that Amalie had heard of, but there was a rough element in the village of Last Island itself that was unpredictable.

Inside the cottage, M'mere stood with a hand over her heart for a long moment, then gave a sigh of relief. Amalie echoed it. Shaking her head, teasing Tige for seeing things, and talking in a light vein of the success of the ball, she waited until Lally had brought the older woman's maid to her. She saw the pair into M'mere's bedchamber, then turned with tired steps toward her own.

She did not sleep. The increasing dirge of the wind as it whipped against the shutters made her restless. The thunder of the sea seemed to shake the foundations of the cottage, rattling the rings of the mosquito baire that hung above her bed. She lay staring wide-eyed into the dark, thinking, though trying not to think.

How different it would be if Robert were beside her. She would turn to him and spread her fingers over his chest, smoothing down, down to the hard flat plane of his belly and lower still to where he was ready for her. She would press herself to him, twining her legs around his, naked, abandoned in her need of him. She would explore his mouth with her lips and tongue, twist her fingers in his hair, breathe in the scent of him, reveling in his strength, his cherishing tenderness, the power of his loins as she took him into her. The need of him was so strong that she turned her face into the pillow, holding it to her as the tears soaked into the feathers under the linen cover and ticking.

It began to rain toward dawn, a light, wind-driven mist that fell endlessly from a sky the color of pewter. Still the clouds rolled and the sea churned onto the shore, beating the sand as if it meant to pulverize it. The waves were reaching higher with each mighty roll, while in Caillou Bay the water was crowding the north shore, steadily rising. There seemed nothing to keep the two from narrowing the small distance that separated them until they covered the island.

Amalie, who had been pacing around the house in her wrapper for hours, put on her clothes by the light of a lamp, donning one of her older, more serviceable black gowns with a single petticoat and leaving off her hoop. She packed a trunk against the possibility of leaving should M'mere wish to go, and always supposing that the *Star* would arrive after all. Smelling coffee, she left her room for the salon where Marthe had come down from the sleeping loft to brew the hot drink over a small fire in the fireplace.

Breakfast was a sketchy meal of cold rolls washed down with more coffee. Time dragged. M'mere did not feel well, but insisted on getting up. She lay on the settee in the salon, talking distractedly of going to the hotel. It might be safer, she thought. Amalie did not encourage her, for she was not certain one structure was better than another in the rising wind, but was sure the older woman did not need to make the effort to cross the sand that separated them from the island's main building. Nor did she think it was a good idea any longer to try to reach the steamer, even if it came.

Marthe, with nothing to do after the morning meal was through, sat rocking back and forth before the glow in the fireplace, perspiration beading on her forehead and upper lip as she hummed a slow tune. M'mere's Pauline joined her some time later and the two women sang softly to themselves. Lally and Tige huddled together in a corner, holding hands, and Isa followed Amalie as she moved from window to window, copying her as she tried to peer through the cracks between the shutters that covered the openings. He was underfoot every time she turned so finally she set him to drawing a picture of the sea to prevent herself from screaming at him.

It was toward noon that she caught a glimpse of what

appeared to be the lights of a steamboat at one window, shining through the rain that had turned into a downpour. She whirled, moving to the door, flinging herself out onto the gallery before anyone knew what she was doing. M'mere called after her from where she lay with her rosary clasped in her hands, but Amalie did not answer.

From the end of the gallery, she could see the *Star,* a dark shape with the glow of lights at her portholes through the gray curtain of rain. The steamer was standing out in the bay at anchor, the smoke from its engines flattened, torn by the wind. It appeared that Captain Smith did not mean to land just yet, that he might be having trouble finding the outlet of Village Bayou because of the blowing rain and high water or else feared being driven onto the bay shore by the wind that pushed at the ship's high housing. She supposed that he was waiting for a lull in the storm to try landing.

There was little to see other than the steamer sitting on the bay. Amalie was driven inside after a few minutes by the rain and wind-driven sand that threatened to abrade the skin from her face. Noon came and went, but no one was hungry. They ate finally because it was the normal thing to do and it seemed important to keep to some kind of ordinary schedule.

Afterward, Amalie wandered out onto the gallery once more with a fried apple pie in one hand and a cup of coffee in the other. She finished the pie while standing against the wall where there was the greatest protection from the wind, holding her cup carefully to keep it from being snatched from her hand. She watched the tumbling, boiling surf. It was breaking nearer the house, almost halfway between the cottage and its usual line. She shivered a little, then clasping the empty cup for its last lingering warmth, moved to the end of the gallery to see if the *Star* was still there.

She was, a faint outline through the sheets of rain that now obscured, now revealed her. Amalie watched for a moment, braving the wet that spattered against her skirts. The vessel was straining on her anchor cables, her superstructure acting like a giant sail to catch the wind.

Without warning, the forward anchor cable that held the steamer snapped. There was no sound for the noise of wind and sea, but Amalie saw the heavy chain crack in the wind like a whip, then dangle as the vessel swung around. The second anchor could not hold the full weight of the loaded steamer. It broke also and the boat was driven like a child's toy before the gale. It slammed into the muddy shore of the bay with a crash that came faintly to where Amalie stood. The steamer heeled slightly, but remained upright.

There appeared to be little damage, but in a moment men—what must have been the crew and every available male passenger—began pouring from inside her with what appeared to be hammers and saws and crowbars in their hands. They attacked the superstructure above the line of the gunwales, smashing at the bulkheads of the ornate cabins, knocking away the railings while the rain and wind flapped their oilskins and even ripped those of one man from his back. Amalie was not certain, but it seemed as if they meant to keep the ship from being pushed farther across the island or sucked back out into the bay with a damaged bottom that could sink her.

She turned toward the hotel where she was sure there

must be many who had been waiting to go aboard. If so, there was no sign. The hotel was a solid bulk, tightly closed in with its barred shutters, the palm trees to one side bending with the wind. As she watched, a green frond was torn from one and sent flying away into the wind-torn sky.

A hand closed on her shoulder. She started, swinging around with eyes narrowed against the wind and her skirts billowing. Even as she turned, she made ready to scold Isa for following her.

Patrick Dye stood before her, a crude grin on his features. The wind flapped his oilskins around him and flipped the brim of his battered, wet hat. His eyes were avid, oddly feral in his face that was shadowed by several days' growth of beard. His grip on her shoulder tightened as he stared down into her startled brown eyes.

With a quickly drawn breath, she stepped back against the end railing breaking his grasp. "What are you doing here?"

"A matter of business," he drawled, leaning near to be certain she heard, breathing his whiskey-fouled breath into her face. "Let's get inside."

She moved away from him in the direction of the door, but stopped when she was beyond the reach of the rain sweeping in at that end. "This is hardly the time for such discussion," she said with a lift of her chin. "Couldn't it wait?"

"I don't feel like waiting." The Irishman stepped close, catching her elbow to give her a push toward the door. "I've wasted near two weeks already, thinking Farnum was still here, and I don't intend to be put off any longer."

"You—it was you Tige saw last night, spying on us." She

could not have said why she was so certain.

"Oh, yes, that was me," he agreed and allowed a smile of bold intimacy to curl his mouth. "It was me looking through the cracks in the shutters into your room, too, or didn't you know that?"

She gave him a cold glance, jerking at her arm to release it, but his fingers bit into her. It suddenly seemed wiser to seek company instead of being alone with him there on the dim gallery. She went still. "Let us go inside, then."

"Let's," he agreed, giving her a wolfish grin.

She swung around toward the door and he moved with her until she halted to allow him to open it. It was a relief when he let her go to perform that habitual service. Being careful not to touch him, she stepped into the hall.

To ease the shock for her mother-in-law, she called out in strained tones before entering the salon, "Look who I found in the storm, M'mere. It's M'sieu Dye."

The older woman looked up and a yellow tinge appeared on the parchment of her face. She made a gallant recovery, however. "Why so it is."

The overseer stood with his legs spread and his hands on his hips. "Sure, now, I suppose you were expecting me?"

"I was expecting no one," M'mere answered with dignity. "Won't you sit down?"

"I would rather have a word with you, Madame Declouet, alone, if you please."

"Oh, really," Amalie exclaimed, "there can be nothing you have to say that can't be said here."

Patrick gave her a hard look, then back to the older woman. "Well, now, I don't know about that. What do you say, madame?"

The cocksureness of the man grated on Amalie's nerves and she did not like the look on M'mere's face, one compounded of dread and resignation. She had opened her mouth to set the overseer firmly in his place when the older woman spoke.

"Perhaps it would be best if we stepped into my bedchamber."

To hear M'mere make that suggestion, highly improper regardless of her age, was more amazing than anything that had happened so far. Her voice sharp, Amalie said, "That will not be necessary; I will step into my own chamber, while the others go into the dining room."

In her room, Amalie stood behind the door, listening without compunction. She could hear the grate of Patrick's voice, but nothing else. Outside, the wind was rising even higher, howling around the eaves of the house, drowning other sounds. A number of reasons for the overseer's presence presented themselves: trouble at Belle Grove, news of Julien's killer, a threat to Robert because of the case. She rejected every one of them. She had a good idea of his true purpose and sought only confirmation before she routed him.

Reaching out, she grasped the doorknob and turned it with slow care, letting the heavy panel swing open a crack. That was better.

". . . wasn't very nice of you to go away without seeing me," Patrick was saying. "It's put me to no end of trouble, bringing me down here to his God-forsaken place, forcing me to kick my heels until I could talk to you without that nephew of yours interfering. You owe me not a little, old lady, and I intend to collect."

"I paid you well for what you did."

"It wasn't enough, not by a long streak. I nearly got myself killed!"

"Julien did die," M'mere said, her voice quavering.

Amalie frowned. It was not what she had expected.

"That wasn't my fault. But it makes no difference, no difference at all. I've kept your secrets and now I expect you to take care of me. You're rich as be-Jesus. It's certain you'll never miss it."

"I—I don't have much with me," M'mere said haltingly. "This isn't Belle Grove."

"I'll take what you have now and you can gather up more later, when we are all back on the Teche." Patrick's tone was gloating, as if he relished being in a commanding position, giving orders to the woman who was, in a sense, his employer.

Amalie stayed to hear no more. She pulled the door open and crossed the hall, stepping into the salon. "So," she said, her voice laced with contempt, "you are here to blackmail M'mere, just as I thought. I knew you were despicable, but not quite the depths to which you could sink."

M'mere clutched at her chest, a spasm of pain crossing her features. Patrick spun around in a crouch, slowly straightening as he saw her there, alone and unarmed.

"You're bound to stick your nose in my business, aren't you now?" he said slowly.

"Your business being the slimy, sneaking sort it is, it seems necessary!"

"I could just make you a part of it, then you wouldn't have to go eavesdropping on what doesn't concern you." He shifted his weight to one foot, moving toward her.

"Thank you, no. I want you to leave this house, to cease harassing M'mere over Julien's past, to cease bleeding her of money. I would advise you to go back to Belle Grove, pack your belongings, and get out, for when Robert hears of this you will be without a job."

"Amalie, no," M'mere whispered, but no one paid any attention.

Patrick smiled deliberately into Amalie's eyes that glinted dark brown with anger. "I don't think so."

"Then you don't know Robert Farnum!"

"I think I do. He won't like Julien's little secret being spread about, but most of all, he won't let the story of how his precious cousin really died get out."

Horror made Amalie's throat numb. It was all she could do to force out coherent words. "What—what do you mean?"

"Don't you know?"

Did the overseer mean that Robert had in truth killed Julien? It could not be. She knew with sudden overwhelming certainty that it could not be. "I know there can be nothing so terrible as allowing a swine like you to rule us with your demands and innuendos!"

"How hot-blooded you are beneath that cool, ladylike front you put on," he said, the timbre of his voice dropping as he came closer. "I always suspected as much. Too bad you wasted it on Farnum. But that's all right. I don't mind another man's leavings, not when it's a woman like you. I think I'll enjoy taming you, teaching you to please me. I think I'll make having you a part of the deal. It seems just payment to me."

"No!" M'mere cried, casting aside the shawls that covered her and coming to her feet.

"You must be mad to think I would agree," Amalie said with a twist of her lips. "Tell your crude tale and see who will believe you when I am seen to be carrying Julien's child."

Surprise wiped the expression from his face, then he gave a harsh laugh. "Julien's? More likely Farnum's."

"Julien's by law and because I will certainly say it's his if you speak a single word against the man who was my husband." She felt strong and positive as she spoke.

"And what will you say about his murder?"

"Ah, don't, don't," M'mere pleaded, tottering toward them.

"It—it was an accident—" Amalie ventured, confused by the hard, self-satisfied look she saw in his hazel eyes.

Patrick grunted. "Was it?"

"It must have been."

"Don't be a little fool. Julien held his liquor well. He had been swimming in the Teche all his life. He thought he was invincible, able to dole out money or cut it off just as he saw fit. He thought he could keep his secret forever, have another man father his children, keep his place in the community, keep you for a wife as a front for his odd tastes. He wanted it all and thought it was his due. God, he was a bastard! But I'll show him. I'll have everything he had, including you."

He reached out to catch her around the neck, dragging her against him. His wet mouth seared the side of her face as she twisted away and his other hand came up to close over the globe of her breast.

"Stop it, I say stop!" M'mere screamed, catching his arm

and tugging at it.

He pushed her away. "Stay out of it, old woman."

"No, you shall not do this!" She caught at his sleeve again. "It isn't Amalie's fault, none of it is her fault."

"Get out of my way!" He swung around, driving his elbow into M'mere's chest so that she cried out, stumbling backward. She struck the end of the settee and fell, slumping to the floor. She tried to rise, gave a smothered gasp, and lay still.

"What have you done?" Amalie cried, pulling away from him and trying to go to M'mere. He grabbed for her, shoving her back against the wall. He came up against her, grinding his crotch into her through her skirts, making her feel the hard lump at his groin.

"Forget her," he growled "you've got other things to worry about."

She pushed at him, turning her head from side to side as he tried to capture her mouth with his. "She's sick, she—"

"She's an old bitch who tried to send Julien off for his own good and wound up killing him."

"What? No—"

"Yes! I should know, I rounded up the men who were supposed to take him away for her."

He took advantage of her stunned surprise to fasten his hot, thick lips on her own. His breath was sour, tainted with whiskey; the feel of his mouth slick, disgusting. She kicked at him and as he turned aside to avoid her knee, ducked her head, twisting from his grasp. He lunged after her and she skipped away, putting the settee between them. Those men had been the seamen, she was sure.

Breathless from their struggles, she said, "You arranged

for the men who killed him. That makes you equally guilty."

He stalked her, moving in a crouch with his arms spread, his eyes bright as he waited for her to make a move to escape. "Oh, they didn't kill him. He was too much for them, even knocked one out and pushed him in the river. It was me that had to use my gun barrel on him."

Pain stopped her voice for a moment. Her voice was hoarse as she said, "And you who decided to throw him in the bayou."

"It seemed the best thing to do, when all was said and done. He had threatened to quit paying, you see, on account of you, and there was always the chance that they wouldn't be able to hold him until the ship sailed. With him gone, I knew I could handle the old lady."

She watched him, her brown gaze shadowed, yet wary. "Until the ship sailed?"

"He was to go to China. Wasn't that fine? By the time he came back, his dear maman hoped he would have forgotten his unfortunate liking for boys."

Amalie spared a glance for M'mere. Her lips were blood-less, tinged with blue. She needed help. At the end of the room there was a movement and Amalie saw Isa sidle in from the dining room, standing in the door opening with his hand still on the knob.

Patrick, a hard grin spreading across his face, leaped for the settee and put one foot on the cushion, vaulting over it. He caught Amalie before she could move more than a single step, pulling her against him, swinging her around the end of the small sofa and forcing her down upon it.

"I've wanted under your petticoats since the minute I saw

you. I knew, one way or another, it was only a matter of time."

He put one knee across her legs, catching her wrists in one hand while with the other he yanked at the neckline of her gown. Feeling his fingers gouging into the softness of her skin, Amalie arched her back, turning, twisting her wrists. His hold broke for an instant and she lashed out to rake at his face above her with her nails. He jerked his head back, but four deep furrows appeared on his cheek.

With an oath and a writhing grimace, he raised his hand and brought it slashing around against her cheek. Her head snapped to one side and she tasted blood as her teeth cut into the side of her jaw. Like a raging wildcat, she came up, throwing him off, scrambling to her knees. He lost his balance and fell backward to the floor. Off the settee she came, half tripping over him in her effort to get away.

He was after her in a moment, his boots thudding on the floor. She dived for the door to the hall, plunging across it into her bedchamber, wrenching around to fling the panel door shut and to throw her shoulder against it as she fumbled for the key. She was thrown back as he charged against it. She backed away, feeling her hair slipping from its soft knot at her nape, losing its pins, gliding down over her breasts like a silken coil unwinding.

She watched him come, saw the anticipation in his eyes, saw his enjoyment of her resistance and his confidence in his ultimate triumph. She sent quick glances around the room for a weapon, anything to thwart him. It was not his physical possession of her she dreaded so much as being forced to submit to his mastery of her and to see it reflected in his eyes.

She whirled toward the bed, grabbing the heavy rolling-pin-looking bar that sat on top of the headboard used for smoothing down a feather mattress when one was in use. It made a formidable weapon and she swung it with a fierce exultation, feeling it thud against his shoulder. He reached around with a hand and grasped the bar, yanking it from her hands. It crashed against the wall as he flung it from him. In desperate haste, she backed away from the bed, dashing to the side as he lunged toward her. He caught her hair, wrapping it around his fist, and she was jerked to a halt.

Tears of pain rose to her eyes, but she blinked them away. She doubled up her fists, clenching her teeth as she was drawn toward him. As his face loomed above her, she drove upward from the level of her waist, aiming for his chin. The blow was off center, but it wrenched his head back and sent him staggering so that he released her hair. She danced away from him once more, but with a growl in his throat he threw himself after her, catching her around the waist and sending her crashing to the floor. He fell on top of her so that the air was driven from her lungs and a red haze appeared before her eyes.

She lay dazed, unable to breathe. She felt him tearing at the fabric of her bodice, exposing her breasts to the cool air. He closed his mouth on one with heated viciousness, biting, while his other hand grappled with her skirts to drag them upward.

There came a high, keening sound. The room was filled with shadows. The noise resolved into words. "No, no, no, not the *petite maîtresse!*"

It was Isa with a blue glass vase in his hand. He swung it, catching Patrick on the neck. The vase broke, the pieces scattering, and blood began to trickle down the overseer's collar. Behind the boy came Tige with a chair held by its back and Lally grasping a flatiron. Hovering in the doorway was Pauline with a shell-encrusted box held in both hands and Marthe, her kerchief on crooked and her eyes big, but clutching a silver pitcher by the handle with one massive fist.

Patrick cursed in a voice thick with rage. He jumped to his feet, standing over Amalie. He put his hands to his neck, looked at it, then cursed again as he saw the blood.

Amalie gasped, pushing herself slowly erect as Isa caught her hand to try to help her to her feet. She clutched at the front of her gown, pushing herself to one knee and standing with difficulty.

Patrick reached into his coat pocket for a handkerchief to dab at his scratch, watching as Isa caught Amalie in a hug around the waist. The moment the attention of the others wavered, he whipped out his pocketknife from the folded handkerchief and flicked it open. Shoving at Isa and snaking an arm about Amalie's shoulders, he snatched her against him and held the long, narrow blade to her throat.

"Get out, every one of you niggers. Go back where you belong and think about how much of your hide I'm going to tear off for daring to mix in a white man's pleasure."

"And what shall I think of?"

The words, quiet and hard, dangerously drawling, came from the doorway. It was Robert who spoke.

There was an instant of frozen stillness. Isa had not released Amalie, keeping his hold as if he would join in a tug-of-war with Patrick over her. He still held the neck of the broken vase in his hand, for she could feel it pressing into her hip. Slowly, she reached back, closing her fingers around the boy's and prising the piece of vase from his hand.

"Anything you damn well please," Patrick rasped, "but get out unless you want to watch me carve on your cousin's wife."

"A waste, that," Robert commented, making his way between Pauline and Marthe and stepping around Lally to stand beside Tige.

"I'm warning you," Patrick said, his grip tightening on Amalie's shoulders, the knife not quite steady as it hovered near her neck.

Fury for her own lack of strength that had placed her in this position crowded into her chest. She clasped the vase neck with convulsive pressure, then brought it up and around in an awkward left-handed swing, stabbing at the arm that gripped her. The jagged glass ripped into Patrick's hand. He yelled, snatching it away, then as he saw the spurting blood at his wrist, he plunged the blade he held toward the white softness of her throat.

It did not strike. Robert caught his hand in an iron grip, then sent a hard fist smashing into the overseer's face. Patrick went crashing backward to slam into a shuttered window. Glass broke with a musical clatter and the wind rushed into the room through the slatted opening. The overseer swayed, shaking his head, then as he saw Robert advancing on him with his face a hard mask of scorn, he bolted. He flung Lally aside, clawing his way out the door. The thud of his boots sounded on the planking of the hall, then came the crash of the front door as the wind slammed it behind him.

Robert let him go, turning toward Amalie. A second later, she was in his arms, clinging to him. His hold closed around her, warm, safe, strong. His lips brushed the top of her head while his hand smoothed the hair that streamed down her back. She took a deep, shuddering breath and was still.

It was only then that she noticed how wet he was: his hair dripping, his coat and trousers clinging to him, his boots soaked. It was only at that moment that she saw the water running in the hall, creeping in at the door, spreading across the floor. The island was flooding. Human strength did not count, warmth was gone, banished with the hot sun of summer, and safety was an illusion.

Chapter 20

M'mere lay as she had fallen. They lifted her up out of the water that sheeted the floors two inches deep, steadily rising, and put her on the settee. She was dazed, opening her eyes for brief moments, but could not speak. Amalie ran for her medicine, giving it to her, then brought dry clothing and put her into it with the help of Pauline and Lally.

Tige and Isa were banished once more to the dining room while they worked. Robert stood at the end of the room with his back turned. He had returned to Île Dernière because of Sir Bent, he said. The old man had told him there was going to be a storm, a big blow that would be bad at St. Martinville, but worse along the coast. The trip out had been so rough that he was afraid several times that Captain Smith meant to turn back. The captain had been well aware, however, that they were caught on the island and only he offered any hope of reprieve.

It had been bad luck and the severity of the weather that had driven the *Star* aground. Robert had helped with the tearing away of the upper decks so as to provide less wind resistance, to keep what was left of the vessel from floating off and sinking. As soon as he could get away, he had come straight to the cottage.

His voice was deep, ragged, he said, "I'm sorry, Amalie, more sorry than I can say, that I was not sooner."

Her hands were still upon the buttons of M'mere's dry gown. "You came," she said quietly, "and that is all that matters." There was so much else that needed to be thrashed out between them, but now was not the time, not with water pouring in around their feet and the wind tearing the shutters from the house.

"What are we going to do now?" she asked when he made no reply.

"It depends on the storm. We will have to stay here as long as possible, for M'mere's sake."

Amalie drew a shawl around the older woman's frail shoulders, then got to her feet. The possibility that they might have to move M'mere was why she had been put into a day gown, rather than nightwear and wrapper, why she was still in the salon instead of tucked into her bed. "You can turn around now."

He swung, the lamplight slanting across the bronze planes of his face, plumbing the dark blue depths of his eyes as they raked over her, resting a moment on the torn front of her gown. He looked away at once, but she was made aware that, though she had rebuttoned her bodice, three of the loops that held it shut over her breastbone were pulled loose.

She pulled her own shawl closer around her, hurrying into speech once more. "You don't think it would be better to go to the hotel now while we still can?"

He stood a moment with his head cocked, listening to the wind, then moved from the room out to the front door. It slammed back against the wall as he pulled it open. The wind tore at his hair and clothes, sweeping down the long hall. Leaning into it, he stepped out onto the gallery. Amalie, holding her shawl tightly around her as the wind tore at it, ducked her head and followed him. They turned toward where the hotel stood, narrowing their eyes to see through the flying spray. Amalie caught her breath.

The building was taller with its two stories plus dormer rooms, with more bulk to catch the force of the wind. On the roof, the dormers were gone, leaving gaping holes, and even as they watched, the roof lifted, settled, then shifted with a cracking explosion and went spinning away into the darkness. There came the sound of faint cries. The hotel walls sucked in and out like the sides of a bellows, windows shattered, and shutters were wrenched away to go flying; then on the north side the frame of the building toppled inward and the air was filled with debris.

Thunder rumbled and roared overhead. Lightning flashed. Behind the hotel could be seen several men, women, and children in the water. They were clinging to barrels and doors, floating, screaming at each other.

"*Mon Dieu,*" Amalie said almost to herself, "can't we help them?"

"Get back inside," Robert shouted, sweeping her with

him, putting his shoulder to the door to shut it once they were out of the wind.

"Those people—" Amalie began, a look of horror in her eyes.

"We may be next."

The words had scarcely left his mouth when the shutters were torn from the windows of Amalie's bedchamber. The glass remained intact, however, and she ran into the room. Through the cleared opening, she could see the cottage belonging to the Pughs. It was off its foundations, sitting on the ground with water past the windows.

"Amalie," Robert called urgently, "come in—"

The words were drowned in the growl of thunder. Amalie felt the floor under her lift, then drop away so that she went sprawling. She came up against the bedstead and lay winded, then rolled over, getting to her hands and knees. She could hear screaming and the gurgle of water. It was uphill to the door, but she made it, grasping at the frame and pulling herself into the hall. The others were there in that stronger center section, the servants in the low corner at the end where the house had left its pillars. Robert was standing with his legs spread for balance, holding M'mere in his arms.

The older woman's eyes were open, filled with intelligence, though the sounds she made had no meaning. There was a confused sound of cries and moans coming from where the servants huddled. Glancing in that direction, Amalie saw Isa crawling up the canted floor toward them, while Pauline was being helped out from under a wicker chair, one of those brought in from the gallery by the others. She was holding her shoulder at an odd angle, her face gray with pain.

Abruptly there came the sound of breaking glass. The wind howled, rushing in at the broken windows. On the lower side of the house, water began to rise, creeping up the sloping floor so that Tige and Lally and Marthe had to drag Pauline higher in the hallway. Then came a creaking, groaning sound. Robert looked up. Amalie followed his gaze and saw the ceiling above them straining upward, the plaster crumbling, falling like snow. There was a booming, a rending roar, and then the sound of rain falling on the ceiling just above them. The roof had gone.

"We've got to get out before the walls collapse," Robert shouted. "Tige, over here."

Amalie knelt on the floor and Robert placed M'mere with her head in her lap. He gave a few terse orders and Tige, Marthe, and Lally leaped to help remove the dining room and bedchamber doors from their hinges, piling them near the front door on the crazily slanted floor. There was no time for more. The storm was tearing at the house like some evil monster, wrenching it apart piece by piece. The walls were swaying, the water pouring through the ceiling, lapping higher on the floor. Robert swung, going to one knee to gather M'mere in his arms again. The servants crowded close. They stood for a moment, staring at each other with sober faces. Robert nodded to Tige and he pulled the door open.

Amalie hesitated, looking back at the tumbled rooms, thinking of food, clothing, and M'mere's valuable jewelry. She swung around to Robert, calling, "What shall I take?"

"Nothing," he shouted, "you'll need your hands and every ounce of strength you have to hold on."

He was right. The wind hit them like a wall the moment they left the shelter of the gallery, and the pounding waves washed down on them, wetting them in an instant, threatening to knock them off their feet. M'mere was placed on a door, with Robert on one side and Amalie on the other. Isa insisted on being beside Amalie and clutched at the door with both hands as if he meant to hold it up, instead of it supporting him in the water that was over his head. Tige was in charge of the women servants, sharing a door with Pauline since she was in need of help. It was easy to see that he wanted to be with Lally, but Amalie's maid was paired with Marthe on a third door.

The water came to Amalie's chest, surging, pushing against her. The wind caught her unbound hair, sending it swirling around her face so that she did not see the great wave, like a tidal surge, that rushed down on them. It broke over her head, knocking her from her feet for an instant, tangling her in her skirts, though she scrambled upright again. It had washed Isa under the door. He was clinging with one hand and Amalie grabbed it, dragging him out, helping him to gain the support of the door, holding him as he coughed.

"Are you all right?" Robert shouted from his place on the other side. A flash of lightning shed its blue light upon him, making him seem ghostly with his hair plastered to his forehead by the rain and his face twisted with concern.

"Yes," she called in answer as she wrapped the end of her shawl, still miraculously around her shoulders, about Isa, binding him to her by tying the corners in a knot. She looked down at M'mere, lying there so pale, very nearly covered with water as her slight weight bore down on the floating door. She glanced back toward the others who had fallen behind. They were still there, struggling against the wind. Behind them, the walls of the cottage bulged, then those on the east side toppled inward. In an instant the air was filled with flying splinters, boards, pieces of window sash, and deadly slivers of glass. Amalie saw a plank hit Tige and go spinning away in the gray gloom. Then, as a missile grazed her face, she turned her head sharply, reaching out to shield M'mere with her upper body.

Before the barrage was over, another wave washed over them. They were ready, but it was still an effort to keep their feet. The wind and the water was driving them over the island. In a few short minutes, they would be beyond the land and out into the bay. Their only chance was to find something, anything, to cling to, to stop their progress.

"Where are we going?" she shouted.

"To the *Star*!" came Robert's reply.

It seemed a doubtful haven, but what other choice was there? All around them now were floating sills and sections of walls. Looking back, Amalie could see only the brick cone of a cistern, a few studs here and there still standing where the line of beach cottages had been. Where Muggah's Hotel had once stood there was only emptiness.

And yet they were being driven in the opposite direction from the steamer by the wind. All of Robert's strength could not overcome that vicious force that sent rain and sand grinding into their faces. They were being taken farther and farther away from the dim beacon of the *Star*'s lights, out into the chill waves.

There came a cry from somewhere to the right. Amalie turned to see a man and woman struggling in the water.

Even as she watched, a flying timber struck the man on the head. He sank without a sound beneath the water and the next wave washed over the woman as she stood transfixed, knocking her down. She did not get up.

Slowly, Amalie, watching for the oncoming waves, became aware of cries and screams all around them, a part of the whistling wind, the rain and thunder and booming roar of the water. She saw a child clinging to a sill with its nurse beside it, holding to the back of its gown; a young couple clinging in a close embrace, turning over and over in the waves; an elderly man with streaming white hair and beard with one arm over a barrel and his face pressed to its side, his hoarse voice raised in a prayer.

Swinging away, she closed her eyes, though they snapped open again at a scream just behind her. She turned to see Marthe and Lally shouting, calling, pointing to where a door floated, empty. An instant later, Amalie saw Tige swimming in the water, trying to reach Pauline who was being carried away. The maid, of an age with M'mere, was unable to help herself because of her injured arm and her frailty.

Amalie heard Robert's imprecation as he watched, unable to help, saw a moment later what he had also realized, that they were being borne away from the others by some odd cross-current. She heard Lally calling her name, calling for Tige, and then there was nothing except the wind and the rain, the moving water, the piece of buoyant wood to which she clung, and the increasing effort it took to hold on to it.

"Over there," Robert called, "the whirligig. Can you make it?"

The thing loomed out of the near darkness, a skeletal shape of angles and crosspieces against the gray mass of the clouds. Its sturdy shaft was deep in the ground, however, and it stood firm. Amalie did not bother to answer, but used her failing strength to fight toward it.

The water was as high as the first crossbar. Amalie caught the piece, trying to steady the door as Robert reached to lift M'mere. Then he motioned for Amalie to go first. It was a wrench to leave the safety of that slab of floating wood for the unstable whirligig that threatened to turn even as she held it. She managed to free herself from Isa, to be certain that he had a handhold, then found the stirrup mount under the water and stepped up, climbing out onto the crossbar. The rush of the wind nearly knocked her off balance, but she grabbed the overhead bar, then leaned to hold out her hand to Isa. He scrambled up beside her, nimble despite his foot, then leaned out of the way as Robert, with M'mere over his shoulder, swung to the bar.

Holding on with one hand, Amalie reached to help Robert lower M'mere to stand between them, steadying the older woman until he could put his arm around her. M'mere made a valiant effort, but she could not lift one arm, and when she reached up to hold on with the other, her grasp slipped away. The older woman wavered on the bar, unable to cope with the gale winds that snapped at her skirts and sent the shawl that had been wrapped around her sailing into the clouds. Without Robert's support, she would have fallen.

Lightning flashed overhead. In its brief glow, Amalie looked at Robert. He met her gaze, his own stark with pain. Without words, they knew that M'mere had had another stroke, that she was slipping away from them, aided by the exposure and the fury of the storm, and that she did not care.

Time ceased to have meaning. The rain beat upon them and the wind slowly shredded their clothes, whipping them into tatters. The evening waned though it could scarcely be told because of the continuous flash of the lightning, a blue-white shimmer around them. Another man came and climbed up on the whirligig, then a pair of men, a man and a woman, a woman and a young girl, and finally another man until there were fourteen of them clinging to the stout play-piece. The water continued to rise, creeping up to their ankles, their calves. The whirligig, weighted by its human cargo and a sandbank that had built up under one side, held steady.

Then dark shapes came floating toward them. They were logs rolling in the waves, washed from the shores of the mainland. They shot through the openings between the bars so that they had to throw themselves out of the way or be picked off like birds on perches felled by arrows. Their worst fear, however, was that a log would hit the shaft directly, breaking it off and casting them all into the water. Amalie, straining to watch for the deadly lengths of log in the gloom, was reminded of that first day she had met Robert, of his gallant rescue of her from the breaking logjam. He could not help her now; he needed all his strength to hold on to M'mere.

The logs were gone as suddenly as they had appeared. There was a small respite and then the wind shifted, twisting, becoming a small tornado. The sandbank that had helped to steady the whirligig eroded. The thing began to move, slowly revolving. It picked up speed in a cruel parody of children playing, spinning faster and faster while in the silence of grim terror they floundered for purchase on the narrow bars, flapping, swinging, slipping, and regaining their footing, always sliding toward the narrow ends, slung by centrifugal force.

It lasted only a few seconds before the wind lifted and the whirligig slowed to a stop. It was just as well, for if it had not they would all have been thrown one by one into the water.

It was after this incident that Amalie, looking down at M'mere, saw her eyes open and staring. She reached out to touch her and her skin was cool; there was no pulse at her wrist.

Amalie was still for a long moment as tightness caught in her chest and tears pressed achingly at the backs of her eyes. Finally she moved closer to Robert and, with her hand, found his arm that was locked around his aunt, moved it down to his hand, and tried to prise his clenched fingers away. Her voice croaking with pain and the sea-water she had swallowed, she called above the wind, "Let her go."

"What?"

He had not understood. "M'mere is gone. You must let her go."

He lowered his gaze to the woman he held, the woman he had tried so hard to save. His features hardened and a muscle bunched in his jaw. His grip became tighter.

"It's what she wanted, needed," Amalie said, wishing that the words need not be shouted, wishing they need not be said at all. "It's better this way. Let her go."

He stood immobile, frozen in his resolve. Then she heard the sighing release of his held breath. His eyes closed, then opened again. Bending his head, he pressed his lips to the forehead of the woman who had been his aunt, then, leaning as far as he could reach and still retain his overhead grasp, he lowered M'mere into the hungry waves. With slow care, he relaxed the tense muscles of his arm, releasing her. She slipped beneath the water and it closed over her, taking her away in its angry flood.

Robert straightened. He reached out for Amalie and she came against him, pressing her tear-wet face into his neck. They stood with the wind shrieking around them, feeling the steady flow of the warm blood in their own veins, the joy and the guilt of it. Then Amalie lifted her head, looking around for Isa, holding out her hand to him. He sidled to stand beside her in the curve of her arm. Standing with their backs to the wind and their heads down, with their arms held painfully above their heads, gripping with bloodless fingers, they endured.

A short time later, toward the time of sunset, the wind died away and the rain became a drizzle. The clouds lifted, and in the west there was a swath of lurid red touched with green. The water began to recede, though it was still high and tossed with rolling waves.

The wet, bedraggled scarecrow forms that shared the whirligig stirred. The woman and her daughter started to laugh uncontrollably. One man said a prayer of thanksgiving to the Lord, while another began to look around in search of a landmark.

There was little enough. Not a house stood as far as the eye could see, not a tree. All that could be seen behind them and to the side was a vast stretch of water, with no way of distinguishing between the gulf and the bay though ahead of them some distance away and at a slight angle from where they stood were the tops of what might have been an enclosure for sea turtles and, beyond that, the bulk of the *Star* rising up like some latter-day Noah's ark.

Amalie looked around her at the women in their wet gowns that were molded to their forms, the parts not hanging in ribbons about their arms and knees. Their hair straggled down their backs and their faces were deathly pale. The men were in only a little better state because of the heavier materials of their clothing. Glancing at Robert and down at herself, she found they were in the same condition. It did not matter. There was no time for modesty or vanity.

"I'm heading for the steamer," said the man with his wife beside him.

"I wouldn't advise it," Robert answered. "This may be the eye of the storm, the calm at its center before the winds change direction. If that's so, you may not make it."

The man grunted. "I'll take my chances rather than hang here like a condemned man on the gallows."

One of the older men shook his head. "Won't hurt to wait a bit, just to see."

The man and his wife paid no attention, but jumped down into the water that came up to the woman's neck and began to wade in the direction of the steamer.

"I suggest that we even the weight a bit now," Robert said, "three to each side of the frame."

They complied and also shifted so that the taller ones were put with those smaller in stature. Robert, Amalie, and

Isa were already well spaced and so did not need to move. The others had hardly taken their new places when the wind began to pick up, hurtling out of the southwest now, and darkness closed in once more.

It was an endless night, a protracted fight for life. At some point in its passage, it occurred to Amalie to wonder at the tenacity of the child she carried. Neither the rough handling of Patrick Dye, the horrors she had witnessed, nor the rigors of the storm had affected its firm seat in her womb. It held to her as firmly as she grasped the whirligig, and with as much determination.

Dawn finally came. Sometime near midnight, the wind had abated and the water begun to recede, though the rain still fell. It was only as the pale light of dawn crept upon them that they could look down and see that there was sand and not water under the whirligig. Too exhausted to cheer or even to comment, they climbed down one by one and began to walk in the direction where they hoped the *Star* still lay.

The storm was over. The elements had exhausted their fury and resumed their proper places. On their right was the bay, crowding the shore, gently rolling. To the left was the gulf, lashing the beach; but unable to reach them. And all around them was devastation: bits of shingles and boards, a broken chair, an armoire on its back, uprooted trees. There were long lines of seaweed and bark mixed together with splinters and nails, empty bottles, a perfectly sound china cup. They came upon a child's rocking horse and, a few feet farther on, a young boy of no more than four years sprawled in death with his uncut curls matted with sand.

The bodies, young and old, master and servant alike, lay

along the shoreline where the sea that had taken them had brought them back again. Some were at the water's edge, some buried in the sand with only a hand or a leg showing to mark where they lay. They passed by them with hardly a look. There was nothing else they could do.

The smell of food cooking drew them as they neared the steamer. It was the scent of bacon frying, the most delectable fragrance in the world. People came out to meet them, staring into their faces as if hoping to see the features of missing loved ones and asking eager questions of who they had seen, when and where. Bacon and bread were pushed into their hands, along with glasses of champagne to alleviate the shock.

"Mam'zelle! M'sieu Robert!"

Amalie turned at the cry to see Tige coming toward them with Lally at his side. Behind them was Marthe with an apron over her tattered dress and a cooking fork in one hand. They held hands, laughing and crying, before they sobered to speak of those who had been lost, Pauline as well as M'mere.

The same scene was repeated a hundred times around them as the day wore on and men and women straggled in from all over the island. Some had found refuge among the turtles in the stout pens, though they had watched the great beasts escape as the water rose to float them to freedom. One man had held on to a fence post the night through, another family had found refuge behind a cistern, while a woman and several older children told of linking arms and standing firm, bowing into each wave as it washed toward them to decrease its force against them. And they all mourned the loss of relatives, friends, and servants. One couple spoke brokenly of losing a baby and a young son, then looked up to see a manservant coming toward them with the boy by the hand. Not many were as lucky.

They had food and shelter from the rain in the hull of the steamer. Modesty was also served by Captain Smith and his crew, who gave sheets and blankets and the contents of their sea chests to fill the need. They bandaged each other, caring for the more severely injured as best they could; there were not many of the last, for those too badly injured had not survived. Finally they turned to the task of searching for those who were lost.

The line of bodies lying in the falling rain grew. Among the first to be discovered were those of Augustine and Mary Ida Magill, the children of Frances Prewett by her first marriage. She was not among the survivors at the steamer, but neither was her body found. They came upon M'mere late in the afternoon, but there was no sign of Pauline. They discovered Patrick at nightfall, a great gash in his head, as if he had been hit by flying lumber. The search was called off at dark, though there were torches seen in the darkness through the night. The morning brought distressing tales of looting of the dead, presumably by men from the village or the surrounding islands, of rings cut from fingers and other atrocities.

Thus ended Monday, August 11. Tuesday came and the sun broke through the clouds. The supply of water began to dwindle and there were several cases of sunstroke because of lack of shade. The flies began to gather, and it was decided to bury the bodies in shallow graves. Many began to stand on the shore watching the bay, waiting for the rescue that must come if they were to live, wondering if anyone even knew of their plight there on Île Dernière.

Still the search for bodies went on. Robert and several other men came upon a pair of looters at the far west end of the island during the hottest part of the day. They would not speak of what they saw or what was done, but there were a pair of shallow graves near the spot.

Wednesday brought the steamer *Major Aubrey.*

There had been some four hundred visitors to the island by all accounting and of that number, as near as could be told, one hundred and seventy-four had perished, with an unknown number from the village. That left over two hundred people to be taken off the island, too many to be carried in one trip. Those with children were detailed to go first, along with the injured and any single women. For the rest, lots were made up to be drawn. Robert refused his turn, preferring to wait, and Amalie, overriding his objections, did the same. Promising the arrival of another steam packet as soon as possible, the captain of the *Major Aubrey* sailed away.

There had been too much to do to have time to think, much less to talk. Now there was nothing. Robert turned away from the wreck of the *Star,* walking across the sand in the direction of the gulf shore. After a moment, Amalie followed. She caught up with him as he stopped where the hotel had stood. He glanced at her, then stood staring out to sea.

There was another layer of bronze on his face and now lines about his eyes that had dark circles beneath them. She reached out to touch his arm with her fingertips. "It wasn't your fault."

"Wasn't it?"

"You did not make Julien the way he was, nor did you cause the grief that killed M'mere."

"It isn't that simple," he said, lifting a hand to clasp the back of his neck.

"But there's no reason to make it harder for yourself than it is."

"If I had not left you and M'mere alone here where Patrick could find you, or better still, if in the beginning I had never touched you, then it might not have happened."

"You are human and you acted for the best at the time. What else could you have done?"

"I could have considered something besides my own desires—but even when I tried, when I left you, it was wrong." M'mere may well have been right, he had left Île Dernière for her sake. There was no time to savor the gladness inside of her, however. "It's over now, ended in a way that may be for the best. You can't go on tormenting yourself."

"It isn't over," he grated, swinging from her, staring down at his hands, "not when a woman like Madame Callot can insult you to your face, not while the old ladies point and whisper as you pass by."

"What's done is done. We can't let the past rule our lives."

"I won't be the cause of more pain, more humiliation for you."

His voice was flat, remote. She looked at him and saw a stranger, one who could not possibly have held her with the tenderness, the passion that she remembered so well.

"I—I am not the only one who has been hurt or humiliated. I said some things that were—were unforgivable. I know they weren't true; I think I always knew, but I—"

"Forget it. I have."

"Have you really?" she asked, her voice low.

He lifted his head and squared his shoulders, staring out at the blue gulf. His answer was immediate. "Long ago. It was never important, but this is. I want you to go back to Belle Grove. It's yours now, yours to do with as you like. You can sell it, go away, find another place to live without—without the memories. Or you can live there. The hurricane will supplant you as a subject of conversation, and in time, if nothing else happens, you will be able to live in peace."

In peace. Alone. Was it a sacrifice for him or was he telling her the way it must be now that he was no longer obligated to her? She could not tell. "And what of the child I carry?"

"Name it for Julien. He would have been pleased, and it is his due."

At Belle Grove there was chaos. The cane crop had been blown flat and less than two-thirds of it had sprung back up again. The ditches were filled with standing water that bred mosquitos by the millions, and there was an outbreak of fever and dysentery in the quarters. The roof of the stable had been torn off and two of the large oaks in the front had been uprooted. Several patches of shingles had been dislodged on the roof of the big house and the seeping water had damaged the plaster in the ceilings of the upstairs rooms. The only thing to escape was, apparently, George's shrubs; they had only benefited from the rain.

There could be nothing done, of course, until after the

funerals for M'mere and for Pauline, disinterred from their shallow graves and returned to Belle Grove. Then came hours spent with the family lawyers going over countless papers, reading, signing, trying to comprehend her new position and its duties. It was necessary to consider her financial situation, only fair due to the ravages of the storm. She needed to make inquiries about the possibility of acquiring a new cane factor in New Orleans or else come to an understanding with Monsieur Callot that would pre-clude visits from his wife. She must then look to the future, make plans for the crop that must be made next year and the year after, as well as for the birth of her child. Then there was Isa. Some provision should be made for his talent. She would write the Declouet family connections in France and, if they were in agreement, send him to them in a year or two when he was older. Matters could be arranged so that he could study art in Paris. He would prosper there, she was sure, where the color of his skin would not matter as much as his genius. And once out of the country, he would be free.

Finally the paperwork was done and Amalie could throw herself into the task, healing, mind-dulling, of restoring the plantation to normal.

The first order of business was the health of those in the quarters. Amalie ordered a strict quarantine, sending everyone who looked even remotely ill to the hospital building with a trio of older women to see to their needs. With that out of the way, she set about finding an overseer, someone who could see that the heavy work was done.

It was not an easy task. No one wanted to work for a woman, to be subject to her orders and caprices. She was near to despair or to pulling her hair in rage when Robert rode up one morning with a young Scotsman. By noon, the hands had been set to cleaning the drainage ditches once more, to sawing up the trees and carting the wood and branches away, and to repairing the stable.

After that, Robert was seen about the place nearly every day, though he seldom came into the house. If she needed to ask his advice or to request his aid with a problem, she had to talk to him on the front gallery while he remained standing on the steps. He would accept a cup of coffee or a glass of water from Marthe at the outdoor kitchen, but refused every offer of refreshment made by Amalie. He would not come in to look at the water damage, but would only walk around the house on the outside, craning his neck to look at the loose shingles. To the question of whether a steel or cypress-shingled roof would be best, he had referred her to her banker, it being a matter of finances, of what she could and could not afford.

If George and his Chloe were aware of the constraint between Amalie and Robert, neither of them mentioned it. Knowing how little the old Chloe would have minded asking what was wrong, Amalie could only suppose that marriage had taught her discretion or that the rift was not as obvious to others as it seemed to her.

Matters came to a head on the day the itinerant priest came to visit. There had been much hardship from the storm among the Acadians along the bayous and in the swamps. Flooding had been severe, and priests had been sent out to officiate at funerals, weddings, and christenings among those who could not easily get to town. It was con- sidered an honor to have one of the clerics stay for a meal or a night. Père Francis, a young man not long appointed to holy orders, promised to do both at Belle Grove and to say mass in the chapel for Amalie and those in the quarters.

Amalie had been visiting in the quarters hospital that afternoon with Père Francis, also showing him the nursery building she was having constructed and the baby cribs that were being made by her own people. Her aunt had always made it a practice to bathe and change clothing when coming from the hospital and it was a habit that Amalie had acquired. As Lally was preparing the water, Amalie glanced out of the window and saw Robert walking his horse around the side of the house toward the back road through the fields. She had meant to ask him to dine since they had a guest she knew he always enjoyed talking to, but there had been no opportunity. She had already removed her clothes, but now she snatched up her wrapper and slipped it on, hurrying through Julien's old room out onto the loggia.

"Robert?" she called, leaning over the railing, holding the wrapper closed at her throat.

He appeared between the house and the *garçonnière* and came slowly forward with his horse following on a rein. He stopped below her and looked up. As he saw what she was wearing, all expression was wiped from his face and his voice was hard as he spoke.

"Yes?"

"I wanted to ask you to dinner tonight, with Père Francis."

He brought his mount around and stepped into the saddle. From that higher perch, he looked up at her again. His gaze rested an instant on the rounded softness of her breasts with the peaks outlined by the soft cotton of her wrapper, dropped to the open front where the length of one leg from above her knee to the ankle could be glimpsed, then returned hastily to her face. The brown of his face was a shade darker as he demanded, "You came out here half dressed to ask me that?"

"You have seen me in less," she said tightly, touched on the raw by the condemnation in his tone.

"Shout it to the world, why don't you?"

"I'm not ashamed of it, even if you are!"

"Not ashamed, Amalie, afraid."

He wrenched his horse around and rode away, galloping as if the fields were after him. Amalie stood watching him for a long moment, a suspended look in her blue-shadowed brown eyes. Then with a slow, sweet movement of the lips, she smiled.

By dark her plans were made. She had spoken to Père Francis, made her confession, and received absolution and a promise. She had had Lally lay out her riding habit and sent to the stables for a pair of horses to be brought round after dinner. She sat down to the meal, but ate little, though the priest, talking with quiet charm with George and Chloe to cover her silence, made up for it. They sat for a time over glasses of wine in the salon, then Amalie, with a quick, almost frightened, glance at Père Francis, excused herself.

She changed into her habit in her room, then went through the now-empty salon to the front stairs. The priest was waiting for her. Her voice hushed, she asked, "Did you tell them?"

"They will come in the carriage, an hour behind us."

She nodded, then moved to the mounting block where a

groom stood holding their horses, his face impassive, though his eyes were alight with curiosity. She hesitated a moment with the reins clutched in her hand, then squaring her shoulders, Amalie swung onto her mare. The priest mounted also and they rode slowly away from Belle Grove.

The Willows loomed dark and quiet as they rode up the drive. They did not go to the front door, but drew their horses to a halt in the dark, spreading shade of huge old oak, made darker by the brightness of a half-moon. Here they dismounted. Amalie held out her hand to the priest. "Thank you, Père Francis."

"You may thank me when it's done, my child. Until then I will pray for you." He pressed her hand and released it.

A qualm assailed Amalie. This good man did not know the methods she meant to use to gain her purpose and she could not tell him, for he might not agree that the end justified the means. She meant no harm, however, and must trust she would cause none. "Yes," she answered before she turned away, "if you please."

She moved toward the house, a darker shadow among the shadows. Her footsteps were quiet and sure. She paused to listen at the front stairs that led up to the upper gallery, then mounted with slow care. Before her on that wide veranda was a line of French windows, but only one set was open to the night. She approached them with care, for she did not wish to wake Robert, not yet.

Inside the door, she could make out the bed draped in the white of the mosquito baire. She eased closer, one step, then two. She could see his form in the pale moonlight through the windows, his bronzed darkness in contrast to the white linen of the sheet. He lay on his back with one arm flung above his head and the other outstretched, with the sheet cutting across his body below the waist. There was a faint odor of brandy in the room and the glint of a bottle and glass on the far bedstand. The last was good; it might well make her task easier.

Her heart was jarring in her chest and her palms felt damp. Her stomach was balled in a knot of apprehension and she had to keep her teeth clenched to prevent them from chattering, but she would not run away. Slowly she reached up to take off her hat, bent to place it on the floor. Her hands moved to the buttons of her jacket, slipping them free one by one. The jacket landed beside her hat and the poplin of her habit skirt made a soft, sighing sound as it joined them. She levered off her riding boots, setting them aside, then stripped off stockings, removed pantaloons and camisole, and dropped them onto the pile. Finally she took the pins from her hair and shook out the long, satin length, feeling it glide warm and soft against her hips, releasing its fragrance on the warm night air.

She approached the bed with hushed stealth and lifted the mosquito netting. As she climbed onto the mattress and let herself down upon it by gentle degrees, it occurred to her to wonder if this was how Robert had come to her, with excitement pounding in his veins and the aching warmth of love in the region of his heart.

He did not stir as she settled herself beside him on one elbow, nor as she placed her hand lightly upon his chest. Emboldened by his stillness, the steady rise and fall of his breathing, she spread her fingers to enjoy the tactile sense of his skin against hers, the roughness of the curling hairs that grazed her palm. Slowly she slid her fingertips to one of his paps, touching it with a delicate brushing motion, enjoying its instant tightening. She lowered her head to touch her tongue to the other, letting her hair drift across his arm as she moved her head back and forth until that pap was contracted into a small bud.

She eased higher then, trailing upward with her lips tasting the skin at the hollow of his brown throat, the molded turn of his neck, placing the smooth surface of her mouth on his. She traced the line of his closed lips, that most sensitive area, with the edge of her tongue, while with her free hand she reached downward, over the shallow indentation of his navel and the flat hard plane of his abdomen. She encountered something smooth, resilient, and most rigidly tumescent.

In that instant her wrist was caught in a biting grip. His muscles coiled and he heaved her up and over onto her back, pinioning her wrist to the bed. His face inches from hers as he hovered above her, he grated, "What in God's holy name do you think you are doing?"

Her heart was pounding with sickening jolts and a faint trembling she could not control shook her, still her voice was steady as she answered. "Returning a favor."

He drew back. That he was startled by her answer was plain from the delay before he demanded, "Doing what?"

"You came to me in the night. Now I will come to you."

"You can't," he said with flat finality.

"You think not? What is to stop me?"

"I will."

"How? I will come when you least expect me, come when you are asleep and without defense, come again and again until the countryside rings with the scandal of how poor Farnum is being hounded by his dead cousin's wife. I am more sorry than I can say that I doubted you, that I hurt you. I love you, and only you, with every ounce of my being. I want you as I will never want another man. I need you with me at night to hold me, need you at my side when I bear your child, need you to hold my hand as I grow old. I am no Evangeline to become a nun or an Emmeline to pine away for lack of love, when I have only to come to you. Can you deny me?"

The proof that he could not lay between them, heated, throbbing. He ignored it. "You speak lightly of scandal, but it isn't something I will let you risk, not for me, not again."

"Don't be damned noble," she answered in a fierce rush. "We have all, you and I and Julien and M'mere, tried to live by conforming to what others expect us to be and to do. If we had not, your aunt and your cousin might be alive. I respect your sense of honor that would protect me, save me from censure, but the cost of approval and respectability is too high. I will not pay it, nor will I allow you to pay it for me, Robert Farnum. I want you. The choice is whether it is to be in wedlock or like this, without."

"You are very certain of your charms, aren't you? What is to prevent me from throwing you out, like this?"

He thrust up with hard grace, dragging her with him, hauling her over the mattress and catching her up in his arms as he bounded to the floor. He swung with her toward the open French windows, moving so swiftly that her hair swirled around them in a soft brown cloud, shimmering in the moonlight.

As she saw his purpose, she went stiff, clutching at him. "No! Oh, please, no, Robert! There is a priest out there."

He halted as if he had been roped from behind. "A what?"

"A priest," she repeated in ragged entreaty, "and maybe even George and Chloe as—as witnesses."

The grip of his arms tightened. "What is this?"

"A—a wedding."

"You are that certain?" There was a strange, tentative sound in his voice, but no anger.

"I have never been more certain of anything."

He lowered her feet to the floor, allowing her to stand, though he retained his grasp upon her upper arms. He stroked the smooth skin with his thumbs almost as if he could not prevent that small action. "The kind of man you once thought I was would agree."

"And so would the kind I know you to be, if you truly wished to save me from the scorn of the world, if the love you spoke of once was not a lie told from compassion."

"It was no lie, *chèr* Amalie. I do love you and have done so since the moment you walked into M'mere's sitting room that day with your dripping cloak and your hair damp with rain. Why else would I have agreed to so base a charade? Why else would I need so desperately to protect you? You flow in my blood like wine and walk my dreams at night, haunting me with remembered sweetness. Without you I have no purpose, no goal except that by my sacrifice I serve you."

"I need no sacrifice, my love, nor want one."

"And yet one seems required."

Her heart stopped. She had thought, had hoped, had been

so sure that he was going to agree.

"It was a mistake to take you in my arms again just now," he said, his voice rueful, warm, rich with love. "I fear that it will be hard to let you go, even for the little time it will take to be wed."

She flung herself upon him with tears rising in her eyes, locking her arms about his neck, burying her face in the curve of his neck. He held her, rocking her gently back and forth, his chin resting on the silk of her hair.

After a moment, Amalie swallowed hard, saying with the catch of a tearful chuckle in her throat, "There may be time. George and Chloe were to come behind Père Francis and me. It may be at least a half hour, or more, before the ceremony can begin."

His chest lifted in a deep drawn breath, then he released it in a slow sigh. There was answering amusement and quiet promise in his tones as he put her gently from him. "That won't be long enough, not nearly long enough."

Author's Note

Belle Grove. The words have a feeling about them of grace and tranquility. There was once a real plantation by that name. Located on the Mississippi River above New Orleans, the house was a Greek Revival mansion of some seventy-five rooms, one of the largest ever constructed in the South. It is gone now. It crumbled to ruins, finally, sometime in the late 1940s. The naming of the plantation in *Midnight Waltz* after it is a salute to the memory of this grand old place.

The physical description of the house on the plantation in *Midnight Waltz*, however, coincides more closely with the houses that were built in the early days of the antebellum period along Bayou Teche, one French in flavor and more adapted to the subtropical climate. The way of life in the big house, along with the duties, obligations, and concerns of the chatelaine of such a place, was much as given in the novel. The conventions that bound the lives of women, and of men, were possibly even more rigid.

There are a few characters mentioned in passing in *Midnight Waltz* who actually lived. Adrien Persac was an itinerant artist who painted many of the plantation houses along the Teche, though he glued cutouts for his people. Frances Magill Prewett was a member of the Weeks family of the famous Shadows-on-the-Teche who died with her two children, Augustine and Mary Ida, in the storm at Île Dernière. The tombs of the children can be found today on the grounds of the Shadows in New Iberia, though the body of Frances was never recovered. Rachel O'Connor was a widow, half sister to David Weeks of the Shadows, who ran a plantation alone for many years. The hotel proprietor at Last Island was a genial host named Dave Muggah, and the Pugh and Schlatre families had summer cottages at the gulf resort. All other characters are fictional, though in the history of Louisiana there can be found a dilettante husband who floated up and down the Mississippi and its back bayous on a pleasure barge with colored sails, and an Irish overseer in the Felicianas in the 1830s who left his mark in the slave quarters.

The gulf resort of Île Dernière, playground of the plantation owners of Southwestern Louisiana known as "Little Deauville," with its gentle pastimes and amusements, was as depicted. The hurricane that destroyed it on August 10, 1856, was one of the most destructive ever to strike the coast of Louisiana. The approach of the storm, its force and aftermath happened just as is written. Also factual is the means used by the survivors to escape from the winds and rising water that it brought, including the long hours spent clinging to a children's whirligig. The true hero of the hour was Captain Abe Smith of the steamship *Star*, whose last-minute arrival and grounding on the island saved many lives that would otherwise have been lost.

As always, there were numerous research sources consulted in the writing of *Midnight Waltz*. A few were particularly helpful. For details of the architecture of the buildings of Southwestern Louisiana, and especially those of St. Martinville, I am indebted to Paul F. Stahls, Jr., for his *Plantation Homes of the Teche Country. Rachel of Old Louisiana* by Avery O. Craven, based on the letters of Rachel O'Connor, was invaluable for the flavor and conditions of everyday plantation life, as was *Daily Life In Louisiana, 1815-1830* by Liliane Créte. *Eating, Drinking, and Visiting in the South, An Informal History* by Joe Gray Taylor provided many insights and much help with menus. And without the wealth of information contained in *Last Island* by James M. Sothern, *Midnight Waltz* would have been a very different, and much less complete, book.

There are many people who helped make *Midnight Waltz* a reality. Among them are Zella Barras Abrahams of Lake Charles, Louisiana, who spent several hours researching in the courthouse and newspaper files of St. Martinville. I sincerely appreciate her efforts and the lovely impulse that made her volunteer them. I would like to thank the staff of the St. Martinville Parish Library for their aid and for unearthing old maps of St. Martinville and the vicinity for me. To Jane Stone, Faye Hood, and all the rest at the Jackson Parish Library, Jonesboro, Louisiana, my gratitude, once again, for a thousand favors granted, large and small. And to the staff at the National Trust home, Shadows-on-the-Teche, I would like to express my appreciation, not only for their fine presentation of the history of the old home and their gracious answers to many questions, but also for their diligent efforts to insure that the Shadows, unlike Belle Grove, will remain for future generations.

Jennifer Blake
Sweet Brier
Quitman, Louisiana

Center Point Publishing
600 Brooks Road ● PO Box 1
Thorndike ME 04986-0001 USA

(207) 568-3717

US & Canada:
1 800 929-9108

S F